Caution to the Wind

by

Mary Jean Adams

American Heroes Series

This is a work of fiction. Names, characters, places, and incidents are either the product of the author's imagination or are used fictitiously, and any resemblance to actual persons living or dead, business establishments, events, or locales, is entirely coincidental.

Caution to the Wind

Contact Information: info@thewildrosepress.com

Cover Art by *Tina Lynn Stout*

The Wild Rose Press, Inc.
PO Box 708
Adams Basin, NY 14410-0708
Visit us at www.thewildrosepress.com

Publishing History
First American Rose Edition, 2013
Print ISBN 978-1-61217-878-3
Digital ISBN 978-1-61217-879-0

American Heroes Series
Published in the United States of America

Amanda pasted a smile on her lips and whirled around to face him. “I am a member of your crew, aren’t I?”

The question sounded more direct than she had intended. Backing a wolf into a corner might not be such a wise thing to do, but desperation had driven her to the point of recklessness.

“I thought you would be leaving with your father now that you know he is alive. I thought he would insist on it. I would, if I were him.”

“He thinks you’re an honorable man.” Amanda lifted her chin.

“And you? What do you think?” Will’s question held a note of uncertainty.

“I think you are as well,” she took a deep breath to steady her resolve, “but I’d really rather you weren’t.”

Amanda waited for his reaction, glad his quarters were lit only by weak shafts of moonlight through the high windows. She hated to think he might witness the desperation she knew to be written on her face. She could hear the despised emotion in her own voice.

She threw back her shoulders and stuck out her chin. She would need courage to carry out her plan.

Other Titles by Mary Jean Adams

LE CHEVALIER
available from
The Wild Rose Press, Inc.

Dedication

To Marjorie, my second biggest fan
and the best mother-in-law a girl could wish for.
And to my own parents, Darlene and Gerald,
for their years of love and support.

Chapter One

Baltimore 1778

The American Revolution had become a drawn out battle between the ragtag American Army and British forces. General Washington's troops, decimated by the previous winter at Valley Forge, were a sickly group of soldiers ill-equipped for battle. On land, it was a war of attrition.

At sea, a different scene prevailed where privateers, ships given the legal right to pursue and capture English vessels supplying the British forces, combined American capitalism with patriotic fervor. A combination of bravery and enlightened self-interest provided General Washington a powerful ally in the War for Independence.

Amanda Blakely twisted around to take a critical survey of her appearance in her floor length bedroom mirror. Her father's work clothes were large, but not so large that a few tucks here and there, and a wide leather belt couldn't make them fit her tall frame. She grabbed the aged leather strap from the dresser and fastened it about her slender waist using one of the notches she had added with nail and hammer.

She had bound her chest, an almost unnecessary effort since her curves weren't exactly the kind that drew attention. Still, without her shift, the soft woolen bindings were all that protected her delicate skin from the coarse cotton weave of her tunic.

She scrunched her nose at her reflection. Turning from a grown woman into an adolescent boy had taken less of an effort than she expected—certainly less than she would have hoped. If nature had been kinder to her, it wouldn't have been this easy. She leaned closer to assess her youthful face in the mirror. Sixteen? No, no stubble to make anyone believe she was quite that old. Even fifteen would be a stretch. Fourteen, a year older than Neil, would be much more believable. In her father's clothes, she looked far more a fourteen-year-old boy than a twenty-one-year-old woman.

Amanda stared at the visage of the young boy reflected in the wavy surface of the old mirror. What would she do if Neil refused to come back with her? Would she follow him onto a ship? Could she? She had always considered herself a sensible young woman, but with her little brother's life at stake, she would do whatever it took to protect him.

However, she must consider the possibility that she would not make it in time. Neil had left sometime during the night and, even if she left soon, it would be well on noon when she reached the harbor. What would she do if he had already signed on to a ship? Or that ship had already sailed?

Whatever it took.

She took a deep breath and crossed her hands over her racing heart. Better to focus on getting ready so she could find Neil before he had a chance to do anything foolish.

Amanda picked up the scissors from the nightstand

next to the bed. Sighing, she took a last look at her long, honey-blonde curls. "For my brother," she said, her voice echoing in the empty bedroom.

An unexpected shudder shook her. *Excitement or fear?* She forced the question from her mind and resumed cutting, the cold metal heavy in her trembling hand.

Once finished, she leaned in and tugged at a lock beside her temple. When released, it sprang back, a cherubic curl against her cheek.

"Humph, it will have to do I suppose." She tied her hair back into a short tail that hung just past her shoulders with a scrap of old leather.

Satisfied, she picked up her father's aged felt hat and flopped it onto her blonde curls. Then she spun on her heal, snatched her canvas sack off the end of her bed, and sped down the back stairs.

****

Amanda urged Homer, her sturdy plow horse, toward Baltimore. By the time they reached the edge of town, he whistled and wheezed, occasionally releasing a lungful of air in a shuddering sigh that promised to be his last. She sold him to a skeptical farmer, probably for far less than his worth. However, if she hoped to stop her brother before he did anything foolish, she did not have time to waste on negotiations.

Without a mount, Amanda forced her way on foot through the busy portside streets, wondering just how many people inhabited the growing town. Despite the early hour, it seemed most of them had business at the docks and all in the opposite direction.

Bracing herself against the oncoming tide of people, she stood on her toes and craned her neck to peer over the faces in front of her. What Neil lacked in height he made up for in strength, but at this moment, she would have given anything to put a couple inches on him so she could spot his dark brown head above the masses.

Amanda pushed forward again, sidestepping murky puddles and drawing up the lapels of her father's coat to protect her mouth and nose from the stench. At times, the ground became so muddy she had no choice but to move forward on tiptoe. Water soaked her leather shoes and greenish brown droplets of foul-smelling ooze spotted her cotton stockings.

"I bloody well can do the job, and I challenge any man who tells me I can't!"

Amanda placed her fists on her hips, raised her chin and turned full circle, trying to pinpoint the owner of the familiar, belligerent tone.

"And, I tells you, you can't!" came the cantankerous reply.

She buried her chin to her chest the way Homer did when working a new field filled with roots and plowed her way toward the voices through the tangle of idling sailors. She could smell the tang of the ocean, but the sea of elbows, backs and broad shoulders made it difficult to see anything but the bodies in front of her. A burly man in a pair of striped pants and a tattered shirt threatened to cuff her ears for her rudeness. Amanda quickened her pace. She shouldered her way past one stalwart frame after another, holding her nose against the sour onslaught of unwashed bodies.

She dodged the elbow of a sailor lost in a fiery debate with his shipmate, and at last, the sea opened up before her. Amanda gasped, letting the fresh, salty air fill her desperate lungs.

"I can!" the familiar voice roared.

Amanda spun about so fast the disheveled crowd became no more than a blur, like the oily surface of the puddles she had tried so hard to avoid.

At the edge of the wharf, she spotted Neil's sturdy form.

A stocky, old man with wiry gray curls leaned half way over a rough-hewn table. Her brother matched the old man's aggressive stance until barely a paper's breadth could fit between their noses. Two gazes wrestled with each other, each vying to dominate the small space above the table.

"Neil!"

Neil jerked his gaze away from his adversary, but his glare remained. "What the hell are you doing here?"

Amanda thought about chastising him for his language but checked herself. A "boy" her age would be unlikely to have a problem with it. In fact, she probably ought to pay more attention to her brother's colorful word choice from now on. She might do well to try a few of the phrases herself.

"Just who the bloody hell might you be?" The crusty sailor scratched the stubble on his chin and sat down on his stool with a hard thump.

"I'm his brother," Amanda replied, forcing her voice deeper into her throat.

Heavens! Surrounded by the low rumble of male voices, hers sounded more feminine than ever.

The old man squinted watery eyes, letting his gaze trail over her. He lingered on her blonde curls, her narrow waist, her long legs. A salty breeze from the ocean cooled the sweat forming on the top of her upper lip, yet Amanda forced herself to stand still. Just when she was sure he would call her bluff, he turned his attention to Neil and gave him the same cynical perusal.

"You don't look like brothers," he said.

"That's 'cause we ain't," Neil said.

Amanda's stomach did a flip. Would Neil give her away? She turned to him and tried to think of some way of persuading him to stay quiet without making the old man suspicious. Her mouth opened and closed, like a fish trying to breathe air, not yet willing to surrender to the inevitable.

"At least not real ones anyways," Neil added. "He's my adopted brother."

Amanda relaxed, an audible sigh escaping before she had a chance to stifle it.

Ignoring her, the old man sucked his teeth and let his gaze roam Neil's short, stocky figure once more. "So did your father give ya permission to join a privateer at—"

"Fifteen," Neil replied.

"Uh-huh." The man rubbed the stubble on his chin again.

It was a wonder that the man could manage to grow facial hair at all with the way he kept scraping his gnarled fingers against his whiskers.

"Father's dead," Neil answered, his voice flat, his gaze unwavering.

"I see. No family then," the corner of his eye twitched, "except a brother, of course."

He turned to Amanda next. "And, how 'bout you? You fifteen too?"

The man's voice was heavy with sarcasm, but Amanda paid scant attention. Her mind raced to form an answer that made sense.

If Neil was fifteen then–

No wait, I am taller. I have to be older. That would make me–

"Are we about ready to sail, Bull?" a voice boomed from behind them.

Amanda gasped. Neil shot her a warning glance before they both turned to face the owner of the powerful set of lungs.

Standing straight, the top of Amanda's head barely reached the man's shoulders, and she stared at a stylized carving of a she-wolf on a bone button midway up the finely woven, blue woolen waistcoat that stretched across the broad expanse of his chest.

Amanda's gaze crept upward, past the last she-wolf, past the narrow frill that adorned his starched white shirt, past his equally pristine neck stock until it rested on the steady pulse beating under the shadow of an angled jaw. She willed her gaze to continue its upward path, away from the safety of the slow, even beat.

His cheekbones were set high on his deeply tanned face, his nose straight and narrow at the bridge but flared slightly outward toward the tip so that it softened an otherwise harsh and unyielding countenance. From beneath straight black brows, he skewered the old man with golden eyes so wild they appeared almost feral.

To Amanda's amazement, the old man he had called Bull stood his ground, undaunted by the withering glare.

"No, we ain't 'bout ready to sail." He slammed his fist on the table, making the logbook and quill jump. "We won't be done loadin' supplies 'til tomorrow, and

I got two more spots t' fill."

"What about these two?" asked the man, equally impervious to Bull's gray glower.

"They ain't got no experience!" With each word, Bull's voice rose in volume.

"That so?" He turned golden eyes on them.

Amanda's heart fluttered in her chest, but she could not look away. He had the outward appearance of a man, but the essence behind those golden eyes was that of an animal, untamed but unafraid, confident of his dominion over the lesser creatures around him.

Strength radiated from him in waves that washed over her and curled about her limbs, binding her wrists and ankles with an unseen force and robbing her of the will to move. He was taller than many of the men around him, perhaps broader of shoulder too, but with a lean build that could not match the bulk of the men loading crates behind him. His power came not from sheer size, but from an energy buried deep within. A shiver rippled through her.

Pursing his lips, he clasped Amanda and Neil by one shoulder each and gave a sharp squeeze. Her shoulder fit easily inside his palm, and his strong fingers dug into the tender flesh below the joint. His touch seared her as though nothing separated skin from skin.

She tried not to flinch when he frowned and ran his hand down her bicep. Instead, she followed her brother's lead and returned the man's scowl with one of her own, attempting with every ounce of her being to match his ferocity while her insides took on the consistency of melted butter.

"And they be calling me stubborn," Bull muttered.

Amanda could swear a smile tugged at the corner of the man's lips, but judging from the look in his hard eyes, she changed her mind. He wasn't the smiling type.

Trapped in his gaze as well as his grip, Amanda prayed he would finish soon. Surely, his sharp eyes could see though her disguise even if Bull could not. Amanda's stomach tightened as though turned on a screw.

Instead, he took his time, assessing, calculating, judging. Everywhere he looked her skin heated. Held tight in his palm, she thought her arm might burst into flames.

Amanda studied him while he studied her. His hair was so black it looked almost blue. Dark lashes framed his golden eyes. She had never seen eyes that color before, not on a man anyway. She might have called him handsome, were it not for the firm set of his jaw and the way he probed her face with his heated gaze.

Her breath rushed across her bottom lip, and she realized she had been watching him, slack-jawed. She snapped her mouth shut and focused on taking slow, even breaths through her nose while he finished prodding and squeezing her.

He slid his palm to the front of one shoulder and pushed as though testing her steadiness. She did her best to hold her ground when he pushed again. She gasped and stumbled backward when he slid his hand lower. The heat that rose to her face matched the heat that outlined the form of his hand. She felt it all, fingertips, thumb, palm, as though his hand still lay across her breast.

Beneath her father's wool coat, his course tunic,

and her wool bindings, her body responded. At twenty-one, she might be inexperienced, but she was not so naïve as to not understand the tightening of her breasts, the tingling in her belly, the weakness in her limbs. That she had never experienced any of these things didn't stop her from recognizing her uncivilized reaction to an uncivilized man.

"They'll do," he said, with a nod to Bull. "See that they're on board and understand their duties by the time we shove off." Without waiting for Bull's reply, he walked away.

The dockside masses parted before his long, languid strides. Amanda stood frozen until his broad back disappeared, swallowed up by the throngs that closed in around him and filled the wake he left behind.

"If that's what ya be wantin' then I suppose they'll do just fine," Bull scratched a few notes in the ship's registry. "'Course, it'll serve ya right, questioning my judgment. You'll be getting just what ya deserve with these two."

Bull chucked and Amanda scowled at him. What did he find so amusing if he disapproved of Neil and her so much?

"Well, ya heard the captain," said Bull, this time speaking to the new recruits.

Amanda's eyelids fluttered. "Th-that was the captain?"

A chill filled her, replacing the residual heat of the captain's slow scrutiny.

Of course he was! That his self-possessed assuredness of his position hadn't tipped her off made her question her judgment. Her reaction to him made her question her sanity. Either way, he posed more of a danger to her than she had first thought, and she would do well to avoid him.

"That he is. Captain Stoakes is his name, but that's not what his enemies be callin' him." Bull's toothy grin showed a number of gold teeth, but his words were thick with warning.

"What do his enemies call him?" Amanda asked before she could stop herself.

"The Sea Wolf." Bull's eyes twinkled beneath bushy brows.

Before Amanda could determine whether the old man was teasing or trying to scare them, Neil chimed in. "Really? How come?"

He sounded far too enthusiastic for his own good.

"On account of the way he stalks his prey." Bull's voice dropped to a grinding whisper, like the stones of a gristmill. She and Neil leaned in to hear. "Like the wolf, he is bloodthirsty and merciless. No one who is his enemy is safe. Be glad you're part of his crew." The acrid smell of tobacco on his breath assailed Amanda's nose, but she could not muster the will to pull back, opting to hold her breath instead. "But you'd better be careful not to get on his bad side or..." His voice trailed off, leaving them to imagine the unspeakable horrors the Sea Wolf brought down upon those who displeased him.

The old man paused, and Amanda assumed he had had his fun. Her breath had just returned to her lungs, when he continued, "If there are women or children on the ships he takes," Bull leaned back and crossed his arms, "well that just don't matter none. He tosses them over the side and pretends they were never there." He spat a dark stream at a gull that had wandered close.

The bird squawked in distress and hopped sideways to a safer distance. "Well, sometimes he keeps the women for awhile."

Amanda scrunched her nose. For a man who hadn't smiled even once until now, Bull seemed to be grinning a bit too much. Then she remembered the captain's golden eyes. Hunter's eyes.

Maybe he hadn't been teasing.

"Well, make your mark," Bull said, his voice normal as though he had never spoken of the Sea Wolf. He dipped the quill in the inkpot and handed it to Neil.

Neil signed the book, then passed the quill to Amanda. Amanda held the sharp point above the yellowed parchment, but hesitated. She couldn't very well sign her real name, but she had never considered, not even once, that she would need a boy's name in order to complete her disguise.

"If ya can't write, ya can just put an X on the line, and that'll do," said Bull.

She cast a glance upward but read nothing of Bull's earlier mistrust in his grizzled face. He believed her. Either that or he followed the captain's orders without question. Either way, she was in the clear, for now.

Turning her attention to the book, she scrawled the first name she thought of in big, bold script...*Adam Blakely.*

"Off you go, then." He waved a dismissive hand toward the narrow boards leading from the dock to the upper deck of the small ship. "Check in with Mr. Smythe when you reach the top. He'll be showing ya where to stow your things and be explainin' your duties to ya."

Amanda and Neil grabbed their sacks and turned to

go. Before starting up the ramp after her brother, she glanced at the page she had just signed. The name of the ship that had become her home ran across the top in large, flowing script. *Registry of the Amanda.*

Amanda sucked in a breath. Good omen or bad?

Neither, she decided, releasing the air from her lungs. Amanda Blakely no longer existed in this new world. From now on, she was Adam Blakely, and she would do well to remember it.

A tingling in her shoulder reminded her of the man with whom she would be spending the next few months. Nothing in those hard eyes suggested he enjoyed a good ruse. She would need to be especially mindful of her new status around him.

Amanda gripped the rough rope handhold running along the gangplank with white knuckled fists and trudged up the steep incline. At the top, she stepped over a small rise and onto the deck below. The bustle that greeted her looked more like an anthill than a ship, with all of the worker ants readying themselves for a long winter. Each and every ant knew its job. Not a one shirked his duties.

"Oh, dear," Amanda tightened her grip on her canvas sack and pulled it higher onto her shoulder.

She had forgotten to follow her own plan. The whole idea had been to stop Neil from signing on to a privateer. Yet, she hadn't even tried. Instead, she had signed the ship's registry every bit as eagerly as her brother.

A sailor in striped trousers and canvas shirt shoved her, and she stumbled toward the center of the activity. A circle of other new recruits closed in, blocking her only avenue of escape.

Chapter Two

"Well, it is *your* choice." Will held up his glass in a half-hearted toast. "And, James, since it is your choice, I wish you every happiness."

"Oh, come on, Will," Captain James Stoddard raised his voice above the groans of the two officers standing behind his chair and the din of the post-suppertime crowd in the small inn's cozy taproom. Unlike his lieutenants, he had earned the right to call the dreaded Sea Wolf by his first name, and his forthright tone spoke of their long association. "You can do better than that. I'm getting married for God's sake, not joining the Royal Navy."

Will gave a small nod of acknowledgment.

He opened his mouth to reply, but one of the enthusiastic young lieutenants beat him to it. "I should hope not, sir. Not when we have them right where we want them."

The other young officer, emboldened by drink, clapped his friend on the shoulder and spoke as though each syllable presented a bit of a challenge. "You got that right. Our Cont'nental Navy'll have 'em runnin' back to ol' England," he paused, his blonde brows on a slow march toward the middle of his forehead. Then, slopping beer over the side, he poked his glass in the general direction of England, "tail between their legs."

He punctuated his point with a sharp nod, spilling

more beer onto his friend's polished boot.

Will grunted. "You Navy men are so sure of yourselves. You've only been a Navy for what—three years now?" His dismissive shrug pulled at the seams of his blue velvet coat. "Your enemy is the most powerful fleet in the world and has been for almost two hundred years."

"Yeeees!" The flickering light from the oil lamp in the middle of the table illuminated a fine spray of spittle. "But you've seen how weak they are now. We've almost as many ships as they do, and ours are much newer!"

He leaned forward, propping a fist on the table, and brandished the glass in his other hand as though fighting an unseen enemy. Will watched the golden waves slosh from side to side, hoping the young man would find an even keel before he upended the entire table.

"No matter how inelegantly my drunken friend makes his point, Captain Stoakes," the lieutenant beside him righted his friend and cast him a warning glance, "I think he has a good one. The British Navy is weak."

"They are tired," Will interjected before the upstarts could make complete fools of themselves by defending the Continental Navy's anemic forces.

"Tired?" James asked.

Will sighed into his glass, before taking another swallow. His beer had grown warm in the packed tavern, too warm.

He and James had been friends since serving together in the Royal Navy in the years before the colonies declared their independence from England. The closest thing Will had to a brother, he also admired the man's sense of duty to God and country. James had proven himself a damned fine officer and loyal to the cause. He continued to serve in the Continental Navy long after Will had had enough.

Nevertheless, he found himself dismayed at how little some of the Continental Navy officers, even the best fighting captains, could see of the complete canvas of war between nations.

They saw the power of their ship's guns. They saw the health of their men. They saw the fullness of their stores. However, rare was the captain who fully understood the political and financial implications of modern warfare. Beyond the bow of their own ship, most were blind.

Will sighed again, resigned to explaining what should have been obvious. "Yes. They have been fighting on two continents." He twisted his glass, making small wet rings on the linen tablecloth. "In Europe they fought the Seven Years War, and here, in America, they fought the French and Indian War."

"But they fought the French in both," the lieutenant argued. "That makes it the same war."

"A war fought on two fronts is as good as two wars." Will's frown deepened at the bemused look on the faces of his audience. "And with the war fought in America, it might as well have been three."

He waited, his gaze roaming from face to face, hoping for a small glimmer of understanding. Only the flame in the oil lamp flickered.

Perhaps he expected too much. James's lieutenants couldn't be much more than twenty. Could either of them remember the savage conflict between the French, their Indian allies and the British? He studied their unlined faces, the vibrant enthusiasm in their eyes and the lack of observable scars that marked so many men tested in battle.

They had been too young to fight, but perhaps they were old enough to hold at least some memory of the bloody struggle. Those who had been there told the stories of the colonists, many women and children, brutally massacred by Indian tribes with a savagery unimaginable to the regimented British forces. Those who had not seen the bloodshed themselves had certainly heard about it. Subsequent years and multiple retellings had done nothing to diminish the horror.

"Do you think you'll ever join the Navy again, sir?" the sober lieutenant asked with polite deference.

Will knew the young officer referred to the Continental Navy even though the only Navy he had ever *officially* belonged to had been the Royal Navy. He took a final swig from his glass, grimacing at the bitter tang of the foamy remnants. The sour taste in his mouth matched his mood.

This was supposed to be a celebration of the betrothal of his closest friend. With the *Amanda* not ready to sail until tomorrow, he had decided he might as well join James and his officers for a celebration supper at one of the finer inns in the small port town of Baltimore. Although a humble establishment, the Horse Head Inn boasted a card room that readily attracted American privateers, flush with cash from recent prize auctions. Later, they planned to join the tables where they would spend the evening putting considerable sums at risk in the hopes of even more substantial gains.

Except now, not yet midnight, all Will could think

about was how to extricate himself from the betrothal party and return to his ship. He had a new crew waiting for him, and he wanted time to get to know them before they got underway. He needed to take their measure; assess their strength and their heart.

A pair of emerald green eyes, framed by long lashes, slightly turned up at the corners, flashed in his memory. The boy's eyes? No, these were not the eyes of an adolescent boy.

But, if not the boy's eyes, whose eyes were they? No matter. He shoved the image aside. They were probably the eyes of some long-forgotten paramour, the kind of entangling connection he could mercifully cast aside once his *Amanda* weighed anchor.

Will raised his glass to his lips, then remembering he had already drained it, set it down with a thud. Looking about for a barmaid, he realized his companions seemed to be waiting for a response.

"No," Will said, answering the lieutenant's question, "I don't think I'll be joining the Navy again." *Continental or Royal.*

"Of course not." The drunken officer teetered, catching himself just in time. "Money's better as a pirate."

Will gave the man a look intended to make it clear to even the most inebriated of the group that he had overstepped his bounds. The young officer flushed to the tips of his ears and took a swig of ale. Foam dripped from the ends of his wiry, blonde moustache when he finally pulled his face out of his glass.

"Ah, yes, well I think I'll see what kind of ac—" the lieutenant's voice broke, and he cleared his throat, "action I can find at the tables."

"I'll join you." The other officer clasped his friend about the shoulders and ushered him away from the two captains who remained seated.

"Seriously, Will," James said once they were alone, "we could use a man like you in the Continental Navy. With your skills, your reputation...your *luck*. Sailors would be signing up in droves."

Will caught the eye of a girl of no more than seventeen or eighteen. Carrying several pints of beer in her sturdy hands, she wove her way through the crowded taproom until she reached the table next to them. She flashed him a crooked toothed grin over one shoulder, then set her burden down in front of a table full of young merchants who seemed as interested in her as the brew. She said something to them that made them laugh, with the exception of the one who appeared to be the youngest. His face took on the appearance of a ripe persimmon.

Turning, she wiped red, wet hands on a stained apron.

"Get you another one, Captain?" Her brown eyes roamed over Will's well-tailored form with obvious appreciation.

Noting the lines at the corners of her eyes when smiled, Will reassessed his initial impression of the girl's age. Not so young as he first thought. Old enough to have the experience of a woman, yet young enough to give the impression of innocence.

She leaned forward, far more than necessary, to take his glass.

Well, almost innocent.

"No, but thank you. That will be all. For now."

The barmaid gave a throaty chuckle and regarded

him through her lashes. “Well now, Captain, you just let me know when you might be needin’ something else.”

She sashayed toward the taps, holding their empty glasses in her hands, her skirts swishing from the exaggerated sway of her hips.

James rolled his eyes, cleared his throat, and turned back to Will. “Forget the Navy, Will. When will you realize the sea does not offer everything a man needs?”

“I have everything I need.” Will said, staring at the woman’s voluptuous backside even while his mind strayed to thoughts of his ship.

James glanced over his shoulder, then leaned forward. “You know what I mean,” he said in a conspiratorial whisper.

Will turned his full attention to his friend. “Yes, I’m afraid I do.”

Of course, he did. This was hardly the first time James had lectured him on the need for a wife.

The barmaid glanced up from refilling a glass at the tap and caught Will’s gaze. She dipped her eyes until her long lashes brushed her cheeks. A knowing smile touched her lips.

Hell! What had made him say something to give her false hope?

“I am not talking about companionship of that sort,” James protested, bringing Will’s gaze back once again to his friend’s earnest, but annoyed face. James ran his hand through his hair, his fingers leaving furrows in his brown locks. “Look, Will, our work is dangerous. Our lives may be short. I want you to find the same kind of happiness I’ve found with Isabella in whatever time you have left.” He paused, “Isa has a cousin who has come to visit—"

"Perhaps I will find it tonight," Will interrupted his friend before he could hear, again, all about Isabella's wonderful cousin. It seemed Isabella had an unending supply of cousins, all fresh from Spain and in search of husbands.

He heartily approved of his friend's choice of a bride, the small, dark-haired and quite delectable Isabella. The two had overcome their initial differences, her hot temper and James's colder English demeanor, and settled down to a largely peaceful courtship that eventually ensnared his best friend. Of course, James's work kept him at sea most of the time so he didn't expect he and his young bride would see much of each other, at least not until the war ended.

Will coughed into his hand to hide a cynical chuckle. The end of the war may bring peace to America, but perhaps not to his friend.

"Whoring is still more your style, I suppose," said James, giving the barmaid a disapproving glare when she bent forward to serve another round of ale, the rough fabric of her skirt accentuating her plump, inviting derriere.

Will made a show of studying the woman. "I doubt she is a whore."

At least she wouldn't be with him. Women never named a price before they shared his bed, and they never asked for a thing afterwards. And Will never offered. He would take what they willingly gave, but he wouldn't be the one to turn them into whores.

Now, with the passing of the years, this little game of self-absolution wore thin. Occasionally, he felt guilty about using the women, despite their willingness. It left him disgusted with them and his needs never fully sated regardless of their expertise and his physical fulfillment.

This time, maybe he would pay her but not bed her. He still wouldn't be turning her into a whore, and she'd get something out of it. It would be a refreshing change.

He tossed some coins on the table and said his goodbyes to his friend before signaling for his coat. On his way out, he caught the girl's eye with a look that promised he'd be back sooner or later.

Stepping into the darkness and a cold spring drizzle, he knew he never would.

****

"Well, Captain." A tall man with a refined bearing and a crisp New England accent came to stand beside Will at the ship's stern. "Our fresh water stores are replenished, we are just about re-supplied and the men have all reported to duty. We shall be ready to sail on the evening tide."

"It's about time, Buck," Will grumbled, watching the loading of the last of the stores, an interminably slow business.

He clasped his hands behind his back, one tight fist firmly locked in the palm of his other hand, and watched two sailors struggle to carry a crate of chickens up the steep slope of the gangplank. The birds flapped about with such fury that the sailor who had the misfortune of being in the lead and walking backwards stumbled and fought to keep his balance.

"Careful there!" a corpulent man in a white butcher's apron yelled from behind the men "or ya'll be drowning the Captain's breakfast, and I'll be sending ya in after it."

He followed them up the walk, his close-set eyes darting back and forth between the crate of chickens and the murky water below.

"Bull hasn't yet found a real cook, eh?" Buck asked, his voice casual.

In no mood for jests, Will merely grunted. Cookie's lack of culinary skills were the one dark cloud hanging over what looked to be a promising voyage.

"What duties did you assign to those two?" he asked, changing the subject with a nod toward Neil and Adam.

The boys stood back to back, Adam appearing confused and Neil belligerent while the men about them loaded the ship and readied it for sail. If they didn't move their asses, they were likely to be trampled.

"Hmm, Adam and Neil Blakely..." Buck tapped his chin with one long index finger. "To tell you the truth, I haven't decided. The taller one goes by the name of Adam. I've thinking of making him your cabin boy. He doesn't seem cut out for manual labor." He cocked his head at his captain. "A bit bonny to make it as a sailor, don't you think, Captain?"

Will gave a small snort. Those had been his thoughts exactly. What had possessed him to go against Bull's better judgment?

Will's stomach rumbled, reminding him that he had not yet eaten breakfast. Normally, his stomach was nothing to trifle with as it directly influenced his state of mind. "The Captain's Curse" one of the ship's boys had dubbed it, not realizing his captain stood directly behind him. Luckily for the boy, Will had eaten ashore that morning and the lad got away with no more than deck-swabbing duties for the whole of the month.

A scuffle by the railing caught Will's attention. Judging from the scene, young Neil Blakely had taken offense at being jostled by one of the sailors loading supplies. The boy now stood toe to toe with a man a foot taller and at least twice his breadth. Neil's strong voice carried on the breeze, and Will heard him call his adversary several names rarely known by boys not long removed from their mother's apron strings.

When his mates started laughing behind him, Roger, a craggy veteran of more than two decades at sea, overcame his surprise at being upbraided by the scruffy young pup. His neck and ears changed to an alarming shade of crimson, and he lurched forward, clearly determined to teach the new recruit a lesson.

Beside Will, Buck tensed and leaned on the balls of his feet, ready to intervene. He looked over at his captain in anticipation of orders. Will considered letting him go. After all, the value of experience was limited if it left a member of his crew dead. Then he relaxed when he caught sight of Bull watching the scuffle from the other side of the ship. His crew master would intervene if called for. Neil was in no danger, other than receiving a cuff to the ears for his insolence.

However, Will thought with a frown, Adam might be in real peril if he didn't get out from between Neil and Roger.

Roger froze, confusion flashing across his weather-beaten face when the lanky boy put one slender hand on his brother's chest and then one on his.

Then confusion turned to irritation and neither combatant seemed too pleased. Their glares pinned the boy between them. Adam turned his head from one to the other, but the stiff shore wind swept his words away. By the look in his eyes and the rapid movement of his lips, Will would swear the boy scolded them.

Will laughed, then turned to stare at the open sea.

There was something about his two newest recruits. Neither looked fit to be a sailor. But earlier, when he had given them an appraisal that would have set older men to staring at their toes, they had returned his gaze without flinching. The shorter, dark-haired one had deep brown eyes laced with a strong streak of rebelliousness. Good to a point, Will supposed. Rebellious independence was the hallmark of a good privateer. If he could temper the boy's natural instincts with some discipline, he might stand a chance.

The taller, thinner boy had eyes green as a troubled sea, but instead of defiance, they held something Will was at a loss to explain.

Those eyes, glaring up at him while he assessed the strength of their owner, had nearly made him lose sight of his duty. The boy didn't look like he had done a hard day's labor in his life, and his arms felt thin as twigs in Will's grasp. Yet the boy's eyes held him captive, threatening to pull him in, to drown him in their depths.

When he found his voice again, Will went against Bull's judgment, something he rarely did.

How old was the lad anyway? He was tall, almost statuesque, with a lithe build and narrow shoulders. Dress him in a gown; he could pass for a woman and quite a fetching one at that.

Will scowled at the absurd thought.

"Buck, I want you to assign both of them to the same duties you would any waif who fancies himself a sailor. We need to work them hard to see what they've got."

In time, they would prove his instincts right. He would see to that.

"You're the captain." Buck turned and strode toward the boys who had taken to yelling at each other to the amusement of the crowd of sailors gathering around them.

"You there!" he bellowed. "If you don't have any work to do, I'll see to it that you do. Don't let me catch you idling. This isn't the Royal Navy!"

Chapter Three

Amanda scoured the grain of the wooden deck with a holystone, the rough edges of the block abrading her palms. A late spring sun beat against her shoulders with a penetrating heat rare for early March, and a trickle of warm sweat ran between her shoulder blades. She sat back on her heels, abrading her brow with the gritty cotton sleeve of her shirt and shielding her eyes from the glare of the sun's rays bouncing off the endless sea.

By her estimation, it had been a little more than two weeks since the *Amanda* weighed anchor and sailed far enough out to sea to lose sight of Maryland's sylvan coast.

In answer to her queries, one of her shipmates explained they were no more than a day's sail from shore. Amanda squinted her eyes against the unyielding sun and tried to spot even a hint of coastline. Perhaps he had been mistaken.

The ship rolled on a wave, and she placed a palm flat against her stomach to quell the nausea. According to Bull, the small bouts of sickness she suffered were less severe than those that afflicted most new recruits. She had to ask him to repeat his small piece of wisdom because her head had been in a bucket at the time.

He suggested spending time in the open air of the main deck and attending to her duties. She took a recuperating breath and admitted his self-serving advice worked. That and the fair weather for which her more seasoned shipmates assured her she should be grateful.

Nausea past, Amanda looked about, letting her senses steep in the beauty of her surroundings. At sea, the sky looked bluer, the ocean a deep aquamarine, and the snow-white clouds close enough to touch. She raised a slender hand to the sky so that it overlaid an ephemeral ball of fluff. She curled her fingers, one by one, into a fist, and imagined capturing the cool, cottony mist in the palm of her hand.

Amanda closed her eyes and drew a breath between parted lips. She savored the air drifting over her tongue and filling her lungs. It was salty, almost sweet. To her, it tasted like freedom. Turning her face skyward once more, she let her skin drink in the sun's heated caress. Most women her age went to extreme measures: parasols, creams, bonnets, anything to avoid the sun's rays. That thought brought a momentary twinge of guilt. Although she hadn't seen herself in a mirror for days, she did not doubt the number of freckles spattered across her nose and cheeks had grown. Her face probably resembled a speckled hen.

What did the captain think of her freckles? The question popped into her mind, unbidden, and it startled her. He wouldn't notice her freckles anymore than he would notice those that made the face of Jimmy, another one of her young shipmates, look like a mass of polka dots. He wouldn't notice because the captain still saw her for what she pretended to be. For reasons she couldn't fathom, or didn't want to, that she could so easily deceive the captain bothered her. Was she so plain that a man who could sight a sail two miles out to sea against a backdrop of white clouds couldn't see what was right in front of him?

"Oh, who cares!" She returned her focus to the deck, scrubbing with renewed vigor and watching the water-darkened boards dry to the color of old bones.

She loved the sea. It didn't demand she be beautiful, or for that matter, even pretty. At sea, she had more freedom to be herself than she had ever had in her entire life. The irony of it made her lips curl. For the past two weeks, she had pretended to be something she was most definitely not.

Perhaps her love for life on the ocean was what had surprised her most. Despite the short bouts of seasickness, she hadn't expected to look forward to each new day with such anticipation, such joy. Every morning, when Bull called "out or down" in his most menacing voice, she was among the first to have her hammock rolled and stowed and be on deck ready for whatever tasks awaited her. She enjoyed working side by side with her shipmates, all of whom were exceedingly polite men, despite their rough edges.

But more than anything, she loved watching the captain go about his duties. Not that he did much. In fact, most of the time, he wasn't even on deck. When he did emerge from his quarters, it was usually to walk amongst the men, inspect their work, say a few words to Buck or Bull, then take a position at the rear of his ship and stare out at the ocean. In that position, she could let her gaze linger on him as long as she liked.

Though she scrubbed at the deck, the memory of him filled her vision. He stood with feet planted shoulder width apart. Beneath his tight fitting breeches, his muscles danced as he adjusted to the swell of the ocean. His golden eyes scanned the horizon. She liked it best when he left his hat behind because she could watch the wind play with his dark curls as though it were trying to untie the leather thong that held back his hair. Silently, she cheered the wind on.

Every now and then, he tipped his chin as though catching the scent of a distant enemy on the breeze before turning his sharp eyes back to the horizon. He reminded her of a wild animal, patiently stalking his prey, waiting for the right opportunity to pounce.

A faint odor tickled her nostrils, and the image faded. Face tilted, nose twitching, she searched for the wisp of a scent lingering in the air. It smelled vaguely familiar, like a hearth in the morning before the lighting of a new fire, musty and thick.

She squinted toward the horizon. Had they sailed closer to land, even if she couldn't sight it yet? Baltimore's chimneys were choking enough when one walked through the town. The sharp odor could have drifted out over the open ocean.

Amanda set the holystone in her bucket to let the seawater seep into the brittle sandstone. She pulled it out, water dripping from its pores, and set to work on a dark, stubborn stain. She hadn't expected sailors to be as fussy as old nurse-maids about the tidiness of their ship, but the *Amanda* was their home, and they insisted everything be—what was it they called it—*shipshape*.

The odor, stronger now, pricked Amanda's senses. She covered her nose and mouth with her grimy sleeve and scanned the open deck. Sailors were busy at their tasks, unperturbed by the foreign scent hanging in the air. One man, perched high above her on a platform, scanned the horizon like a bird of prey searching for its next victim. Two more coiled a rope the thickness of her forearm. A third group cleaned the guns even though they had seen only limited use in training exercises.

The captain and Buck Smythe stood amidships, their heads bent together in consultation over a map. The captain's cocked hat was nowhere to be seen, and sunlight streaked his dark hair with golden highlights. He looked up and his gaze captured hers. Amanda's breath caught in her throat, and she twisted her face away.

The sound of a familiar ditty drifting on the breeze caught her attention. Bull leaned against the bulwark, whittling, whistling and keeping an eye on his charges. Amanda shrugged and dipped her stone in the bucket again. If Bull and the captain weren't concerned about the smell, she supposed she had no cause to be.

She scrubbed the deck and watched the seawater evaporate, appreciating the way her efforts reawakened the sun-bleached oak, giving the dull, lifeless planks an ivory glow that sparkled in the sunlight. She didn't mind hard work. Her assigned duties absorbed her every moment, from sunup to sundown, and sometimes longer if Bull decided something needed done. In the evening, she crawled into her hammock, muscles aching and so tired that even the thunderous snoring of the men didn't keep her awake.

Life at sea and a constant stream of duties kept Neil out of trouble as well. At first, he and Amanda had been assigned the same tasks, but Neil's sharpness of mind and interest in sailing soon earned him the right to learn at the side of any man with the patience to withstand the endless questions of an intelligent, inquisitive boy.

Amanda overheard him ask the navigator how he could navigate when the skies were cloudy and one couldn't see the stars. He asked the bosun the names of each of the different types of sails and when they were used. He asked Buck about the differences between nNaval ships and privateers. And Neil, not having the sense to give the captain a wide berth, trailed him as if he had the captain at the end of a line. Whenever Captain Stoakes got too far away, Neil pulled him back, asking questions about the business of privateering, how Letters of Marque were issued, what ships they were allowed to attack and what happened at the prize courts.

Much to her surprise, the captain didn't seem to mind being Neil's captive. With the passing of the days, he and Neil spent more time together than apart.

Buck Smythe returned to other duties, and Captain Stoakes joined Neil at the bulwark. Neil spoke, the snapping of the sails in the crisp breeze drowning out his words, but the left corner of his mouth turned up in a half-smile, the way it always did when he was up to something. She held her breath when Neil balanced against the bulwark, hands gripping the gunwale, and leaned forward until his toes just skirted the deck. The captain grasped the back of Neil's breeches with one hand when the weight of her brother's shoulders threatened to topple him overboard.

Amanda sat back, resting her backside on her bare heels. What could he be doing?

The captain yanked Neil back aboard ship, but instead of giving him the scolding she expected, he took his turn at the bulwark. To the delight of the grinning boy, the captain let lose a straight stream of spittle aimed at something out of sight in the water.

Amanda's jaw dropped. Neil had challenged the captain to a spitting contest and he had complied!

A wave of malodorous fumes washed over the deck, yet the captain and Neil remained bent over the bulwark, seemingly oblivious to the odor. Nose burning and eyes stinging, she peered over their posteriors at the horizon, half-expecting to see another ship aflame on the open sea. Nothing but blue sky and shimmering water.

She twisted about to look behind her. What was wrong with the captain and this crew? Could she be the only one who smelled it? She tossed her stone into her bucket with a sigh. Placing damp, red hands on her knees, she pushed herself up and strode to where Bull leaned against a railing, whittling wood chips onto the spotless deck.

"Excuse me, Bull, but it smells like something is burning."

"Sure is," Bull replied without missing a beat with his knife.

Amanda watched him whittle and wondered if he planned to make a toothpick. With each stroke of his blade, he tore away great chunks of the narrow strip of wood.

"Well, isn't that a bit of a problem on a boat?"

"Ship," Bull scowled at the abused wood in his hands, turned it over and started anew on the other side.

"Excuse me?"

"This here's a ship. That there's a boat." He jabbed his knife at one of the small, tarpaulin-shrouded shapes hanging suspended at the rail.

Amanda set her hands on her hips. She learned that

lesson her second day aboard ship when she called the *Amanda* a boat in front of the captain. An eerie silence fell over the deck in the few moments before the captain threatened to toss her overboard if she ever insulted "his *Amanda*" again.

"As I was saying, isn't that a problem on a *ship*?" She cringed, realizing how petulant she sounded. She had seen ship's boys have their ears cuffed for far less.

To her relief, Bull chuckled. "Not unless you're the captain."

Amanda pursed her lips. What kind of insane logic was that? Only the captain should be worried about whether the ship was aflame? She waited for him to add more, but Bull continued his assault on the wood.

Amanda looked about. Bull may not be worried about a fire on the ship, but her gut told her something was amiss. She hurried back to her bucket, pulled out the holystone and dropped it with a dull thud onto the deck. Then she raised her chin and sniffed the air.

A long-forgotten memory of Neil making his own breakfast surfaced. *Burnt eggs*.

She picked up her bucket and headed toward the hatch leading below deck. Struggling to maintain her balance, water sloshing, Amanda felt her way down the narrow steps with bare feet. Once her feet met the solid planks of the floor below, she breathed a sigh of relief and looked about, her eyes adjusting to the relative darkness.

The sharp smell surrounded her now, filling her nose and burning the back of her throat. Somewhere in the dark, a man cursed. At least she believed it to be a curse. She couldn't make out the words, but they were reminiscent of the Gaelic she sometimes heard the Irish immigrants use on market day. Still, a curse sounded like a curse in any tongue. She didn't need to understand the words to recognize an oath.

Amanda shuffled toward the galley, gripping the heavy bucket with both hands. Tendrils of gray smoke snaked about the edges of the open galley door. A man wrapped in an apron that might have been white at one time, waved a towel toward the galley as though he meant to extinguish the fire with the breeze. Amanda shoved him aside, bringing more strangled oaths, this time directed at her. She ignored them and squinted into the smoke-filled room. Coughing, she covered her mouth with the back of her hand to keep the soot out of her lungs.

A small flame licked around the sides of a blackened pan set on the edge of the stove. The contents within emitted a steady stream of noxious fumes. Amanda marched forward, heaved her bucket of seawater over the stove and emptied it into the pan.

"Now what in the hell do you think you're doin', laddie!" The cook grabbed her shoulder and shoved her away from his stove.

The force of his shove spun Amanda toward the door, and she stumbled. She reached out through the smoke, grasping for something, anything, to steady herself. Her fingers found stiff wool laid over a unyielding frame. She grabbed a fistful in both hands.

Blinking to clear her vision, she stared at the fabric she held. Blue wool. A man's coat?

"Ahem."

The sound of someone clearing his throat came from in front of her, right in front of her. She had felt the rumble beneath her balled hands. Eyes burning and tears blurring her vision, she raised her chin to find a hard face just inches from her own. Amanda dropped the wool as though it burned.

"That's just what I want to know." The captain's golden eyes demanded an explanation.

Her heart beat like a caged bird while she searched for the words to clarify the situation. Even if he hadn't seen her dump water on the fire to save his ship, surely he could smell the smoke. Did he think she had caused the fire?

Amanda opened her mouth, but before she could say anything, the cook spoke up again.

"Here I was, sir, cookin' your breakfast, and this boy comes in here and dumps his bucket of dirty water on it." He pouted and wrung his apron between fleshy hands.

The captain reached around Amanda and yanked a towel off a hook on the wall. He wrapped it around his hand and pulled the hot pan off the stove. Frowning, he looked at the charred, wet remains of his breakfast. The blackened eggs had disintegrated and floated on the surface of the greasy water like a pair of charcoal dumplings.

"And I was so looking forward to breakfast," the captain said, staring at the unidentifiable remains.

Amanda's stomach churned. Even if his ship hadn't been in any real danger, he would not have emerged unscathed if he had eaten those eggs.

The captain leveled his gaze at her. "So what are you going to do about my breakfast, boy?"

What did he expect her to say?

Her heart threatening to break free of its prison, she suggested the only thing she could think of. "Make it for you?"

The captain stilled for a moment, then gave her a look that made her knees tremble. Had her suggestion given her away?

"You can cook?"

His question did much to explain away the speculative look on his face, and Amanda's heart slowed its frantic pace.

"Well, a little bit, sir." Her voice cracked on the last note.

He folded his arms over his chest, and she shifted her stance from one foot to the other under the heavy weight of his gaze. Silence filled the small room, and he seemed to be waiting for an explanation. Amanda improvised again.

"You see," she licked her dry lips and did her best to control her wavering voice, "my mother wanted a daughter, but she never got one. I guess she figured I would do, so she taught me how to cook."

Amanda held her breath. Her hastily contrived cover story rivaled anything Neil could fabricate. Best of all, part of it was true. She could cook. It was fairer to say, she *loved* to cook, especially for people who loved to eat. Despite his lean build, the unholy gleam in the captain's eyes suggested he fell into that category.

"Well then," the captain slapped his fist into the palm of his other hand, "from now on you have a new job."

"But Cap'n!" Cookie's extra chin wobbled in protest.

Captain Stoakes held up his hand, "Let me finish. Adam, you are to be Cookie's assistant. It's his kitchen and you do what he tells you. Understood?"

"Yes, sir," Amanda answered.

He flashed her a smile and liquid warmth seeped all the way to her toes.

"Splendid! If you want to stay on my good side, you'll have my breakfast in my quarters in the next twenty minutes!" He turned on his heal and strode out the door.

Amanda placed the palm of her hand against her chest and blew a shuddering breath between pursed lips. Then, she turned to face her next challenge.

"Name's Ama…Adam Blakely." She held out her hand.

The pudgy cook returned her gaze with watery eyes but ignored her hand. "Cookie is what they call me," he muttered, his fleshy bottom lip protruding below his thin top one.

"Cookie?" she repeated, trying to sound as though his rebuff didn't sting.

Amanda dropped her hand. She barely knew the man for heaven's sake. What difference did it make if he didn't like her?

"Real name's McCoughnehey." His whiskered chin quivered. "Bull named me Cookie."

Amanda felt sorry for the man. He held a position that didn't suit him. The crew had given him a nickname, obviously in jest. He had been made to look the fool in front of his captain. Even though Amanda knew she was not to blame, she could see how Cookie might not see it the same way.

To make matters worse, the captain had given the job of cook to her. Even though technically only the cook's *assistant*, his parting orders for breakfast suggested he expected her to do the actual cooking.

When she told him she had some slight ability, she swore his stomach growled. She studied Cookie's rounded shoulders, slumped over his empty stove. It just wouldn't do to start off on the wrong foot by taking over his kitchen.

Cookie pushed away from the stove and waddled over to a side table shoved into the corner of the room. He gathered up a fresh batch of eggs in his meaty fists.

"Actually, Cookie, I'm really not that good at cooking." Amanda hoped he wouldn't squeeze the delicate brown shells too tightly. "But, if you'll show me what to do, I'll try my best."

"Suit yourself." His eyes met hers for the briefest of moments before he turned and scooped a ladleful of lard into the freshly scraped, cast iron pan. "Think you can crack an egg?"

"It's been awhile. Maybe you could show me?" She joined him at the stove.

Cookie nodded and gave her a half-smile. He clutched a small brown egg in his wide palm, gave it a sharp rap on the edge of the stove, and held it over the pan. Bits of shell hung suspended in the thick ooze dripping through his fingers to the lard sizzling below.

"You've gotta be real delicate about this. First you stick your thumbs in the crack, then pull the two halves apart." He demonstrated the technique.

Amanda pinched her lips between her teeth to suppress a grin when Cookie's two thumbs, the size of sausages, crushed the small egg, and half the shell fell to the pan along with a viscous mix of yellow goo.

Cookie stared down at the pan and uttered another unintelligible oath.

Amanda helped Cookie fish the pieces of unbroken

shell out of the hot grease, her slender fingers doing a much more efficient job.

"That looks difficult. Mind if I try?" she asked when they had retrieved the last of the fragments.

"Hmph." Cookie stepped aside and crossed his arms over his chest, resting them on the considerable girth about his waist.

Amanda picked up one of the eggs, pretending she hadn't done so a thousand times before. Holding the egg against the edge of the stove, she cast him a questioning glance. When Cookie nodded, she gave the egg a gentle tap. Then she held her egg over the pan and, with just the slightest pressure of her thumbs, pulled the two edges apart. The egg dropped to the pan and formed a perfect pool of clear liquid with an island of yellow floating, edges intact, at the center.

"Huh," Cookie said, peering into the pan.

Amanda shrugged and held up her hands. "Mama always said cracking eggs is easier if you have little hands." It was a small lie, but since Cookie's feelings were at stake, it seemed justified.

Cookie studied Amanda's open palms as though he had never seen hands like hers.

Amanda picked up another egg, cracked it, and dropped it in the pan to fry beside her other perfect egg and Cookie's swirling blend of white and yellow. Then she took up a perch on a stool next to the stove to stand guard over the pan and ensure this new batch of eggs didn't meet the same fate as the last.

Bare feet hooked about the legs of her stool, she watched Cookie prepare the beans for the captain's coffee. Eventually, his eyes stopped shifting in her direction. Perhaps it signaled a good time to strike up a conversation and get to know her workmate a bit better.

"Have you been with the captain long, Cookie?"

Cookie spun the handle of the coffee grinder. "Only a couple o' voyages."

The pungent aroma of freshly ground coffee filled the galley, chasing away the remaining smell of burnt eggs.

"Where are you from?"

"Ireland." He turned the handle faster.

Amanda pursed her lips. She could have guessed that much, but she had hoped he would say more.

Cookie opened the grinder and scooped dark, fragrant granules into a linen pouch, hung it in the coffeepot, and set the pot on the stove. Amanda had to grip the edge of her stool when he opened the oven door and stoked the coals until they sprung to life again.

"Have you always been a cook?" she asked, restraining herself from pointing out that more heat would only make it easier to burn the captain's breakfast.

Cookie looked up, his face as twisted as the apron he held in his hands. "Look, I know I ain't the best cook, but I try." He strangled the apron in front of him and looked over his shoulder. Then he leaned forward and lowered his voice to a whisper. "If I let you cook, you gotta promise me you won't tell the cap'n you're the one doin' it. Will ya promise?"

"Of course, Cookie," she promised, her voice quiet as though they shared a secret.

Surely the man's lack of cooking skills weren't exactly a mystery.

"I got nowhere else to go." Cookie sniffed and swiped the back of his meaty fist across his eye. "If I leave the cap'n's employ, I'll wind up rottin' in a debtor's prison. It's only 'cause the cap'n thinks I can cook that he keeps me."

Amanda choked and then coughed to cover it up. If Cookie had served the captain for any length of time, there was no possible way the captain harbored any illusions. Still, the cook seemed so frightened she refrained from pointing out the obvious.

She laid a hand on Cookie's broad forearm. "Between the two of us, I'm certain we will muddle through."

Cookie stared down at her hand. Then he glanced up at Amanda. "Thank you," he said, his grin making apples of his chubby cheeks.

He leaned forward, and for a fleeting moment, Amanda thought he might enfold her small body in those beefy arms of his, but he pulled back at the last moment. When he turned to slice a loaf of bread for the captain's toast, Amanda shrugged. She returned her attention to the stove, wondering which of her carefully chosen words had so effectively mollified the emotional Irishman.

She flipped the eggs in the pan and removed them a moment later, sliding them onto the waiting plate. Afterwards, she stood guard over the stove from her post on the stool while Cookie finished making the captain's toast. She rolled a couple of sausages around in the pan, ensuring they browned evenly and didn't stick to the bottom.

When Cookie suggested she "let it boil," she snuck the coffeepot off the stove anyway and retrieved the slices of bread he had slapped on the stove and then forgotten.

Finally, the captain's breakfast complete, Amanda helped Cookie arrange everything on a tray.

"Wait a moment, Cookie," Amanda said before he could head out the door, tray in hand. She grabbed a sprig of rosemary from a strand tacked to the wall and arranged it on the plate.

"What's that for?" he asked.

"It's what my mother would have done." Amanda shrugged.

Cookie grunted and disappeared down the hall. Silently, Amanda vowed to maintain a tighter rein over her more feminine instincts. If she weren't careful, she'd give her secret away, and then the captain would have her off the ship for sure.

She let out a sigh and leaned against the wall, tired yet pleased with herself. She had cooked a breakfast she suspected the captain would enjoy, she had allowed Cookie to maintain his self-respect, and she had been assigned a duty she had far more talent for than cleaning guns or scrubbing decks. Not that she minded hard work, but cooking for the captain promised to be much more satisfying.

The captain's smile flashed in her memory, and a small voice told her it was more than just her love of cooking that made her look forward to this duty. She shushed the voice before it could say more.

Amanda hoped the captain would appreciate her efforts. They were just eggs after all, but she thought they had turned out quite well. At least two out of the three had. The one Cookie cracked resembled a scrambled egg, but it would still be edible.

Cookie returned through the galley door and interrupted her thoughts, "Cap'n wants to see ya."

"Did he say why?"

Had he not liked his breakfast?

"Cap'n's not goin' to tell me." Cookie cocked his head and grinned. "And I ain't gonna ask."

Amanda made her way to the captain's quarters at the rear of the ship. Taking a deep breath, she knocked on his door. When he bade her enter, she pushed the door open and peeked in.

"Come in, Adam. I'm not going to eat you." The captain waved Amanda forward and then returned his attention to the piece of parchment in front of him.

The captain scratched out some notes, his head bent over his work, his quill dancing across the page.

Amanda clasped her hands behind her back and braced her bare feet apart. She shifted her weight to adjust to the constant rolling of the ship. She took no issue with being made to wait. It gave her a moment to study the Sea Wolf in his lair.

The captain's quarters appeared smaller than she expected, but then this was a small ship. Even the captain would have to make do with the space available. She noted with interest that he had a hammock instead of one of the stationary boxes filled with bedding she had heard other captains preferred. Who could blame him? She shuddered and averted her eyes from his bed. Sleeping in a box would be too much like sleeping in a coffin.

His cleaned plate and cup lay stacked in the corner of the table that served as his desk. Large enough to seat three or four guests, it left little clearance between the table's edges and the planked walls of his quarters.

She supposed the captain didn't entertain much. After all, they were at sea. It's not like ship's captains called on each other for tea. Amanda stifled a giggle.

Several trunks, stacked one on top of the other, took up most of the rest of his room, along with a mishmash of scattered charts, papers, and books. The room could be described as clean, but certainly not tidy.

She glanced at the breakfast tray balanced on a stack of books. His empty plate showed streaks of yellow from where he had used his toast to mop up nearly every remaining bit of fried egg.

He was such a formidable man, aloof, stern, commanding. Everything she might imagine a ship's captain should be. Yet his actions were different from his reputation and the façade he wore at all but the most unguarded of times. Why, for instance, would a man who so obviously enjoyed eating keep a cook who couldn't even fry an egg? Did he understand more about Cookie's situation than the cook realized? Perhaps he wasn't quite the wolf he pretended to be.

Warmth stirred within her. If she weren't careful, she could fall in love with a man like him, and that would never do.

She glanced down at her homespun tunic, the color of dead leaves where it was still clean, darker elsewhere. Even if he could see past the grime that covered her, her other flaws were almost too numerous to mention. There was her unflatteringly flat chest, made even less flattering by the tightness of her bindings, her chipped fingernails, her narrow hips and spindly legs, her curly hair that refused to be tamed, the freckles across her nose... No, a man as handsome as the captain no doubt had women waiting for his return in more than one port.

Besides, she needed to keep up her disguise if she

had any hope of remaining aboard ship. On her second day, one of her shipmates had struck up a conversation while they were scrubbing the decks. Although he looked to be about her age, he had served with Captain Stoakes for a number of years. From him, she learned the captain had one hard and fast rule—no women aboard ship.

While it stiffened her resolve to keep up her ruse, she wondered why the sailor saw fit to warn her. Did he think her likely to sneak a woman aboard? Laughter caught in her throat and came out as a snort.

Captain Stoakes looked up. He pushed aside the parchment and leaned back in his chair, folding his hands over his stomach. “I wanted to thank you.”

“Did you like it?”

Amanda knew she should try to sound more impassive, but she couldn’t help herself. While she might never be able to attract his attention with her feminine appeal...she almost laughed again at the notion, she could at least make him happy with her cooking.

“It was the best meal I have had in…well, a long time.” The captain paused. “A *very* long time.”

His eyes crinkled at the corners, softening his strong features. A grin carved well-formed lines around his mouth.

Amanda dropped her gaze to her toes when she felt her cheeks flame. *Had she tamed the wolf?* She made a silent promise to him to do her very best to keep him well fed for as long as she remained part of his crew.

Perhaps someday she would become so indispensable that he could accept her for who she was. Not that it would change their relationship, but she wanted him to see her, really see her, not the boy she pretended to be.

"Captain!" A young man in a sweat-stained, striped shirt and loose fitting canvas trousers stood in the doorway, gasping for breath.

Amanda shot him a smile, trying hard to remember his name.

"What is it?" the captain asked in a clipped voice.

"British merchant ship on the horizon!"

"Looks like breakfast is over." Captain Stoakes pushed back from his desk, scraping the chair over the wooden floor.

Amanda glanced about, unsure what to do next. The sailor's words reverberated in her brain. *British merchant ship on the horizon.* Did that mean they were going into battle?

Chapter Four

Amanda picked up the captain's empty plate and carried it to the galley. Her hands shook when she set the plate in an oak washtub alongside the cast iron pan. She scoured bits of dried egg while guilt did the same to her conscience.

She should be on deck and preparing for battle with her shipmates. Yet, regardless of how much she knew where she should be, her feet refused to obey. For the first time in two weeks, it occurred to her that joining the *Amanda* might have been a grave error.

She stacked the dish next to the oak tub and strained her ears to make sense of the sounds coming from the deck above. The dull thuds of running feet shook the planks, there was a muffled shout, then silence—a silence so all encompassing that the soft, ever-present lapping of waves against the hull seemed to fill the small room.

Amanda dried the last of the dishes then wiped her hands on her apron and hung it from a tack on the wall. She straightened her shoulders in an effort to stiffen her resolve and left the galley, venturing into the dimly lit open space that served multiple functions, dining room for the crew, sleeping quarters…and surgeon's operating room during battle.

With three shifts, hammocks filled with snoring sailors almost always swung from the sturdy beams overhead. Or there would tables lined with hungry men to wend one's way through before reaching the stairs leading to the upper deck. Not now. The area below deck stood empty, the hammocks neatly stowed and all but a couple of tables turned sideways and pushed against the outer walls.

Amanda slowed when she came to the two upright dining tables covered in canvas sailcloth. She ran her fingertips across the space that might soon hold one of her fellow shipmates, his blood soaking the stiff white fabric beneath him, life draining away.

The ship groaned, rolling on a wave, and the lanterns rocked back and forth, rattling like the chains of a ghost. Amanda hurried toward the ladder. She needed to assure herself that her shipmates were still among the living.

She grasped the railing in a white-knuckled grip and pulled herself up to the main deck, poking her head above the planks.

Men stood motionless at their stations. The breeze rustled the sails and the rigging creaked. Overhead a gull circling the ship called out, its wraith-like cry echoing against the waves.

She peeked about, eyes level with the crew's feet. Every face angled toward the captain. He stood at the rail, his looking glass to one eye, peering out at the thin, hazy line where the choppy gray ocean met the cerulean sky. If she moved slowly, she just might make it to her station without drawing undue attention.

Bull caught her eye, pointed to her station, and mouthed something unintelligible. Her absence had been noted. Hunching her shoulders in a futile attempt to become invisible, Amanda scurried to her assigned position.

Lowering the glass, Captain Stoakes turned and shouted to the sailor standing on the platform high above the deck. “Any sign of an escort, Nate?”

“No sir!” the lanky, young man yelled down through cupped hands, one elbow hooked around a rope.

The captain bared a row of strong white teeth, and his eyes reflected the late morning sun. Amanda shuddered. Gone was the man whose soft smile had charmed her so just a moment ago. The wolf with the golden eyes had returned.

From her station, Amanda followed the captain’s every move. A shiver of excitement rippled through her when he called out orders to those standing around him. He was in his element, his enjoyment evidenced not so much by his expression as by the unwavering confidence in voice and action. Once, to get a better sighting, he leapt gracefully onto the ropes as though it took no more effort than climbing the stairs. Amanda’s heart leapt with him.

In long, fluid strides, he moved to the base of the main mast where Buck stood, squinting at the horizon, no glass to assist him. Captain Stoakes handed him the glass, and Buck raised it to his eye. Moments later, he shut it with a resounding click and handed it back. Buck’s lips were set in a firm line, but even from her post, Amanda caught the steely look of anticipation. He said something unintelligible to the captain that made them both laugh.

Stationed near one of the center guns, Amanda strained to hear what they said. Curiosity winning out over fear, she crept closer, then a little closer still.

The captain spoke to the dull gray smudge taking shape in the distance. "Well, my little lamb, didn't anyone ever tell you there are wolves in these waters? Best not stray too far from the flock."

Buck gave a low chuckle. "Shall we give chase, sir?"

"Hmmm," the captain squinted at the horizon again. "Odd for a ship of that size not to have an escort."

It didn't seem like a question to Amanda, but Buck offered an opinion anyway. "She could have been separated from the rest of the convoy by a storm." His voice held the childlike eagerness of a little boy asking for permission to play in the garden.

"Could be." Captain Stoakes tapped his looking glass against his open palm. "Or, it could be a trap."

A trap? Amanda crept closer, dread and excitement warring in her stomach. She focused her eyes on the distant sea and tried to make out which of the dark patches might be the enemy ship and which were low-hanging clouds.

Without warning, the captain turned and shouted over her head, "To stations!"

Amanda grasped the mast to steady herself while she waited for her ears to stop ringing. She had just managed to regain control of her wobbly legs when Buck turned to take a position at the rear of the ship and almost tripped over her. He made only the briefest eye contact and then stepped around her. Amanda's face flamed.

Captain's orders given, the ship sprang to life with sailors rechecking guns, powder, and ammunition. Bull shouted orders at the less seasoned sailors, Amanda and

Neil included, directing them to where they needed to be and giving them last minute instructions. Both she and Neil were assigned to carry powder and shot to the men at the guns. Theirs was a menial task, but its importance had been drilled into them, none too gently, by Bull.

Within seconds, every man stood ready, and again, there was nothing to do but wait. Eager anticipation roused some chatter, but one quick order for "quiet on deck" from the captain stopped it in an instant. The heavy silence descended once more.

Amanda strained her eyes, trying to make out the form of a ship in the dark smudge on the horizon. Feature by feature it materialized, the outline of a sail, the glint of copper in the sunlight, the curve of a hull.

Still at a distance, it grew obvious the *Amanda* couldn't match it in size. The sides of the other ship were well rounded and the upper deck rose high above the deck of the small schooner in pursuit. The ship's towering sails blended with the swollen clouds scuttling across the spring sky.

The Cross of St. George fluttered from the ship's foremast. It snapped in the stiff breeze, like the heavy, oppressive hand of the king himself extracting retribution from his rebellious subjects. The warm sun ducked behind a cloud, and a cool breeze cut through the thin cotton fabric of her loose tunic. A shudder rippled through Amanda. This ship belonged to the enemy.

Bull stood next to Amanda, and she couldn't help but voice at least one of her thoughts aloud, "Bull, that is a merchant ship, isn't it?"

"Aye, it is," Bull replied, without taking his eyes

off their quarry.

The sailing master called for more sails. Sailors took to the rigging, and the air soon filled the canvas sheets. The *Amanda* gained on the massive vessel.

"Isn't it rather large?" Amanda asked, finishing her thought.

"Aye. That it is. She'll be loaded with supplies for the Tories," Bull's gold teeth glinted as the sun slid from behind the clouds, "of which we shall be happy to relieve them."

Amanda could see the ship clearly now, and she marveled at Bull's confidence. The merchant ship looked to have three decks with several small hatches propped open on each. She couldn't yet see in the open ports, but she had a feeling she knew what lay within those dark recesses.

"Are merchant ships armed?"

"That they are," Bull confirmed.

Of course, she had known they would be armed, but had long-since convinced herself the guns on a merchant ship were for nothing more than show. Likewise, she had convinced herself the guns on the *Amanda* would be enough to induce any ship they encountered to drop their defenses and surrender post haste. She eyed the nine-pounder next to her. How foolish she had been!

The *Amanda's* guns had filled her with awe and dread when she first came aboard, but compared to the massive ship looming on the horizon, they seemed little more than toys, her namesake no more than a sailboat.

The *Amanda* glided ever closer to the merchant ship, and she tried to count the number of open ports. She gave up when she reached thirty.

“Aren’t we outgunned?” She asked in a cracked voice.

“Yes, we are,” Bull answered, with characteristic bluntness.

“But why would the captain attack a ship when he is outmatched?”

Bull looked fully at her this time, and there could be no mistaking the reproach in his eyes. “I agreed we was outgunned. I never said we was outmatched.”

With every ounce of her concentration on the merchant ship, Amanda hadn’t noticed the captain leave his position at the main mast to perform a quick inspection of the crew’s readiness.

“Where are you supposed to be?” His strong voice snapped her out of her stupor.

“P-p-preparing the powder,” she said, mortified that he might have overheard her questioning his decisions.

“Then get to it!”

****

Will watched Adam scurry to his station, careful not to let his concern show. The boy had arrived late on deck. Moments before he took up his glass, he noted Adam’s absence. Then when he called “to stations” he nearly tripped over him. Adam had had the audacity to eavesdrop on his conversation with Buck. That he didn’t mind so much. In the young, courage often mingled with curiosity. However, he also noticed the young sailor conversing with Bull, an unusual thing in the moments before battle, especially since Will had ordered silence. He took his inspection tour close enough to hear the exchange.

The fear in the boy’s voice concerned him. Fear

was natural. Not to have fear before going into battle could get the lad killed. Yet, to voice fear aloud did not speak well of the young man's courage and the effect he might have on the crew's morale. Not that Adam had expressed his fear in so many words, but Will could hear it in the high, tight pitch of the boy's voice.

Of course, Adam was hardly the first new recruit to let his fear show. It wasn't unheard of for a ship's boy to dissolve into tears during their first battle or soil themselves the first time they heard the roar of a gun. Either the lad overcame his fear, or he returned the boy to his family with the gentle suggestion that their son take up farming or some suitable trade.

He'd hate to have to leave Adam behind. He liked having the boy around. His skill with a stove had been evident, but there was more to it than that. The boy had a gentleness not often found among sailors. Will found it...soothing.

Will shook his head at his own foolishness. A gentle soul did not belong on a privateer anymore than a woman did.

"All men at the ready, sir," Bull reported.

Clasping his hands behind his back, Will walked past each of the nine-pounders, Bull trailing behind him.

"Will you have trouble with that one?" he asked when his inspection took him to the far end of the ship and out of earshot of Adam.

"No, sir," Bull responded, turning for a moment toward the gun where Adam stood, waiting for orders from the captain of the gun crew.

Will wondered that Bull didn't have to ask to which of the new recruits he referred. Several sailors still had a hard time keeping their grog in their bellies and their feet underneath them when the *Amanda* pitched without warning. More than a few were still unsure of their duties. Many of them had eyes glistening with fear.

Had he done something to lead Bull to believe he had a special concern for Adam? He would have to guard his expressions better to avoid having his crew think he had gone soft.

"So you believe the boy can do his duty?" Will asked, his voice harsher than he intended.

"He will or I'll toss him over the side meself," Bull said. Then his tone softened, "It's his first battle, Captain. Everyone has to have a first battle."

Truer words were never spoken. Will's stomach roiled as he remembered his own first battle on the *HMS Triumph* in the last days of the French and Indian War. Until then, the life of a lieutenant in His Majesty's Royal Navy had seemed easy compared to that of an officer in the army. On a ship, one could spend days on end without so much as spotting the enemy. Battles often lasted only a short time, and some captains struck their colors after the first warning shot across their bow.

Then he witnessed first-hand the carnage left behind when ships of war engaged in a full offensive, and he knew the illusion of a bloodless battle to be just that, an illusion.

However, the real test of character was not to quell one's fear before battle, but to perform one's duties during battle in spite of the fear. He still held out hope that Adam would do himself credit.

He could read the name on the back of the merchant ship now. *Duckworth.*

The boy would soon have his opportunity.

With any luck, the *Amanda* could rake the side of the larger ship and then draw past before the merchant ship's twenty-four-pounders made toothpicks out of her. The superior speed of his Baltimore schooner over a heavily laden merchantman gave him more than enough advantage to overcome the mismatch in firepower. However, not every captain had as much skill at leveraging that advantage. Nor as much luck.

Time slowed. Every eye focused on the captain. Every ear, alert for his next order. Even the wind whistling through the rigging quieted as though to listen for the captain's command.

"Fire!" Will's cry split the silence and bounced across the deck a fraction of a second before a series of explosions rocked the small ship. The pungent aroma of spent gunpowder permeated the air.

Several of the shots fell clear, but a number of them hit their mark in a spray of splinters.

Although clearly better armed, the merchantman's crew didn't appear to be well-trained or well-supplied. Many of the enemy's guns were not fired, and those few that were, fell short. Tell-tale shouts of confusion rang across the short expanse of sea separating the two ships.

"Above the water line, men!" Will yelled, before ordering the helmsman to bring the ship around. "We don't want to sink our prize before we get a chance to see what she offers, do we?"

A raucous cry rose from the deck. A good sign for a new crew.

The *Amanda* came about to take another shot at her prey, giving the men time to reload the guns. Will spent the few minutes of respite considering his good fortune to have a crew so hearty and capable and a merchant ship so defenseless on which to cut their teeth.

Crews aboard a privateer were neither pressed into service nor required to serve for a specified length of time. Many men returned to shore once they had made enough money to pay off their debts or start a new life. For sailors aboard a skilled privateer, it often didn't take more than a year or two.

Still others stayed on, either for patriotic or personal reasons. With each new voyage, Will prayed he would have enough seasoned sailors joined by willing, capable new hands to continue the almost legendary string of the *Amanda's* successes. A lucky captain was a good thing, a skilled crew even better.

Will laughed when Bull sent a sailor sprawling to the deck with a boot to his backside. Never vicious in his discipline, when he felt the men were shirking their duties, Bull made sure they knew it.

He had been crew master on a whaler, but eager to join the fight when war broke out at last. With Bull's rough edges and his disregard for authority, he made a natural privateersman, especially under Will's command. He had great respect for Bull's experience and trusted the grizzled old veteran without question. On the rare occasion when Bull argued with him, Will listened. Bull respected his captain too, and if he saw fit to resist an order, he usually had good reason.

Although Will trusted Bull's counsel, he trusted his own instincts more. He watched Adam go about his duties. The boy juggled three of the nine-pound balls while his brother yelled at him to keep up.

Had he been wrong this time?

After more than two weeks of hard work, Adam still looked like he might snap in a stiff wind. Struggling with his load, fear showed in the boy's wide eyes and colorless lips.

As if sensing Will's gaze on him, the boy looked up. He gave Will a look that was clearly apologetic, then tightened his grip on his load.

Sighing, Will focused his attention on the rest of the preparations. With the *Amanda* bearing down on a much larger vessel with vastly superior armament, he couldn't allow himself to be absorbed in concern for one ship's boy.

"I don't think we've woken her up yet, men," he bellowed. "Prepare to give her another round."

"Fire!" The boom of his voice was echoed a moment later by a chorus of cannons.

A momentary chaos descended on the *Amanda* when shot from one of the merchantman's guns struck a railing. Wood splinters rained down on the crew, a man screamed, and Buck and Bull shouted orders above it all.

Once the smoke cleared, Will assessed the damage. Minimal, he thought with relief. A railing could be replaced. Masts and men and guns were not so easy.

One man lay on the deck, his face chalky. A large piece of wood pierced his thigh. He struggled to get up while another sailor held him down.

Another good sign, Will concluded. He had seen men have an arm blown off and still want to fight. This man had heart. Will hoped the sailor's wounds weren't serious, and he would be able to rejoin them in the next fight. However, for now, he was in the way.

"Take him below!" he ordered.

****

Amanda stared at the jagged wood protruding from the sailor's thigh. A red stain seeped through his canvas trousers.

With the captain's order given, Bates, the sailor who had been holding the man down, grabbed him under the arms and motioned with a sharp nod for Amanda to take his feet. With a grunt and an effort not to stare at the red ooze seeping around the wood, she grabbed both legs and struggled to carry the wounded man toward the steps. A couple of times, she had to readjust her grasp, and the sailor groaned in pain.

Going first down the ladder, Amanda bore the brunt of the man's weight. Her legs burned and her back ached. His blood, hot and sticky, trickled down his leg and seeped into her sleeve. When she somehow managed to descend the few steps and gain a solid footing on the planks below, she offered a quick but silent prayer of thanks.

"First patient, Doctor!" Bates called.

They carried the man into the erstwhile dining hall.

"Set him there," the doctor said, looking up from a tray of instruments.

The sailor grunted when they laid him on the nearest table. His lips paled when Bates and the doctor adjusted his position, and Amanda winced along with him.

"You're going to be just fine," she whispered in his ear, setting her hand on his shoulder to calm him.

The man looked at her with some surprise before saying, "Thank ye, kindly." He sighed and his shoulder relaxed beneath her fingers.

Bates gave her a nod of thanks and retreated to the

main deck. Amanda watched him go, her hand still resting on the wounded man. Perhaps she would stay just a few minutes to comfort him while the doctor saw to his wounds. Then she would return to her station no matter how much she dreaded it.

She searched for something soothing to say. "What's your name?" she asked.

"Simon, m…" He mumbled the rest of his answer, but at least she caught his first name.

"Well, Simon," she said, trying to sound cheerful, "it doesn't look too bad. I am sure the doctor will have you fixed up in no time."

Simon gave her a week smile. In truth, his leg looked awful, and she had no idea how the doctor would go about removing the large piece of wood and repairing such a ghastly wound.

Setting aside her doubts, Amanda continued to whisper words of encouragement to her shipmate, and Simon closed his eyes. After awhile, she stopped paying attention to what she said because it didn't really seem to matter. So long as she kept speaking, Simon kept his eyes closed and continued to breathe in a slow, even pattern.

"Well, let's see what we have here." Doctor Miller laid his instruments on a side table.

With a pair of scissors, he cut open the man's canvas trousers, revealing his large thigh, the dark, curly hairs matted in blood. Poking around the splinter, he examined the damage.

"Are you well?" He peered at Amanda over the top of the round spectacles perched on the end of his nose.

"Yes," Amanda replied. Remembering her duty, she added, "but I really should return to my station."

The doctor ignored her comment and returned to prodding his patient. “First time in battle?”

“Yes, sir.”

Amanda caught a glimpse of herself in the mirror over the washbasin in the corner of the room. She looked as white as a sheet, the paleness of her face accentuated by the soot smudges across her forehead and chin and the blood staining her filthy shirt.

She looked terrified. The captain had noticed it too. The look of disappointment he gave her just before turning away had torn at her insides as surely as if she had been struck by the grape shot whistling past her ear.

“Well, you have a good bedside manner. The damage here isn’t too great. No major arteries hit, just ripped the flesh a bit.” The doctor stood and met Amanda’s gaze. “Still it’s going to sting a bit when I take this out and clean him up. Mind staying down here awhile longer?”

“No, sir,” Amanda replied.

Not at all!

The battle raged on deck. Even in the cool, shadowed darkness, the acrid odor of cannon fire hung in the air and mingled with the metallic smell of fresh blood. She gave Simon a reassuring smile. Gratitude shone in his bloodshot eyes when he tried, without much success, to return her smile. If she could do anything to ease this man’s pain, maybe it would be best to stay awhile.

The doctor removed the splinter and cleaned the wound with a dark liquid that made the sailor suck air through his teeth.

“Hold this against his leg, will you?”

He handed Amanda a patch of folded gauze,

already stained crimson from the man's blood. More blood seeped through the thin fabric, wetting the tips of her fingers when she held it against his wound. Amanda wondered at the absurdity of calling the offending matter a "splinter." To her, the jagged piece of wood lying in the refuse basket at the end of the table looked more like a garden stake.

She held the gauze with a firm but gentle hand and watched the doctor thread a needle thinner and sharper looking than her sewing needles at home. This one also had a slight curve to it.

A boom shook the timbers, and Amanda instinctively leaned over her patient to protect his open wound from the flecks of oakum and dust falling from the beams overhead.

"There now, that looks good," the doctor said, peeling Amanda's hand and the gauze away from the man's leg. "Looks like the bleeding stopped, but we're going to have to sew this up before we get any more patients."

The doctor made the first stitch, dabbing at a rivulet of blood with the edge of a fresh piece of folded gauze. Despite the difference in the needle, his motions looked much like sewing, and Amanda wondered why there were not more female doctors if the skills were so similar.

Roger came down the stairs, his beefy arms supporting two sailors about the waist. "Doc, that ship's givin' us more trouble than we bargained for."

The two men were bleeding, but both moved under their own power, although with considerable assistance from their uninjured shipmate. Roger deposited them against the wall, and the doctor glanced over his spectacles, assessing their condition. One man's arm hung limply at his side. It looked broken. The other had a trickle of blood running down his temple.

"Can you hold the gauze against the wound again while I make sure those two aren't in immediate danger?" the doctor asked.

Amanda nodded and pressed her hand against the rough fabric. The needle and thread, still connected to the skin where the doctor had made the first several stitches, dangled freely.

"Does it pain you much?" she asked Simon.

He raised himself on his elbows with a small groan. "No, but I would like to get it over with." His voice held a hint of a suggestion.

Amanda chewed her lower lip and considered the needle dangling from the end of the thread, recalling the doctor's tiny, even stitching. It was slightly different from that which one would use to sew cloth, as was the needle, but she could perform just about every type of stitch imaginable. She could reproduce his technique.

"Doctor, is it all right if I finish up here?"

Doctor Miller stopped his examination of the man with the broken arm. "You can sew?" Despite the question, he didn't seem surprised.

"Yes, sir."

"Very well," the doctor agreed. "But sewing a man isn't quite the same as sewing a shirt. If you think you're in over your head, let me know right away."

Amanda glanced at Simon. Even though he had given her the idea, his knitted brows resembled a wooly caterpillar.

"It's all right. I've done this before," Amanda assured him, wondering how soon she would be called to account for all the little white lies she had told in the past two weeks.

Simon lay back on the table and released a long-held breath. Amanda peeled back the gauze, careful not to reopen the wound. Picking up the needle, she glanced at Simon to be sure he hadn't changed his mind. Then she attempted the first stitch.

Keeping a firm hand on Simon's lower thigh, she pushed the needle into his warm flesh. She felt the resistance of his skin and then a sudden release as her needle penetrated the tough outer layers. The sensation wasn't all that different from sewing through leather, although a bit easier in living tissue.

Except with Simon, she couldn't help but be aware of the pain she caused with every stitch. She spoke softly to him while she worked and kept her efforts slow and steady. The muscles of his thigh relaxed under her hand, and she glanced up to be sure he hadn't passed out. To her amazement, he gave a weak smile, then closed his eyes and lay back on the table.

A small bead of sweat ran down Amanda's forehead and caught on her eyebrow. She wiped it away with her sleeve, feeling the scrape of soot and dried blood.

She would be gentle but quick, and only when she had finished would she stop to assess the damage. If the splinter hadn't killed him, she could be reasonably certain her ineptness with the needle wouldn't either. After a half dozen or so neat stitches, she tied off the thread, cut it, and set the needle on the tray. She glanced up at Simon, relieved to find him smiling at her. She smiled back.

"Battle seems to be over," Simon said in a voice

tinged with regret.

Focused on her work, she had stopped listening to the din of the battle. Cheers of a victory celebration shook the timbers. She had made it through!

"Where the hell is he?" The voice rose above the din and echoed into the hold.

Amanda's smile faded. She had no doubt whom the captain sought, and he sounded none too pleased.

Reaching the doctor's makeshift operating room, the captain grabbed Amanda by the front of her shirt. Luckily, Neil had helped her find a solitary corner that morning in which to rebind herself or the captain might have grabbed more than he bargained for. Amanda almost giggled at the thought, but the hard look in his eyes stopped her.

"Do you know what the penalty is for abandoning your post?" he roared, his face just inches from hers.

Anger radiated from him like waves of heat from the galley stove. Even though he had pulled her up so that the tips of her toes scarcely brushed his leather boots, she still had to peer up at him to meet his gaze. She wanted to look away but, like looking into the eyes of a wild animal, it seemed more dangerous to take her eyes off him than to meet his golden glare.

A thin layer of soot covered the angles of his face, and his hair, damp with sweat, curled about his ears. He had discarded both neck stock and coat during the battle, and his shirt lay open to the middle of his breastbone revealing the thick mat of dark hair that covered more hard angles.

He smelled wonderful, Amanda thought, surprising herself with the inappropriate reflection. She had been around enough sweat-soaked farm hands to know that men didn't always smell great after working hard, but his scent held an intoxicating mix of spice and sea air. She inhaled deeply, letting his essence sink into her.

When she tried to refocus her attention, a dark slash of soot over the planes of one cheek captured her attention. She reached up to wipe the smudge away with her thumb.

The captain jerked his head away when the soft pad of her thumb made the briefest of contact with the day's worth of stubble on his cheek. Amanda yanked her hand back, knowing in an instant that she had given herself away. Her eyes shut and fingers curled into a ball against her chest, she waited for him to condemn her actions.

Several long, silent moments passed.

Amanda cracked open one eye, then the other. Something in the captain had changed. His brows were still dark slashes, but the rest of his face had softened into something that more closely resembled confusion. He no longer stared at her eyes, but at her lips.

Was something amiss with her lips? Amanda licked the dry chapped skin. The captain's gold eyes followed the sweep of her tongue, and he pulled her closer, as though to inspect her thoroughness.

"Captain, please don't be angry." Simon's voice was a jolting reminder that they had an audience, and both Amanda and the captain swung their heads to look at him.

"Please don't be angry," Simon said again, casting a quick glance at Amanda, "at the boy. He was fixing me up while the Doc was helpin' them fellas who was hurt worse than me."

"Fixing you up?" The captain eyed Simon, but

didn't release Amanda.

After a quick scan of the sailor's stitched wound, he set her feet back on the floor. Amanda wobbled, thankful he still held her in his grip. It would be a moment before her knees would support her.

"Yes, sir. After Doc removed the splinter and cleaned me up, the boy did the stitchin'. I have to say, I've gotten stitches from near on a dozen doctors. They all hurt worse than this. He was real…delicate."

Delicate? Amanda cringed at the feminine description of her work that she would have taken to be a compliment only a few weeks ago. The captain released her, and she tugged her shirt back in place. No boy should ever be called delicate.

The doctor and the captain leaned over the man's leg. The doctor peered through his spectacles, and the captain glared at the stitches as though he could unravel them with his gaze and prove their unworthiness.

Finally, the doctor straightened up and gave her a thoughtful appraisal. "You learned to sew from your mother?"

"Yes, sir. She wanted a girl and…"

The captain raised one dark eyebrow, ending her story. Amanda had the distinct impression he did not care to hear the details.

"He did a good job, didn't he, Doc?" Simon suggested.

"Yes, he did, Simon," Doctor Miller agreed. "I doubt you'll even have a scar."

Doctor Miller turned to Amanda. "How would you like to be my assistant?"

Amanda opened her mouth to respond, but didn't know what to say. Out of the corner of her eye, she glimpsed the captain leaning against the wall, his arms crossed. He, too, waited for her response.

Did she even have the option to accept the doctor's proposal? She didn't think so. That decision belonged to the captain. Didn't it?

Besides, he had just assigned her to a new role serving as his personal cook. She couldn't do both, could she?

"I don't think I can, sir. I'm already Cookie's assistant, and I have my regular duties to attend to." Her face heated at the reference to the duties she had so recently neglected.

"Cookie doesn't cook anything when there's a battle going on." The captain pushed away from the wall. "If you think you are up for it, you can be Doctor Miller's assistant. Bull will just have to do without you during battle."

Amanda thought she detected a hint of sarcasm in the last, but before she could be sure, the captain was gone.

The doctor gave Amanda's shoulder a squeeze. "Well, I guess we won that battle, didn't we?" he said, a touch of wry humor in his voice.

Amanda stared at the doorway through which the captain had departed. "I don't suppose the war is over, is it?"

The doctor laughed. Shaking his head, he returned to his patients. "No, I don't suppose it is."

Chapter Five

"Doctor, do you have a moment?" Will hesitated at the door to the doctor's quarters, not certain whether he wanted his surgeon to invite him in or send him away.

The doctor looked up from his papers. "Certainly, Captain. Please come in." He stood and offered his chair to Will with a wave of his hand. "Would you like a seat?"

"No. No, thank you, I'll be fine standing," Will said. He mustn't get too comfortable. He might stay too long, reveal too much.

Will leaned against the wall. Then again, what did it matter if he availed himself of the doctor's counsel? He had nothing to hide. Besides, Doctor Miller's professional ethics would not allow him to disclose the details of their conversation to anyone. If there was anything he could be certain of in this world, it was the doctor's capacity to guard matters of a personal nature.

Doctor Miller regarded Will with a quizzical look. "I hope you don't mind my saying so, Captain, but you seem troubled. Are you ill?"

"Oh, no." Will gave a choked laugh. "Nothing like that."

"Then what did you wish to speak to me about?"

Will shifted his stance. He really had no idea where to begin. Perhaps a direct tack. He cleared his throat, "I wanted to thank you for the books."

So much for being direct, but his thanks had been overdue. At the beginning of the voyage, Doctor Miller had given him several small crates of pamphlets and treatises written by great men like Franklin, Paine, and Dickinson. That he hadn't found time to read them was no excuse for being lax in his manners.

"Oh, I'm glad you're enjoying them." Doctor Miller searched Will's face. "But that's not why you came to see me, is it?"

"Well, no," Will folded his arms across his chest. His ship's surgeon was a most perceptive man. Leave it to him to see through any pretense. "I thought I might get your opinion on some of the crew."

"Anyone in particular?"

"No, no one in particular." Will's forced the words, scratchy and uncertain, through his dry throat.

What was wrong with him? It's not like he had never asked the doctor to offer his opinion on a man's fitness for duty before. Why should this time be so different?

He licked his lips and began again. "Let's start with the new recruits. What do you think of Adam, for example?" His words sounded casual, perhaps too casual.

"Are you asking for my professional opinion?"

"Yes." He did need a professional opinion, but was this something in which surgeons received training? Somehow he doubted it.

The doctor sucked in a breath, then let the air rush from his lungs. "Well, since he's never come to me with any sort of ailment, I can only surmise he's in good health. Although he doesn't appear to be as strong as his shipmates, he's a tireless worker and has an excellent bedside manner. To me, he's—"

"No, that's not what I mean, Doctor." Will tucked his hand back into the crook of his arm. "Adam's a fine crewmember...if a bit unusual."

"Then perhaps I don't understand what you're asking." The doctor tipped his head, inviting Will to elaborate.

Will unfolded and refolded his arms. "Have any of other men commented on him? Said anything that might cause concern?"

"Commented?" The doctor thrust out his chin and considered the first question. He brightened. "I suppose they have, now that you mention it."

Will's gut tightened. "What have they said?"

"Nothing in particular, but they seem to enjoy having the boy around. I suppose you could say the more they get to know Adam, the more they like him."

Will sighed and ran his hand across the back of his neck. "That's a relief."

"How so?" the doctor asked.

"As you said, he's not as strong as his shipmates, and in most things, the things that count to the men, he's not as capable. I'd hate to think of Adam being tormented just because he's...different. Sailors can be cruel to anyone they believe to be shirking their duties."

The doctor grinned, "I think your crew might surprise you."

"How so, Doctor?"

Doctor Miller set his elbows on the arms of his chair and steepled his fingers. "They're getting to know Adam, coming to appreciate his true worth to the ship...and to you."

Will patted his stomach. "I have grown accustomed

to having him around."

While still lean, the snugness of his breeches around his waist suggested he might have gained a pound or two in the last week. He would have to remember to ask Adam to cut back on the lemon cake.

"I would not worry," the doctor said with a touch of humor. "A man can't help but liking Adam."

Will looked up, warning bells pealing. "What do you mean?"

There was, of course, another concern, one that made Will queasy even considering. He had been ready to dismiss it altogether, but the doctor's words, nay, his tone suggested he needed to confront the possibility. As captain of the ship, the responsibility for the welfare and morality of the crew lay with him.

"Adam does things for them."

"Like what sorts of things?" Will asked, not sure he wanted to know the answer.

"He spends time with them. Holds their hand while I tend their wounds. Brings then treats while they are recu–"

"He does *what*?"

Confusion wrinkled the doctor's brow. "Brings them treats?"

"No, before that."

"Holds their hand?"

"Yes...*that*." Will growled.

"I'm sure he doesn't mean anything by it, and the men are soothed by his presence. Short of having a woman to comfort them, he's the next best thing."

Will's blood ran cold at the doctor's choice of words. With no woman aboard, would they consider Adam the *next best thing*?

"The men show no untoward attention to the boy." The doctor added, showing he understood at least some of Will's concerns.

No untoward attention now, but Adam was clearly an innocent. Encouraging the men, however unintentionally, wouldn't help his situation. Who knew when he would give the wrong idea to the wrong man?

Will's long sigh did little to relieve the strain, but it did give him an opportunity to consider another possibility. Perhaps this was simply a phase Adam was going through. In time, he might add some weight to his slight frame, lose the roundness of his features, and learn to stop blushing like a maid whenever he became nervous. If he could just protect Adam through this awkward time in his life, the boy would learn to fend for himself.

But how long would this phase last? Will had never experienced anything even remotely similar so he had no way of knowing.

"Doctor, do you think Adam is, well, developing normally?"

"As a sailor, you mean?"

"No, no," Will waved his hand then tucked it back in the crook of his arm. "I mean as a man. He's a bit...underdeveloped, don't you think?"

"Underdeveloped?" the doctor repeated.

"Yes. The boy has no noticeable muscle, no facial hair and skin that looks as soft as a baby's. Don't you think he's a bit too...pretty for a man?" Will snorted. "I've met women who were less enticing."

"Ahh," the doctor said with that irritating tone that all doctors used when they thought they had their patients figured out. "You think he's enticing?"

"Well...you know...interesting." Will paused, realizing that he might be giving Doctor Miller the wrong impression. "Not to me, of course. But I do wonder the affect that such an attractive boy might have on the rest of the men. Not all men have such leanings, of course, but sailors can be at sea for months at a time with no woman in sight."

"Thanks to your rule," the doctor reminded him.

"It's for the good of the ship." Will shot back. "How would I ever get the men to work as they do if I allowed women aboard ship?"

"Perhaps women would give the men a reason to work hard, finish their duties in record time, even fight harder to save the ship if it came to that." Doctor Miller's chair squeaked as he sat forward. "And perhaps if you allowed wives and sweethearts aboard, you wouldn't have to worry so much about boys like Adam."

Will gave the doctor a lopsided smile. "Have you seen some of the women the men leave behind? An attractive boy like Adam would still need to watch his back."

The doctor raised an eyebrow.

"I mean, I'm not attracted to him," Will said, realizing the doctor had misunderstood him again.

The doctor nodded but said nothing.

Will remembered how the touch of the boy's thumb on his cheek had sent a ripple of pleasure coursing through him. For one horrifying moment, he had contemplated the softness of the boy's lips.

He checked the shudder that ran through him. He would never have acted on the impulse. He had simply been taken aback by the boy's overt femininity, but he had come to his senses soon enough. Anyone might have had the same reaction. Will's stomach added another knot. That was precisely the problem. The boy was too damn feminine to serve on a ship full of men.

"The boy is just too pretty for his own good, Doctor."

"Ahh," the doctor said again, the sound grating on Will's nerves. The doctor's grin didn't sit much better with him. Doctor Miller and several of the men had been witness to Will's confrontation with Adam. Had they noticed his reaction?

"How old do you think he is?" Will asked, eager to keep the focus on Adam.

If Adam weren't of age, there was the hope that his youth would throw off any men intent on using the boy for their own purulent amusements. He knew some captains looked the other way, but he had always agreed with those who thought men who preyed on younger boys should be strung up by their—

"I don't really know. Fourteen? Maybe fifteen?" the doctor said. "Bull usually records that in the logbook for all ship's boys, doesn't he?"

"Yes, but for some reason he did not this time."

"And you're concerned he might be too much of an innocent to fend for himself?"

"Yes," Will agreed, relieved the doctor finally understood.

"Captain, it's clear you've developed an affection for the boy. I wouldn't worry about it though. It's only natural when you spend that much time around someone."

"Yes, I suppose that's true," Will said.

"As for your other *feelings*, I wouldn't worry about

those either."

Will pulled away from the wall. "But you misunderstand me, Doctor—"

Doctor Miller raised his hand. "It's quite possible you're simply responding to the boy's natural inclinations."

"If those are the boy's natural inclinations," Will ground the words out, "don't you think he's in danger on a ship full of men? There's always the possibility that someone will try to take advantage of him."

He was in no mood to defend himself. He had no *need* to defend himself. His concern was for the rest of his ship and for Adam.

"Would you prefer it if Adam were a woman?"

"Naturally I would prefer it if Adam were a woman. If Adam were a woman, he wouldn't be on my ship in the first place. And if, somehow, he managed to get onto my ship, I would toss him, or rather her, off at the next port."

The doctor looked almost horrified at the thought, and Will drew breath to calm his outrage at the very idea of a woman on his ship. "It is a moot point, Doctor. Adam is what he is, and whether you or I would prefer him to be different is of no matter."

"No, I suppose not." The doctor gave him an enigmatic smile. "At any rate, my professional recommendation is to keep a watchful eye on the boy and be sure he comes to no harm. I am certain, in time, the situation will work itself out."

A knot tightened in Will's gut. Time was perhaps the best cure, but it might also be the most painful.

Chapter Six

Amanda discovered Neil at the bulwark, a book propped open before him, peering at the coastline in the pre-dawn light. The ship lay at anchor, having picked up supplies the day before. Bull and Buck had gone ashore to recruit more men to replace the seasoned sailors assigned to sail their latest capture to the prize court in Boston.

Sounds of snoring rumbled up through the minute crevices where the oakum had worn away between the planking. A sudden, powerful snort tickled the bottom of Amanda's feet through the soft leather shoes she wore.

With only the night watch on duty, the deck stood nearly empty. Amanda waved "good morning" to Nathan, the young sailor standing watch on the platform some forty feet above her head. He returned her greeting. Even in the dim light, she could see the young man's cheerful smile.

The ever-present lapping of waves against the hull of the ship and the soft creaking of her timbers lulled Amanda into a peaceful stupor. She leaned against the bulwark, twenty feet or so from where her brother stood, to savor a precious moment of solitude.

"Hey, Mandy!" Neil called out, his voice reverberating off the morning air, thick with dew.

Amanda shot a glance about her to see if anyone

else might have caught the nickname only Neil used.

"Oh for heaven's sake, we're fine." Neil rolled his eyes and turned his gaze back to the shoreline. Dawn had lit the haze lingering amidst the craggy beaches and rocky promontories with a soft glow. "Nate and I are the only ones on duty right now, and he can't hear us from up there."

Amanda pushed her anxiety to the side. She hadn't spoken to Neil in what felt like forever, and she missed her brother. She joined him at the rail. Crossing her arms atop the rough wooden surface of the bulwark that ran the perimeter of the ship, she leaned forward and rested her chin against them. For several moments, she gazed down at the mist skimming the surface of the water. Spiraling tendrils of vapor danced and then disappeared like fairies of the deep.

She breathed remnants of cool misty morning air, letting it fill her nose and escape through open lips.

"It's beautiful, isn't it?" Neil asked, sparing her a quick glance before turning back to his book. He flipped a few pages. "Smells much better than the farm, anyway." He traced an outline on a page with his finger.

"Mmmm." Amanda had never minded the musty smell of animals, but much preferred the fresh, clean scent of the sea.

She propped the tips of her toes against the bulwark and, grasping the top beam, leaned back, rear end first. She twisted this way and that. Her spine creaked and popped. The last battle had seen numerous injuries. None life threatening, but she had helped more than one hefty sailor into the operating room. She was growing stronger by the day, but some days tested her limits.

Stretching the knots from her muscles, Amanda watched her brother's eager fingers flip the pages of the book. He lifted his face to the jagged coastline, and despite his boyish countenance, she could see the man he was becoming.

Was it selfish for her to long for their relationship to return to its former terms? Neil was turning from a willful boy into a reliable young man. Without a doubt, much of the credit belonged to Captain Stoakes. Somehow, he had known how to give her brother just the right mix of instruction and encouragement, of discipline and freedom. She had never managed to master that recipe. Soon, perhaps even now, her brother would no longer need her.

Amanda raised her eyes to watch the gulls dart in and out of unseen nests along the rocky shore. Distance and the morning breeze softened their plaintive cries. Did they think about the future? They had homes among the cliffs, plenty to eat, and each day played out much like the last. She, on the other hand, had no idea what her future held.

She couldn't very well remain a sailor. Although she had done a credible job fooling a ship of sixty men, she couldn't keep it up forever. Once Neil no longer needed her, there was no reason to stay.

Sadness fell like a fog over the beauty of the morning. The men of the *Amanda* had become her family...Cookie, Bull, Buck, every one of her shipmates. Of course, they weren't the only ones she'd miss. Sadness turned to despair, though Amanda was at a loss to understand the ache that settled in her heart.

In her mind's eye, she saw Captain Stoakes sitting

at his desk, his quill scratching across a piece of parchment. Nigh on three times a day for the past several weeks she had come upon him this way, the captain working diligently at whatever kept the commander of a successful privateer occupied while she brought him the tray of food that kept him content.

Her heart skipped a beat, just as it always did when she encountered him. Walking into his quarters felt much like walking into the den of a wild animal. Over time, however, apprehension turned into a sort of reckless enjoyment. She would set the tray on the corner of his desk, lift the cover off his meal, then stand off to the side, watching for that moment when the tantalizing aroma pulled him from his work. He shoved his papers aside and reached for the tray, and a sense of satisfaction warmed her.

In her imagination, he was without his neck stock and wool jacket. His muscles rippled beneath the finally woven silk of his snow-white shirt when he added more butter to his toast, then took a bite. A drop of melted gold clung to the corner of his mouth. Amanda licked her lips when his tongue darted out to catch it.

The captain reached up and tugged at the strings that held his shirt closed. The soft fabric fell away to reveal a broad chest, tanned, with a smattering of curls as dark as his hair. The urge to touch him, to dip her hands beneath the silk folds, to run her fingers over the broad mounds of his pectoral made her palms ache.

He looked up from his half-eaten breakfast, and his golden eyes burned like embers. Everywhere he looked, her skin quivered as though his gaze were a physical touch. The heat seemed to suck the air from the room, and her breath came in short quick gasps. The hunger in his eyes beckoned and pulled, urging her forward until she had no recourse but to obey.

She rounded the corner of his desk, and he rose to his feet. She walked forward until the tips of her soft leather shoes brushed the tips of his boots. She raised her chin. His golden eyes darkened to amber with a need so deep it made her breath catch in her throat. Emboldened, she slid her palms up his chest and over his shoulders. His eyes widened and his pulse quickened when she ran her hands up the side of his neck.

Running her hands around to the nape of his neck, Amanda tugged at the leather thong that held his queue. It came off easily and his dark curls fell to her shoulders. She buried her hands in the dark mass, and leaned in until she could smell the sweet scent of butter on his lips.

The captain dipped his head to–

"How's Captain Stoakes?" Neil asked.

Amanda jumped at the intrusion into her private thoughts, daydreams so far removed from reality she wondered if they didn't indicate an addled mind. She gave her little brother a sidelong look, reminding herself that he was not a mind reader. Neil alternated his attention between the coastline and his book, the barest hint of a smile on his lips.

"He's doing well, I'm sure," she replied, her tone cold.

She could tell by the casual way he asked the question, as though just passing time, that he had a point to make. That it involved the captain, the subject of her intensely sensual daydreams, didn't bode well.

"You see him several times a day, don't you?" Neil

thumbed a couple of pages.

"Yes, I do, but only to bring him his meals," Amanda said. "I don't ask after his health or state of mind."

She did actually, but Neil didn't need to know that. Besides, the captain never told her much. Whenever she greeted him, he gave her a startled look, then indicated where to set the tray down, usually with a grunt or a wave of his hand. He'd go back to work until the scent of a cooked meal reminded him of his hunger. Even then, he generally ignored her until she left. Her thrice-daily encounters were far less satisfactory than the one she had just imagined. Once, when she had tried unsuccessfully to engage him in conversation, she had heard him sigh just before she closed his door. The small sound carried an unmistakable note of relief, as though he were happy to see her go.

"What with all that, you must be getting *close*, right?" He turned innocent brown eyes on her. "I mean you can't spend that much time alone with a man without getting to know him a bit, can you?"

Amanda frowned. "I'm not alone with him. I simply bring him his meals and then leave him to them. That's it."

"Very well...*Adam*." He drew out the sound of the name. "Whatever you say."

The way Neil avoided meeting her gaze told her all she needed to know. He always avoided looking at her when trying to keep a straight face. Amanda scowled, the tranquility of the morning forgotten. She would have set him straight, but several men of the first watch joined them on deck, making private conversation inadvisable.

Besides, what he said held a kernel of truth. Although he rarely spoke to her, she had gotten to know the captain. She knew how he liked his eggs, yolks still soft with lots of pepper. She knew how and when he liked his coffee, with breakfast and after supper but never in the middle of the day.

She might be the only person on earth fully aware of the captain's little quirks. Cookie had been surprised when Amanda told him about the captain's preference for black coffee over sugared and how he really didn't care for haggis. Of course, she broke the latter news gently to avoid any perceived insult to Cookie's revered Scottish grandmother.

There was more to it than just the captain's moods and his preferences. She often stood in his quarters while he finished breakfast, studying him as he ate, waiting to see if he required anything else. When she shut her eyes at night, she could see every angle of his face, the way he stopped chewing when focused on a particular thought, the way he used his toast to clean his plate, and the way he sighed, a little satisfied sound, after swallowing the last bite.

She knew as much about the captain's eating habits as his wife, should he ever decide to marry. Perhaps more than any future wife would, unless he gave up privateering or decided to break his cardinal rule and allow women on his ship. The thought of the captain bringing a wife on some future voyage made her stomach clench.

Could it be jealousy? She had little experience with the emotion, except perhaps when she was six and a friend had shown her a pretty piece of ribbon her mama gave her for her birthday.

Besides, jealousy would be completely irrational. First of all, the captain didn't have a wife. Second, even if he did, he held so steadfastly to his rules, he wasn't likely to break them for her. And thirdly, why should she be jealous in the first place? She was just another member of his crew. She had no claim on him.

"What's gotten into you?" Neil asked.

"What do you mean?" she asked.

As a child, she had developed the tendency to speak her thoughts aloud. Had she reverted to old habits? Amanda felt herself pale.

Neil chuckled. "If I didn't know better, I would have thought the beam you are strangling had wronged you in some way."

Amanda looked down at her white knuckled hands. She held the top of the bulwark in a vice-like grip and the muscles in her back screamed from being overstretched.

"What are you doing?" she asked Neil, straightening and changing the subject in an effort to distract herself from her tortured thoughts.

"Trying to figure out our position from the shape of the coastline and this book," replied Neil.

"Where did you get that?" She peered over his arm. The rough pages of the small leather-bound notebook held what looked like nautical charts with handwritten notes and drawings in the margins. The penmanship looked familiar.

"It's the captain's," he answered, confirming her suspicions.

Amanda narrowed her eyes at him. "Looks important. Does he know you have it?"

Neil held his finger skyward and traced the outline

of a distant headland that jutted into the sea. Then he flipped a couple of pages in the book.

"I got it!" He thumped a page with his forefinger. In his excitement, he lost his hold on the book and it plopped over the edge and into the sea below. It landed, face up, floating on the surface of the calm water.

Amanda peered over the side in time to see the book ride a small wave, the breeze ruffling its open pages. It wouldn't be long before the notebook became waterlogged and the captain's charts were lost forever. Without another thought, she set one foot on the bulwark and dove over the side. With two short strokes, she traversed the distance and plucked the book from the water. It appeared largely undamaged, a little wet but only a few of the pages smudged.

"It's all right. I have it!" she yelled up at Neil, holding the book aloft and waving it over her head in triumph.

As though she had forgotten how to tread water, her legs seized and she dipped beneath the surface. She inhaled a mouthful of brackish water then bobbed to the surface, sputtering and coughing, while trying to brush wet hair from her eyes with her free hand.

Captain Stoakes had joined Neil at the bulwark. He held the end of a rope for her to grab onto, his face like that of the hangman waiting for his next customer.

Chapter Seven

"Someone want to tell me what that was about?" Will sat at his desk, his finger tapping a random beat against the blotter.

Adam and Neil faced him from the other side.

Adam's clothes dripped from his swim in the bay and formed a puddle at their feet. A shiver racked his narrow shoulders. In late spring, the Atlantic would still be frigid, but Will suspected the shudder was from more than just the boy's impromptu swim.

The boy had the right to be afraid. Anger ate at Will. However, it warred with the panic that assailed him when he recalled the image of Adam diving off the bulwark. Sailors had an odd relationship with the sea. Many never learned to swim for fear it would tempt the fates. He had no way of knowing that Adam could swim like a dolphin, and the thought of losing him had given him a rare moment of terror. He rubbed his throat, the same constriction that had prevented him from calling out the boy's name now made it difficult to breathe.

"I'm sorry, Captain," Adam offered. "It was my fault the book dropped into the water so I went in after it. I can swim."

Will caught the fiery look Neil gave his brother. Clearly, he was not happy with Adam claiming responsibility.

"Yes, I could see that," Will said. "But how was it your fault?"

He didn't really care whose fault it was, so long as Adam was safe, but the question gave him an opportunity to regain his composure. He needed to behave as a captain should, not as a man given to emotional outbursts and inappropriate sentiments.

"I startled him, causing him to knock the book into the water." Adam ignored Neil's glare.

Will narrowed his eyes and regarded Adam. He had been watching them while they were together at the railing. He could see Neil had discovered their location, and in his excitement, he knocked the book off the railing.

He couldn't believe one of his own crew would tell such a brazen lie. Any other captain would have Adam punished. Neil, too, for the disgrace of allowing his brother to take the blame.

"Is that what happened, Neil?" Will kept his tone formal, if only to prove to himself that he controlled his emotions.

"No, sir," Neil replied, equally formal.

"Yes, it is." Adam cut him off with a high-pitched denial. "If I hadn't caught you unawares, the book would never have fallen in." He spoke to Neil as though Will didn't exist.

Neil swiveled his head to look at his brother. "Would you, for once in your life, just shut up! I don't need you protecting me."

Adam paled, and Will leaned back in his chair, crossing his arms over his chest.

Neil had given his brother a wide berth ever since the day they came aboard. This confrontation had been a long time coming, and he wanted to let it play out a bit. He would intervene when the time came, but for now the boys needed to work out whatever lay between them.

Then he could work out his own inner turmoil when it came to his highly competent but disconcerting cabin boy.

"But the book belongs to the captain!" Adam turned to Neil and placed his hands on his hips in a gesture that reminded Will of something he had seen his mother do long ago.

"Yes, and he loaned it to me. I know I should have been more careful with it, but that's between him and me. I don't need you sticking your nose into it."

"If I hadn't been there, it would be at the bottom of the ocean by now." Adam's voice trembled.

"Better to have it at the bottom of the ocean and me in irons for losing the book than to have you protecting me."

"But I can swim!"

"So can I!" Neil turned fully away from the captain, his arms flailing as he railed at his brother. "What makes you think I wouldn't have gone in after it? I would have if your fat arse hadn't already been over the railing and in the water."

"Fat arse!" yelled Adam, his voice rising in pitch.

Will stifled a chuckle. For an insult from a sailor, it was mild, but Adam's chin quivered nonetheless. Things were getting out of control. He leaned forward to propose a cease-fire but stopped short when Neil turned to him.

"Captain, it is entirely my fault." Neil's dark eyes were determined and unafraid. "Even though I can't take responsibility for my *brother* being an idiot, please don't punish him." Neil directed a pointed look at Adam, and Will wondered what silent communication exchanged between them.

"Neil, no—" Adam raised a hand to stop Neil from saying anything more.

"Why shouldn't I punish Adam?" Will asked. "He seems eager to take responsibility."

"Because he's not my brother," said Neil.

"Not your brother?" Will asked, one eyebrow raised in mock surprise.

There was nothing enlightening about that revelation. The boys looked nothing alike. He presumed they had grown up together, perhaps under the same roof, but it didn't surprise him to learn they were not truly blood-relatives.

"*He* is actually my incredibly irritating, domineering, busy body *sister*." Neil spat out the last word as though it were an accusation.

The breath escaped Will's lungs in a rush as surely as if he had been punched in the gut. He tried to inhale, but his thundering heart seemed to leave no room for air

He took in "Adam" standing before his desk, wet clothes clinging to skin. Even a blind man could see the bindings underneath the loose folds of the sodden cotton shirt clinging to her chest. Her slender figure narrowed at the waist far more than a man's and then flared out again at the hips. The cotton fabric of her men's breeches clung to the mound at the juncture at her thighs, eliminating all doubt.

What's more, she probably wasn't even a girl. She had the willowy figure of a young woman, but the self-assured tilt of her chin and directness of her gaze spoke of a mature adult. He had seen this in the steely-eyed glare she gave him when they first met, but had put it down to that attitude of faux self-possession adolescent males, eager to be adults, sometimes adopted. How wrong he had been!

"I see." He pinched the bridge of his nose between thumb and forefinger.

He looked down at his desk, trying to make sense of his jumbled thoughts. The room spun and, for the first time in his life, words eluded him.

He should be angry at having been made the fool, but anger only flitted at the edge of his thoughts. He tried to grasp it, to hold onto it as an anchor against his whirling emotions, but each time he tried, it vanished like the ephemeral remnants of a recent dream. Will looked up again, expecting to see Adam, the boy who had served him so well these past weeks. The boy was gone.

In his place stood a young woman of such undeniable femininity that she assaulted his senses. Her appeal, even in her bedraggled state, overwhelmed him. Fighting to hold his wits about him, he searched for the right course of action.

He needed to get her off his ship!

Yet, with that conclusion, a sense of loss enveloped him. He had enjoyed having her at his side, cooking his breakfast, keeping him company while he ate, tidying up his quarters when he wasn't around. He had never been so well-fed, and for the first time ever, his charts and logbooks stood in organized progression on his one bookshelf.

But there was more to it than just the allure of a full stomach and clean quarters. He had done his best to ignore her when she came into his quarters, but he liked having her nearby while he ate. He had even grown to enjoy her silly chatter when she tried to get him to speak. Although he hadn't allowed himself to admit it at the time, he loved the sound of her voice, especially when she tried to deepen it to sound like a man. He had stayed strong, saying little, sensing that to give into his desire to talk with her would bring him closer to his cabin boy than was wise.

Perhaps he had been afraid to confront the evidence that was right in front of him.

"I don't suppose your name is Adam, is it?" The question sounded inane.

"No, it's Amanda."

The reply, soft and feminine, brought him to his senses, and a wave of anger broke through his confusion. Had lying become a habit of hers? Did she have so little imagination she could only come up with the name of his ship?

Seemingly reading his thoughts, she added, "It really is. I won't lie to you anymore."

Will studied her face, green eyes beneath soft blonde brows that, for once, weren't knit together in vexation, a sprinkle of freckles across otherwise flawless skin, and lips set in an uncertain smile. With her face, the ruse couldn't have been easy to pull off.

Except she had, which either meant she had exceptional skill or he was the biggest dolt in America. That his men hadn't figured it out either provided little consolation.

He forced himself to look into those sea-green eyes. "Although you are not his brother, is Neil really yours?"

"Yes, sir. Well…no, sir," Amanda's eyelids fluttered. "Yes, sir," she finished, with a decided nod of her head.

"What she means, sir, is that we aren't related by blood," explained Neil with an exasperated sigh. "Her father took me in and raised me until he left for the fight. For the last couple of years, it's been just Mandy and me. She's every bit a sister to me even though we aren't related. I'm sure the confusion in her response is because she couldn't figure out which answer would seem less like a lie." He laughed. "She's not very good at deception."

"Like hell she isn't!"

Both Amanda and Neil jumped at his outburst. Will ran a hand through his hair while he fought to regain control. He centered his gaze on her face because every time he let his attention slip to her narrow waist and long shapely limbs, his concentration crumbled. If he could barely hold a thought with her in the room, his ship would be in chaos if he let her run loose among his men.

But what to do with her? He grimaced, recalling his conversation with Doctor Miller. He could hardly just drop her off at their next port of call and leave her to fend for herself. She couldn't be more than, what? Seventeen? Eighteen?

"I suppose you're not as young as you claimed, either?" He held his breath, waiting to see if she would reveal her true age.

"No, I'm twenty-one." Defiance flashed in her eyes, and he couldn't blame her. It had been a rather ill mannered question.

But twenty-one? He would never have guessed she

could be past her teens. However, it had taken spirit and courage to do what she did, face what she faced in her short time aboard ship. The rebel in him admired her pluck, despite her deception. He sat back in his chair, staring at his two charges, not sure what course to take. He had never been so flummoxed in his life.

"Captain, lone ship off the port bow," Buck said from the doorway.

Will stood, a sigh of relief escaping his lips. The English merchants were something he could handle, and he didn't think he had ever been so grateful for their appearance. "I'm needed on deck," he said to no one in particular. To Neil he added, "Get to your station."

Neil flew out the door in a shot.

Amanda turned to follow, but Will grabbed her arm. "Not you."

"Excuse me?" she asked, bewilderment reflected in her wide eyes. "The doctor won't need me for awhile, but I should at least get out of these wet clothes."

"I want you to stay in my quarters where it's safe," Will said, his voice making it clear it was a command not a request. "You can dry off with one of my towels and wrap yourself in a blanket until your clothes dry." He tried to ignore the image of her lithe, naked body wrapped in his bed sheets.

"Safe? Why?" A red flush crept up from the base of Amanda's neck to her temple. Had she been holding a similar image?

Amanda tugged at her arm, but Will didn't let go. Her stormy green eyes were only inches from his. Her blonde hair, curled about her cheeks and forehead, invited him to brush it back. How had this delicate creature survived on his ship for so long?

"Because women don't belong in a fight," he said without thinking, noting with some surprise that he didn't say they didn't belong on a *ship*. "It may be some time before we return to Baltimore. I will return you to your family, but in the meantime, it's my duty to protect you."

"Protect me? It's your duty to protect all your crew. Why should I be any different?" She stared up at him, green eyes blazing, and issued what amounted to a challenge. "I am a member of your crew, aren't I?"

Will ran his hand across the back of his neck. She had a point. She did the work of two men with her role as the doctor's assistant and his personal cook, and her performance had been exemplary. But looking into her eyes, Will couldn't block out the undeniable fact that she was female.

Amanda stretched to her full height, yet her forehead only came to the top of his collar. An attempt to intimidate him perhaps? His pulse quickened, but it wasn't intimidation that stirred his blood.

The pressure proved too much for Will. He had a potential prize off the port bow. He really had no idea how far off, yet he couldn't bring himself to care now that all the repressed desire of the last few weeks flooded his veins.

He struggled to refocus his thoughts. Did the English ship look low in the water, implying they were heavy with cargo? Did the *Amanda* have the advantage? Had the other ship struck her colors, or did they turn to fight? None of those concerns mattered anymore. If he was to have any hope of composing himself and taking charge of his ship, he needed to take action.

He lowered his face to hers and inhaled her soft scent. She smelled like a woman. How could he not have noticed that before? Mustering every ounce of self-control he still possessed, Will brushed his lips against Amanda's. He couldn't risk more than that. He would be needed on deck soon, and it would be all too easy to get carried away, to lose himself in her.

Amanda didn't close her parted lips when Will caressed them with his own. She stiffened, but just for a moment, when he pulled her to him. Then she melted in his arms, molding her body against his.

He ran his hands up her arms and trailed his fingers across her neck before cupping her face in his hands. She rewarded him with a soft sound, half moan, half whimper, in the back of her throat.

He would have stopped if she had shown the slightest resistance. She didn't.

Amanda kissed him back, inexpertly perhaps, but there could be no doubt about her intent.

With a sigh, he pulled away before passion consumed them both and he lost all sense of duty. She wobbled for a moment then settled herself against the edge of his desk, a faraway look in her eyes.

"When I get back, we'll talk about how to return you to your family." He snatched a key from his desk and left the room without looking back.

Chapter Eight

Amanda steadied herself against the hard edge of the captain's desk. She brought hesitant fingertips to her tingling lips. The captain had kissed her. Why had he done that?

The harsh click of a key in the lock brought her back to her senses, and anger swept away her confusion like a spring tide. The man had locked her in his quarters!

"What the…!" she yelled at the heavy oak door.

She still couldn't bring herself to swear even after more than a month of living with sailors, but her mind easily filled in the missing words. She strode to the door and gave it a kick. Pain radiated through her toes and up her calf. She cursed her own impulsiveness, the door and the captain—all in a single breath. Toes still smarting, she turned to pace the limited space afforded by her makeshift prison.

"I am just as much a part of this crew as any man aboard." She advanced on one wall, spun on her heel, and hobbled the five paces that brought her up against the door. "More than some." She shook her fist at it.

She pivoted on her heel again, grinding the momentary shame she felt at such an uncharitable thought into the rough planks. "But I do two jobs," she informed her own conscience and the captain's empty chair.

She spun and did another turn about the room. “Granted, I’m terrible at fighting, and I hate every minute of it,” she stopped and stared at his chair, seeing his implacable face instead of the chair’s slatted back, “but the doctor told me, more than once, how indispensable I’ve been to him.”

She hobbled once more about the room.

When she had completed the small circuit, she waggled a finger at the phantom captain. “And where would you be without my cooking? Probably dead at the bottom of the sea from burnt toast and charcoaled eggs. That’s where you’d be!”

She covered an unladylike snort with the back of her hand. Scolding an empty chair would get her nowhere.

“The captain and his stupid rules.” Amanda fell into his chair with a thump and crossed her arms over her chest.

She hadn’t changed from the person she had been an hour ago. Just because he knew her secret didn’t make her any less competent, any less useful, any more *female*. The word reverberated in her skull. Never did she think she would come to despise who she was, but right now she would give anything to cast off the anchor that her own sex had become.

She had been a valuable member of his crew, both as cook and the doctor’s assistant. She had! She let her head roll back and stared up at the ceiling. Men passed over her, preparing for battle, and slivers of daylight streaming in from the deck above flashed on and off, on and off, on and off.

Why couldn’t he see he needed her?

His parting words drifted back to her, and she

stopped seeing the flashes of light and darkness, stopped hearing the running footsteps and excited shouts of the men. What did he mean by take her back to her family? She had no family to which to return. Did the captain think Neil had lied when he said their father was dead?

The skin around her eyes tightened until she thought her eyeballs might sink into her skull, leaving her a soulless shell. Amanda took a few deep breaths and rubbed her temples. Focus. She needed to focus.

She had been locked in his quarters, a virtual prisoner during a battle with an English ship off the bow no less! She set the side of her index finger against her lips. She had once heard Buck tell a young sailor to keep a close eye on a group of captives because, as he put it, "a prisoner's primary duty is to escape."

"Well, then," Amanda pushed herself out of the captain's chair, "that shall be my first priority too."

After that, she would find a way to make the captain see her worth. But for now, she would fight one battle at a time.

She strode to the oak door and rapped on it, her knuckles making a dull thump against the solid surface. With her light frame, it would be foolhardy to try to break it down. Perhaps if she knocked harder she might convince someone to open it for her. No. Before a battle, everyone would be on deck. No one would hear even if she pounded on the door until her fists were bloody.

Except, perhaps, Doctor Miller.

He would be busy, readying his equipment and preparing the common area for casualties. Amanda put her ear to the door in a futile attempt to detect sounds of activity beyond her prison. She might be able to yell loud enough for him to hear, but in all likelihood, the captain had already told the doctor she would not be attending him.

What more had he taken the time to share?

She straightened and rested her fists on her hips. Well then, if she couldn't break the door down, nor enlist help from the outside, she would have to find a third avenue of escape.

She studied the lock...copper, faint patina about the edges, familiar design. The room about her faded, replaced by the memory of an eleven-year-old Neil standing triumphant in the hallway outside his bedroom. She had threatened to lock him in his room. He dared her to try, claiming he didn't need a key to unlock the door. When she told him she didn't believe him, he proved it to her by showing her how to do it. It took a couple of tries, but with Neil's teaching, she mastered it soon enough.

"Thank you. Neil," Amanda whispered, for once grateful for her brother's antics.

Amanda scanned the captain's quarters for something long and thin but sturdy enough to do the job. Her gaze landed on the brown and white turkey quill in a silver stand at the edge of his desk. No, the hollow tip would break too easily and could jam in the lock. Although he deserved it, she'd hate to have to explain to Captain Stoakes how she had broken his lock and his favorite quill.

Then she remembered a metal instrument—V-shaped and about the size of her hand—she'd often seen lying atop the pile of charts on his desk. One of its pointed arms might be thin enough to slide into the keyhole.

Amanda strode to the desk and rummaged through chaotic stacks of charts, resisting the urge to tidy the captain's belongings while she searched. She rifled through the papers a second time, still failing to turn up the mysterious device.

"It's got to be here somewhere!" She yanked open the flat middle drawer on his desk and shoved a stack of parchment to the side.

"Ouch!" Amanda brought her finger to her lips and sucked at a spot of blood forming at the tip. "For a man who runs a tight ship, you could do with a little personal organization," she mumbled, still sucking on her sore finger.

She pulled out the item she had been seeking and held it up to the light streaming in from the high windows. The slim shape might do well, but would it be strong enough? She tugged at the tip of one metal arm.

"I hope that was supposed to happen." She scrunched her nose at the single arm that had come off in her hand.

"Oh well, no hope for it now." She shut the drawer and tucked the remains of the instrument into the waistband of her breeches.

Kneeling before the door, she inserted the slender, metal arm into the keyhole. Her hands trembled, partly from the delicacy of the task, partly from residual anger, mostly, she admitted with some reluctance, from the memory of his kiss.

She probed into the dark recess. With her plan of escape in motion, her anger receded, leaving room for other more perplexing thoughts. Her lips tingled anew with the memory of the warmth of his mouth on hers.

She had never been kissed by a man. Although some of her more adventurous friends had said it could be quite enjoyable, that didn't even began to describe it. A picnic at the lake on a warm summer afternoon was enjoyable. Or a good book in front of the fire on a winter's eve. Or…well, a million other mundane things, his kiss not included.

Her hand stilled. His kiss was like the warmth of the sun on her face.

Amanda pounded her fist against the door. *Focus*.

Why had he kissed her? Kissed her and then told her they would talk about putting her ashore after the battle? He said he would return her to her family, but the only living relative she had was aboard this ship. But then he knew that, didn't he?

She scowled and rattled the pointed metal around in the darkened hollow of the keyhole. Perhaps he meant he would find a way to return her to the farm where she could waste away, scratching out a meager existence among her few remaining chickens. She stabbed at the inside of the lock. Maybe he thought she could marry one of her snaggle-toothed neighbors. Anything to get her, a *woman*, off his ship. He acted as though her sex posed a bigger threat than the English!

Perhaps he had kissed her to remind her of her place in the world. Her jaw tightened and she stabbed again with the metal arm. His strategy had worked. His kiss had so knocked her off course that he had imprisoned her in his quarters before she regained her senses.

Amanda shook her head, knocking a blonde curl in front of her eyes. She blew it away with a sharp puff and jiggled the metal arm, feeling for the lever that meant her freedom.

Enough thinking about the captain. May he rot for all she cared!

But *why* had he kissed her? The question poked and prodded her brain while she felt for the unseen lever that would release her.

And she had kissed him back, without any attempt to protest his boldness. What had he thought of that? Had he expected her to withdraw from his advances, to play the frightened maid? Maid though she might be, and surely her inexperience in kissing had to be evident, how surprised he must have been when she didn't resist. Instead, she had melted like butter against him. Heat pricked the tips of her ears.

A boom shook the *Amanda.* A split-second later, the ship listed, throwing Amanda against the heavy door.

She swore softly and pulled the metal arm out of the keyhole. She put her eye to the darkness, trying in vain to see the mechanism within. It had been years since she had last done this, and this lock had proven more difficult than those at the farm. She shoved the instrument inside the lock again. The battle overhead would not make her task any easier. She must free herself soon.

At last, Amanda felt the little lever move inside the lock. She eased the latch in the mechanism upward with a satisfying click. One tug on the door handle freed her from her prison. Brushing sweaty palms against her tunic and breeches, she considered her next move. It had been some time since her swim in the sea and her clothes were nearly dry. No longer in need of a change of clothing, she might as well do as she normally did.

Shutting the heavy oak door, she relocked it in one deft maneuver, surprised at how easy it was now that she had learned the lock's secrets. She smiled with satisfaction, imaging Captain Stoakes returning to find the door still locked, but no prisoner inside. She stashed the metal arm in her waistband alongside the rest of the instrument. Let him stew on that one!

Amanda found Doctor Miller, hands bloody, in the common area, examining a man with a jagged wound on his leg.

"You know he's going to be quite angry, don't you?" Doctor Miller peered through his spectacles at the man's injury, his eyes lacking their characteristic sparkle.

So he had stopped to tell the doctor.

"Not sure what you mean, Doctor." She strode to the basin and poured water from a pitcher over her hands.

"Amanda…" he began.

She held her hands frozen in midair. "So he told you everything? Even my real name?"

She watched a rivulet of water roll down the back of her hand and pool into a mirrored drop at her finger's tip.

"Told me?" Doctor Miller snorted. "I am the one who should have told him long ago."

She whirled to face him. "You knew?"

"Well. Not your name perhaps, but that you were a woman? Yes. One would have to be blind not to see that."

"So what's the captain's excuse? He certainly sees well enough when he's sighting the enemy."

"Yes, but he's looking for the enemy. In a way, the

captain is blind to you. Because he expects his men to be obey his rules without question, it never occurred to him that you might have broken them all on your own."

Doctor Miller waved her toward the man he had been examining. "Could you help Martin, dear?"

Martin's beaming face suggested he was more interested in the discussion than in the bloody gash across his shoulder.

"Martin, you can't tell anyone what you just heard. Please." She threaded a thin needle.

"Your secret is safe with me, Miss," Martin said. "I won't tell a soul that don't already know."

Amanda wondered at his choice of words until Doctor Miller broke into her thoughts. "Amanda, don't worry about the captain. He is more concerned for your safety than angry at you. In fact, if he's angry at anyone, it is himself."

Amanda snorted. "He's concerned for his ship. For some reason, I pose a danger to him and his men, although I can't imagine what it would be."

"Can't you?" The doctor's eyes shone above his spectacles.

"No, I can't," Amanda said, feeling contrite when Martin stiffened under the first jab of her needle. "It's not like I'm in the way during a battle. I'm down here helping you. The rest of the time, I'm in the galley cooking just to feed his insatiable appetite."

"I think he understands your value," the doctor replied, "even if he hasn't admitted it to himself."

"He wants to put me ashore," Amanda said, knowing she sounded miserable.

"Did he say that?" the doctor asked.

Even Martin's face showed doubt.

"Yes," Amanda said. "He told me we would discuss it after the battle. Who is to say that I am in any more danger here than on land? For all we know, the British took Baltimore last week and burned my family's farm to the ground."

"Perhaps..." The doctor shrugged. "But, on land, you would at least have had neighbors, *female neighbors*, to whom you could turn to for help. On the *Amanda*, you've been forced to bunk with sixty men."

"There were never sixty of them at once." Amanda took another stitch. "My shift only had thirty-five."

Martin chuckled his appreciation of her humor.

"I'm not in any danger," she said, her tone turning serious. "The men of the *Amanda* are honorable."

Martin looked up from the needle poking halfway out of his shoulder to nod his head, a look of pride at her defense on his blunt features. She steadied him with her hand and resumed sewing.

"Yes, they are, but at one time, the captain thought the rule necessary. Perhaps it still is for all but the most exceptional cases. Either way, the captain is, right now, at war with his rule about 'no women on my ship.'" He did a poor impression of Captain Stoakes, and her hand shook from stifled laughter. "He's only just discovered his rule has been broken and nothing dire has happened because of it. Perhaps we need to give him time to come to terms with that."

"He does love his rules, doesn't he?"

The doctor must have heard the doubt in her voice. "Amanda, you are as much a member of his crew as anyone else on this ship. If nothing else, you have been a godsend to me. I could have managed. I have before, but the men have definitely fared better under your ministrations." He smiled thoughtfully. "Even old Joe seems to be recovering well. I had no idea chicken soup and lemon cake could help a man recover from a broken arm."

"Chicken soup cures everything," she said, her mood, if not her hopes, lightened by the doctor's praise.

"Yes, well, the point is that every man on this ship, me included, will fight to make the captain see you have earned the right to be here."

Amanda frowned. "I hope so, but he is a stubborn man."

"That he is," agreed the doctor. "And there's always a chance that we won't have the opportunity to come to your defense before he's made up his mind."

Amanda glanced up, her frown deepening. Was he trying to cheer her up? If so, his approach needed refining.

"But, mark my words," the doctor continued. "I have known the captain for a long time. You won't stay ashore for long. You've become a member of his crew. You've become a part of him too. You are one prize he will not be so willing to let go."

Amanda blushed at being compared to the captain's quarry. She hoped the doctor was right, yet she did not quite share his confidence. She agreed the captain needed her, but perhaps he did not realize it yet.

She knotted off the thread and clipped the end with the scissors.

If she couldn't convince him of her worth through the needle and his stomach, she would have to find another way.

Chapter Nine

The battle lasted well into the next day, the two ships circling each other like vultures waiting for death. Bright flashes of cannon fire rocked the moonlit night.

Before a final volley brought down the main mast of the English ship, she battered the *Amanda* with everything she had. When she ran out of shot, her crew used the captain's silver. Forks and knives tore through canvas like grape and sunk deep into the white pine of the *Amanda's* main mast.

A steady stream of wounded kept the doctor and Amanda busy. Above their heads, shot peppered the deck, shattering the ankle of one man. Amanda held his hand when the doctor forced a block of leather-covered wood between the poor man's teeth. She tried not to flinch when he set his saw to the pulpy mass that had been the man's bones. The soft thud of the dead foot falling onto the straw-covered floor would haunt her dreams.

Her shipmates descended the stairs in a steady stream of blood, bodily fluid and broken limbs. Some hobbled to a table under their own power; others had to be carried. Alternately sewing, setting and comforting when that was all she could do, Amanda didn't give even a passing thought to what the captain would think when he found his quarters empty.

****

The first thing Will noticed was the gaping hole in the wall where an uncommonly well-aimed English cannonball had found its mark. The shot left a breach about the size of a man, surrounded by shattered planks. Beyond, lay nothing but open air and a choppy sea.

"Amanda?" His voice echoed off the walls of the empty room.

Only the soft whoosh of waves and the distant trill of an albatross answered his call.

His gaze swept the room, and he fully expected to see what remained of her bloody, mangled body. Splinters covered his desk, his chair, and his bed, but no blood, no mangled corpse, no dead Amanda.

His heart tightened as though squeezed by a giant fist. If not in his quarters, where could she be?

Clinging to the jagged edge of his wounded ship, Will squeezed broad shoulders past ragged planks. A tight fit for him, Amanda's small frame could slip through without effort. He looked past the tips of his blood-spattered boots to the white-capped crests licking at darkened planks just a few feet below. Could she have become disoriented by the blast and fallen in? Or perhaps her sense of self-preservation had driven her to madness, the opening her only means of escape. The door, after all, had been locked.

He scanned the sea, hoping to catch sight of a small head bobbing on the waves. Hope dwindled with each passing second, surpassed by reason and what Will knew to be true. Whether disoriented or mad, for surely she would never have slipped through the rent in the wall on purpose, more than five minutes in the cold, choppy Atlantic would be enough to overcome the strength and will of the sturdiest man, let alone a fragile woman.

God! He brought his palm to his mouth. He had sought to keep her safe by locking her in his quarters. Had he gotten her killed?

Death was a constant companion in war. Will had witnessed his share of death, come close to experiencing it himself on many occasions. However, for Will, and probably for most men, attention to duty and the constant call to action offered the antidote to fear. Amanda didn't have the soul of a fighter, or the strength of a man, but she had performed her duties well even if she weren't an official member of his crew. As much as any man aboard, she had earned the right to go to her station and not simply wait for death with nothing more to do than contemplate her own fate.

Even before he reached the open deck, he had decided to let her out, but the *Amanda* had drawn within enemy range. Too much time had been wasted to turn around and release her. He would send someone below as soon as a man could be spared. That moment never came.

Now she was gone.

A torrent of emotions swamped Will—remorse, dread, fear, and an overwhelming sense of loss that bore down on him like a hurricane. He drew back into his quarters and leaned against the wall. His legs folded beneath him, too weak to hold the weight of his emptiness and the loss in his heart.

"She's gone." Will stumbled into Doctor Miller's quarters some time later.

It might have been an hour or it might have been a day. He would never know how long he remained propped against the wall of his empty quarters, as lost to time as Amanda was to him. Even now, the world about him, his ship, his men, the doctor seemed unreal. Trying to focus on the wavering forms was like trying to seize the remnants of a dying dream.

He teetered and grasped a support beam just in time to keep from toppling forward. Through vision that had grown blurry, he saw the doctor's face. Confusion mixed with concern puckered the brow above his nose. The doctor helped him to a chair, then turned and spoke to someone standing nearby. The words were garbled as though they traveled through water before reaching Will's ears.

A moment later, Doctor Miller tried to hand him a glass half-filled with a tawny liquid. Will reached for it, but he had little strength left. He only managed to raise his arm a few inches before the energy left him and his arm fell to hang limply at his side.

A warm hand curled his fingers around the glass. Then the hand moved the glass closer until Will could smell the buttery warmth of the liquid. He gazed into the glass for several seconds, then downed it in one gulp. The last of his strength spent, he let his hand fall to his side. The glass dropped from his limp fingers and rolled into a corner, a casualty of the battle raging in the captain's soul.

Will's hazy world wobbled for a moment then stilled. Then it wobbled again.

He wanted to lash out at whatever tormented force would not allow him to slip into a mindless oblivion. He longed for the dark emptiness that would ease the crushing pressure around his heart.

Once more, the room swam in front of his eyes, but this time he registered a slight force against his shoulder. Will tried to raise his hand to swat it away, but found he lacked the strength. Mustering what little remained, he managed to turn his head.

Will stared at the hand lying on his shoulder—small, delicate and soft. It was attached to a thin arm, smooth skin sprinkled with almost invisible soft blonde hair. That arm disappeared beneath a grimy sleeve. His gaze drifted upwards, small shoulders, blonde curls and a face that looked familiar, yet somehow out of place. Where had he seen that face? His head throbbed, as though his brain resisted the effort he forced upon it.

The pulse at the base of a delicate throat beat fast. Green eyes regarded him with concern. Lips the color of rosebuds puckered and opened, forming sounds he could not comprehend.

The words were garbled and far away, as if they came from under the waves. He struggled to make sense of them. Was this soft creature a sea imp come to take him to his eternal rest at the ocean's bottom?

The lips moved again.

Those lips. He remembered those lips, the way they melted under his own, the way they opened up to him, the way they willingly gave him what he sought.

"Amanda!' Will jumped from his chair and pulled her slight form against him. "I thought I had lost you," he breathed against her ear.

He released her, only to entwine his fingers in her curls and draw her closer. After he had kissed just about every inch of her face, including the tip of her nose, his lips found hers.

This time he kissed her as though he had been trapped under water and she were air, hard, greedy kisses that left her little opportunity to pull away.

Amanda started when his tongue darted into her mouth to tease her own, but she soon matched his actions, pouring life back into him with each stroke.

Doctor Miller cleared his throat. “If you are done manhandling my assistant, she still has work to do.”

Chapter Ten

The laughter of men skylarking in the rigging filtered through the planks above Will's head, dissolving the residue of grief left behind after the deaths of so many of his crew.

From the shouts of the men, he guessed a competition had begun. The younger, more agile boys and even a few of the men would race to the pinnacle of the main mast then slide down the backstay. The first to plant his feet firmly on deck would be the winner.

A cheer rose, a sound of joy and of healing.

Last week's battle had been hard won. Those killed were good men and valued crewmembers, and Will couldn't shake the idea that had they served under a better captain, they might still be alive. Writing letters to their families had been difficult enough. Those who spent their days working side by side with the fallen men would grieve their loss even more.

Though the loss of crew always left him adrift, his fear of losing Amanda had left him grasping at his surroundings, in sudden want of something solid to hold on to. Worse, his fear, an immobilizing emotion he hadn't felt in years, left him questioning his fitness for command.

He could still taste panic in his throat when he glanced at the pine boards that covered the opening to his own private hell. Bull had promised the last of the repairs would be complete on the morrow once the carpenter had finished more vital parts of the ship like mast and rail.

Tomorrow could not come soon enough.

Will set his elbows on his blotter, entwined his fingers and rested his forehead against them. Did other men question his suitability to captain a ship? He never had. In all his years commanding the *Amanda* and serving on ships before her he had never once questioned his capacity for courage or the prerequisite self-control. Now he wondered whether that unshakable belief hadn't been blind ignorance.

He could hardly be faulted for a sense of relief at finding Amanda alive, but his loss of control, kissing her like that in front of a roomful of injured men, evidenced the depth of her influence on him. Luckily, the promise of an extra share of rum had been enough to earn the silence of those who had witnessed his indiscretion.

However, Amanda's near loss and his uncensored reaction reminded him of an undeniable truth. He had proven himself as human as any man. For however long he allowed her to remain aboard ship, he endangered her life and the lives of his men.

Whenever she was near, her soft scent and the memory of her sweet lips drove away all else but his need for her. He found himself reflecting on what it would be like to have her beneath him, her legs wrapped around him in sweet surrender. He yearned to discover what type of body she concealed beneath her tight woolen bindings and shapeless clothes.

Fingers digging into the arms of his chair, Will turned away.

That he would never know. He could not jeopardize her safety, no matter how much he enjoyed her charms. He would not jeopardize his crew with a bemused captain. His wall would be repaired tomorrow even if he had to do it himself. Then, he would make plans to return Amanda to Baltimore so he could return to being the captain his men needed him to be.

Shouts sounded from above, and Will rose to join the men. Perhaps their joy would be strong enough to chase away his doubts.

He climbed the stairs, his mood lifting with each step.

Who had inspired such enthusiasm in his tired crew? Had young James overcome his fear of heights to challenge one of the older boys? Or perhaps a wager had been cast among the more seasoned hands to see which were still able enough to compete.

"Bet he never makes it to the top!" Roger's rough growl rose above the other voices. "His lunch will be rainin' down on all of us before he reaches the yardarm."

Will averted his eyes from the men tossing coins, tobacco pouches and other personal effects into a pile. Had his been a ship of the Navy, he would have been forced to take action. But even as captain of a mere privateer, it would not do well for him to be seen encouraging wagers.

Skylarking in the rigging on the other hand… Will shielded his eyes from the midday sun to search the sky for the competitors. Fun for the lads, this kind of activity also turned boys into sailors. After all, a boy who feared heights or couldn't climb the ropes, whether to take his turn at the watch or to work the sails, would be of little use on a ship.

Far above the deck, a lone figure clung to the ropes. The boy raised a cautious foot and planted it on the next level. A raucous cheer went up from the men. More coins clanked as they were added to the pile.

"That's it, my boy. Just a little further." Will clenched his fists, remembering the first time he had clung to the ropes, the deck spinning below him, his stomach spinning within.

The lad froze like a fly caught in a spider's web. The late morning sun outlined his pitiful plight.

"C'mon, you're almost there," Bull bellowed. "You'll never be a real sailor if ya can't make it to the watch platform! Get your arse moving!"

The boy looked down then turned a resolute gaze toward the platform. Buck clapped Bull on the shoulder, and the two men exchanged grins.

"Captain Stoakes," Buck said, catching sight of Will over Bull's grizzled curls. "Shall I call the men to attention?" Laughter resonated in his voice.

"No, that's all right. Let them have their fun." Will squinted against the glare, trying to make out the identity of the sailor with the wobbly legs inching his way along the ropes.

It couldn't be James. The lad's short, stout bearing would make the ropes bend and groan under his weight. Besides James had yet to make it more than three rungs off the deck. Doubtless, he never would. This boy had climbed so high the sun haloed his darkened silhouette, showing long limbs and a lanky frame. Definitely not James.

Will scanned the deck with an inquiring gaze. Nate's simian build made him the ideal climber, and he spent more time on the watch platform than on deck. However, having proven himself long ago, he would not have warranted the crowd nor the pile of coins and tobacco. It couldn't be Nate anyway, for he stood at the foot of the mast, one long-fingered hand resting on the wood, eyes turned skyward, jaw agape.

The lithe, little sailor set his foot on the platform and pulled himself up. Another cheer, louder than the first, rose from the deck. He turned and looked down at his mates. Will's breath caught in his throat when the boy gave a victory pump with his fist that threatened to knock him off the platform. At the last second, he latched onto one of the ropes with his other hand.

Will scanned the sailors laughing at the boy. Among the seasoned old tars stood several ship's boys, clinging to each other like barnacles. He mentally ticked off the names in the registry. James stood by the bulwark, freckled face red from his exuberant cheering-on of his mate. The twins, Randall and Fredrick, tow-headed boys of about nine, clung to the tails of James' coat. Neil stood behind them. Nate, the oldest and almost a man, stood apart, gawking from the foot of the mast.

A sickening wave caught Will's stomach and the deck spun for a moment. "Bull."

"Yes, sir." Bull joined his captain, still chuckling. "What can I do for you, sir?"

"Who is the brave lad up there?" Captain Stoakes kept his voice even.

Bull stroked his chin. "Well, sir, I'm not sure I'd be calling him a brave lad exactly, but that's Adam."

"A…dam?" Will choked.

"Yes, sir," Bull confirmed, his gray eyes filled with

an almost fatherly pride. "It's his first time making it that far. Next time, mark my words, we'll have him out on the yardarm."

"Whose idea was it for Adam to climb the rigging?" Will asked.

"Oh, he was all for it," Bull said, deaf to the tightness in his captain's tone. "I have to say, he surprised me with the request, him being so...*soft* and all. Maybe he decided it was about time he became a real sailor."

"He is my personal cook and the doctor's assistant," Will said between gritted teeth. "He has no need to learn to climb the rigging."

Bull's bushy eyebrows rose as one. "Adam said he had served your noon meal and you wouldn't be needin' him till supper. 'Sides, Captain." He gave Will a conspiratorial grin. "If he falls, ya still have Cookie."

Falls? The deck heaved again. One misstep and they'd be scraping Amanda off the planks as if she were no more than a casualty of battle.

The vein in Will's forehead pulsed; he wondered that Bull didn't see it. Had he done so, he would surely have beaten a fast retreat. Yet Bull stood next to him, gawking at Amanda, a grin of almost sadistic delight on his wizened face.

"Adam is unfit to serve on deck," Will said, his jaw even tighter than before.

"Unfit? Captain, he's hardly been on the ship a full two months. Came aboard same day as young Jimmy." He waved a gnarled hand toward the red-faced boy staring upward with unmasked adoration at his more accomplished shipmate. "In fact, Adam's better than Jimmy at most things, and I don't see you telling me that lad's unfit."

"James can't cook," Will said.

"I see." Bull gave a small chuckle more insolent than any verbal reply ever could be.

"The moment Adam sets one foot on the deck, I want to see him in my quarters," Will growled.

"In your quarters. Aye, Captain." Bull turned away, his grin wider than ever.

Will pivoted on his heel before he succumbed to the temptation to strangle his crew master.

****

By the time a timid knock sounded on Will's door, his world had slowed to a near normal rotation and the knot in his stomach had loosened—at least enough to allow him to breathe. He had also had time to rehearse the discussion to come a dozen times.

It had been days since he had spoken to Amanda, other than a few polite words when she brought him his meals. "Please" and "thank you" hardly sufficed for the type of conversation he needed to have with his would-be cabin boy, but it had been all he could manage. The sight of her robbed him of the ability to form more than the simplest of thoughts. He lived in a state of almost constant apprehension should his crew start to notice her undeniably feminine attributes.

In truth, he hadn't known what to say anyway. If she were any other crewmember, he would have taken her to task for defying his orders regardless of how misguided. He had been wrong to confine her, but even when wrong, a captain expected to be obeyed. A crew who questioned a captain's orders was not an effective fighting force.

But Amanda was not a member of his crew, and

the time had come to explain where she fit into the small world that was his ship. She must be made to understand that her position was temporary and at his discretion.

The knock came again, louder this time. Will steeled himself for the first waves of desire.

"Come in," he said, rising to his feet.

Amanda ducked inside the door and stood at attention.

Will shook his head at her appearance, bare feet, grimy shirt, frayed canvas trousers. A stray blonde curl peeked from beneath a wool cap so old it gave no hint to its original color. A line of soot accented one cheekbone. He never met a woman so content to look like a common street urchin. He never met a street urchin more beguiling.

Amanda nipped at her lower lip with even white teeth, and Will sucked in a breath. Not for the first time, he appreciated how the current fashion helped conceal his body's reaction beneath a knee-length coat.

She stood silent, uncertainty marring her clear brow, while he studied her. It was the first time he allowed himself the pleasure of looking at her fully since the discovery of her sex, and he came to understand something of himself. Even disheveled and dirty, she affected him in ways no woman ever had.

The desire he felt coursing through his veins was not the result of having been without a woman for months at a time. He had been months at sea before only to find himself in a port surrounded by beautiful women, some courtesans, but also the daughters of wealthy merchants and equally wealthy widows. Whore and socialite alike had tried to tempt him, only to fail time and again.

Even on the occasion when he did satisfy the need that every man felt, his was a controlled reaction, a simple satisfying of a thirst much like drinking a glass of water on a hot day. Never had he felt the need to drown himself in a woman the way he did with Amanda.

His reaction to her only served to strengthen his resolve and prove his course of action correct.

"Amanda, have a seat." He waved to a wooden chair across from his desk.

She gave him a skeptical glance, but did as he asked.

Will considered taking his chair and sitting across from her but decided against it. He could think better if he didn't have to look into those green eyes of hers. Plus, he always thought better when standing. Perhaps it came from years of standing on deck during battle.

No, better not to think of this as a battle. He and Amanda needed to be allies, not enemies—if not for the sake of his ship, then for her own safety.

Will clasped his hands behind his back and paced the small space behind her chair. "Amanda, it may be several weeks before we return to Baltimore."

He stopped pacing long enough to glance at the back of her wool-clad head. She didn't turn around or respond, but then she didn't interrupt either so he continued.

"I'm sure you understand, I can't drop you off at just any port. Neil has told me you have no family other than him." He spoke in a measured pace designed to give her time to come to terms with her situation.

It occurred to him that although he had spent more

time with her than possibly any man on the ship, except perhaps Buck, they had never really spoken. He knew nothing about her save what her brother had supplied, and that was far too little. Which of life's experiences had given her the courage to sign on to a privateer? The act required more fortitude than most men had. What kind of life had she given up? Did she have friends, a sweetheart? Did she have hopes for the future? Perhaps for a husband and a home filled with children?

A part of him mourned for the conversations they were never to have.

"Even if we were to spot a packet ship," he paused, wondering if she understood that a packet ship carried the post but decided she must know that by now, "I could not entrust you to their care, knowing they could be beset by the British."

Amanda shifted in her chair, but didn't turn around.

Will began to wish he had sat across from her. That way he could see her face and perhaps have some idea of the thoughts behind her clear green eyes.

He cleared his throat, the sound as obtrusive against the backdrop of silence as a cough at a funeral. "Therefore, I am forced to keep you on my ship for the time being."

Amanda might have been made of wood, for she gave no more indication that she heard him than did the chair on which she sat. Surely, his decision should elicit some response, perhaps even an expression of gratitude. He hadn't said she could stay on the ship indefinitely, but he would allow her to stay for now.

He had seen silence used as a weapon. His own mother had been a master at it, but he had never understood why his father always lost the argument at that point—until now. He hadn't realized how razor-sharp a woman's silence could be.

Then again, Amanda considered herself part of his crew. Perhaps she simply waited for permission.

"You may speak," Will said.

Amanda sighed. "I wasn't aware you said anything requiring a response. So far, you have informed me of things I already know. Then you informed me of your decision." She gave a nonchalant shrug that chipped away at Will's carefully erected facade. "What response are you wanting from me?"

Not two minutes into the discussion and they were already at odds with each other. In some ways, Will missed his malleable, obedient cabin boy.

He took a deep breath. "We must have a discussion about your future," he said, using his best captainly voice.

Amanda stood and pivoted her chair on one spindled leg until it faced Will. Then she sat back down with a decided thump. Her eyes had the look of a storm-churned sea.

"It is rather difficult to have a conversation with someone who insists on pacing the floor behind me." She waved a dismissive hand before crossing her arms over her chest. "Please continue."

First Bull and now Amanda. Insubordination had become the order of the day. However, Amanda was not a member of his crew, so he would overlook it for now. Besides, he found he much preferred anger over silence.

Will cleared his throat again. "The point is, you will be forced to remain on the ship. That is, at least until we get back to Baltimore."

"You mean," Amanda spat from between tight lips, "you will be forced to have me on your ship until we get back to Baltimore."

Will saw no point in arguing. "Yes, well, since that is the case, I thought perhaps we might reach an agreement on certain…standards of behavior."

"Am I to understand you object to the way I conduct myself?" Amanda stood, fury flashing in her eyes. "When have I done something inappropriate?"

"I don't approve of ladies climbing the rigging," he explained, trying to douse her ire with his cool captain's demeanor.

Just as he commanded his ship, he would maintain control of this conversation no matter how emotional she became.

"But I am not a lady." She gave a flip of her hand he assumed was intended to resemble a feminine gesture, although it looked more like casting a fishing line. "I am a sailor."

"Only by accident," he said, his voice radiating calm logic.

"What accident? I did not accidentally show up at the docks. I did not accidentally sign the ship's registry. And you," she stabbed at him with an accusing finger, "did not accidentally order Bull to sign me on."

Will bristled at the reminder of perhaps the gravest error he had ever made. "That's where you are wrong. Had I known you were a woman, I would not have done so."

"Why not?" Amanda rested her hands on her hips. "You obviously saw something in me that made you think I'd be a decent sailor."

He had. A pair of bright green eyes glared back at him now with the same determination they had on that fateful day. Determination was perhaps the best trait a man could have if he hoped to be a successful privateer. She had it in abundance.

"Look, Amanda, it's simply bad luck to have a woman on a ship."

"Oh, ballocks," she said with a snort, then a faint flush crept up her cheeks and she averted her eyes. "You can't possibly believe that nonsense."

Will ignored her vulgar language although he considered it clear evidence she had been surrounded by men for far too long. "I may not believe it, but some of the men do, and that's what matters. I can't have them thinking I've brought a Jonas on board." Amanda glared at him in silence, so he started to explain. "A Jonas is—"

"I know what a Jonas is. I've heard the men talking about the many things they believe bring bad luck, and I concede you may have a point." Her lips looked as though she had downed a tot of vinegar. "So what do we do about it?"

"First, we must conceal your identity," Will said, relieved that Amanda at least appeared amenable to a pragmatic approach. "So far, only Doctor Miller and I know you are a woman."

Amanda opened her mouth, then shut it again. After a moment's hesitation, she asked, "Won't I have better luck blending in, so to speak, if I act like one of the crew? Taking my turn at watch, for example?"

A soft sweetness replaced the sharp determined look in her eyes, and Will had no doubt he was being played. "But you're not a member of the crew,

Amanda."

Amanda gave him spun-sugar smile. "Then shall I have Cookie make your meals again? I mean, if I am not a member of the crew then…" She shrugged.

"I will allow you to continue that duty." Sacrifices would have to be made eventually, but for now, he saw no harm in allowing her to continue.

"You will allow…you will allow," Amanda sputtered, her sugary smile dissolved. "I rather think you have the better end of that bargain. But I will make a deal with you. You *allow* me to prepare your meals for you, and I will *allow* myself to continue assisting the doctor."

Will narrowed his eyes at her. In truth, he didn't mind the arrangement, but he couldn't let a member—a woman on his ship undermine his authority. One did not negotiate with the captain.

"Amanda, I am the captain aboard this ship—"

"But I am not a member of your crew," she reminded him.

Will blew out a breath. There might be an advantage in conceding on one point, if it allowed him to win on more important matters.

"I see no harm in letting you assist Doctor Miller. We must also find a way for you to have quarters of your own."

"Why?" Amanda asked, genuine surprise showing on her face. "If no one knows I am a woman, won't it be rather difficult to explain if I am given my own quarters? They might think you—"

"Yes, but it is necessary," Will said, plowing ahead before she could finish that thought. "After all, there is no privacy on a ship, and…" he paused, trying to figure out how to continue without offending her delicate sensibilities. He needn't have bothered.

"You mean there is no privy in the privy." She laughed at her own joke.

"Yes. I mean how did you—" He stopped himself when he realized what he had been about to ask.

She eyed him, amusement replacing her anger. "Do you mean to ask if I hung my arse over the side like the men?"

Will's collar seemed to be getting tighter by the moment. He stuck a finger beneath his neck stock and tugged. Amanda's smile widened

"No, I will admit to being a bit more creative, and Neil's been a willing accomplice. He might not want me on the ship any more than you do, but since I am here, he looks out for me."

"Nevertheless, I can't have you sleeping with sixty men." Will cringed at the implication in his words.

"Oh for heaven's sakes, I'm not sleeping with sixty at a time." She didn't look offended, just bored.

"And there's one other thing," A trickled ran down his back. When had he started sweating? "You and I cannot—"

"Cannot what?" Amanda asked.

"We cannot be alone together," Will finished in a rush of words.

"You mean like we are now?" Amanda cocked her head.

"No, well, yes," He hated the uncertainty he heard in his voice. "Yes, even though we are alone together now, we should endeavor not to be."

"Why not?" Amanda asked.

"Because it would be improper," Will answered.

One couldn't argue with the obvious.

"Why?" Amanda asked, proving that one could indeed argue the obvious.

"Because you are a woman!" Will's carefully erected façade crumbled in a rush of words.

Pinching the bridge of his nose, Will looked at the floor. His careful rehearsal of the conversation had not included Amanda's unpredictable responses. Her side of the discussion had involved her sitting primly in a chair, giving responses such as, "yes, sir," and "no, sir" when called for.

He raised his head and eyed the comely street urchin before him. How stupid could he have been?

"Then what is the point, pray tell." Her blonde brows furrowed. "I cannot be alone with you because I am a woman. But no one knows I am a woman, so what would it matter if I am alone with you?"

Because you are not safe being alone with me.

Will knew it to be the truth. With each moment that passed, the inexplicable power she held over him strengthened. He should never have agreed to let her stay aboard ship. A wiser captain, one still in command of himself, would have ordered the helmsman to set a course for Maryland weeks ago.

"If you are alone with me and anyone finds out you are a woman, your reputation will be ruined," he growled. "We must have as little to do with each other as possible."

At that point, William Stoakes, Captain of the *Amanda* but better known as *The Sea Wolf*, did something he had never done in his life. He turned and stomped out of his own quarters, effectively dismissing himself.

Chapter Eleven

Amanda had been over every inch of the ship, yet not spotted so much as one glimpse of Neil's dark brown head. In keeping to her bargain with the captain, she searched the ropes a second time—without stepping foot on them. Nate waved down from his usual station on the watch platform. The only other inhabitants of the tall spires were the omnipresent gulls clinging to the ropes, their gray-white feathers blending into canvas and cloudy sky.

She forced a smile and returned the wave. Her mood wasn't Nate's doing, and he didn't deserve the scowl she wore. She would reserve that for the captain.

Her first genuine conversation with him, her very first as a woman, had not gone as she had hoped. She had known he would want her off his ship. After all, her presence was a constant reminder that his cardinal rule had been broken, his command usurped. Although he tried hard not to show it, she could sense his irritation simmering below the surface of his calm demeanor. He was like a heated kettle that had almost reached a boiling point. Thankfully, when her own ire had pushed him that final degree, he had left her in his quarters and blown off steam in some other part of the ship. She hoped none of her shipmates had suffered.

Regardless of the inevitability of his attitude toward her, it didn't stop her from wishing that he might have acknowledged her usefulness. Lying in her hammock at night, listening to the snores of the men, she had even imagined him saying that she had become indispensable. Invariably, as she drifted off to sleep, those imaginings turned into an admission that he wanted her, not for her skills at cooking or caring for his men, but her. In her dreams, he would pull her close and kiss her with a heat at which his previous kisses only hinted. The kisses of her dreams were long, languid affairs, not to be broken by the untimely arrival of an English ship nor the Doctor.

Amanda sighed. Those dreams could never become reality. Captain Stoakes had made it abundantly clear that he neither needed her for her skills nor wanted her as a woman. He had agreed to allow her to remain aboard his ship. That is, until he could find a way to toss her off. Until then, what had she agreed to? To act like a lady while pretending not to be one? To not be alone with him even though that was practically impossible?

She supposed she should be grateful that she wasn't a real member of his crew, for no man would have been allowed the show of temper that she had demonstrated. Not known to have fits of pique, when she had reason to be angry, neither heaven nor hell could dissuade her. In his quarters, the first flames had flickered and sprung to life, fed by the dry kindling of repressed passions. His cold, logical demeanor had fanned the flames until they consumed her.

She twisted around, examining the face of each man. She would worry about the captain later. For now, she needed to find her brother. She wouldn't confide all her troubles to him, but she needed to talk with him, to be reminded by his playful demeanor that very little in life was ever as serious as it seemed.

Emotion still raw from the previous day, apprehension built within her.

Could Neil have slipped off the ship somehow? Fallen overboard perhaps? She looked out across the ocean, trying to glimpse sight of a shoreline through a layer of sea fog. She sucked the thick air into her lungs. Panic's squeeze forced it out.

If he had fallen over during the early watch, it was possible no one was there to witness it. He could swim, but she doubted even Neil's skills would allow him to reach the unseen shore through water she knew to be cold from firsthand experience. What if he had swum in the wrong direction?

No, she would not consider that. If he had gone missing, someone would have alerted the captain by now. Neil had duties, even if she wasn't privy to them. He had to be aboard ship somewhere.

The ropes called to her. If only she hadn't agreed to stay grounded, she could join Nate at the platform and search for her brother from a better vantage point. For the captain to forbid it went beyond reason.

Amanda had requested to climb the rigging but not because she really wanted to. She needed to work off some of her anxiety. Besides, Bull made skylarking sound like fun. He had also hinted, in that odd way he had of saying things without really saying them, that no boy would turn down the opportunity to test himself before his mates.

Deep within her breast, she hoped the captain would come on deck just in time to find her climbing those last few rungs to the watch platform. He would have to admit her abilities rivaled that of the ship's boys, all of whom, with the exception of Neil, had served longer than she had.

She had started climbing to prove something to him, but about halfway up the rigging, her reasons turned inward, and she found she needed to prove something to herself. A sense of accomplishment surged within when she finally set foot on the platform and hauled herself up. The cheers from the men gave her an elation she had never known. She had not feared falling. Standing on the platform, the breeze nudging her back, she thought she might be able to fly.

Then she looked down to see those fierce amber eyes staring up at her and almost lost her grip on the rigging. Legs wobbling, she traced and retraced her steps around the small deck, a memory of the captain's face keeping her company every step of the way.

Neil, where are you? Her whispered words, tight with worry, were carried away by the freshening breeze.

In the past hour, she had checked and rechecked the riggings, the deck, the hold, the galley and even the officer's quarters. All save one, that is.

Amanda halted when she reached the steps leading below deck. She stared into the shadowed darkness. Surely, Captain Stoakes knew what had become of Neil. Maybe she could find a way to wheedle information out of him without appearing overly concerned. On the morning the captain learned of her true identity, Neil had made it sound as if his older sister were a bossy nuisance. Amanda frowned. Nothing could be further from the truth. She was concerned, not bossy.

Amanda gripped the wooden railing and stomped down the short flight of steps. A few determined strides brought her to the captain's door, and without thinking to knock, she shoved it open, banging it against the opposite wall.

****

Will held a piece of freshly baked lemon cake halfway to his mouth. "Yes?" he asked, setting the cake back on his plate. "Is something the matter?"

"I can't find him anywhere!" Amanda's cheeks were flushed and her green eyes sparked with annoyance from beneath the pilled edges of her woolen cap.

Will sucked at a crumb-covered fingertip then examined the end of his finger with exaggerated interest until he regained his self-possession.

After his unsatisfying negotiations with Amanda, he had left his own quarters, in a mood fit for no man. Heedless of the concerned faces of his crew, he climbed to the deck, stripped to his breaches and plunged into the cold Atlantic. It had been a reckless and desperate act, but a short swim had chilled his anger and his ardor. Since then, he had received a few sidelong glances from his crew, and one blatantly speculative one from Buck, but no one mentioned his odd behavior.

His body cooled, he had hoped time would restore his rational mind, at least enough to allow him to assess the situation with a dispassionate eye. It would allow him to see her as she was, a woman, nothing more. At least nothing more to him.

Time had not been so accommodating. With her standing before him, her chest heaving in obvious agitation, his rational mind deserted him. Instead, he found himself in the grip of even baser instincts. The need to protect her stirred within him stronger than ever, but it mixed with something more potent and even more primitive—the need to possess her.

He had reached the edge of his self-restraint, and he longed to lock the door behind her, imprisoning them both in his quarters. The fault would be hers. He had tried to warn her that they shouldn't be alone together.

A rush of color stained her cheekbones as though Amanda sensed the danger she had put herself in simply by coming to the wolf's den.

"He can take care of himself," Will said, smashing little bits of lemon cake with the dampened tip of his forefinger. He tamped each morsel as though it represented an impulse that needed to be conquered.

"But I can't find him anywhere!" Amanda strode, uninvited, into his quarters.

"He's fifteen," Will replied. "Seems old enough to me to be responsible for himself."

She stood a few feet away from his desk, an innocent lamb waiting for the slaughter. He could rise, come around his desk and have her in his arms before she knew what happened. He would teach her what a real kiss was like, not the soft peck on the lips he had given her before, nor the greedy kisses he had stolen in front of the doctor. This time, if he kissed her, he would take his time exploring. He would ravage her sweet mouth until her lips were swollen and her body ached every bit as much as his.

Judging by the sparks in her eyes, perhaps now was not the time. His little lamb looked like she'd put up a fight.

Will sighed. Perhaps it was for the best. He had always trusted his instincts, base though they might be, and right now they told him that his hunger was a dangerous thing. For him, lust was like an ocean wave. He could anchor himself against it, resisting its pull, or give in and ride the wave for as long as it lasted. Like all waves, it swept back out to sea soon enough.

His desire for Amanda was more than simple lust. He sensed her the way the sea senses the moon. Even when he couldn't see her, she exerted a soft pull on him so that he felt her presence in every corner of his ship. If he ever did truly possess her, he would never let her go. Yet, that was precisely what he needed to do for the good of his crew and his ship.

"He's with the prize crew." His steady voice belied the turmoil within.

He waved Amanda toward a chair, but she shook her head. Would she ever learn to follow even the simplest of commands?

"The prize crew?" Puzzlement knit her brows.

Will sighed. "I know you signed on to my ship without the slightest idea of how to sail or to fight," he paused when she flinched, "but don't tell me you joined without knowing what it is we do."

"Of course I know!" Amanda protested.

He cocked an eyebrow. "Just not the specifics, right?"

Amanda's silent glare was answer enough.

Quelling his impatience, he explained how the captain hand-selected a group of his best sailors, the prize crew, to take a captured ship to the prize court. At the court, papers were inspected, the manifest checked, and an estimated value assessed to the ship and its contents. After a successful auction, the owner of the privateer paid off any private investors and distributed the remaining proceeds among his crew according to their rank and length of service. At least that was how he did it. Other captains could be a bit more arbitrary.

"You have been getting your share, haven't you?" he asked.

With the sudden thought that she might have been cheated, annoyance flickered within him. She might not be a full-fledged crewmember, but she did the work of two. She would receive her share.

She nodded, and Will's tension eased.

"Everything must be absolutely in order or the owner of the captured ship could sue, and I could lose my Letter of Marque."

"Letter of Marque?" Amanda asked.

While her expression held confusion, the furrow between her brows relaxed. A good sign.

"Yes. That's the essential piece of paper that makes me a…" he paused and chose his next words carefully "*businessman* instead of a pirate."

"Oh, I had wondered about that," Amanda said.

Will studied her face but detected no traces of mockery, so he continued.

Amanda listened in silence while he explained the intricate code of the privateer and all that could go wrong if the captain proved careless or corrupt. She nodded at periodic intervals and even commiserated when he related a gruesome tale of another captain's misfortune. He assumed he had successfully distracted her from worry over her brother's absence. He was wrong.

"My brother was necessary?" Amanda asked,

leaving not even a beat between his explanation and her question.

"No."

Perhaps he shouldn't have added the details about the hangings or the prison ships, fates that sometimes befell the unfortunate privateer whose papers were not found in order. He blamed the unsettling affect she had on him for bringing out his darker side.

"No, he wasn't necessary?"

"No, he wasn't." Will met Amanda's stormy stare with equal intensity. "It was necessary for *him*. He needed the experience, and he needed to be out from under his sister's wing."

****

Amanda bit back a reply. She wanted to protest that Neil was still a boy. He needed time to mature. He needed her guidance. He needed his sister. She wanted to say those things and more, but if she did, she'd be wrong.

Her brother had spent less time with her the last few weeks than he had spent in years, and in that small span of time, had grown less rebellious and more eager to take on new responsibilities. She hated to admit it, but time away from her may have been exactly what he needed.

Despite her own troubles with Captain Stoakes, her heart held nothing but gratitude where Neil was concerned. She loved watching them together, knowing he gave her brother one thing she never could—the guidance of a man.

She assessed the captain, commanding in his impeccably tailored formal coat, crisp white shirt and neck stock. She could just see the tips of his polished boots at the end of long legs stretched out below his desk. She knew from past observation, the boots would end at his knee, evolving into buff colored breeches that strained against the muscles in his thighs.

He looked every bit the fearless captain. He exuded confidence in the way he walked and in the way he stood, his back straight, shoulders square. His face never betrayed a moment's weakness. His voice never wavered. Amanda hoped her brother would grow up to be a man half as certain of his place in the world.

Familiar doubts resurfaced, gouging furrows between her brows.

How well did Captain Stoakes really know her brother? Neil was only thirteen and barely looked that. How could the captain possibly think him fifteen? Had he really matured enough to handle the kind of responsibility the captain had given him?

"Is there any more of this cake left?" the captain asked, interrupting her inner debate.

"Yes, sir," Amanda said, grateful for the excuse to slip away. She needed time to think.

Amanda spun on her heel, nearly plowing into Buck who had just stepped through the door and forcing him to dodge out of her way. Mumbling her apologies, she ducked her head and scurried on.

****

"Something up with him?" Buck tipped his head toward the door through which Amanda had fled.

"I told him where his brother is," Will replied.

"Ahh," Buck said with a knowing nod.

For a moment, Will considered sharing his troubles with Buck. It would be easier if he had someone in whom he could confide, and Buck had been a friend before he became a subordinate.

He studied Buck's tan face, the sandy blonde curls so many women seemed to favor, the full lips, his manicured hands. With no ladies around, it wasn't so obvious, but Buck was a dandy; exactly the kind women inexplicably adored. Although he would trust his second in command with his life, he wasn't so sure he was ready to trust him with Amanda.

Buck pulled a chair away from the wall, spun it around on one leg, and then straddled it before sitting. He crossed his arms over the back of the chair and rested his chin on them.

"At ease, sailor," Will said, giving Buck a grin, one normally reserved for friends, not subordinates.

"Still trying to look after his brother, I imagine. Strange boy, that one is," Buck said, his voice trailing off, inviting Will to comment.

Will's gaze flicked to Buck's face. Strange indeed, but did Buck realize just how strange?

The man's amiable face held no hint of deception, although the speculation in his eyes unsettled Will. It would be better to leave the topic of "Adam" for another time, lest Buck divine her secret and his captain's peculiar affliction.

"He'll be fine." Will snapped open his logbook. "In fact, they both will."

"Of that I have no doubt," Buck said, then shrugged. "Still, taking a prize ship to court is not without its dangers."

Will shot a glance at Buck, then dropped his gaze to the logbook lest Buck see the depth of his own concerns.

Recapture was always possible, especially when

British blockades rendered many American ports useless. A privateer and her crew didn't always have the latest intelligence regarding which ports were open. Often at the last minute, the captain of the prize ship had to decide whether to attempt a daring run at a blockade or to try to slip away to another port farther up or down the coast.

It made his heart ache to think of Neil spending the remainder of the war locked in the hold of a prison ship or in one of New York's vile sugar houses. In either case, he estimated the boy's chances of surviving the war to be fifty-fifty at best. His incarceration would kill his sister.

Buck's hazel gaze grazed Will's facade, peeling away layer after layer of carefully crafted deception and reminding him why he always had his second in command interrogate the prisoners. He had a unique ability to convey none of his thoughts or all of them through expression alone. At the moment, the fine arch of his honey-blonde brows said he saw the turmoil within his friend's heart.

"Pretty pathetic, aren't I?" Will tossed his quill to the desk. "A privateer does what a privateer does, and taking a prize ship to court is part of the life. The best part, if you ask me."

"Yes, but Neil is still very young." Buck sat up straight, gripping the back of his chair in his fists. "You know, I'm not sure the boy is the fifteen he claims to be."

"You don't say," said Will, with a small snort.

"Still thirteen, fourteen, or whatever, he's almost a man. You've given him an opportunity to gain experience, the kind of experience that can turn a boy into a man."

"So why am I feeling so damnably uncomfortable about this?" Will asked.

"Perhaps, it's his brother who makes you uncomfortable?" Buck said, refolding his arms.

"Am—Adam? Perhaps," Will admitted, grimacing at his near slip of the tongue.

"He seems to put you on edge when he's around," Buck prodded.

Will closed his logbook and set it aside. "I'll admit he's a pain in my backside at times, but he's a good crewmember, in his own way."

"I've heard good things about him." Buck said. "In fact, I was playing cards with the doctor last night and he told me, and I quote, 'Adam Blakely, has the bedside manner of a woman and the nerves of a man.'"

Will cringed at the compliment. "That's just it. He's just so, so, so…delicate," Will said, recalling the word Martin had used to describe Amanda's skills with a needle.

"And pretty," added Buck.

"You're not helping, my friend. *Pretty*—to use your words and not mine—he may be, but that is not what we need on a privateer."

Especially when the pretty crewmember proved such an irresistible temptation to the captain.

How often had he berated himself for kissing her while an English vessel bore down on his ship. Had he not spared those few seconds, would they have been able to get the upper hand? Had some of his men died needlessly all because of his fascination with Amanda? In truth, he knew those few seconds hadn't mattered, but if there were a next time, would he stay longer?

Will grimaced when he realized Buck was studying him with calculating eyes.

It would not happen again. He would get her off his ship, and the sooner the better. She would be safer, and his crew wouldn't have an addled captain putting their lives in danger.

"Why don't you send him with the prize crew next time?" Buck suggested. "That might make a man out of him."

"No!" Will barked then closed his eyes while he regained his composure. "I mean he's needed here."

He had to fight to subdue the churning in his belly at the very idea. Knowing Amanda, she would jump at the chance to go, and she evidently had his crew master following her orders. After seeing her climb the rigging, he would have to make sure Bull understood she was by no means to leave with one of the prize crews, whether she suggested it or not.

"You mean you don't want to lose his cooking skills."

"Yes, I suppose so," Will said, grasping at Buck's logic like a drowning man might grasp for a rope.

"I'm glad for that," Buck said. "Adam's tarts are the best I've ever tasted. And, his chicken pies, the savory filling, the flaky crust..." His voice trailed off, and he rolled his eyes and sighed as though even the memory of Amanda's chicken pies left him in ecstasy.

"Yes, his cooking is good," Will agreed flatly.

Instead of relieving some of the burden, this conversation with Buck had worsened his already dark mood.

Buck didn't appear to notice. "Of course, there are always opportunities to make a man out of the boy right here on the *Amanda*. The English are in desperate need of supplies and that means more ships for us. Maybe next time we take a prize, you can let Adam lead the boarding party. Send him straight over," Buck added with an exaggerated motion of his hand.

"He's not ready," Will said, feeling the blood draining from his face.

"Ah, well, I suppose that's for the best. With his complexion, the English might mistake him for a Frenchman anyway." Buck laughed at his own joke. "Add a little powder, pinch his cheeks a bit, and he'd be right at home in the French Court."

Will shuddered and Buck took note. "Calm yourself, Will. I am joking. No one's going to mistake the lad for a Frenchman. A girl maybe, but a Frenchman?"

Chapter Twelve

"Argh!" Amanda took out her frustration with the captain and her worry over her brother's absence on the cast iron skillet in the washbasin, scouring it with a dishcloth before slamming it into a twin basin filled with rinse water heated to scalding. Using a clean spatula, she fished the handle out of the water just enough to grasp it.

"Ouch!" she said, burning her hand before dropping the pan into the drying rack. She sucked at the tips of her throbbing fingers. At least they were clean from washing the dishes, even if they did taste like soap.

How could she focus on her duties when her brother was God knew where—perhaps even in the hands of the British? She picked up the empty coffeepot and plunged it into the soapy water again and again as though trying to drown it.

Would they torture him? She didn't think the English could be that cruel, but capture might mean slow death in one of the floating prisons the captain had told her about. Neil would be left to rot in the sunless hold with nothing but moldy bread to eat. How could Captain Stoakes be so unconcerned with Neil's life at stake? Infernal man! She slammed the pot down again.

Tossing the pot into the rinse water, she reached for the captain's plate and was about to give it the same treatment when she decided the delicate china might not tolerate such abuse. Instead, she swiped it with the dishrag then set it in the scalding rinse water next to the coffeepot.

She almost needn't have bothered. The man might have no regard for her personally, but he enjoyed her cooking. By the time he finished a meal, nothing remained on his plate to scrub. A mental image of the man they called the Sea Wolf licking his plate clean made her smile, despite her irritation.

"Something amusing?" Bull asked from the door.

"No… Well, yes, but just personal thoughts. Ones I should probably keep to myself."

"You seem to do more thinking than most men I know," Bull said.

Amanda's hands stilled. What had he meant? She studied his weathered face, but he looked as he always did, old and cantankerous. She wondered if anyone else knew about the heart of gold that beat beneath his tough exterior.

"Oh, I wanted to thank you for the book," Amanda said. "How on earth did you come by that on a ship?"

It had been a volume of Voltaire in its original French. Proficient in French, it had nevertheless been a long time since she had practiced. She found her progress slow but enjoyable. The book itself looked quite expensive, with a gilded leather binding and crisp pages. Certainly, one would not expect to find such a fine piece in the library of an ordinary man.

"From the prize we took," Bull replied, looking down at his feet. "Neil told me you can read and write French so I thought you might enjoy it."

"Hmmm," Amanda murmured, fishing the still hot

plate from the water with the tips of her fingers. What kind of English merchant kept a copy of Voltaire in French?

"You know, we, meaning me and the rest of the crew…" Bull shuffled his feet, "we wanted to thank you."

Amanda dried the plate with a towel, then turned to Bull. "For what?"

For the life of her, she couldn't imagine what he should be thanking her for. Although she and Bull had started out on rough terms, and she had surely vexed him with her lack of seamanship, he had shown her nothing but encouragement since the day they set sail. She pursed her lips. Far more encouragement than a certain captain had.

Bull's encouragement had developed into kindness. He, Buck and the Doctor supplied her with a constant stream of books and pamphlets. They kept her busy and her mind off the captain—mostly. Why should he be thanking her when she owed him so much?

"Captain Stoakes has become a different man since you started feeding him," Bull said.

"Really?" She lowered her chin at Bull. Even before he knew her true identity, she seemed to be always at odds with the captain. Lately, the tension had increased to almost palpable levels. She had never considered herself disagreeable, so the fault must lie with him. "You mean he used to be worse?" she asked, before she could stop herself.

Bull laughed. "Hunger doesn't sit well with the captain. Since you've been feeding him, all our lives have become easier."

All of their lives, but not hers. Hers had become a

daily battle between the unsettling emotions the captain aroused in her—anger at the high-handed and medieval views he held toward her sex, fear that she would be sent away from everything she loved, and most of all, a burning need to be near him that grew each time she saw him regardless of how hard she tried to deny it.

Nighttime was the worst. Dreams of the captain tortured her sleep. They were like something from a long forgotten fairy tale with her locked away in a tower. As with many fairytales, this one included a handsome prince and a wolf with pitch-black fur forever trying to devour her. In her version of the fairytale, the captain played the part of both prince and wolf. She never failed to awake in a cold sweat, hot desire coursing through her even while fear chilled her to the bone. Her dreams, try though she might to remember them, faded easily until only her tormented emotions remained.

Perhaps some dreams were best forgotten. Now that he had made his regard for her, or lack thereof, clear, she would bury any hope she might have had.

"Well, let's just say I did it for the crew and for Voltaire." Amanda gave Bull a sympathetic smile that said she understood what a wolf the captain could be.

"Oh, that reminds me." Bull reached inside his shirt and pulled out a thin pamphlet with brown crumpled pages and no outer binding. "Here's another one I picked up last time we was ashore. It looks pretty beat up, but lots of folks are talking about it."

Amanda dried her hands on the apron around her waist. She reached for the pile of rumpled brown pages Bull held out, eager for something new to take her mind off her troubles.

She read the title at the top of the first page. *Common Sense*. She liked it already.

"I read it too," Bull said, sounding a little sheepish.

"Really?" Amanda looked up at him. By no means an ignorant man, neither could Bull be deemed an intellectual. Few former whalers were, she supposed.

"Yup, and either I'm getting smarter or that fella's a hell of a writer. I understood 'most every word of it."

"Thank you, Bull." She laid a light touch on his shoulder then turned to the worn pages.

Scrawled beneath the title were the words, *Written by an Englishman.* She scanned the cover searching for a date—1776. A month had not been listed, but scanning the contents, she surmised the essay had been penned when the Colonies were still debating independence. More surprisingly, given the nationality of the author, he supported the cause.

Her compatriots had declared independence and now fought to retain it. She understood the depth of their passions. Her parents and even her grandparents had been born in the colonies. While England was her mother country, she had never set foot on English soil, never laid eyes on the King, never given a moment's thought to what her life would have been like had she been born in England. She was English without really being English.

Moreover, her colony, Maryland, had always filled her with pride. Her fellow colonists were hard working, pious and kind. To her, breaking away from a country that treated its subjects as inferior to those residing in England seemed a natural course of action.

This author still considered himself English, yet made the same arguments. She flipped through the crinkled, well-thumbed little book, noting the passages that caught her attention were invariably on the most worn and tattered pages. This Englishman's ideas had fascinated many a reader prior to Bull.

She must find a quite place to read. An intriguing sentence caught her eye, and she groped her way out of the galley.

"You're welcome, my dear," Bull said, his soft words blending into the words on the page.

A few steps away from the galley, darkness enveloped her. The narrow shafts of light from the deck above were not enough to illuminate the pages. She clutched the pamphlet beneath folded arms and considered where she might hide herself away for a few quiet minutes of uninterrupted reading.

After spending so much time below deck, cooking for the captain or assisting the doctor, Amanda missed the warm early-summer sun and longed to spend time where the ocean breezes could caress her face and ruffle her curls.

On the other hand, she wanted to be alone with her new acquisition. Some of the sailors could read, but even they rarely took time for more than a letter from a wife or sweetheart or the Bible. She would be an unusual sight, sitting on a tarpaulin or coil of rope, her back against the bulwark, a book in hand.

She would have no peace. Over the weeks, she had been amazed at how friendly the men had become with her. She supposed it helped that she sewed up their wounds, made them a little chicken soup when they were feeling ill, or even treated them to a piece of the lemon cake she often made for the captain when she heard they had done something especially worthy of reward.

Now, they greeted her whenever she saw them, asking how she fared and wishing her continued health. They were such polite men. How could anyone ever confuse a privateer with a mere pirate?

Of course, they would be curious about her book and tempted to stop what they were doing to ask her about it. It would be just her luck to draw the captain's attention by attracting a crowd of idle sailors. In all likelihood, he would accuse her of breaking down order on his ship and order the captain's skiff to row her to Baltimore.

Straining her eyes to read in the dim light, she heard the doctor's voice drift through his open doorway.

"Next time we take a prize, see if you can get me more gauze before you sail her off."

"Yes, Doctor," she heard Buck reply.

Amanda drew back just outside the doctor's open door to listen. She felt bad about eavesdropping, but this time she was the topic of discussion even if Buck and the doctor didn't know it.

"I know I asked for more to be brought on board before we sailed, but we must have used it faster than I anticipated." The doctor paused and Amanda could imagine him polishing his glasses as he usually did when deep in thought. "That would be odd though, since our casualties have been light this voyage."

Heat rose to Amanda's cheeks. She had neglected to consider one element of her transformation to an adolescent boy. Still, even if she had thought about it, she could have done little. She may look like a boy on the outside, but her body still worked like a woman's no matter how much she wished it wouldn't.

At any rate, packing more than a month or two of her own paddings in her small sack would have been impossible. If someone had chanced to open her sack, her monthly supplies would have been hard to explain away.

Buck turned to leave and Amanda ducked further into the shadows. She held her breath and hoped he wouldn't notice her skulking in the corridor. When he headed in the opposite direction, she let herself breathe again.

"Oh," the doctor said with a start when he discovered Amanda standing just outside his door. "Were you looking for me?"

"I was searching for a quiet place to read," Amanda said, glad to have a ready excuse for lurking in the dark corridor.

"What do you have there?" The doctor held out his hand for the pamphlet. "Ahh, *Common Sense*," he said, taking it from her and reading the worn cover in the lamplight that shone through the door of his quarters. "I remember this."

"You're familiar with it?" Amanda asked.

"Oh, yes." His eyes sparkled behind the round wire-framed spectacles perched on the end of his nose. He handed the pamphlet back to her. "Very familiar with it. In fact, I think the captain may have a copy."

Amanda's heart beat faster. Could Bull have borrowed the pamphlet from the captain? If he had, why hadn't he said so? At the very least, she hoped he asked permission before loaning the captain's belongings to her. Captain Stoakes already thought her a nuisance. She didn't need him thinking her a thief.

"You could read in my quarters," the doctor offered. "Fortune seems to be smiling on us, and we have no patients at the moment. I'm sure you won't be bothered. Plus, I have business elsewhere that I must attend to."

"That would be wonderful!" Amanda replied, delight at finding a place to read outweighing her concerns about the source of the pamphlet.

The doctor removed his glasses and started polishing. "Actually, I have been thinking, would you like to move your hammock to my quarters?"

"Your quarters?" Amanda asked.

She would have sworn he blushed, but she couldn't tell for sure with the shadows playing against his face in the dark corridor.

"I can assure you all the privacy you need to uh…read and such," the doctor added, his voice wavering.

Amanda considered for a moment. Oddly enough, privacy was the one benefit she had not thought of. She had spent the last several weeks in the company of men and had grown quite adept at finding privacy when needed. Still, changing the arrangement so she shared a room with only one would ease matters considerably.

Doctor Miller had always been so kind and courteous to her. She guessed him to be around sixty, and more than once, he mentioned his wife while they worked together. Sharing quarters with him didn't seem scandalous in the least.

To have her own private quarters, or at least semi-private, seemed a luxury beyond comprehension. Maybe she could even find time to wash at a basin while the doctor was away. The thought of washing in something other than salt water, even standing at a basin, seemed heavenly.

"Thank you, Doctor!" Amanda said.

"That's the spirit!" The doctor grasped her elbow and led her into his quarters. "Now let's work together and see if we can't make some more room in here. Here, grab the other end of this desk."

Sometime later, he and Amanda managed to rearrange his personal quarters to provide enough room for Amanda's hammock plus a small sea chest with a beautiful, intricately carved mermaid gracing the lid and tiny shells at the corners. When Doctor Miller asked about it, Amanda explained that Roger had given it to her as an apology for being so rude on her first day.

The doctor smiled.

A few of Doctor Miller's experiments and supplies had to be moved into the hold, but when Amanda expressed regret at his having to accommodate her, he told her he had been meaning to do a better job of clearing out some of his older things anyway. In the end, she judged the arrangement cramped but cozy. Although less than a foot separated their hammocks, the doctor had hung a sheet between so she had at least the illusion of privacy.

Doctor Miller excused himself, saying he had some business to attend to, and Amanda flopped into her hammock with her copy of *Common Sense*. The solitude, the quiet, the *privacy* felt almost decadent compared to what she had been living. Her hammock swung in time to the gentle rocking of the ship, the hypnotic rhythm soothing her mind and body.

The pamphlet proved fascinating, but in the stillness of the small cabin, her thoughts wandered back to how Bull had come by it. She chuckled. Pestering him would be pointless. But obstinate though Bull may be, he would have never stolen something from his captain. Would he?

She sighed and flipped a dog-eared page.

Of course, Captain Stoakes wasn't always the man he appeared to be either. She could see he cared about his men. Whenever a man lay in bed, recuperating from anything from injury in battle to a sore stomach, he always found time to speak with the doctor about his condition. It would be natural to be concerned about a sick crewmember, disease spread like fire through the close confines of a ship, but the captain's questions showed genuine concern for the man's comfort.

She snuggled into the flock-filled padding in her hammock, a gift from Cookie who had said he didn't find it comfortable.

The captain had proven to be more than just the Sea Wolf his enemies knew him to be. With his amber eyes and fierce grin, the name was apt, but not always.

She flipped another page.

Then again, wolves had a softer side too. Her father had told her stories of how they traveled in packs with the alpha male and female mating for life and caring for their pups together. They were deadly predators and a danger to livestock, but, to her, their fierceness always seemed to carry a strain of nobility, a sense of honor and of duty.

It suddenly occurred to Amanda that the captain resembled a wolf in many ways. Did the alpha male take his obligation to the pack and his mate as seriously as the captain took his responsibility toward his crew? Did he have a mate?

She shifted in her hammock. That line of thinking would not help. Better to concentrate on her reading since the captain's personal life was none of her business. True, he had kissed her twice, but that meant nothing. The first kiss in his cabin had been no more than a gentle touching of lips that left her dazed. His intention had undoubtedly been to throw her off guard so she wouldn't react quickly enough to prevent her confinement in his quarters. He had succeeded.

But that second kiss... She ran her fingertips across her lips, remembering the way his kiss had robbed her of all sense of time and place, made her forget she stood in the doctor's operating room, half a dozen pairs of eyes on her and the captain.

Amanda chuckled, remembering the varying looks of surprise and shock on the faces of the injured men conscious enough to bear witness. Undoubtedly, they were hoping he wouldn't kiss them in the same manner!

She settled herself further into the hammock. That kiss could be just as easily explained away. He had been overjoyed to see her alive. At least her death wouldn't be on his hands. She gave the pamphlet a rueful smile.

"Argh!" Amanda groaned again, realizing she hadn't registered a single word for several minutes. She flipped back a few pages searching for passages that looked familiar.

If she were to think of the captain at all, she needed to think of him as her commander, not as a man. Her top priority needed to be convincing him she did not pose a threat to his ship or his men. That way, she could continue on, living the life she loved, surrounded by men she had come to consider her family.

In the quiet stillness of the empty cabin with only the lapping of the waves and the creak of the hammocks to break the silence, Amanda could hear her inner voice as clearly as if the words had been spoke aloud. *Why do you so desperately want to stay?*

Because I am a good sailor, she argued without saying a word.

Are you?

Amanda shifted in her hammock, trying to find a comfortable position. She should have known there would be no point in arguing. She was a horrible liar, even to herself. Although she adored life at sea, she wasn't particularly well-suited to it.

The voice spoke again. *So why stay?*

Neil needs me.

No he doesn't, and you know it.

Probably not, she agreed with some reluctance.

So why stay? Her inner voice had become impatient, demanding.

"Because the men need me," she whispered, knowing how demented she would sound if anyone should happen to hear her arguing with a phantom.

No they don't. Some will die with or without you. Others will live on, sailing, fighting, living just as men of the sea have done for thousands of years.

Amanda closed the pamphlet she had no hope of reading while her own conscience demanded she confront her deepest desires with brutal honesty.

"Because I can't bear the thought of never seeing him again." She said in a fractured voice that sounded suspiciously close to a sob.

The admission had the impact of a physical blow. To leave the ship would be to leave behind the captain.

She inhaled a ragged breath. Regardless of his lack of feelings for her, she didn't think she could live without him.

So do something about it!

Chapter Thirteen

After nearly two weeks of idleness, the prize crew returned, Neil among them. Joy settled in Amanda's bruised heart when she glimpsed his ardent face between the shoulders of shipmates jostling for position, eager to hear accounts of their adventures.

Neil seemed to have grown a couple of inches and broadened about the shoulders. Or maybe he just stood a little taller. Caught in the excitement and relief of seeing her brother again, she wedged her way in and reached to give him a hug.

"Remember yourself!" he said for her ears only, then pushed her away.

Relief at seeing him safe mingled with the pain of the rebuff made her eyes well with tears. "So, how did it go?" Amanda asked, the forced cheer of her voice pitching it above the clamor.

"It was magnificent!" Neil said, looking at the other men and largely ignoring his sister. "The court accepted the legitimacy of our claim and we sold the merchant ship at auction. That took some time though."

"What did you do with yourself while you waited?" Roger asked.

Neil's gaze skittered toward Amanda then back to his mates. For the briefest of moments, he reminded her of the little brother he had once been.

"We spent most of our time at the tavern," Neil

said.

"Enjoying the entertainments and such," Simon nudged him with his elbow so hard that Neil nearly toppled.

Neil righted himself, but a blush covered his cheeks. The color took Amanda by surprise. For all the trouble her brother had gotten himself into over the years, she couldn't ever remember him blushing.

"Did you consort with any locals?" one man asked, his leering grin leaving no room for interpretation.

The implication of their questions dawned on Amanda, and she glared at the sailor.

She could protect her brother on the ship to some extent, but if his mates insisted on introducing him to *whoring*...she could barely say the word even to herself, well then, there wasn't much she could do about it.

She would speak to the captain. He might think she coddled her brother too much, but this was different. If ever Neil needed a steady male influence, this situation surely called for it.

Then again, perhaps Captain Stoakes approved of this sort of behavior. He allowed no women on his ship, yet they could be at sea for weeks or even months at a time. He might encourage the occasional romp with a tavern wench. For all she knew, he engaged in all sorts of sordid activities while on shore.

She gritted her teeth. The captain could use his shore leave however he pleased, but he really should keep more careful watch over his younger charges. He had to know Neil wasn't the fifteen he claimed to be. To expose a boy to such depravity was unforgivable!

The men were now talking in some sort of code of

which Amanda could make little sense. She guessed many of the phrases referred to lying with a woman given the leering grins on their faces and the way they were elbowing each other and slapping each other on the back. Maybe she had given their honor too much credit. Men were men after all, and the captain was one of them!

A small corner of her mind told her she was being *slightly* unreasonable, but the larger part, the part that held absolute sway at the moment, disregarded the fact that he hadn't personally introduced her little brother to the seedier side of life. As captain of the *Amanda*, he was responsible for the conduct of his crew.

"...blood everywhere," Neil finished saying.

The words yanked her from the fog of her anger, and she refocused her attention.

The crew had been given transport to the *Amanda* on the *Venture*, a ship of the Continental Navy, under the command of Captain James Stoddard. It seemed luck followed the *Amanda's* crew like a pod of dolphins, and Stoddard had served with Captain Stoakes aboard a Royal Navy ship when they were both lieutenants, long before independence had been declared. Although they chose different paths, they remained friends.

Fortunately, at least in Neil's opinion, they engaged a 64-gun frigate outside the port of Boston. Equally matched in sailing skills and firepower, the ships were like cocks in a fight, each determined to claw the other to pieces. Neil's large hands flew in all directions as he mimicked the scenes for his audience. He expressed surprise at how slippery blood made the scrubbed planks of a wooden deck. Even though it ran off into the scuppers in glistening crimson ribbons, he ended up on his backside more than once.

Amanda choked back the bile rising in her throat.

After what seemed like hours of bloody fighting, the *Venture* brought down the enemy's main mast with a well-aimed shot, and the English merchantman struck her colors. There were many casualties, and he had found himself with the insides of a man clinging to his sleeve, too busy to notice it until victory had been won.

The seas rose like the appreciative laughter of the men around her, and the deck heaved under Amanda's feet. Her brother's answers to the fervent questions of the men grew distant and indistinct. She knew she had mere moments to make her way back to the privacy of her quarters before her breakfast pushed past the constriction in her throat.

Legs like ropes, she made her way down the narrow steps. Holding her hand against the rough planks of the wall to steady herself, she groped along to the quarters she shared with the doctor and fell into her hammock. The world still spinning, she squeezed her eyes shut and willed the images of her brother covered in blood and viscera to go away.

"Sounds a bit too gruesome to be real, doesn't it?" a deep voice said.

Amanda's eyes flew open. "I'm sorry, Captain, I was feeling a little ill." She forced herself into a sitting position in her hammock. "We've had such nice weather, and now that the seas have become a bit rougher, it appears I may not yet have my sea legs."

She couldn't let him think the violence had overwhelmed her. It would give him one more reason to get rid of her.

The captain's smile was understanding, but not accusatory. He didn't question her resolve nor call her bluff. Nor did he mention the small puffs of wind that ruffled the smooth surface of the sea like the breath of an angel.

"How do you handle it?" she asked, without preamble, hoping he wouldn't take her question as a sign of weakness.

"Not well," he said with a sigh. "Believe it or not, I hate the violence of war."

Surprised at his candor, Amanda gave him a questioning look. He pushed himself away from the doorframe and came to sit next to her. His greater weight made her side of the hammock lift up, and she had to force herself to sit upright to avoid falling against him. Unable to resist, she let herself lean toward the captain, not touching, but close enough to let the comforting heat from his shoulder wash against her cheek.

"I was too young to fight in the French and Indian War, but I followed my father's regiment and helped in any way I could; drummer boy, stable hand, latrine digger."

The self-deprecating smile he gave her with that last admission warmed her heart.

"The Indians had a vastly different idea of warfare from the British. Their battles could be bloody and merciless. Many of the tribes didn't even consider the notion of sparing women and children." His voice caught. "I was there when my father died…"

The pain in his eyes said more than words ever could. He had yet to recover from the death of his father. In a way, she understood his pain, having experienced a similar loss. However, she could only imagine the horror of being a young boy and watching it happen.

He lowered his head until his chin rested against his chest and closed his eyes. Amanda looked at his strong hands, resting in his lap. She wanted to lay her hand on his, to comfort him while he wrestled with the demons from the past. Fear that her touch would end the fragile connection they had formed kept her hands balled in her lap while she grappled for something that would keep him talking.

"Did you have brothers and sisters? A mother?" If he couldn't talk about his father, maybe he could talk about the rest of his family, assuming he had one.

"A mother, yes. No brothers or sisters though, at least none I was aware of." His soft laughter held no humor this time.

Amanda could have kicked herself for asking. With a mother who, for whatever reason, he felt bitter toward, and no brothers or sisters, he must have grown up a lonely young man. No wonder the role of captain, separated from the rest of the men by rank and duty, suited him so well. He had grown used to being alone.

"As soon as I was old enough, I decided to join the English Navy." He opened his eyes and looked down at his hands. "For a time it was wonderful. On the open sea, you could see the enemy, but not their faces unless you boarded the ships. Since I was still quite young, I didn't join a boarding party for over a year. When I did, I realized the idea of a bloodless battle was no more than an illusion." He rubbed his palms over his knees as though they were sweaty. "People still died."

The need to comfort him exerted almost a physical

pull on Amanda. She gave up trying to maintain her ramrod posture and allowed herself to fall a little closer, her head inches from his broad shoulder. The heat from his body enveloped her even though no part of her touched him.

"Didn't men on your own ship die?" she asked.

"Of course. But that only made me more eager to fight our enemy. They were responsible for the deaths of my shipmates, and I wanted revenge. But that was before I actually had the *pleasure* of killing my first man." Bitterness rang in his words.

"He probably wasn't much older than I am now. Big brute of a man though. I remember a gold tooth flashing through his thick beard. When I ran him through with my sword, I thought perhaps I had missed until I saw the gold turn red. Blood seeped through the gaps between his teeth, and I barely had time to scamper out of the way before he dropped to the deck like a felled tree."

"But you kept fighting?" Amanda asked, although she already knew the answer.

"I did," the captain said, his face a mask of determination.

"But why? Why would you continue to fight if you hated the violence so much? You didn't need the money, or at least you don't now. Why continue?"

Amanda's questions came in rapid-fire succession. She needed to know the answer, for somehow, she knew in her heart the answers held the key to the man behind the captain's façade.

"Because there are some causes worth fighting for. If you're lucky, the causes you fight for are also worth dying for, if that is to be your fate."

Suddenly it all became too much. The pain he had endured, her own difficult life, and the thought of losing the captain bore down on Amanda. This man, so suited to be captain of a ship, abhorred the violence that came with it. Yet he was willing to sacrifice his happiness for a cause he believed in. His sacrifices had led him to great wealth, but what good would that do him if his head were taken off by a cannonball in the next battle?

She tried to blink back her tears, but one escaped and slid down her cheek.

"Hey there, sailors don't cry," the captain said.

"But you said so yourself. I'm not a sailor. I'm just a woman."

"That you are." He put his arm around her shoulders and drew her to him.

Amanda turned her face into his shoulder, her tears soaking his coat. "I'm getting you all wet," she said, dabbing at the sooty streak her tears had left on the blue wool.

He must be disgusted with her. She had tried her hardest to act like a sailor so he might give up his hardheaded notions about women, yet here she was, acting more like a woman than ever.

"That's all right." His smile crinkled the corners of his eyes. "Your face looks like it could use the cleaning."

Amanda gave a sputtering laugh. "I've been teaching Cookie the finer art of biscuits and he hasn't quite got the knack of it yet." She dried her tears on her sleeve, then laid her head back against his chest, amazed at her own brazenness.

"Is my galley still serviceable?" he asked,

resettling his arms around her.

She couldn't see his face, but she could hear the humor in his question. Only he would think of food at a time like this.

"Don't worry, you'll get your precious eggs in the morning," she said, her voice light.

He had shared something of himself, memories of the past she suspected few men had heard. Now, he held her in his arms, allowed her to stain his wool coat with her tears, and jested with her about mundane things like the state of his galley. She snuggled against the captain, taking comfort in the slow steady beat of his heart against her ear. He tightened his arms around her.

The tender moment had an illusory quality about it. Amanda shut her eyes, daring to imagine sitting with him like this in a townhouse in Baltimore, a roaring fire at their feet, children sleeping in another room. They would talk of many things, politics, literature, what they should have for breakfast.

That last thought brought a smile to her lips until guilt chased it away with a sigh. Her actions were those of a woman, but did it matter anymore? The moment she had allowed the first teardrop to spill from her eye, she had proven the captain right. She didn't have what it took to be a true sailor. She never would. Why not enjoy being held in the captain's strong arms for just a few more minutes? The chance might never come again.

"What is it?" Captain's Stoakes' concerned voice rumbled against her ear.

"I don't suppose you comfort all your men this way, do you?" she said, hoping her humor would help hide her sorrow.

The captain chuckled. “I most certainly don’t. For one thing, I don’t think my arms would fit around some of them. For another, I don’t relish the black eye I’d get from Roger if I tried to hold him like this.”

Amanda’s sad smile pressed her cheek into the warmth of his chest. “Well, if you ask me, they don’t know what they’re missing.”

“How’s that?” His breath ruffled one of the curls that had escaped from beneath her cap.

“It’s very comforting. I can’t recall the last time I’ve felt so warm and safe.”

Beneath her cheek, the captain’s chest ceased its steady rise and fall. His arms felt like lead pipes wrapped around her waist. She pulled away and looked into his face.

“I’m sorry, did I say something wrong?”

“No.” His voice was as hard as his eyes.

Perhaps Captain Stoakes couldn’t abide a woman’s tears. That might explain his insistence that no women be allowed aboard his ship. He had seen her distress at Neil’s gruesome tale and come to make sure she hadn’t taken ill. Her tears undoubtedly caught him by surprise, and he reacted as any man would, giving into the need to comfort her until she stopped crying.

Then he remembered himself and where they were. The captain probably saw tears as a sign of weakness. They might be acceptable in a woman, but they certainly weren’t something he should have to contend with aboard his ship. Amanda had never been prone to tears, but he had no way of knowing that.

“I know I’m not behaving as I ought. It’s been a trying week, but I’m sure I’ll be back to my usual annoying self after a good night's sleep."

Her attempt at humor did nothing to ease the harsh look he wore.

"You do not annoy me," he said.

Amanda straightened and realized he still had his arms about her. Her heart beat a little faster.

What had he meant? With his crew, his demeanor was often benevolent if demanding. With Neil, he was kind and even paternal. More often than not, he treated Buck and Bull as friends instead of subordinates. With her, he behaved as though he found her as irritating as a bur under his shirt.

But whenever she came near, it was almost as if he donned a uniform he kept handy just for such occasions. His shoulders grew rigid and his spine straight as though someone had slapped a corset on him and cinched it tight. His moves became as precise as the doctor's during a difficult surgery. Even his speech changed. He said little, if anything at all.

Sometimes she even saw traces of the wolf in the way he watched her as though she were his enemy moving about his quarters, serving him breakfast and straightening his things.

Her inner voice prodded her. *He kissed you—twice.*

Yes, but he had kissed her once to make her docile, and twice because he had been under extreme duress. His ship had been battered, and they had lost many men. He had found comfort in kissing her, and she had gladly given it.

Since that day, however, his unease around her had grown worse. Perhaps he regretted his behavior, thinking she might read more into it than there was. Then he had informed her that he did not wish to be alone with her. How could she not think her very existence annoyed him?

Although the captain's arms were still about her waist, he hadn't moved. It was like being held by a statue, except instead of cold metal, she could feel his heat wrapping about her, drawing her in. She raised her chin to look into his face, certain his eyes would hold the same aggravation they always did when he looked at her.

The hard amber orbs had turned to molten gold, and he looked at her with a heat that threatened to melt her to the core. His darker side, the side she had come to think of as the wolf, had emerged.

The urgings of her inner voice echoed in her head. *Do something about it!*

But what? she nearly asked aloud. How did one master a wolf?

The day had grown late, and dark stubble covered the captain's jaw. Amanda found herself drawn to the uniquely masculine trait. Instead of making him look unkempt, it emphasized the hard lines of his face, making him look more commanding than ever.

His questioning gaze swept over her face. She wasn't sure what he expected from her anymore than she knew what to expect from herself. Her inner voice seemed to want her to take action, but her rational mind had no idea what to do.

"Are you hungry?" she asked.

"Yes," he said, his voice a low rumble that was more vibration than sound.

He made no move to stand, and neither did she.

Without stopping to consider the appropriateness of her actions, Amanda reached up to touch the dark stubble that covered the captain's chin. The muscles of his jaw twitched beneath her fingertips, but he didn't pull back. His beard scratched like the bristles of a brush when she ran her hand down the sculpted contours of his cheek. A sudden flash of boldness enticed her to draw her thumb across the fullness of his mouth. His lips opened as if compelled by her touch. They were warm and soft, a delightful contrast to the rough maleness of his unshaven jaw. Currents of heat ran from the tips of her fingers to the pit of her belly.

She lay her other hand flat against his chest and the rumble of a low growl against her palm sent a thrill of power coursing through her. The wolf was hers to command, at least for now.

His gold eyes watched her, wary but ready to take her lead. His nostrils flared slightly as though catching her scent. He would kiss her again if she wanted him to. She need only lean in a little closer, slide her hand around his neck, tilt her chin just a little, part her lips...

"Oh, pardon me," the doctor said, pushing back the curtain that separated his side of the room from hers. "I was bringing something for Amanda. I didn't realize you were here."

Heat rushing to Amanda's face, the captain pushed her away and stood up. With a curt, "Excuse me," he strode past the doctor and left the cabin.

Chapter Fourteen

Will sat at his desk, fingers drawing circles at his temples while he stared at the accounting of the auction of their latest prize. Normally, he loved this part of commanding a privateer. He had financed the *Amanda* with the last of the money his mother hadn't had the chance to spend. With his first few prizes auctioned off, he had successfully built back his father's fortune. Now, with his continued success, he could claim wealth exceeding even that which his mother had squandered before her death.

After he took his share, generous yet smaller than what some captains allotted themselves, he divided the rest among his crew. He loved that part most of all, seeing the faces of men who earned more money from one captured ship than many of them earned in an entire year, some in an entire lifetime.

But this evening, his thoughts were on one specific crewman, or rather, would-be sailor.

What in the hell had gotten in to him? Only a thin sliver of self-restraint kept his desire for Amanda in check. Why had he gone to her quarters?

The doctor's timely interruption had led to a later dressing down. The ship's surgeon informed him, in no uncertain terms, that he would not allow any harm to come to Amanda. The hard gleam in his spectacled eyes told Will exactly where the doctor thought the greatest danger lay. He could just imagine what Doctor Miller's reaction would have been if he had been caught in the act of deflowering his assistant!

He grunted in self-loathing and looked down at his books. The crew expected their allocation in the morning. By midday they would be in a Portsmouth tavern doing their best to spend every last cent before they passed into a rum induced oblivion or lost themselves in the arms of a comely wench.

Maybe he should do the same. He might be able to quench some of his desire at one of the higher-class establishments in town. With his more base needs met, Amanda would lose some of the sway she held over him.

He reflected on the perfumed and pampered ladies at Madam Lydia's. An establishment intended for men of wealth and position, he could spend the night drinking only the finest brandy, playing cards with men of similar means, and if one of the lovely ladies caught his fancy, engage in a discreet interlude with one of the finest prostitutes in New England. Lydia's Ladies were so elite, it seemed almost unfair to call them prostitutes. Mistresses would be more like it. Most of them ended up with a small list of exclusive clients who paid enough to assure the girls were kept in style and relatively unencumbered.

Not being a regular client of Madam Lydia's—hell, he had never been a client—he would have to settle for one of the newer girls. However, because Madam Lydia had her pick of the crop, his choice would be young and fresh, even if no longer virginal.

He imagined the heart-shaped face of a dewy-eyed woman staring up at him with faux admiration. She would have blonde hair, not too long, piled atop her head in a style that took forever to release, but with short curls that wound around his fingers when he buried his hands in them. She would have green eyes that glittered like emeralds in the candlelight, but softened when he kissed her. A sprinkle of freckles…

"Damnation!" he said when he realized the woman he had imagined finding at Madam Lydia's had transformed into Amanda.

He knew better than to think he would find anyone like Amanda at Madam Lydia's, but he had to find one who could wipe the green-eyed wench from his mind, at least for a while. He blew out a breath and pushed the manifest away. Then he leaned back in his chair and stretched his long legs in front of him, crossing them at the ankles. Closing his eyes, he contemplated going ashore for a night of dissipation that would leave him spent for weeks to come.

Maybe he would just read a good book.

****

Amanda flipped the pages of her book, not really seeing the words. From the deck above, she could hear the sounds of the men preparing to go ashore. They hadn't invited her.

Shouts of laughter reached her ears. One of them had probably made a lewd suggestion. There had been many this afternoon, enough to make her seek refuge in her quarters.

Not that she would have wanted to go even if they had invited her. The first couple of times, a few of the sailors had tried to get her to go along telling her "there was a first time for everything." She presumed they were referring to her virginity. She found it odd they didn't treat Neil like such an innocent, he being younger than her.

She recalled Neil's recent trip with the prize crew and scowled at her book. Thanks to the captain's loose attitudes toward his crew, Neil might no longer be innocent.

She flipped a page with more force than necessary, frowning at a small tear she created in the delicate paper. She didn't want to go the taverns or the brothels of Portsmouth, but still, it would have been nice to have been *asked*. That she had not been was just one more sign she didn't fit in. Her shipmates might not realize they had a woman in their midst, but even they could see she didn't quite belong in their world.

"Doctor, have you seen my copy of Locke's *Treatises*?" Captain Stoakes flipped back the curtain separating her "quarters" from the doctor's and poked his head in. "Oh, I beg your pardon. I thought you were Doctor Miller."

Her dark mood having festered into animosity toward all members of the opposite sex, Amanda narrowed her eyes and frowned at him. He arched his eyebrows in surprise.

"Didn't feel like going carousing with the rest of the horn-mad cockroaches?" she asked, horrified at her coarse words and the contempt she heard in her own voice. Anger did not excuse vulgarity.

"I beg your pardon?" asked the captain, taking a step into the room.

A flush crept up her cheeks. She thought the meaning of the euphemisms had been obvious. Maybe she had misunderstood its usage. Or, quite probably, it was an improper thing to say to your captain, and she really had crossed the line.

This time she did stand up, clutching the book to her chest, her ire overwhelmed by her mortification at her behavior. "I-I thought you were someone else."

"Who?" he asked, his voice skeptical.

Her ears grew hot. There was no way the captain could be mistaken for any other sailor. His voice, even when calling after the doctor, had a resonance no one else on the ship possessed. And, no one quite filled the space in the little room the way he did. She shifted her stance under his direct gaze.

"Did you need something?" she asked before he could comment on the obvious lie.

"Actually, I was looking for something the doctor gave me," the captain's voice trailed off when he noticed the book she clutched against her chest. "What are you reading?"

"A book," she replied.

"Yes, I can see that." His jaw tightened. "What book would that be?"

"This b-book?" she stammered, holding the book out for him.

"Milton, eh?" The captain took it from her hands and examined the cover. "Isn't *Paradise Lost* a bit much for a common sailor?"

He didn't seem to be expecting a response, so Amanda decided the wisest course of action would be to say nothing. For reasons she dreaded contemplating, he didn't appear too pleased to find her reading Milton.

"Since you are so fond of reading, I don't suppose you might have a copy of any of Dr. Franklin's works, would you?"

He crossed his arms and leaned against the

doorjamb, his face a mask of indifference, but the rhythm of his pulse beat against the chords of his neck, and the muscles in his thighs twitched. He looked ready to pounce.

Her instincts had been right. Of course all those books, pamphlets and papers Bull and Buck loaned her had belonged to the captain. She had seen stacks upon stacks of books and pamphlets in his quarters when she served his meals. Some part of her brain had refused to acknowledge what her eyes told her.

Her knees turned to pudding.

Now what was she going to do? She clutched the book until her fingers turned white. She couldn't very well lie and say she didn't have them. She held the incriminating evidence in her hands, and she had an entire sea chest full in the corner behind her.

For a moment, she considered making a dash for the doorway, but where would she go on a small ship in the middle of the sea? Besides, his large frame filled the path to the door, so even if it hadn't been an absurd idea, it was impossible. It would be better to confess and get it over with. Still, with him standing over her, looking at her with those feral amber eyes, she couldn't will her lips to speak.

"Perhaps, I'll just check for myself." He pushed away from the door and made a move for the small locker she kept tucked in the corner.

Amanda jumped out of his path just in time to avoid being knocked over.

The captain threw open the lid and pulled out his belongings one by one. "Voltaire, in French." He tossed the volume to the floor. "And Dr. Franklin. No wait, several copies of Dr. Franklin's works. And, several of

Mr. Shakespeare to keep him company." He fixed his eyes on her each time he read off the title of a book or pamphlet.

The pile grew with alarming speed; she sensed his anger filling the room. She opened her mouth a couple of times in a futile attempt to protest that she didn't steal the books, but her dry throat could produce no words. As he pulled out book after book, she started to feel like she really was the guilty party.

Finally, when the locker was empty, he stood up and faced her. "Do you know the penalty for stealing?" His eyes shone like burnished gold in his hard face.

She stared at the wall behind him, her thoughts racing for something, anything she could say to defend herself. Now he wasn't going to just kick her off the ship, he was going to kill her.

"I..." she croaked, her mouth felt as though it had been stuffed with cotton.

The captain took a step toward her and she stepped backward, stumbling over an uneven floorboard. He grabbed her arm and pulled her up against his chest. His golden eyes seared her face for only a moment before his mouth descended on hers.

With her last rational thought, Amanda decided whatever she thought the punishment for stealing might be, it certainly hadn't involved kissing. The ship rolled on a wave, and Amanda and the captain were thrown off balance. Lips never losing contact, they stumbled through the curtain to the wall adjacent to the door. The breath rushed from Amanda's lungs when her back slammed into the rough planks, but she paid it no heed. She didn't need air at the moment.

The captain pinned her to the wall with his body,

his palms flat against it. He tore his lips from hers, giving her a moment to catch her breath while his lips seared a line of kisses from her collarbone to her ear. Amanda gasped when he nibbled her sensitive lobe. She entwined her fingers in his hair and held on while he traced the outline of her ear with his tongue.

"Amanda," he groaned against her temple.

He still had his body pressed against her, but the pressure eased.

No, don't go! She didn't want the captain to come back. Right now, she much preferred the wolf. He was not nearly so guarded as his master.

Amanda grasped his face in her hands and held her to him. His ragged breath washed over her. She had to do something, anything, to make him stay.

She reached behind his head and tugged the small leather tie that held his queue in place. Dark locks fell about his shoulders, and her breath caught in her throat. With his golden eyes, tanned skin, and dark flowing hair, he looked more feral than ever.

The captain lowered his face to hers again, and Amanda parted her lips. Remembering the way he had tasted her with his tongue, she teased him with her own, tempting the beast she knew lived just beneath his controlled façade.

"Amanda," he said again, his voice held a note of anguish as though he knew he couldn't win the battle he fought with himself.

He tugged at her shirt and she quivered when his calloused hand touched the sensitive skin at her midriff. His hands gripped her hips, and he caressed both sides of her navel with his thumbs. When she sighed against his chest, he ran his hands higher still, over her waist and ribcage stopping when he reached the bindings that encircled her chest.

Silently, she urged him onward. Her bindings were coming loose already. He could release them as easily as she had released his hair if only he would give a small tug on the right one. *Oh, please, captain, now is not the time for retreat!*

"Stop!" Bull yelled from just inside the door.

Bull stumbled forward when Buck and the doctor plowed into his back.

The captain stepped away, and Amanda had to catch herself to keep from falling to the floor.

"He didn't steal them," Bull said between gasps for breath. "I loaned them to him."

"As did we," added the doctor.

He and Buck squeezed around Bull to stand at his side.

For a moment, Amanda had no idea what they were talking about. Then she remembered the captain's belongings that lay scattered about her hammock.

Had they heard the captain's shouts when he first discovered his books in her locker? He hadn't actually raised his voice, but even his normal voice would be more than enough. Perhaps his words had carried up through the planks where one of the men had heard and gone to fetch the others.

Amanda stole a glance at Captain Stoakes. Except for the hair cascading over his ears making him appear atypically unkempt, he didn't appear to be a man recently returned from the throes of passion. His eyes hard and his lips set in a thin line, she would have guessed him to be angry. She was a little disgruntled herself.

Captain Stoakes glared at the three officers filling the cramped quarters. "Correct me if I'm wrong, Doctor, but aren't these the books you gave me at the beginning of our voyage?"

"Well, yes, they are." the doctor studied the incriminating pile in the middle of the floor. "However, we had a bit of an emergency."

"An emergency?" The captain had lowered his voice, but his eyebrow twitched, and Amanda knew the storm had not blown over yet. "Pray tell, what was the emergency?"

"They kept the lad from drinking," said Bull.

Drinking? Amanda wondered if it wouldn't have been better to be accused of stealing.

"He has a drinking problem?" The captain's blank expression showed his confusion.

The men looked at each other in silent conference. Amanda would have sworn the doctor gave a small nod.

"No, not really a problem," the doctor began, his words measured as though he were trying to decide how to describe the issue.

"No, not really," added Buck, less than helpfully.

"More of a predicament," said Bull, looking pleased with himself for finding just the right word.

Doctor Miller and Buck nodded in agreement.

"And, what is this *predicament*?" the captain asked, emphasizing the chosen term.

"Well, you see." The doctor spoke slowly, as though he were explaining an illness to his patient. "I'm guessing that growing up with his mother and all, the boy hasn't had much experience with alcohol."

"No, sir, he hasn't," added Bull.

Buck nodded in agreement.

That part was true at least. Actually, no experience would be more precise. Her first taste of hard liquor had been the mug of rum Bull gave her only a couple of weeks after setting sail. When she tasted it, she had sputtered and coughed. Bull had yelled at her, saying something about "not inhaling it."

After that, she sipped slowly until she grew accustomed to the taste. Rather more, she liked the sort of soft warm glow it gave. It took the edge off her aching muscles and relaxed her head until her troubles didn't seem quite so overwhelming. However, that had been her first and last taste of rum because she most certainly did not like the headache she had in the morning. Cooking the captain's eggs had been a most nauseating experience and not one she wished to repeat.

"And as such…" the doctor was saying.

"Yes, as such," Bull added.

The captain shot him a dark look that suggested he would throttle him if Bull repeated one more word. After that, Bull joined Buck, silently nodding in agreement with everything the doctor said.

"As I was saying," the doctor continued as though he were discussing one of his scientific experiments, "With such limited experience with alcohol, I find he doesn't tolerate it well."

"So he gets drunk easily. Is that it?" The captain looked at the three men in disbelief. "That's the problem, I mean the *predicament*?"

They nodded in unison.

"A little alcohol, or a lot, doesn't matter." The captain snorted. "Most of my crew will be lucky not to be facedown in a gutter by the end of tonight."

"It's not that he gets drunk," the doctor interrupted.

"Well then, what the hell does he do?" the captain asked, running his hand across the back of his neck. He had clearly had enough of whatever game they were playing.

Spellbound, Amanda wondered where this story was going. She had to admit she hadn't really remembered climbing into her hammock the night she tried rum. Had she done something *improper* under its influence? The room growing warmer by the minute, she tried to recall the rest of that evening.

"He giggles," the doctor said with a shrug.

"Giggles!" the captain and Amanda exclaimed together.

"Yes," said Bull, finding his voice again. "And, we just figured it was kind of unseemly and all for a sailor to giggle, drunk or no."

"Hmm hmmm," murmured the other two in agreement.

They all looked so satisfied with themselves that Amanda was sure they had to have made the story up. Besides, she had more self-composure than to giggle when she had a little rum. Well brought-up ladies, even ones raised in the country, avoided giggling.

"I have had enough!" the captain bellowed, and Amanda's knees wobbled.

"You three are hereby ordered to remain on this ship until further notice. Your shore leave is canceled." He paused as if to think what else he could do to them, but simply added, "And, before you go borrowing any more of my books, you are to ask my permission. Am I clear?"

"Yes, sir!" all three men said in unison.

"And you." He looked at Amanda, but she could

see the fire had gone out. Giggling appeared to be less of an offense than stealing.

"No shore leave for you," he growled but then stopped and regarded her. "Not that you look like you were planning to go anyway." He turned to go but stopped again. One hand on the doorframe, he swiveled to face her. "And stay away from the rum!" he bellowed before turning and slamming the heel of his fist against the doorjamb on his way out.

Chapter Fifteen

The following morning dawned clear and bright. All those given shore leave the night before were back aboard by midmorning. They looked and smelled a little worse for wear, but since Buck and Bull had both had a good night's sleep, they were in fine form to make sure no one shirked his duties.

Shortly after the noon bells, Captain Stoakes spotted a lone English merchantman on the horizon. He glanced around at his crew with their glazed eyes and slack jaws. An unescorted ship presented too promising an opportunity to pass up. Perhaps fast sailing and a well-fought battle would shake the cobwebs from the addled brains of his men. He gave the order to give chase.

The captain got the speed he craved, and the *Amanda* overtook her quarry with ease despite the merchantman's relatively low profile and fast lines. The battle, on the other hand, was not to be had. One shot over the bow and the captain of the English vessel hauled down her colors.

Only a short time later, Amanda understood why. She had been below deck helping the doctor re-stow his unused operating instruments and supplies when the hard thud of booted feet sounded on the steps.

"Captain wants you on deck when you're finished with your duties here, Adam," Buck said, climbing halfway down before ducking his head under the planks to relay the orders. Before she could ask why, he disappeared through the hatch.

She caught the doctor's eye then turned back to wrapping the doctor's clean bone saws in a sheet made of wool. "What do you think he wants?" she asked, trying to sound casual.

Her nerves were still a little rattled from his kisses the day before. Had they not been interrupted, how far would she have allowed his advances to go? She had grown hungry for more than his kisses, and even now, she could feel the imprint of his warm hand against her belly.

She had managed to avoid him all morning and had been hoping to extend the reprieve awhile longer, at least until she could pull her wits about her again. Her knees still grew week every time she thought of his strong hands encircling her waist.

The doctor shrugged. "You know the captain. He works up a powerful hunger chasing the British. He probably just has a request for dinner tonight."

Amanda laughed, but only to cover her nervousness. "Or, maybe he just wants a mug of coffee," she suggested with false cheer.

Doctor Miller gave her a look that told her he had heard the forced nonchalance. He hadn't said anything, but she doubted he had been fooled by their performance yesterday. After all, he knew her secret and had interrupted their kisses once before. This morning, when she returned to the cabin, she found the captain's black leather thong sitting atop her pillow. She had torn it from his hair while he had her pressed against the wall on the doctor's side of the room. Where it went once it left her fingers, she had no idea, but she doubted it crawled into her hammock on its own.

She took her time packing the doctor's remaining instruments into his storage chest, making sure each one lay properly nestled, the blades protected from impact by the soft wool. When she unfolded and folded a protective cover around a sharp blade for the third time, trying to get it right, the doctor came and put a hand on her shoulder.

"I can finish that. You know how the captain is when he's hungry. I think you'd better get up on deck."

"Yes. Thank you, doctor," she said, turning the task over to him.

Amanda climbed the steps to the upper deck. What could the captain want? Certainly not a repeat of last night's performance since he had asked to see her in such a public place. Considering how often their private exchanges had ended in passion lately, perhaps meeting on deck, surrounded by her shipmates, was the safest place for both of them.

She expected the captain to be waiting on deck. Instead, she found him talking to a man, not nearly so tall as himself but almost twice as wide. They were engaged in a cordial, if somewhat stiff, conversation. The captain even laughed at a comment made by the other man, although his smile did not quite reach his eyes.

He must be the captain of the English ship. His velvet coat, cut in a stylish fashion, looked finer than anything most Americans could afford or would choose to wear even if they did have the funds. He had layers of lace about his wrists and neckline and carried a lace handkerchief in one hand, with which he repeatedly dabbed his nose. Since the man appeared in good health, Amanda suspected snuff or force of habit more than any lingering illness.

She didn't think she had ever seen the captain talking to the commander of another ship so soon after battle. The code of the privateer usually dictated the enemy captain be held prisoner aboard his own ship in the comforts of his own cabin but under armed guard until they reached port.

She stopped several feet from the captain to give him his proper due and because it seemed wiser to keep a good distance between them.

Captain Stoakes stood with his back straight, his hands clasped behind him. When he spoke to the English commander, his tone was light, convivial, but his eyes were always on the English captain. He gave the impression of watching the man, assessing his strength and his weaknesses. How very like a wolf.

But if her captain behaved like a wolf, the English commander looked more like a fat partridge, unaware of the predator nearby. Amanda ducked her head to hide her grin.

The breeze shifted and carried the captains' voices across the deck. The commander of the merchantman, in his clipped English accent, told Captain Stoakes his ship had been separated from their escort by the recent storms. As fortune would have it, they had survived the gale, but wound up lost until the *Amanda* arrived.

The captain of the merchantman didn't seem at all displeased to have met up with an American privateer. In fact, he sounded rather eager to hand over his "very special cargo" with the understanding that Captain Stoakes would see it safely cared for and to its proper destination.

Amanda inched closer to see what more she could hear. The "proper destination" for most cargo was public auction in a port such as Boston. However, she had heard there were prize courts as far south as Martinique. Her spirits soared at the thought of sailing to such an exotic locale. Then they returned to deck. Not being an official member of the crew, she would hardly be chosen for the prize crew. Life could be so unfair.

"I hope you and your officers will do me the honor of joining me for supper this evening," Captain Stoakes said.

The invitation startled her. Did privateer captains often invite their prisoners to dine with them? They had captured several ships, and so far, no one had been invited to supper. Did the captain expect to entertain them in his quarters? Where on earth would he stow all those books, charts and papers?

Amanda shook her head when Captain Stoakes bowed to the other captain before signaling for Buck to escort their guest to the ladder. She found it hard to believe that just minutes after they were trying to kill each other these two captains could have a genial conversation and agree to dine together that very evening. She knew women who held a grudge for years after the smallest slight. Men could be so simple at times.

Buck steadied the Englishman at the elbow and assisted the portly man over the side.

The captain turned toward Amanda, and she held her breath. How long he had been aware of her presence? The glow in his eyes suggested he had known the moment she stepped onto the deck. Perhaps she was the partridge.

His gaze softened as though he had called a momentary truce. For whatever reason, he needed her assistance.

"We're going to have guests tonight. Do you think you're up for cooking a meal for eight?"

"Yes, sir. Anything in particular you would like to serve?" she asked, trying to sound more like a ship's cook than a woman with a supper party to plan.

Captain Stoakes pursed his lips and considered. "No, you choose. I don't think you've served me a bad dish yet."

Amanda's insides melted like butter. She would prepare the best meal he had ever tasted—within the limits of his larder, of course. His unexpected praise emboldened her.

"Captain, is it usual for a privateer to entertain…his prisoners?"

She had been uncertain what word to use for the captured ship's crew. Buck had always called them prisoners, but she didn't suppose one invited prisoners to supper.

"Not unusual," he replied, not appearing put off by her choice of words. "At least not on a privateer, anyway. The code a privateer sails under requires us to treat the crew of any captured ship with the utmost dignity and respect. Some privateers make a regular habit out of entertaining their 'guests,' sometimes lavishly, although often raiding the stores of the captured ship to do so." His words ended with a chuckle.

"Have you ever done that?" Amanda asked.

"That *would* be illegal," he replied with a mischievous grin and a slight wink that told her he wasn't denying anything.

Amanda heart raced.

"But no matter. Before you became my cook, I'm afraid I didn't have a choice. I would have been violating the privateer's code of honor if I subjected them to Cookie's fare."

Although true, Amanda wondered if that was a joke. Then the captain's eyes crinkled at the corners and she laughed.

"There will be eight?" she asked.

"Yes. Three of our people, four of their officers and a guest."

"A guest?"

"Hmmm," the captain murmured. "A young lady apparently."

A young lady? Now that was interesting. She searched his face to see if he thought so too, but his smile had dissolved, and he stared off at the horizon. A dark cloud shadowed his features, and Amanda rubbed her hands over her arms to warm herself. She guessed the idea of two women on his ship didn't sit well with the captain.

****

Captain Stoakes watched his crew haul a young woman on deck in a contraption that looked much like a tree swing. Apparently, she had claimed to be too weak to climb the ladder. More than likely, she enjoyed the attention of the men watching her carefully perched backside on the makeshift hoist. She swung her silk-slippered feet and swayed above the deck, all while proclaiming the experience to be "most frightening."

Women don't belong on ships, Will thought for at least the tenth time that morning. Judging from the way she mesmerized his crew, this woman in particular did not belong on a ship, especially not *his* ship. He noted with disgust the slack-jawed faces of several of his crew. He would have to talk with Bull and Buck about increasing their workload to keep them out of trouble.

He must safeguard her even though she was his "prisoner" as Amanda had called her. He smiled at that. The woman hardly seemed to mind being a prisoner. Even so, as his prisoner, his duty required him to make her as comfortable as possible.

"Oh dear," the woman said when her feet touched the solid planking. She spoke to no one in particular but to any man willing to listen, which at that moment seemed to be any man within earshot. "I didn't think I would make it through that. I can't swim, you see." Her eyelashes fluttered, and her gaze dropped to her expensive satin skirt made full by the numerous petticoats beneath. "At least, not with this dress on."

Will ignored the hint of suggestiveness in her tone and stepped forward to assist her.

"Do not fear, miss." He bowed, taking her small, white-gloved hand and kissing the air just above her knuckles. "I am certain more than one of my men would have jumped in to save you before you even hit the water."

The girl blushed. Up close, Will could see she was no more than a girl. Maybe seventeen. Possibly eighteen, but certainly no older. Her wide-set blue eyes complimented her ivory-complexion. She must have spent much of the crossing from England below deck, lounging in her hammock and complaining of seasickness. If she hadn't, her complexion would have been marred with freckles or at the very least sport an unfashionable sun-bronzing.

Thoughts of Amanda's glowing skin, dotted with freckles across a pert nose sprang to mind and he pushed them away, forcing himself to concentrate on the preening, sallow-skinned woman before him.

The wind tugged at her large straw bonnet and threatened to shred the flimsy parasol she carried. She straightened her delicate lace over gown with elaborate fastidiousness, the breeze unmaking her every effort.

Why would a father send his daughter to a country in the midst of a war? She clearly hadn't been bred for the frontier, and although the North Carolina territory didn't classify as wilderness, she would have her share of hardships. Did she realize just how hard plantation owners, including the women, had to work to make a plantation profitable?

Although he couldn't tamp down his immediate dislike for the girl, he couldn't help but feel sorry for her at the same time. If he guessed correctly, her aristocratic family in England had fallen on hard times. This girl had drawn the short straw when they decided which of the children they would ship off to the rich uncle in America. Undoubtedly, they hoped the rich uncle's connections would help restore the family fortunes. She would be expected to make a match with a wealthy man as soon as possible, the wealthier the better. He had his own experience with more than one such unfortunate sniffing around his bank accounts.

The girl stumbled and took a halting step forward. Buck reached out to steady her. She assessed him from beneath the sweep of her dark lashes, and Buck flashed his most disarming grin.

Will cleared his throat before the girl had time to take in Buck's velvet coat and silk shirt. He needed his second in command on his ship, not tied down to a demanding aristocratic wife who refused to accept that her blue blood meant nothing in America.

"You must be the pirate captain." She tucked back an ebony curl that had escaped from beneath her bonnet and let her fingertips linger at the side of her cheek while she raked him with her dark eyes.

The girl knew her part in the scheme.

"Privateer, miss. Welcome aboard the *Amanda.* I am at your service." He made another elegant bow.

"There's a difference?" she asked, a small frown of disappointment on her delicate features.

"Most definitely, miss," replied Will.

There was, of course, but he'd be damned if he would take the time to explain it to this little chit.

"Well, I'm happy to be on your boat, sir." She curtsied.

A suspiciously feminine gasp came from somewhere near the steps. Someone, and Will had a good idea who, watched from the safety of the hatch. He checked his grin just in time. Amanda had made the same mistake, calling his ship a boat, on her first day at sea. He had threatened to toss her overboard at the time. The blood had drained from her face, and he had felt contrite over the harsh treatment of a new recruit, but the fault did not lie entirely with him. Cookie had served him a haggis that morning and it lay in his stomach like a rock.

He had been well fed this morning, so the Captain's Curse couldn't be blamed for the desire to grab this woman by her laces and toss her back over the side to see if she really couldn't swim. He distracted himself from the urge by estimating how long it would be before he could get her off his ship and away from his men.

Perhaps being a woman herself, Amanda might enjoy the opportunity to spend time with their guest. At the very least, she could keep the chit away from his men. Had he been alone, Will might have snorted. Given the vast dissimilarities between the two, he had the uncomfortable feeling he would be handing Amanda a duty worse than scrubbing decks.

"Hmm," the girl said, looking around, then she gave the captain a pointed up and down perusal. "I had rather expected a pirate ship to be larger."

Had she just insulted his ship, his person, or both? Will wanted to laugh. Given the girl's own lack of charms, he doubted she wanted to start that battle.

Keeping a tight rein on his expressions, he offered her his arm and said, "Shall we go below? My cook is putting the finishing touches on a meal you are sure to enjoy. While we wait, perhaps you would care for a glass of sherry?"

"Oh, that would be delightful," she cooed. Instead of resting her hand on the arm he proffered, she slid her dainty fingers between his arm and torso, latched on to his bicep and squeezed. Apparently, she hadn't finished assessing him. "Do excuse me, Captain, but I'm afraid I've still not got my sea legs."

Will looked down at her oval face, and forced a polite smile on his unwilling lips. After more than a month at sea, she most certainly would either have her sea legs or be dead from nausea. At the very least, her ample curves wouldn't be quite so well-rounded.

He also couldn't help but notice that the way she clung to him forced her generous breasts upward and to their best advantage. Her stays already pressed her breasts so far upward that they threatened to spill out over the top of her bodice. He only hoped her barely restrained flesh would wait until he had her out of sight.

With the girl clinging to him and tittering like a sparrow, Will's irritation intensified. It would be a long night, but at least he could look forward to the pleasure of watching Amanda while she served their supper. He immersed himself in the thought of having her near until the sound of the girl's voice melted away, and his impatience eased.

Chapter Sixteen

Amanda set a steaming tureen of turtle soup on the table. Later, she would have to admit she had outdone herself with dinner, but right now, she was too amazed at the transformation that had taken place to pay much heed to the visiting officers' keen interest in the succulent aromas wafting from the stone tureen.

She had been stunned to learn a dining room existed on the ship. Actually, it didn't normally. The *Amanda* was too small to have a permanent dining room, but like many ships refitted for battle, certain walls were removable. From somewhere the crew had produced a large, mahogany dining table, a linen tablecloth edged with lace, and china decorated with delicate blue flowers inlaid with a silver filigree. She wondered if the captain had borrowed the finery from his English guests.

Captain Stoakes had told her she could cook whatever she pleased. There were plenty of chickens on board, and her sense of humor got the best of her. While she had to improvise a bit with the ingredients, she made a passable *coq au vin* for his guests.

She hoped serving a well-known French dish to English guests didn't go against the privateer's code, but with the chicken simmering in the pot, it was too late to turn back. Perhaps no one would notice the subtle jab at English pride. But, whether or not they caught it, these were Captain Stoakes's guests, and she really had no right to be rude. She would make up for her thoughtlessness by serving a fabulous desert.

Maybe a *crème brulee*? Amanda cringed. Apparently, her dark sense of humor went even deeper than she knew.

Now, she and Cookie brought out one perfectly prepared, although somewhat improvised, dish after another, and she watched their guests attack each with gusto.

The captain's table seated eight that evening; Captain Stoakes, Buck Smythe, Doctor Miller, and four of the officers of the captured merchantman, including the captain whom she had seen earlier and his ship's surgeon. To Captain's Stoakes left, a woman of stunning beauty hung on his every word, and when she could manage it, his person. Amanda couldn't help but stare, both at the girl's beauty and her boldness.

Seated next to the captain's tall, powerful frame, she appeared almost fairy-like, something to be seen yet not quite believed. She had dark blue eyes set in porcelain skin. Her rosebud lips smiled demurely at everything the captain said, and she often cast sideways glances at him from beneath her long dark lashes. Unlike her own complexion, this woman had no freckles and certainly no sun-bronzing. Amanda raised her hand and trailed her fingertips across her wind-roughened cheek to settle for a moment on her chapped lips. She let the hand drop.

Tearing her gaze from the woman's face, she ladled the soup into elegant, sculpted soup bowls then handed them to Cookie so he could set them before the guests. She was no one's idea of a beauty, and never would be, so what did she care? Still, the graceful appeal of this woman made her all the more conscious of her own shortcomings.

Amanda served the last of the soup, enraptured by the woman's voice. She said very little to anyone but the captain, but when she spoke to him, her soft English accent tinkled like little bells. Dimples danced in her cheeks whenever she laughed at something the captain said. In Amanda's opinion, she laughed more often than necessary, since the captain said little that could be taken to be humorous.

Eavesdropping on their discussion, Amanda discovered Miss Violet Bowersley was really no more than a girl despite her sophisticated, elegant demeanor. She explained to the captain, in animated detail, how her father ordered her delivered from her home in England to her rich uncle's plantation in North Carolina. For once, the girl's voice trailed off, giving Amanda the impression more lay behind the story than the girl wished to share. Pain flickered in her dark eyes, only to be replaced by hard determination.

"Have you ever been away from England, Miss Bowersley?" the captain asked in a somewhat stiff but polite voice.

"I have not, sir," she replied. "Can you imagine how frightening it is for me to be so far from home on my first trip abroad? I had imagined my father would allow me to visit the continent, but instead he sends me to America where I shall have much to learn about living with savages."

Savages? Was her uncle an Indian, Amanda wondered. Did Indians own plantations?

"I assure you America is much more civilized than

your English friends have led you to believe, Miss Bowersley," the captain said.

"I should love to know what the country is like. Are there shops?" Hope shone in her wide blue eyes.

"You should visit the—" Buck started to say.

"Shops for dresses, and hats, and gloves and all the necessities a woman of breeding simply must have?" Miss Bowersley asked, cutting Buck off without so much as a glance in his direction.

Amanda shot a sympathetic look toward her shipmate, surprised Miss Bowersley didn't welcome his attentions. He was handsome with a refined manner. He dressed even better than the captain, preferring velvet to wool and rich colors like forest green and mauve. Despite being aboard ship for months at a time, his shirts and neck stock were always crisp and immaculate. Amanda often wondered if he didn't perhaps have a new set of freshly laundered shirts delivered each time they called at port. Surely, he was the type of man who would catch a young girl's fancy.

Buck smiled at Amanda as though sharing a private joke.

"Yes. America has towns and even a few cities filled with shops much like those you'd find in England," the captain replied, treating Miss Bowersley's question as though it were more than mere prattle.

Amanda thought it rather silly, but then she had never been to England. Perhaps their cities and towns were much different.

"What do people do for entertainment? Do they go to teas? Are there parties?" Miss Bowersley asked, her voice rising in pitch with each question.

"My wife loves to—" the doctor started to say.

"Do they have balls and soirées?"

This time, the girl's eyes shifted to the doctor, a look of unveiled irritation flitting over her face before she donned her beguiling mask again.

"I suppose some do," the captain replied.

Amanda caught the knowing glance the doctor cast in Buck's direction. Buck didn't acknowledge it, but he dabbed at his lips with his linen napkin, a familiar devilish sparkle shining in his eyes.

Amanda's jaw dropped and she snapped it shut. The two men weren't besotted with their female guest any more than the captain. They were simply playing a game to see if either could distract the girl from her intended victim; a game they were both losing.

Amanda picked up a carafe of wine to fill the glass that sat empty before the English captain. He seemed determined to drink an entire bottle by himself, and with her desire to stay in the room and watch their guests, Amanda stood at the ready.

The English captain hadn't once tried to join the conversation, and neither had his men. Instead, they attacked each new dish with relish, smiling their appreciation at her with greasy lips, while leaving Captain Stoakes to fend for himself in the face of Miss Bowersley's unrelenting attention.

"Do the Continental officers look as handsome in their uniforms as the English officers?"

Amanda choked, jostling the carafe she held and spilling a crimson drop on the snowy white tablecloth. Captain Stoakes shot her a silencing glance, and she quickly looked down.

But really! How on earth did Miss Bowersley

expect the captain to answer that question?

Luckily for him, she didn't seem to require a response. She continued on, describing in a breathy voice how divine the English officers looked in full dress uniform.

She must be talking about the military officers, Amanda decided. She took up her post in the corner of the room and watched the merchantman's officers greedily wolf down another serving of *coq au vin.* The occasional drop of brown sauce stained the ruffles around their sleeves. Still, she couldn't help but feel generous toward them. Miss Bowersley had probably been quite a lot to endure during their voyage from England, and Amanda admired their ability to suffer in silence.

Captain Stoakes withstood it all in stoic silence too. He continued to answer questions when propriety demanded it, and when Miss Bowersley stopped chattering long enough to allow it. He was neither rude nor expansive in his responses, but when he finished speaking, his lips never failed to return to a thin slash above his squared chin.

"Captain Stoakes," Miss Bowersley asked after an expansive but futile line of questioning concerning the latest fashions in America, "do you have any women on your ship? Perhaps even a wife tucked away somewhere?"

For a moment, time stood still and silence filled the small chamber. Amanda froze, her hand holding the carafe over the crystal glass of one of the English officers. A small cough from Buck snapped her out of her reverie in time to avoid overfilling the glass.

"No, Miss Bowersley, I do not," the captain

replied.

Miss Bowersley cocked her pretty, oval face in innocent surprise. "Why ever not? I would imagine your voyages are long, and the addition of female companionship would be most welcome."

Miss Bowersley's bottom lip jutted out in a small pout that Amanda assumed the girl intended to be charming. The hard set of the captain's jaw and suggested he didn't find it so.

Amanda poured wine into the glasses of the men at the table, even those that were nearly full. She could feel the captain's tension from across the room, but she could no more leave the room than she could leave the ship. Miss Bowersley had asked the unthinkable, yet Amanda would sooner die than miss the captain's answer.

When the glasses could hold no more, Amanda stood, holding the carafe at the foot of the table, and stared at a knot in the planked wall on the opposite side of the room just over the captain's head.

"Women do not belong on ships, Miss Bowersley." The air in the small chamber grew thick with tension.

The others at the table stopped eating. The English commander had the boldness to look at the captain, but his officers studied the remnants of the meal before them.

Amanda's heart beat so hard in her chest that the carafe in her hand twitched to its rhythm. She placed it on the sideboard before it gave away her distress.

"Perhaps not *American* women," Miss Bowersley said, oblivious to the mood of those about her. "With some of them you would hardly notice that a woman was aboard, would you? I've heard they can be so coarse!"

She looked around at her male companions, seeking confirmation. None of the men would meet her gaze. Then her dark, speculative eyes fell on Amanda.

Amanda swallowed the lump in her throat. Could Miss Bowersley see what the men could not?

"I assure you, I would know if there was a woman on my ship," Captain Stoakes replied, drawing her attention back to him.

"I suppose a man like you would." She took another sip of wine and regarded him with an intense gaze over the rim of her glass. "Have you ever had a woman on your ship, Captain? I don't mean for the entire voyage, but perhaps for…a shorter length of time?"

Miss Bowersley's voice caught on her words, and her deep blue eyes were bright and shiny. Amanda decided she would watch the speed at which she refilled the girl's wine glass from now on, for her own sake and the captain's.

Amanda risked a glance at the captain's face, marveling at his ability to keep his composure. She could feel the strain, see it in the muscle that twitched along his jaw when he cut into a chicken thigh with his fork and knife. The captain brought a piece to his mouth and chewed with slow deliberation, focusing his gaze on his food, his wine, his other guests, anywhere but Miss Bowersley.

Miss Bowersley, on the other hand, watched the captain take another bite of chicken with unabashed interest. When the captain dabbed at his lips, she leaned forward. With each stroke of the napkin, her long, tapered fingers twitched as though she wished to handle the task for him.

Amanda relaxed. The girl only had eyes for the captain, and for all she cared, Amanda was just a servant. Despite her impertinent comments about American women, the fool had no idea one stood not five feet from her.

When the meal drew to a close, Amanda cleared away the last of the dishes and prepared to bring out coffee and dessert.

Captain Stoakes laid a hand on her arm and stopped her. "Adam, you really outdid yourself tonight. Supper was superb."

"Here, here!" the other officers in the room raised their glasses and echoed the captain's praise.

Amanda returned their smiles, relieved that no one appeared offended by her choice of a French dish for a main course. She nodded and reached for the bottle of Port sitting on the sideboard.

"Here, boy," Miss Bowersley said, her voice sharp. "I don't care for Port, but I've been ignored, and my wine glass has been allowed to sit empty."

If you hadn't drained it in one gulp the last time I filled it, it wouldn't be empty now. Amanda bit back the retort, and set the Port bottle back on the side table. She brought the carafe to the crystal wine glass Miss Bowersley held aloft.

Amanda filled her glass, this time right up to the rim, while Miss Bowersley puckered her lips and managed to look down her nose at Amanda, despite being seated.

Amanda's hand shook a bit when she set the bottle back on the side table.

"Captain, I wonder if you might let this boy go

with me to North Carolina? I'm sure Uncle Theodore has a cook, but it is probably one of those Negro women brought in from the fields. I've heard their cooking is dreadful, and you can never be sure exactly what you are eating." She sighed. "But I suppose they do their best to learn our ways, and they can't help it if they aren't able."

For a moment, Amanda remained focused on Miss Bowersley's thoughtless words. Having been raised in Maryland, she had been exposed to slavery, but her family had never owned any. Their farm was too small to profit by it, but her father had also felt it wrong for one man to own another. The whole idea had never sat well with her either. Apparently, Miss Bowersley considered it an inconvenience, for herself if not for the slave. Any charity she felt toward the girl faded.

Then the meaning behind the words sank in, and her mind raced. Would the captain seize the opportunity to get rid of her? After all, if Miss Bowersley's uncle had the wealth she claimed, he could give her a job and assume responsibility for her. She would no longer be a member of the crew and, therefore, no longer Captain Stoakes' responsibility. Whether she chose to stay with Miss Bowersley or leave her employ would be up to Amanda, but Captain Stoakes would be free to wash his hands of her.

She couldn't leave the ship, she just couldn't! She needed more time. Time to prove her worth to the captain. Time to prove she could be as valuable as any man. Time to prove he needed her. The blood rushed to Amanda's head, and the world around her took on a tinny sound. Boys didn't swoon, did they? She clung to the thought like a life raft to avoid losing control of her senses.

Amanda caught the captain's eye for a moment, but he looked away.

"I'm afraid I can't allow Adam to go with you." He laid his napkin across his plate. "He is indispensable to me."

Chapter Seventeen

With Miss Bowersley clinging to his arm once again, Captain Stoakes escorted his guests to the upper deck and called for the transport boat to take them back to their ship. Amanda wondered if Miss Bowersley could walk under her own accord. If the captain let her go, would she weave her way over to the side of the ship and topple over?

The image, although delightful, could not have raised Amanda's sprits any higher. The captain had called her "indispensable." Had he meant it?

Perhaps he had been so put off by the way Miss Bowersley made the request to take Adam with her to North Carolina that he hadn't been inclined to be accommodating.

Regardless of whether he had been sincere or not, he had made it clear she would not be sent with Miss Bowersley to her uncle's plantation. And the more she had thought about it while she and Cookie cleared the dishes and poured more wine, the more she doubted he would dump her off on an English captain. After all, he wouldn't want her feeding the enemy, would he?

Despite the few moments of tension, Amanda had never been so entertained, and she hated to see the evening end. Their guests, for she no longer thought of them as prisoners, were so unlike any of the people she knew. Prior to life on the *Amanda*, her circle of friends and acquaintances didn't extend much beyond farmers, local merchants and their families. None of the *Amanda's* crew, even those with telltale British accents, were as uniquely alien as the officers of the merchantman and the girl.

Especially the girl, Amanda decided, standing at a discreet distance so she could watch their departure. Despite Miss Bowersley's foolishness and her absorption with the captain, she regretted not having the chance to sit and chat with another woman. Perhaps she wouldn't be so bad when no men were around to tempt her.

However, while she didn't want her guests to leave, the captain did. While stacking the dishes in the galley, Cookie told Amanda the captain had given Bull orders to hand-select a prize crew of only the most reliable, most honorable men and to have them aboard and in command of the ship before morning. Cookie, with his thick Irish accent, had done a poor imitation of the captain saying he "would not have this foolish girl accusing his men of mistreatment and cause him to lose his Letter of Marque, all for her own amusement."

Amanda wondered if he had actually said those words, or if Cookie had made his little piece of gossip a tad juicier by dressing it up. Surely, the captain didn't think Miss Bowersley would go that far, did he? Would a mere girl have that kind of power?

The galley cleared, she mumbled an excuse to Cookie, saying she needed to go on deck to speak with her brother. She struck up a half-hearted conversation with Neil by the main mast, but her gaze kept straying to the captain and his guests. She barely noticed when her brother drifted away to join Nate at the ship's bow.

The transport boat had been lowered and the makeshift hoist readied, but Miss Bowersley still didn't seem inclined to let go of her tight grip on the captain's arm. Amanda waited to see how Captain Stoakes, his restrained politeness back in place, would extricate his arm without causing undue offense to her or embarrassment for himself.

"Oh, Captain, I do have a request that I hope you'll grant," Miss Bowersley said, removing her hand from his bicep and placing it on his chest in an intimate gesture that made Amanda squirm. "I wondered if I might be allowed to remain on this ship tonight."

"On this ship?" The outer corner of one of his dark eyebrows twitched.

Amanda cringed at the breathy tone in Miss Bowersley's voice, and she imagined the vulnerability in her blue eyes had helped her win many favors in the past. Wrinkling her nose, Amanda waited to see if the captain also had a weakness for helpless women with luminous blue eyes.

The captain of the merchantman cleared his throat and shrugged. "She would like to be able to tell her future friends in North Carolina she spent the night on a pirate ship." His tone held a note of apology.

Captain Stoakes didn't comment on the insult of being called a pirate for the second time that evening, but Amanda felt the air around her thicken the way it did when a storm approached.

"Besides," Miss Bowersley chirped, "you agreed to transport me to my uncle's plantation in North Carolina. I will have to be with you for several days at least. Why not begin our journey tonight?"

Amanda didn't care for the way she leaned in when

asking the question.

"My prize crew will take your ship and all its passengers to North Carolina." Captain Stoakes stepped away from Miss Bowersley so she had no choice but to remove her hand or appear to be clinging to him like a monkey in a tree. "That way, you will not have to transport your belongings to the *Amanda,* and you will not be forced to spend several days on such a small ship in cramped quarters."

"Oh, but I don't—" Miss Bowersley started to protest, but before she could finish, the captain of the merchant ship interrupted her.

"Won't that delay the auctioning of your prize, sir? North Carolina is hardly on the way to Boston."

The man's shoulders were slumped and his voice a near whine. Amanda feigned a cough so she could cover her smile with the back of her hand. She had never seen a captain so eager to give over his ship and his cargo.

"The loss of time is inconsequential," replied Captain Stoakes. "If the winds and seas are favorable, my crew can continue on to the court at Martinique."

Miss Bowersley's eyes widened, even though her tight smile remained. She looked desperate to stay aboard the *Amanda*, and behind those clear blue eyes, Amanda could almost see the woman searching for a way to force the captain to allow it.

"Besides, I regret I have no chaperone for you, Miss Bowersley."

Amanda stifled a groan, disappointed that a man like Captain Stoakes, who could out sail any vessel on the ocean, could not outmaneuver one young woman.

A slow cat-like smile replaced the look of

desperation on Miss Bowersley's delicate features.

"Oh, I do not believe I need one. I am sure your men are all honorable unless..." she drew out the words as though considering them carefully. "Did you think I might be in danger from anyone in particular, Captain?"

Amanda scrunched her face, feeling pain on the captain's behalf. Miss Bowersley was a formidable foe. She had let loose her own volley by impugning the captain's honor. The broadside was made doubly powerful by the implied insult to the captain *and* his crew.

Even if Captain Stoakes didn't understand women like Miss Violet Bowersley, she certainly understood men like him. Amanda sensed he would yield even before it happened.

"Buck, see to it that Miss Bowersley has a cabin to herself, and post guards outside her door," he said with a slight sigh of exasperation.

"Yes, sir." Buck turned on his heel.

"Guards?" Miss Bowersley inquired with a tilt of her delicately pointed little chin.

"I trust my men. All of them. However, I should think you would be more comfortable knowing you are protected should *anyone*," he paused to make his meaning clear, "be less than the man I think he is."

The spark went out of Violet Bowersley, and Amanda was surprised to see her give up so easily. When not playing the flirt, Miss Bowersley looked far more plain and ordinary, but her ordinariness lasted no more than a moment before she cast him an artful glance from beneath veiled lashes.

"Well then, since you trust all of your men, would you permit Adam to attend me?"

"Me?" Amanda squeaked before she could stop herself.

"Yes." She gave Amanda a slow appraisal from head to toe. "I won't embarrass you by making you do the things a lady's maid would do, but I would love the company. I've been sailing with nothing but old men for three months now." She looked apologetically at the crew of the merchantman.

A couple of them rolled their eyes, and Miss Bowersley's lip curled the tiniest amount before her smile returned.

"I know you are younger than me, but it would be like having a brother to talk to. I should so love the company," she said in a voice that might have sounded petulant coming from a girl not quite so winsome.

Amanda thought she might choke when Miss Bowersley batted her eyelashes at her.

"You may go, Adam." The captain gave Amanda a pleading look that had her stifling a laugh.

If she could save him from the designing clutches of this girl, she would gladly sacrifice herself for the evening. With that, Amanda found herself in Buck's freshly made quarters. They had been given over to Miss Bowersley for the evening so she could tell her new friends in North Carolina she had "spent the night on a pirate ship."

Amanda had been right about the ill effects of being around eligible men. *Violet*, she insisted Amanda call her by her first name, improved once they were alone. She supposed Violet considered "Adam" too young and not wealthy or powerful enough to be bothered with, so she felt comfortable allowing her true self to come through. When it did, she came across like a genuine seventeen-year-old, eager to get on with being an adult but often childlike in her view of the world.

Amanda caught the dress Violet flung over the top of the screen, while she changed into her nightgown. Shaking out the wrinkles and laying it over the back of a chair, she listened to Violet prattle on about the things a girl her age would normally talk to a friend about. She talked about the parties and social events she would miss being away from England, what life would be like at her new home in North Carolina and whether or not she would find a proper husband in the savage lands of America.

"I am already seventeen, I'll have you know," she said from behind the screen.

A silk stocking fluttered over the top like a butterfly.

"But, seventeen is still young," Amanda captured the stocking before it could fall to the floor. She readied herself to receive the next one. "You have plenty of time."

"Plenty of time? Plenty of time?" Violet sputtered and Amanda could imagine her ebony curls bouncing with indignation. "You are so lucky to be a boy. *You* have plenty of time. No man is worth marrying before he's thirty, but no woman is worth marrying after nineteen. After that, she might as well give up. No man worth having will want her."

Amanda frowned. What would Violet think if she knew the young boy she spoke to was really a woman the ripe old age of twenty-one? She caught her freckled reflection in the mirror above the basin and her frown deepened. Certainly, nothing about her life would prove

Violet wrong. She would be twenty-two next month, unmarried and with no prospects in sight. Perhaps no man would ever want her.

"Why does a woman really need a man, anyway?" Amanda asked, feeling suddenly argumentative.

Violet poked her head around the side of the screen. "Are you serious?"

Amanda looked at her and nodded.

"Some husband you'll make," Violet replied, ducking back behind the screen. "All women need men to provide for them."

"Provide for them?" Amanda asked.

"You know, take care of them. Put food on the table. Take care of the things woman aren't capable of taking care of on their own."

"Like what sort of things?" Amanda asked. Her farm hadn't been doing that well, but she always managed to provide for herself and Neil.

"You know. Things!" Violet flailed her hand, a dark shadow batting the other side of the screen.

"Like hunt?" Amanda asked, trying to be helpful.

She didn't mind farming. Even butchering a chicken wasn't so bad, but she had never enjoyed hunting. Neil had taken her a few times, but it involved too much idle time, sitting and waiting for their prey to cross their path, or traipsing across cold, damp fields trying to flush out a flock of birds. Either way, her toes always ended up frozen. She preferred to let Neil do the job while she prepared the results of his effort. It seemed a fair trade-off.

"Hunting? I won't allow my husband to hunt," Violet said.

"Do they not hunt in England?" Amanda asked,

amazed Violet thought she could take an American husband and deny him the pleasure.

"Of course they hunt in England," Violet said, "but my husband won't."

The girl sounded so certain there seemed little point in arguing.

Besides, she imagined Violet's future husband would probably spend a great deal of time hunting. She couldn't imagine any man spending quiet days in front of a fire, discussing literature or politics with a wife like Violet Bowersley.

Violet emerged from behind the screen in the nightgown she had sent over from her ship. "If you ask me, men spend far too much time thinking about ways to kill things."

There was nothing at all alluring about Violet's white nightgown, but somehow the shapeless garment, with its ruffles set high about the neck and at the sleeves, made her petite form looked feminine and innocent. Her delicate ankles and bare feet peeked out from under the scalloped lace edging at the hem.

Amanda averted her eyes. She had played the boy for so long; instinctively she knew she had just found herself in a compromising position. Perhaps she should make an excuse and go. Then she reminded herself that Violet had no interest in her. She treated Amanda much the way a young, well-bred girl would treat her lady's maid or perhaps even a little brother if she had no one else to confide in.

"Would you be a good boy and brush my hair for me?" Violet asked, sitting at the edge of the bed.

After a moment's hesitation, Amanda took the brush from her hand. Violet turned her back and then wiggled into the hammock to make herself more comfortable. If there had been a man in the room, Amanda was sure he would have found the move provocative. But with only a "boy" in her presence, perhaps Violet had not intended it that way.

"How about for companionship?" Amanda removed a few hairpins holding the curls on the side of Violet's face. "Don't women need men for that?"

"Companionship?" Violet scrunched her face.

"Yes. Someone to talk to. Someone you enjoy being with."

Violet twisted at the waist to give Amanda a skeptical look. "Have you ever met a man who could hold a conversation?"

"Well..." Amanda began, thinking about how much she loved listening to Captain Stoakes and about her dream of discussing literature with him one day. She felt certain she would find the captain fascinating if he could get over his aversion to her long enough to hold a decent conversation.

"Oh, never mind," Violet said in an exasperated tone. "How could I expect you to understand when you are almost a man yourself?"

Amanda smiled. "Almost a man" indeed!

"But you seem to enjoy talking to me," she said, brushing Violet's long silky strands.

"Hmmm…" Violet murmured. Her shoulders relaxed beneath Amanda's expert touch.

Amanda brushed, remembering the calm that always descended when her mother brushed her own long blonde hair. The warmth of long-forgotten memories came flooding back, and she mimicked her mother's techniques, sweeping slowly with just a light pressure from the front of Violet's scalp and all the way down to the ends of her long hair. She let one of Violet's thick locks slide slowly through her hand, fervently wishing she'd be able to grown her own hair back one day. There was freedom in her short curls, but she missed putting her hair up for special occasions and the feeling of looking her best if not actually pretty.

Lost in her own thoughts, Amanda didn't notice when Violet turned on the bed and rose to her knees. She only had one glimpse of Violet's flushed face before her lips descended. At first, stunned surprise held her motionless, but when she came to her senses, she pushed Violet so hard she sent her sprawling to the floor.

The thud brought Buck in from the hall. "Everything all right in here?" he asked.

His voice held no clue to his thoughts, but Amanda cringed at what he must be thinking. She sat on the bed while Violet sprawled on the floor, the skirt of her frilly nightdress up to her knees and displaying her shapely white calves.

The seconds slowed and no one moved.

Without warning, Violet's screech pierced the air, "He pushed me!"

Stunned, Amanda turned to look at her. She had no idea what to say. She had pushed Violet, but only to avoid the kiss. However, she didn't imagine the vaunted privateer's code looked favorably on pushing a guest, especially a woman, to the floor.

"I think the two of you had better come with me," Buck said.

Chapter Eighteen

Buck led the way to the captain's quarters, Violet marching behind him, head held high. Amanda trailed them, mustering her dignity and trying to make sense of the last few minutes. Should she try to explain the situation before Violet had an opportunity to level her accusations? But why should she feel the need to defend herself against charges that were clearly absurd?

Buck nudged Amanda and Violet ahead of him into the captain's quarters.

"What's this about?" the captain asked.

"There appears to have been a misunderstanding," Buck started to explain, only to be interrupted by Violet.

Miss Bowersley no longer screeched, but she still quivered with indignant fury. Back and forth, she paraded before the captain, seemingly unbothered by her bare feet peeking out from under her nightgown while she informed him all about the "misunderstanding."

"We were having a nice chat while I changed behind the screen, Captain. Then I needed help with a couple of buttons on the back of my dress that I couldn't reach. I should have known by the way Adam's hands lingered something was amiss." Tears welled up in her eyes.

Liar! Amanda wanted to scream. She hadn't

touched a single button on Violet's dress.

"Fool that I am, I asked him to brush out my hair. I'm so used to having my lady's maid do it for me, but I've had to do without these last three months. I thought perhaps it would help comfort me, being so far from home, if I had someone to take care of me." Her face took on the essence of innocent vulnerability.

Amanda opened her mouth to interject something, *anything*, in her own defense, but the captain held up his hand. Why wouldn't he let her speak?

"After he finished with my hair, I bade him goodnight, but he didn't leave. Even so, I wasn't frightened at that point." She clasped her hands together and Amanda thought she glimpsed tears glistening in her big blue eyes. "Oh, I'm such an innocent!"

Like hell you are! A sound escaped Amanda's lips before she could help it, and the captain shot her a look that suggested, for her own sake, she remain quiet.

"Still, I hinted it would be improper for him to remain. Then he... Then he..." A fat tear rolled down Violet's cheek. "He pushed me onto the bed and tried to kiss me!"

Amanda watched in disgust, wondering how Violet could produce tears on demand. The captain had already proven himself vulnerable, but Amanda found the idea of using them to manipulate abhorrent. Real tears were one thing, but these?

They had to be fake tears. In fact, Miss Bowersley had begun to remind Amanda more and more of an actor on the stage–a bad actor. Her indignation, the fluttering of her hands against her chest, the flush on her cheeks, it was all too passionate to be believed.

"Adam, I believe you owe Miss Bowersley an

apology," the captain said, without looking at her.

"But, captain," Amanda sputtered.

He believed Violet, bad acting and all? More than that, how could he possibly think she would try to steal a kiss form the girl? Did he think just because she dressed as a man meant she preferred the attentions of women?

Amanda stood in horrified silence.

"Now, Adam!"

Amanda gritted her teeth. Well, she could be as much an actress as Violet.

"My dear, Miss Bowersley," Amanda clasped one of Violet's hands. "I sincerely regret our misunderstanding. You see, I was so captivated by your company that I simply must have missed your suggestion to leave."

Amanda's stomach churned, and although she tried her best to keep the sarcasm out of her voice, it crept in through her words. "As for the kiss, although it would be heaven to be permitted to kiss an angel such as you, I realize I am a mere boy and not fit to kiss the ground on which you tread."

Buck coughed, and Amanda could feel the captain's eyes boring into the side of her head. Violet preened like a parakeet.

"I would never try to take advantage of an innocent like yourself. I'm afraid I lost my footing on the uneven boards and, unfortunately, knocked you over when I tried to catch myself. I do hope you will forgive me and we can remain friends."

"Well, I suppose it could happen to anyone," Violet said, in a haughty and condescending voice, but at least she no longer sounded angry.

Amanda gave Violet her biggest smile. *What a fool!* Either that, or Amanda's deception skills had improved. After all, she'd had more than two months to practice.

Miss Violet held out her hand for a kiss and Amanda's conceit vanished.

Oh, for heaven's sakes. How low would she have to stoop before this was all over? And how did one kiss a hand? She once had a neighbor's boy try to steal a kiss on her cheek, a move he soon regretted, but she had never had anyone kiss her hand. Fighting revulsion, she tried to remember the captain's performance when Violet had first come aboard. Taking her hand, she kissed the air above her knuckles, all the while imaging what Violet might do if she spit on her instead. She lingered over Violet's hand a moment longer while she forced back a grin.

"You may escort me back to my quarters now." Violet's tone would have befitted a queen.

"I think not," the captain interjected. "Buck, escort Miss Bowersley to her quarters, and then make absolutely certain no one is allowed inside."

Or out, Amanda wanted to add, but she decided not to press her luck.

"Yes, sir," Buck waved his hand to allow Violet to precede him through the door.

Amanda turned to follow.

"Not you," the captain said.

He didn't sound pleased. Amanda turned back and set her feet shoulder width part so she could bob with the waves and weather whatever recriminations came her way.

The captain rose from his chair and went to stand

beside a small window. He stood there for some time, staring out at the night sea, hands clasped behind his back. After several minutes, Amanda wondered if he had forgotten her presence.

"Captain, I…" she began, but the captain's deep sigh cut her short.

"You have no need to explain, Amanda. Do you honestly think I believe you pushed that woman onto the bed? I sent you with her to her quarters to keep her occupied and away from anyone else she might try to seduce, me included."

Amanda choked back a giggle. So the captain had not been oblivious to Violet's intentions.

"I sent you because you were the least likely to have any interest in her and she in you." He glanced at her. "I had no idea she would use you to further her goals."

"I'm sorry about that, Captain," Amanda said. "I hope I didn't cause any trouble for you."

"No, I am the one who should offer an apology." His lip curled in a sneer. "When I ended the dinner and she saw her chance slipping away, she used you as a pawn in her little game—and I let her." He leveled his gaze at Amanda. "For putting you in that position, I am truly sorry."

His sincerity touched something inside her. "If you didn't believe I pushed her, why didn't you allow me to tell my side of the story?"

"Because you obviously don't have much experience with women."

Amanda bit her lip, not sure whether she had just been insulted. She was a woman!

"Sorry, I didn't mean that the way it sounded," he

said with an embarrassed laugh. “What I mean to say is that you don’t have much experience with women who will do whatever it takes, use whomever they will, to get their way.”

“That sounds suspiciously like a compliment,” Amanda said.

To her surprise, the captain returned her smile. “If she felt her reputation had been damaged, she might complain to some authority or another, and I could lose my marque. Her uncle may not be as powerful as she claims, but I don’t want to take any chances.

“I see.” Amanda had no idea the stakes were so high.

“Plus, I have the suspicion she is husband hunting.” The dismay on the captain’s face suggested he didn’t relish being the girl’s quarry.

“Oh, I can assure you, she is,” Amanda said.

“Yes, well, I don’t intend to get snared in her net. Women like her are one of the reasons I don’t allow women on my ship.” He looked up as though he suddenly remembered to whom he was speaking. “Most of the time anyway.”

A glimmer of hope kindled in Amanda’s chest. His statement hadn’t been a reversal of his cardinal rule, but it was tantamount to an admission that rules could be broken. But could they be broken permanently, or did he still consider her presence a temporary aberration?

“You are lucky she is vain enough to actually believe your outrageous apology.” The captain shot her a grin. “Where did you learn to kiss a hand like that?”

Amanda shrugged. “From you.”

“From me?” The captain’s brows rose as one.

“Yes, I watched you greet Miss Bowersley when

she came on board this evening."

"Ahh, so that's it. Anyway, your performance may have saved my ship, and I am grateful."

"Thank you," Amanda said, humbled.

"However, to avoid further mishap in case she changes her mind, I think perhaps the two of us should stick together tonight."

"Stick together?" Amanda's heart leapt into her throat.

Surely, he didn't mean she should spend the night with him. A sudden image of the two of them snuggled together on his narrow hammock sent heat rushing to her cheeks. If the captain noticed, he didn't comment. His gaze dropped to the manifest in front of him.

"I wouldn't put it past her to drug poor Buck and slip into bed with one of us while we are fast asleep and then claim we put her there."

Perhaps he did know women—of that type anyway—far better than she did.

Amanda grinned. "So you want me here...as your protector?"

"Something like that." He held up a hand. "But before you get too smug, it's for your own protection as well. She could just as easily sneak into your hammock as mine, and I thought you might find that a bit awkward."

"I'll say." Amanda laughed. "Still, I'm happy to oblige you, Captain. If I can be of service..." Her voice trailed off as she started to imagine some of the ways she would like to be of service to him.

Not that any of that was likely to happen.

"Thank you." Captain Stoakes said, his voice warm.

"Captain, can I go fetch something?" Amanda asked.

The captain nodded. "I think Buck has things well in hand for now."

Amanda scurried out the door. Minutes later, she reentered carrying a small tray.

"You ended dinner so abruptly that you missed dessert." She set a French custard and a pot filled with steaming black coffee before him on his desk.

The captain looked up from the manifests. A grin infused his features when he looked into the scalloped custard dish. "Nice choice. I see it was intended to complement the main course."

Amanda grinned, pleased he understood and appreciated her humor instead of seeing it as an affront to his guests.

The captain gave her leave to sit in the chair across from him. She politely declined to share the custard, saying she didn't care much for sweets. In truth, she got far more pleasure watching him enjoy it than she would eating any of the confection herself.

The captain produced a chipped ceramic stein from a desk drawer. Pulling a handkerchief from his breast pocket, he swabbed it out, blew in it, and poured it full of coffee from the pot. Then he offered the dainty teacup to Amanda while he kept the stein for himself. She accepted it as though it were the most natural thing in the world.

Amanda sipped the coffee, reveling in the rich aroma and flavor while she watched the captain polish off his desert. When he finished spooning up the last of it, he stared into the empty dish. From the longing in his eyes, Amanda half expected him to bury his face in it and lap up every last dreg. Instead, he contented himself with the remnants of custard clinging to his spoon. Then, he gave her a sheepish grin and offered to refill her cup.

Amanda shook her head. "No, thank you. Coffee disturbs my sleep."

Not that she would get much sleep sharing quarters with the captain. Where did he expect her to sleep anyway?

"Before you drift off, would you mind brewing another pot?" he asked, refilling his stein. "I have a lot of work to do tonight, and I may be up for hours."

For reasons she didn't want to ponder, his words disappointed her.

Now that Cookie had learned to make coffee, he almost always had a fresh pot at the ready so Amanda returned in a few minutes. Not thinking to knock, she pushed his door open with her shoulder and entered to find Captain Stoakes standing at his basin.

He had removed his white linen shirt and stood bare-chested in front of the mirror, a small cloth in hand. In the reflection, Amanda could see his broad chest covered with a smattering of dark curls, soft and springy.

While he washed himself with the cloth, Amanda watched the play of muscles in his back. He had to be the most beautiful creature God ever created. His shoulders were wide, but his back narrowed to a trim waist. Each movement sent muscles rippling beneath his skin. Above the waistline of his breeches, she found herself fascinated by two indentations in the small of his back that ended somewhere below his belt line. She traced them with her eyes, and then let her appreciative gaze linger over his taught buttocks and long legs. Under his tight breeches, she could see the rest of him was just as well built.

Letting her eyes drink in the sight of him, Amanda realized something had changed. Muscles no longer rippled beneath glistening skin, and she no longer heard the soft swish of the cloth in the basin. She raised her gaze to the mirror.

His golden eyes glowed like embers in the reflection.

Probably an effect of the light from the oil lamp. She set the pot down on the desk, but her skin tingled with awareness. She knew without looking his gaze was still on her. An alertness filled her, and she understood what it felt like to be a rabbit stalked by a wolf.

She settled herself in the hard wooden chair, a foolish rabbit without the sense to flee.

Amanda closed her eyes and attempted sleep, but she couldn't shut out the sounds about her, the glide of cloth over bare skin, the trickle of water returning to the bowl, the small groans of exertion as he tried to reach places on his back that she longed to scrub for him. She squeezed her eyes tighter.

Every fiber in her body hummed to his presence and the intimacy of being alone with him. Perhaps he had been right about not being alone together. However, it wasn't her reputation that concerned her. It was her sanity.

He didn't invite you here so you could try to seduce you him.

Over and over, she repeated the reasoning to herself until it became like a mantra. His invitation might mean they were on the path toward an understanding, but nothing more. That he could be comfortable with her in his quarters all night meant he thought of her as his subordinate, nothing more.

She tugged at the bindings on her chest, wishing she might at least loosen them. They chafed at her delicate skin, but she had grown to hate them for what they represented more than the discomfort she had to endure. If he saw her as less than a woman, the fault lay with her, not with him.

Amanda was still arguing with herself when she finally found a comfortable position on the little chair. Fatigue overtook her, the refrain repeating as she drifted off.

He didn't invite you here so you could try to seduce you him...could try to seduce him...try to seduce him.

****

Will drank the entire second pot of coffee, but got no work done. Amanda talked in her sleep, and although he couldn't make out the words, the way she tugged at her clothing and laughed suggested her dreams were interesting ones. Much of the time, he sat gazing at her and entertaining himself by trying to deduce what enticing visions could cause such sensuous sighs and moans.

When her breathing at last slowed and he thought he might be able to move her without disturbing her slumber, he scooped her up in his arms and carried her to his hammock. As soon as he laid her down, Amanda gave a breathy sigh and snuggled into his pillow.

"What am I going to do with you?" Will smoothed her blonde curls from her brow.

Amanda smiled in her sleep as though his confusion pleased her.

Somewhere over the last few weeks, he had lost all desire to get her off his ship. He hadn't realized that until Miss Bowersley offered the perfect opportunity, but the thought of being without Amanda overwhelmed him with a gut-wrenching sense of loneliness. He couldn't imagine life without her.

But if he allowed her to remain on his ship, how would he keep her safe? How would it affect his crew's morale? His ability to command?

It had been nerve wracking keeping her identity a secret from everyone but the doctor. No matter how well Amanda covered her soft curves with men's clothing, everything she said and did appeared delightfully feminine. It would only be a matter of time before others discovered her secret.

The first ray of dawn stabbed through the darkness in the cabin, haloing Amanda's blond curls with an angelic glow. Will knelt down and placed a light kiss on her cheek.

"Amanda, I surrender," he whispered.

Come what may, he needed her by his side and would not let her go. The rising sun warming Will's cheek, he tucked his quilt beneath Amanda's chin. They would begin anew today.

Chapter Nineteen

Amanda arranged the captain's breakfast on a tray, positioning an array of orange wedges until they resembled a flower. The oranges had been a gift from the English merchant, a thank you for her culinary efforts. She suspected they might also be an apology intended for Captain Stoakes, since he had assumed the responsibility for their "cargo."

She hadn't seen the captain yet today, and she found his absence unsettling. Last night, he allowed her to remain in his quarters in order to keep them both safe from the machinations of a clever young woman.

Amanda gave a soft laugh. If anything, the captain had been in far more danger than she had, and he knew it. She had given the situation considerable thought this morning, wondering why he hadn't suggested she simply go back to her own hammock. The doctor would have made sure Miss Bowersley didn't molest her in her sleep. However, that arrangement would have left Captain Stoakes alone and unguarded.

Still, she couldn't help but wonder if it went deeper than that. Perhaps sleeping in his hammock had given her the illusion of intimacy. Although he had not shared his bedding with her, she had awoken, surrounded by his heady masculine scent almost as if he had lain next to her. Not possible, she concluded, since his hammock was only slightly wider than those used by the men. If two people shared his hammock, their weight would have brought them both rolling toward the middle and they would have had to curl around each other like two pieces of a puzzle.

The image made her cheeks heat, and she fanned herself with the captain's linen napkin until the flames receded. He hadn't been curled around her when she awoke. Disappointment stabbed at her, and she reminded herself she had no right to feel that way.

She set the linen napkin on the tray and made a few last minute adjustments to the arrangement before carrying it out the door.

Walking into the common area, she remembered how anxious she had been leaving the captain's quarters this morning. The impending shift change meant the common area would be crowded with men from the morning shift eating the breakfast of milled oats that Cookie prepared in vast kettles. She had considered waiting a half hour or so until they finished. After that, the much smaller night watch would be preparing for bed. But if she did that, she would be late with the captain's breakfast. Or worst case, Cookie might take it upon himself to try his hand at the captain's eggs again. Amanda flinched just thinking about it.

When she finally mustered enough courage to step into the common area, a few of the men had greeted her with their usual smiles, but none seemed to think it odd that she should emerge from the captain's quarters so early in the morning. Perhaps they thought she had just brought him his breakfast.

Luckily, only the night shift remained in the common area to see her bring this tray to the captain, and most of them lay snoring in their hammocks.

Amanda balanced the tray in one hand and rapped on Captain Stoakes's door with her knuckles. When no answer came, she pushed the door open and peeked in.

"Your breakfast, Captain," she said to the empty room, before setting the tray on the desk.

The overwhelming desire to see him kept her from leaving. Maybe if she waited around a bit, he might return. She folded his bedding and laid it at the end of the hammock. Brushing off the velvet coat that lay slung across the back of the chair, she hung it in his wardrobe. Then she picked up his chipped ceramic stein and peered in, appalled at what looked like months of coffee stains. He could at least let her wash it for him. She tucked it in the pocket of her apron.

She busied herself stacking his papers in neat piles on his desk, picking up those that had dropped to the floor. Most of the papers were charts showing the outlines of various ports along the American coastline, but another showed the coast of England surrounding Portsmouth. There were even charts of the French coast. One in particular showed very detailed if somewhat aged looking sketches of the inlets and harbors around the area of held various missives from contacts whose names she had never heard of, sharing their opinions on the progress of the war. Most were dire predictions, but a few held out hope the King of France would send aid soon. Although the allusions to funds were veiled, it seemed the French were already supplying money. Now these men wanted ships.

Guilt gnawing at her, she perused the letters. She wasn't truly prying. She couldn't help it if she happened to see some of the words while tidying his desk.

...countryside northwest of Baltimore...

Her hand stilled over the scripted words that jutted from beneath a weighty pile of less interesting correspondence.

Her farm was less than half a day's ride northwest of Baltimore. Had the captain been inquiring on her behalf?

She pulled the letter from beneath the pile. The writer noted there had been no reports of violence from that area. The farmers had been particularly hard hit by the needs of the armies, but most still managed to survive. A man suspected of being a Tory sympathizer had been ill-treated in the local village, but he fled before the villagers could do any real damage. They satisfied themselves by burning his home to its foundation.

Amanda skimmed the next few paragraphs, then turned the page over and read through to the end, hoping the writer might give the name of the village. Why would the captain's correspondent bother giving such a thorough report of a sparsely populated area? It held nothing more than a collection of farming villages nestled in the rolling hills. Could it have been mere coincidence that her farm lay not far outside one of those villages? Or had the captain been looking into the feasibility of returning her to her home? Hand trembling, she flipped the letter over, looking for a date.

July 1st, less than two weeks ago. That meant the letter had probably been delivered sometime during the last couple of days. Of course, despite its recent date, that didn't mean the request from the captain had been recent, nor that he had made the request at all. The letter writer might simply have been giving a report on the area he had most recently passed through. Even if responding to a special request from the captain, it might have been one made months ago, before he had deemed her *indispensable*.

Determined not to jump to any conclusions until she had a private word with the captain, Amanda returned to the galley. When she came back an hour or so later to pick up his dishes, his plates were empty, but the man had disappeared again. Was he avoiding her?

Amanda piled his plates on the tray and carried them back to the galley. After drying the last of the dishes, she spent the rest of the morning in her half of the doctor's quarters, lying in her hammock and pondering the letter. She tried to close her eyes and get some sleep before she needed to start dinner, but images of her farm looking forlorn and abandoned in the morning mist alternated with visions of the captain washing at the basin, his bronze skin and golden eyes glistening in the lamp light.

Giving up on the idea of a nap, she went above deck hoping to get a breath of fresh air to help clear her head.

She found Captain Stoakes on deck, inspecting the guns. She smiled in greeting when he glanced her way, but he simply looked her over with an assessing gaze that spoke of a man trying to come to a decision. Amanda walked to the bulwark, determined not to let his presence prevent her enjoyment of the ocean breeze on her flushed cheeks. If he remained on his end of the ship and she on hers, he could avoid her all he liked.

Buck joined her at the bulwark. "Good morning, Adam."

"Good morning, sir," She eyed the dark smudges

beneath his eyes and the pallid look to his skin.

While she had slept soundly in the captain's hammock, Buck had undoubtedly had an eventful night trying to keep the determined Miss Bowersley contained in her temporary quarters.

"You don't sound yourself this morning. Everything all right?" His own voice lacked its usual jovial brightness.

"Yes, nothing to worry about," Amanda reassured him with a smile. "I'm just weary from last night."

"Last night? What happened last night that has you so weary?" Buck made a tired effort at a grin.

Amanda turned to study him. If he weren't such a gentleman, she might think Buck had implied something happened between her and the captain. She gave him a reprimanding scowl, but couldn't stop a smile from erupting in its place.

"You know I'm talking about Miss Bowersley. Speaking of the little vixen, where is she this morning?" Amanda turned her back to the bulwark and rested her elbows on top. She surveyed the deck. "I expected to find her clinging to the captain, but she is nowhere to be seen. Did you actually manage to keep her confined to quarters?"

"I did." Buck sounded pleased with himself. "I also managed to get her bundled off with the prize crew at the crack of dawn. She's headed to North Carolina so she can vex her rich uncle with talk of handsome men in English uniforms. That is, until he manages to find some poor sap willing to marry her."

Amanda turned back to the sea with a sigh. "I'm sure looks and money go a long way. She will probably be married by her next birthday."

"Mmmm," Buck murmured, watching her face.

Amanda ignored his speculative gaze. He did not need to know that her own birthday lurked just around the corner. She pushed the thought away and closed her eyes. She would enjoy the cool morning breeze and the warm sun on her face and leave the melancholy notions for another time.

She wouldn't mind if Buck decided to leave her in peace. She would love to talk with him, unload her burdens on someone who understood the captain better than anyone, but how could she when he knew only half of the story? She stayed silent, eyes closed for several minutes, expecting to hear Buck's retreating footsteps at any moment.

Buck didn't take the hint. Even with her eyes closed, she could feel his gaze linger on her face. Somehow, he seemed to know she wanted to talk, *needed* to talk.

Amanda opened her eyes and stared out at the sea. The mid-morning sun glittered on the gentle swells as though the waves were crested with diamonds. Before she had gone to sea, her image of the vast expanse had been limited. She would have described it as a big body of water that lapped against the land. Now, she appreciated the thousand faces the ocean could wear, from the sublimely beautiful to the ferocious and terrifying.

The *Amanda* had been sailing south, presumably to get Miss Bowersley closer to her destination. Now, looking out at the sea from the starboard side of the vessel, the sun crept slowly toward its zenith.

"Where are we headed now, Buck?"

She didn't really care, but if he wanted to talk it

seemed a safe subject.

"Home," Buck said, with an almost nostalgic look on his face.

"Home? Where is home for you?"

She knew Buck had to come from somewhere, but he seemed to have been bred for the sea. She didn't think home could be anywhere but a ship for him.

"Baltimore."

The deck rolled under her feet.

Baltimore? The mere mention brought to mind the letter and its report of the countryside to the northwest, an area inconsequential to the captain, but home to Amanda.

He is indispensable to me. The captain's words replayed in her head. Had that been no more than a diversion intended to thwart Miss Bowersley?

Buck turned to her and his smile dissolved. "Adam, are you all right?"

The ship heaved again, and Amanda grasped the bulwark. "Yes, as I said before, I'm just tired from last night."

Buck just managed to catch her in his arms before the world went dark.

Chapter Twenty

Dawn of the next day saw the *Amanda* docked in the Port of Baltimore. The scent of rotting refuse and the cloying odor of dead fish brought Amanda to her senses almost as if someone had waved smelling salts beneath her nose. Lying still in her hammock, she listened to the familiar shouts of street vendors and sailors fighting to make themselves heard over the cries of the gulls scrapping over bits of dead fish and other flotsam that rode the waves and washed up on the docks. She had forgotten how noisy and smelly Baltimore could be. She turned on her side, drew her woolen blanket over her head, and willed it all to go away.

Pleading ill, she had managed to convince Cookie to take over her duties for the rest of the day. If Captain Stoakes intended to be rid of her, he would have to reacquaint himself with the Irishman's cooking sooner or later anyway.

Cookie had worn a worried frown and rung his apron between his hands, but didn't protest. She supposed it helped that Buck had carried her below and laid her in her hammock. She had regained consciousness to find herself nestled in his strong arms while he navigated the steep steps. Cookie hovered over her like a mother hen, clucking his tongue and offering her food which Amanda did her best to decline without hurting his feelings.

The doctor checked on her once, measuring her pulse and feeling her forehead with the back of his hand. He pronounced her to be suffering from simple dehydration. Rest and water would be all she needed to get back on her feet.

Even Buck and Bull had come late in the afternoon to assure themselves she was well despite remaining abed through the day. She had tried to rise, but both of them insisted she should get as much rest as possible.

Neil visited last. His worried frown told her how much he cared, even if her little brother couldn't admit it aloud. When she assured him she was feeling better, he said he would relay the good news to the rest of the crew. After all, they were worried about her.

All day she had lain in bed, restless and wondering if the next knock at the door would be his. The captain never came.

Amanda threw back her blanket. She had had enough. A new day had dawned, and they were in Baltimore. If he didn't have the courage to face her, to tell her of his plans directly, she would go to him.

****

"He's not there." Neil said when she knocked on the captain's door some time later to bring him his breakfast. "He's gone ashore with his friend, Captain Stoddard."

"Captain Stoddard?" Amanda asked, trying to remember where she had heard the name.

"Yes, that's the captain who transported us back to the *Amanda* after we auctioned our prize in Boston."

"Oh, I remember." Amanda pressed her lips together.

She remembered all too well. Captain Stoddard had put her little brother's life in jeopardy by taking on a 64-gun frigate.

Women don't belong on ships. The captain's oft-repeated words echoed in her brain, and her stomach plunged to her feet. Had Captain Stoakes gone ashore to make arrangements to put her off the ship? Perhaps this Captain Stoddard was necessary in some way to his plan. Or, as a fellow captain, he might be sympathetic to the dangers of having a woman on a ship and have offered his assistance.

Her shiver rattled the contents of the tray.

"Did they say what they were about?" She tried to hide the small tremor in her voice.

"No." The corner of Neil's lips twitched just before he turned to go.

She scowled at him as he climbed the stairs to the upper deck. Why did her little brother have to be so happy about getting rid of her? Had she been that overbearing?

More than likely, Neil had adopted some of the captain's notions about women on ships. They had spent enough time together these past few weeks.

Amanda took the captain's uneaten breakfast back to the galley, then returned to her hammock and lay staring at the ceiling for the next hour, trying to decide whether she should be more angry or sad. Amanda's emotions were like a storm cloud, each one rolling over the other until only a jumbled mass remained.

Neil popped his head through the open door.

"Captain wants to see you in his quarters." He waggled an eyebrow at her.

Amanda sat up in her hammock, her heart

hammering against her breastbone.

"His quarters?" She tried to swallow but found it difficult.

So this was it? The time had come for her to leave the *Amanda* and the life she loved behind.

Neil came and sat by her, a mix of sympathy and impatience on his face.

"Mandy, he cares for you, you know," Neil paused and squeezed her forearm. "You should trust him and let someone take care of you for once."

Amanda clasped her hands in her lap and looked down at them. "Neil, what can you possibly know of this?"

"I know the way he looks at you. The way he's always looked at you, even before he thought he should." Neil chuckled. "Imagine his relief when he found out you were a girl."

"Relief?" Amanda squeaked. "You saw how angry he was when he found out. He glowered at me for days. He still does."

Neil shook his head. "I don't think it's anger in his eyes."

Amanda nudged him with her elbow. "Oh, what do you know? You're only thirteen." She sighed. "And I'm only a woman."

"I'm pretty sure he's aware of that." Neil nudged her back, his grin suggesting he knew more than any thirteen year old should.

Amanda couldn't help but laugh. "You know what I mean." She gazed into his brown eyes and hesitated. "I will miss you."

"You're not going to start crying on me, are you?" He arched a dark eyebrow at her in a way that reminded her so much of the captain.

They really were two peas in a pod. Knowing he would look after her younger brother made her fate easier to accept, at least at some level.

Amanda swallowed her tears, then set her hand on her brother's shoulder and gave him a quick peck on the cheek.

"I love you, Neil." She tousled his hair as if he were eleven again.

Instead of pulling back or complaining, he gave her his best eleven-year-old grin, his mop of brown hair sticking out in all directions.

Amanda stood and brushed her hands against the front of her breeches, trying in vain to smooth the many wrinkles. With a dignified tug at her stained cotton shirt, she strode out the door, her back straight and shoulders squared.

"Now, that's the sister I know," Neil said as he watched her go.

When she arrived at the captain's quarters, she found the door ajar, but she knocked anyway.

"Hello?" She pushed the door open just enough to stick her head through, expecting to see him engrossed in work at his desk.

His quarters appeared empty. She stepped inside to be sure.

Had she misunderstood Neil? Maybe he had said "on deck", and her overactive imagination had supplied what she wanted to hear.

Amanda's gaze strayed to the captain's clean desk. She hadn't straightened his things, and she doubted the captain had it in him. But somehow between this morning and now, someone had come in and cleared everything so that only a small sheet of parchment remained. She picked it up with a trembling hand.

Dearest Amanda,

I have bought you a gift that I hope you will do me the honor of accepting without questioning my motives. Actually, I have two gifts for you. The first lies in a box on my hammock.

Note in hand, Amanda walked to the captain's hammock and opened a large, white box. In it lay a stylish, emerald-green satin dress, finer and more expensive than anything she had ever owned. She ran her fingertips across the soft material before returning to the note.

I had to guess at your size, but if you need alternations, ask Bull to get the sailmaker to assist.

Amanda held the tips of her fingers against her lips. The thought of turning Bull into a lady's maid was one thing, but the sailmaker into a dressmaker? The curmudgeonly old man excelled at sewing canvas, but she would not let him anywhere near the delicate fabric of her one and only dress.

The other gift is of a slightly more personal nature, and I hope you will forgive me for any impertinence or unintended offense. I know living aboard ship requires one to forego many of the luxuries ladies are accustomed to. As I recall, one of those luxuries is a hot bath—in fresh water.

A bath? Amanda hadn't taken a bath in months. She had done her best to stay clean, but she had to settle for washing at the basin in her spare moments of privacy.

The only other option was a dip in the sea, which had the effect of washing away human dirt only to leave one covered with a thin coating of salt and never giving the sense of being truly clean.

Amanda spied the tub in the corner of the room, steam rising from it.

> *Do not worry about being interrupted. I ordered Neil to find Buck after he escorted you to my quarters. They are to stand guard outside the door while you have this time to yourself. I will not see you until this evening.*
>
> *Yours always,*
> *Will*

Amanda tiptoed to the door and peeked out. From his station outside the door, Neil waggled his fingers at her, delight shining in his eyes. From the other side, Buck stared straight ahead. His lips were set in a straight line, a heroic effort on his part to not show his delight but one that didn't extend to the dimple in his cheek.

Amanda shut the door again and read the rest of the note.

> *P.S. Now that I have hopefully impressed you with my gallantry, I have a favor to ask. My good friend, Captain Stoddard, and his officers will be joining us for supper. I would like you to join us as my guest, but I'm afraid I also need your help in making sure Cookie doesn't kill us all. It would reflect badly on me if one of the Continental Navy's finest officers should die aboard my ship.*

Amanda stared at the paper in her hand, completely

befuddled. She thought he had been ashore making arrangements to return her to her farm. She fingered the cool satin. Instead, he had been buying her a dress.

She scanned the letter again. That didn't mean he hadn't also found time to make arrangements for her departure, but the letter said nothing about it. Only that he wanted her to prepare supper for an old friend of his and to join them.

Surely he intended her to wear the dress. Why else would he have purchased it? That meant he wanted her, Amanda, to join them, not Adam. But why now?

Amanda read through the letter again, searching for clues to his intent.

If she wore a gown, the entire ship would know her secret, and there could be no predicting how they might react. Did this gift signal her imminent departure from the *Amanda*? Perhaps he just required her services one last time before he sent her on his way. If so, he might see no harm in letting his men know who she really was. Perhaps the knowledge would even aid him in his effort to rid himself of her. If some of the crew really saw a woman as bad luck, they'd insist she be removed.

She stared at the letter, her hand shaking so badly she could barely read.

He had signed his name Will and not the more formal Captain Stoakes. Would he bother to give her his Christian name if he intended to leave her ashore and never see her again?

Eyeing the tub, she puzzled over the meaning of his signature, certain only of one thing. She would not let this gift go to waste, regardless of his intentions. She may not have Violet's charms, but she would show him she knew how to be a woman too.

Crossing her arms over her chest, she grabbed the hem of her shirt and drew it over her head. Then she peeled away the bindings around her chest, reveling in the brush of cool air against chafed skin. Shucking her breeches, she tossed them into the pile with the other clothes and stepped into the tub.

While she soaked, Amanda took her time contemplating a dinner menu that would do their ship and its captain credit. Unfortunately, her thoughts wouldn't stay focused on the topic of food.

Will. His name is Will, she thought, sinking deeper into the water until it lapped against her upper lip. Did it stand for William perhaps? He might look like a William, she supposed, but his dark hair and golden eyes spoke of a more exotic heritage. Wilhelm perhaps? She laughed, blowing bubbles in the water. Definitely not Germanic. Willard? No, that wasn't right either. In the end, she decided he must be Captain William Stoakes. A very handsome name for a very handsome man. She sunk deeper into the water, a thrill rippling through her at the intimacy of knowing his full name.

By the time Amanda had washed her hair and risen from the tub, the skin on her fingers puckered, and the water had turned cold, but at least the red welts from her bindings had faded. She would have been happy to stay immersed for another hour or two, even with cold water, but she had a supper party to arrange.

She thought about donning her usual attire so she wouldn't soil her new gown while she cooked, but she couldn't bear the thought of putting on the old, grimy, very unfeminine garments after she had just bathed with lavender soap. She would wear Cookie's apron over her dress and instruct him through most of the preparations from the other side of the galley.

She pulled the green silk from the box, delighted to find the captain had not only purchased a gown, but also the many accouterments to go along with it, including a lady's shift, petticoats, stays, stockings, garters and silk slippers.

She ran her hand across the creamy surface of the satin petticoat, a lighter shade of green than the moss green of the over gown. Then she held the delicate shift up to inspect it in the late afternoon light streaming in through the small windows. Judging from the fineness of the weave, he had spared no expense on her undergarments. Did he really know that much about women's clothing or had some saleswoman taken pity on him? A giggle burst from her lips at the image of the formidable Captain Stoakes selecting a lady's undergarments himself.

She took her time dressing, relishing the cool caress of satin against skin. Then she did her best to brush out her damp curls and arrange them about her face. Her hair wasn't long enough to pile on top of her head even if she had the hairpins with which to do it. Instead, she managed to arrange it in a credibly feminine fashion by plumping them, tucking a few behind her ears, and then pulling out a few strands to curl against her neck and forehead.

Appraising herself in the captain's mirror, she decided it would do. With her short hair about her face, she looked young, very young. However, in the form fitting green dress with its low bodice showing her modest figure to its best advantage, no one would ever mistake her for a boy. The swell of her breasts above the low cut neckline made her feel positively exposed.

The captain's cabin lay not far from the galley. She simply needed to cross the common area. She peeked out the window at the sun melting into the western horizon. The men would already have eaten their mid-day meal and most would be on deck either on duty or idling before the changing of the watch.

If luck stayed with her, she could make it across the common area and into the galley without anyone seeing her. Cookie might be in for a surprise when she raced into his galley, but that couldn't be helped.

Amanda bit her lip and cracked open the door of the captain's quarters. She peered out only to meet Buck's appreciative gaze. She slammed the door shut.

Damn! She had forgotten he and Neil had been ordered to stand guard. She tugged at her neckline, then to assure herself that nothing showed, she ran her fingertips along the lace that skimmed the sensitive skin only an inch or so above her nipples.

They could tease her all they wanted, but she wouldn't give them the satisfaction of seeing her for long. Throwing open the door, she hitched up her skirts and broke into a dead run, heading for the safety of the galley on the far side of the ship.

Chapter Twenty-One

The supper party guests voiced their appreciation when Cookie brought out one elaborate dish after another: leek soup, stuffed partridge, glazed ham, roast squash, fresh greens in a savory cream sauce, and biscuits as light as a cloud, all complemented by the finest wines Will had to offer from his personal stores.

Will, however, tasted little of it, his mind dwelling on the empty seat next to him. Every time the door swung open, he turned his head, expecting to see Amanda. The delightful aromas were always followed by Cookie, balancing steaming hot dishes above his protruding belly. He set each one down, and with an apologetic glance at his captain, served the guests.

His patience nearing the breaking point, Will grabbed Cookie's arm before he could head back to the galley.

"Where is she?" he hissed in the cook's ear.

"In the galley," Cookie whispered back, although his whisper could be heard around the table.

"Can't you do more of the cooking tonight?"

"Yes, sir. I keep telling her she's your guest. She should come and join you." Cookie shrugged. "But she just keeps thinking of something else that needs doin'. If you was to ask me, I think she's not wantin' to come out."

"Not wanting to come out?" Will kept his voice

low while he glanced around at his guests. They appeared engrossed in Captain Stoddard's tale from his naval days when he and Will had sailed together. "Did she happen to say why?"

"Well, beggin' your pardon for saying so, sir," Cookie spoke as though he were considering how best to break a bit of bad news, "but if I was to offer a guess, I'd say she's not happy 'bout being a girl."

"Not happy about being a girl?"

"Well not so much being a girl as being dressed like one," Cookie amended. "She's got that pretty gown on her, but she's all wrapped up from neck to knee in my biggest apron. And as I was saying, she keeps thinking of something else that needs doin'. Every time I suggest she take off the apron and take her seat next to you, her eyes get big as my sauce pan, and she starts stammering about not being finished with this and that."

Will excused Cookie so he could return to the galley, and for the next five minutes he chased a piece of roast squash around his plate with his fork, only half listening to the stories of his misspent youth being told by Captain Stoddard.

"Will, you seem lost in your thoughts tonight," James said, before taking a sip of wine. "Is something troubling you?"

Will looked up from his plate. "No, it's nothing."

"Or perhaps it is *someone*?" James added with a knowing grin.

"What could you mean by that?" Will stabbed his fork into the bit of squash.

"Well, it's just that young Bradley here," he nodded to the young officer next to him, "saw you in town today."

"Did he?" Will glowered at the young man who didn't look too pleased to be the center of attention. If his memory served, this same officer had overstepped his bounds at James' nuptial celebrations.

"Yes," James continued, nonplussed by his old friend's fierce look and offering no mercy to the junior officer at his side trying his best to sink into his chair, and if possible, the deck below. "And at a lady's shop no less. Buying undergarments, I believe it was."

He turned to the officer whose cheeks were almost the same shade as his wine. "Wasn't that it, Lieutenant Bradley?"

"I could have been mistaken," the lieutenant mumbled.

"Is it possible, though, that our perpetual bachelor has at last found a woman who is up to his standards?" James asked with a gleam in his eye,

Will stuck the piece of squash in his mouth and chewed with deliberate slowness.

James raised an eyebrow, took a sip of wine, then took mercy on Will by changing the subject. "Supper was delicious, Will."

"Here, here!" The other officers at the table raised their glasses.

"Was the man you spoke to a moment ago responsible for this culinary artistry?" James asked. "If I'm not mistaken, I detected a bit of Irish accent in the very few words he spoke. If so, he is a rare gem indeed. To find an Irishman who can cook like this."

Dammit. Amanda had done more than enough to honor his guests with an elaborate supper, but her absence left him in danger of being an unforgivably dull host.

"No, he is not the one." Will set his fork across his plate.

"Then pray tell, who is behind this exquisite meal? Bring him out here so I may thank him personally, and perhaps even steal him from you. I am not in need of a cook, but I'd be happy to make room for this one."

Will gritted his teeth at the challenge. He wouldn't put it past James to try to steal his cook. They had played this kind of gamesmanship since they were boys, and his friend excelled at it. This time, James would not win. Amanda belonged to him.

"Cookie!" Will's bellow rattled the china.

Cookie came through the door a moment later and stopped just inside. "You'd be wantin' somethin', sir?"

Damn right, he wanted something. "Bring Amanda out here, and tell her it's an order."

"Yes, sir!" Cookie said, with a grin.

"Amanda, eh?" James' chuckle made it clear he appreciated the irony of the name. Many captains named ships after their wives.

Not amused, Will glowered at him. Then a soft rustle of satin caught his attention and he stood, prepared to order Amanda to take her seat. That is, until his power of speech abandoned him.

Amanda had taken off the big apron worn to protect her gown, or as Cookie suspected, to protect herself. Now she stood clad in emerald-green satin the same color as her eyes.

Soft golden curls framed her face, flushed from the heat of the kitchen. Her skin gleamed from her time in the bath and her long, creamy neck invited a man to follow a trail down past her shoulders to the low cut bodice of her gown. Too low cut, Will thought. No wonder she had not wanted to take off the apron and join them. She should have had the sailmaker make a few alterations, as he had suggested. Then he imagined her with a canvas neck scarf tied over her gown and shuddered.

"Well, who is this vision, Will?" James asked, rising to his feet along with his men.

"Amanda," Will whispered. He stared at her for a moment more before catching himself and giving a proper introduction. "Gentleman, may I present Amanda Blakely. I have given her passage on my ship, and in return, she has been gracious enough to give my cook a few pointers."

The explanation bordered on the absurd, but James was too well-mannered to goad him in the presence of a lady. He satisfied himself with flicking an eyebrow at Will before focusing all his attention on Amanda.

"I am at your service, ma'am," he bowed, "and in your debt. Never have I eaten so well."

"Thank you, Captain," Amanda replied, her voice a gentle whisper.

Like the song of a Siren, calling him to the rocks, Will decided.

"Can she join us, Will?" James asked.

Will realized he had left her standing at his side, her back straight and her eyes level while he had been gazing down at her, his jaw agape.

"Yes, of course." He pulled out the chair next to him so Amanda could, at last, take her seat.

She glided to her chair, the soft scent of lavender and woman and the rustling of her skirt washed over him. Once settled, he poured her a glass of wine, nearly spilling it from lack of attention.

****

Amanda took a tentative sip of the ruby colored liquid. She had tasted wine as a child. Some of the neighbors made their own, and her father often purchased several bottles of it. For as long as she could remember, he had allowed her a small taste with dinner. But this delightful, mellow liquid tasted nothing like the powerful local wines. They left her lips numb and the inside of her cheeks feeling as though she had sucked on a dry cloth.

Amanda ventured another small sip. The heady aroma filled her nose, and she breathed it in as she drank, discovering the sense of smell combined with the sense of taste greatly enhanced the experience. The wine had none of the unpleasant jolt that came with rum. Of course, she had personally carried this bottle from the captain's private stores. Given its position on the top shelf of the rack, she guessed it cost more than any two barrels of rum put together. She would savor this experience, for it may never come again.

For the next hour, Captain Stoddard and his officers regaled Amanda with tales of Captain Stoakes' exploits. The stories told of his bravery, but also of his honor and love of his newly formed country. In his youth, he apparently possessed a love for mischief rivaling Neil's. No wonder he knew just how to guide her brother. He simply considered what trouble he would have caused and ensured Neil didn't have the opportunity.

The captain signaled for Cookie to set a plate of food before Amanda. She smiled her gratitude, but didn't pick up the fork.

She had nibbled a little in the kitchen to ensure the results of her efforts met with her satisfaction, but not enough to satisfy her normally healthy appetite. She had every intention of sitting down to her own supper in the galley once she finished seeing to the needs of his guests. Then Cookie had come, telling her the captain wanted to see her at once. When she brushed past him, concerned the captain might have found fault with one of the dishes, Cookie had snagged the bow of her apron, untied it and pulled it off in one swift gesture. Holding it over her head, he refused to give it back no matter what threats she leveled at him.

Her appetite had vanished the moment she entered the dining room and spotted the captain dressed in a velvet coat the color of midnight. Edged with a golden thread that matched his waistcoat, it made his eyes glow with an amber light.

Instead of eating, Amanda sipped her wine, drinking in every detail of Captain Stoddard's tales, each one adding a new dimension to the man she already admired and perhaps, if she were to be honest with herself, even loved. She chanced a glance at him and found him studying her with his golden eyes. A sip of wine caught in her throat, and she found it hard to swallow. She could not lose her heart to the captain, not when this might be the last time she ever saw him gazing at her with such ferocity.

In between stories, Captain Stoddard and his men toasted to everything. First to honor, then to country, at least once more to her cooking and several times to her beauty. She felt the heat rise in the room every time she took a sip of wine. She attributed it to having spent hours in front of the stove in a windowless galley and the embarrassment at having the full attention of a group of handsome young officers, but just to be safe, she decided to take smaller sips. She would still drink to their toasts, of course. To do otherwise would be rude, and someone kept filling her glass so she really had no choice.

"Cookie," Captain Stoddard called out. "Would you be so good as to open one of the bottles I brought over from the *Venture*?"

Cookie nodded and came back moments later carrying a fresh bottle. He showed it to Captain Stoddard who simply nodded, then he uncorked it and set it next to the captain.

"This one," Captain Stoddard said, pouring wine into Amanda's glass, "is a very special wine that I acquired from a very special Frenchman whilst we were still enemies. It's a, it's a..." He squinted at the label on the bottle. "Well, it's French anyway."

Amanda giggled and took a sip, reveling in the new taste. Even headier than the last, she delighted in the way the tingling on her lips took on a new dimension, and the wine hit her tongue in new places. She savored the beverage in her mouth before swallowing. It was almost as good as kissing.

Amanda quickly put her hand over her mouth when another giggle threatened. She glanced at Captain Stoddard and his officers to see if they had noticed, but they were in the midst of an argument over whether the French could be counted on to help the Americans shake off Britain's tyranny.

Captain Stoddard hadn't noticed, but someone else did.

"Don't you think you've had enough, my love?"

Captain Stoakes whispered, his breath caressing her ear and sending tingles shooting down her arm to the tips of her fingers.

Had he just called her *my love*? She hadn't really been paying attention, so perhaps she had misheard. She raised her gaze to his.

"Perhaps you might want to slow down a bit."

Amanda tried to focus on the words as they formed on his lips. They were such delicious looking lips. His upper lip was well formed, but not at all feminine. And his lower lip was so pleasingly full that she felt an overwhelming urge to nibble on it. To the sides of his mouth, he had creases that grew deeper when he smiled. They weren't visible now though.

She wondered what it would be like to trail little kisses over those lines. She had never kissed a man's face before. She remembered the sharp prick of his whiskers against her fingertips. What would they feel like against her mouth? Her tongue? She licked her lips, tasting the slightly sweet remnants of wine, and imagined the feel of his whiskers as she nibbled on his angled jaw.

"But it is the Spaniards that have the best songs!" Lieutenant Bradley's enthusiastic declaration drew her attention away from Will's face.

"Songs?" Amanda clasped her hands together. "It has been so long since I have heard any. Will you sing one for me?"

****

Good God, what was that? Now that Amanda no longer threatened his self-control by staring at his mouth as though ravenous, he could think.

She giggled when the young lieutenant suggested a

song whose title should have made her blush.

He recalled Bull saying she couldn't hold her rum. He thought that had just been a story his officers had made up to defend her and hadn't given it much thought when he had poured her that first glass of wine. Now into her third glass, her merry laughter and the openly sensual look she had just given him, suggested she had the same trouble with wine.

He had about come undone when her little tongue flicked out to moisten her lips while she stared hungrily at his. And people compared him to a predator? If they could have seen the look in her eye a moment ago, they might have thought twice about whom they called a wolf.

Of course, he might have devoured her if his guests hadn't still been there. For a fleeting moment, he considered sending Captain Stoddard and his lieutenants back to their ship so he could haul her back to his cabin and make love to her.

Then the sprinkling of freckles across her delightful little nose caught his eye, and he remembered himself. Until he could propose a new arrangement, she still served under his command, and he would not take advantage of his position.

Amanda leaned forward and the bodice she couldn't quite fill gapped slightly. Will's body hardened when he caught a glimpse of one rosy tipped breast. It would be best if he sent her back to the quarters she shared with the doctor before he discovered just how far his honor extended.

He watched the three young naval officers serenade a sparkling-eyed Amanda and found he didn't have the heart to end her evening prematurely. She was not to blame for the passions she provoked in him.

Will nudged his nearly full glass of wine away. He hadn't drank much of his wine and alcohol never had much effect on him anyway. Nevertheless, it would be best to keep all his wits about him tonight.

He glanced up when James encouraged Amanda to join in him a song. He taught her the words, and her sultry female voice accompanied the deeper male voices in a harmonious combination. Although not a particularly bawdy song as sailor's tunes went, Amanda's husky tones made it sound suggestive, and Will fought another painful wave of desire.

After the song ended, Lieutenant Bradley took another turn to show off his talents, selecting a ballad that he proceeded to sing while gazing directly into Amanda's eyes. Amanda looked down at her hands, her face flushed, when Bradley began to sing about unrequited love in his surprisingly clear, tenor voice. When he grasped her hand, Will pushed away from the table, the discordant scraping of his chair against the wooden planks turning all eyes to him.

"The night has grown late, and I suggest it is time to retire," he said, ignoring James's knowing grin.

Chapter Twenty-Two

The crew rowed Captain Stoddard and his men back to the *Venture*. Will watched until the dark night swallowed the small boat.

Gazing up at the moon slung low in the sky, he gave a harsh laugh. Poor James's men must think him an insufferable boor. They had dined with him twice, and on both occasions, he had been an irascible dinner companion.

The first time, it had been because of his eagerness to get back to the *Amanda*. His ship represented more than a home, more than his livelihood. For a man like him, being ashore was akin to being cast adrift.

This time, however, it had been a different Amanda—one with green eyes that drew him in until he thought he might drown in their depths. Now that he had acknowledged his feelings for her, they had free rein on his senses, bringing him to dizzying heights then dropping him into the depths of despair. Having her near him was like trying to ride out a hurricane.

But if being near her was this painful, what would it be like after she returned home? In the midst of a hurricane, hope still thrived. Only when it passed could one really see the full extent of the devastation.

A star shot across the sky, vanishing when it reached the hazy horizon where inky black faded to charcoal gray. Will blew out a breath. Unlike his ship, the flesh and blood woman was not his to command. He could not order her to love him, any more than Odysseus could tame a siren.

Will laughed at the stars. Perhaps, if he had his men tie him to his own main mast, he could ride out this obsession.

Speaking of his personal siren, he needed to check on her and make sure she found her way back to her own hammock. He headed for the hatch.

His decision to allow her to stop hiding herself beneath a tattered tunic and canvas trousers had seemed like a good one at the time. Trying to keep her secret from his crew had been driving him insane, and it seemed only a matter of time before the rest of them discovered it anyway. Cookie hadn't appeared too surprised, which led him to wonder if others had discovered what he had.

His gaze slid over hammocks filled with snoring sailors. It would all be a moot point soon.

He had toyed with the idea of keeping Amanda aboard ship, turning it, twisting it, and looking for a solution from every angle. He might not be able to keep her secret, but he could instruct Buck to assign guard duties to men he trusted. He, on the other hand, would have to be conveniently absent or occupied—or tied to the mast—whenever she brought his meals to his quarters.

Then he remembered the way she looked at dinner, a sea nymph in green satin. Even in a dress borrowed from the fishmonger's wife, Amanda would be a distraction for any man. He had to let her go.

He squinted into the darkness, acknowledging the real reason he searched for Amanda. More than ensuring she made it to her hammock safely, he wanted to see her one last time.

In the morning, he would have a boat row her ashore. Buck would escort her to ensure she hired a reputable coach to take her back to the farm. He might even delay his departure so Buck could accompany her the entire way and make sure the British hadn't burned her home to the ground. Even if they had, Buck could see her situated in town with access to her considerable funds.

"Oh, hello, Captain!" Amanda's melodic voice came from somewhere on the other side of the darkness. Like a siren calling him to the rocks. "I'm afraid this ship has grown somewhat, and I seem to have misplaced my hammock. Would you be a dear and help me find it?"

"Would you keep it down?" Will growled, weaving his way between the remaining hammocks toward the sound of her voice.

He didn't need the men to wake and find Amanda dressed like a woman and tipsy to boot.

Groping for her in the dark, his fingers found her delicate wrist, and he pulled her against his chest. His frown deepened when he gazed into her flushed face and heavily lidded eyes.

"The doctor's quarters are at the other end of the ship," he said in a harsh whisper.

"Oh," Amanda's eyes grew round, and she glanced about. "I must have gotten turned around."

Will frowned. From now on, she had a one-glass limit. But it was too late to do anything about it tonight. He could not leave her, alone and unguarded, in this condition.

Dr. Miller had left with the men of the *Venture* to discuss medicine with Stoddard's surgeon, an old friend of his. Last time they caught up with Stoddard's ship, the doctor had lost track of time while discussing his latest experiments with his friend, and Will did not see his ship's surgeon until late the next day. Without the doctor to look after her, Amanda would be on her own.

He couldn't have her stumbling about in the middle of the night, in that gown, with the slight swell of her breasts peeking out above the neckline. He knew all too well the temptation she presented.

He cursed the saleswoman who had assumed he bought the gown for his wife or a mistress. She had assured him the design was just the thing for his ladylove. Of course, he couldn't blame her for making the wrong assumption. No man bought a gown and undergarments for a woman he wasn't bedding. No man except him. He tightened his grip on her arm and pushed her ahead of him into his quarters.

Amanda didn't comment on their destination. Without waiting for him to leave, she reached for the buttons along the back of her gown, chattering on about the evening. She released the top two buttons then struggled with a third until Will took pity on her feeble attempts to undress herself. When he started undoing the row of tiny pearl buttons trailing down her back, she stopped trying to do anything herself and let him do all the work while she prattled on.

He slipped the gown from her shoulders, past her waist, and over her hips, satin whispering against satin. Gritting his teeth against a tug of desire, he helped her step out of it. Then he unlaced her stays and untied her petticoats, letting them fall to the floor at her feet. If privateering no longer paid, he thought humorlessly, he had a future as a lady's maid.

"Your friend, Captain Stoddard, is a very handsome man, isn't he?" Amanda stood before him wearing only her stockings and a gossamer shift.

"I wouldn't know." Will muttered.

The soft, flowing shift brushed her small curves, taunting his self-control. Beneath the thin fabric, twin, pink nipples jutted out, inviting him closer, drawing him in, unraveling his resolve. He cursed the saleswoman again for doing her job all too well. His siren needed no assistance.

Amanda seemed to have no intent of finishing the job of undressing herself, and he considered abandoning her in her shift and stockings while he sought refuge in her hammock in the doctor's quarters. Then he reminded himself that he needed to watch over her. Having her wander the ship in a nearly transparent shift would be worse than the emerald gown. Locking her in his quarters had proved ineffective once, and he wasn't about to chance it again.

Wrapping his hands around her waist, he picked her up and plunked her down on the edge of his desk.

"I understand he is recently married." Amanda set her hand on Will's shoulder to steady herself.

The breathy way she spoke about his friend had Will gritting his teeth once more. Then Amanda leaned in, bringing one pink nipple almost to the edge of his nose, and he thought he might grind them to stubs.

She didn't even pause for a breath when he pushed her shift up to her knees and rolled a stocking down her calf, past her ankle, and off her foot. He reached under her shift to remove her other stocking. The heat from her thighs washing over his fingers, he probed for the garter holding her stocking in place. His gaze locked on her face, he tugged at the bow, pulled off the strip of satin and tossed it aside.

Through her wine-fogged brain, she must have sensed his gaze on her face. Her chattering stopped mid-sentence, and her green eyes focused on his. Her small pink tongue made a brief sweep of her upper lip, leaving it moist and glistening in the candlelight.

Will groaned and scooped her off the desk and into his arms. Without a word of protest, she entwined her arms around his neck and nuzzled his ear. He carried her to his hammock and set her down on his bedding. He stared at her, his resolve flowing from him like molten glass, melted by the heat of her expression.

"What am I going to do with you, my little siren?" He sat on the edge of the hammock and rested a hand on her thigh.

He stroked the fabric with his thumb, the warmth rising from her flesh making him all too aware that only a thin layer of cotton separated skin from skin.

Amanda answered for him. Propping herself up with one arm behind her, she moved her hand to the back of his neck and pulled him to her. Her green eyes shone with the same determination he had seen on that first day.

Will struggled against the storm of desire that raged within him. When her soft lips settled on his, and her mouth opened to allow her tongue to dart out to tease him, he nearly gave in. He wanted her, and from all indications, she wanted him too.

Had he overestimated her innocence? She nipped his lower lip, and he winced. Perhaps not.

She might be lacking in style, ignorant in the ways of making love, but she made up for it with enthusiasm. Perhaps he shouldn't be surprised. Three types of men signed on to privateers: the adventurous, the desperate and the stupid. Amanda certainly wasn't stupid, and although she had signed on to protect her brother, the way she had taken to the sea showed a love of adventure that rivaled most of his men. Perhaps she saw making love as just another new adventure.

His tongue danced with hers, the taste of wine reminding him that she had overindulged. She wouldn't be the first to drink a little too much and regret her actions in the morning. He would not take advantage of her present condition, but there could be no harm in showing her how to kiss properly, could there?

He cupped her face in his hands, deepening the kiss. She rewarded his efforts by drawing her other hand from behind her and putting it about his neck, pulling him so close he could feel the press of her breasts against his chest even through the thick fabric of his waistcoat.

Her inhibitions, had she ever had any, had been thrown to the wind. He would have smiled if his lips hadn't been otherwise occupied, for he suspected only her inexperience kept her from ravishing him.

His mouth not leaving hers, Will put his hands behind her back and gently lowered her into his hammock. With one hand next to her ear, his thumb gently stroking her cheek, he kissed her. With his other hand, he fumbled at the buttons of his waistcoat, eager to remove at least one layer of clothing separating skin from skin. He pulled back to undo the last stubborn button before tossing it to the floor.

Need shone in Amanda's shining, half-closed eyes. Her cheeks were flushed and her breathing rapid. His body ached to respond, but lingering doubt nagged at his conscience. Letting his hand trace the contours of her hip, he tried to sort duty from desire.

His duty was to protect her, both as a member of his crew and as a woman. If he made love to her, she would be his, inextricably bound to him. She was an innocent, and his sense of honor wouldn't have it otherwise. But, deep down, in the part of him that thrilled to the hunt, he knew it was more than that. Like the wolf some thought him to be, he would make her his mate. The need to possess her driving him on, he bent to kiss her again.

With one hand, he pulled her shift over her shoulder to give him greater access to her creamy skin. He nibbled at her throat, then nipped with far more care than she had shown to his swollen lower lip. He grinned when she gasped and arched against him.

His other hand settled on her rib cage just below her breast. When she didn't stiffen in response to the intimate placement, he stroked the full roundness of the underside of her breast with his thumb before moving upward to where her tightened nipple poked against the fabric.

He could make her his wife. Perhaps in time, his attraction to her would mellow into something more manageable. In the meantime, she could live in Baltimore where he could visit her often if he restricted his voyages to this side of the Atlantic.

But would she want to marry him? Her single-minded goal had been to remain on his ship as a member of his crew. What evidence had she ever given that she harbored any feelings for him? The wolf within him may be satisfied with carnal desire, but the man wanted more. If he were to force her to live ashore, she might prefer to do so as a single woman instead of being shackled to an absentee husband who had made her give up the life she loved.

Amanda gave a low throaty laugh and ran a bare foot up the back of his leg. Her shift slid to her knee, exposing a considerable amount of soft, white skin on her thigh.

He needed to lay her options before her. He would be satisfied with her choice, or at least learn to live with it in time. He would do it soon too, but for right now, his body seemed to have a mind of its own.

Fitting her breast into the palm of his hand, he grinned, glad that Amanda couldn't see his face and ask him what he found so amusing. He did not doubt her breasts would be considered unfashionably small by those with enough vulgarity to comment, but the taut globes fit the rest of her willowy frame to perfection and lacked nothing in their ability to entice him.

He kneaded her breast with his hand, then bent to nip at her, grinning to himself when Amanda gasped and reached up to entwine her fingers in his hair and hold his head to her. Encouraged by her uninhibited response, he took her nipple fully into his mouth, wetting the rough fabric and raking his tongue against her.

Will chuckled. He needed to ask her about "her intentions" before things progressed too far. The irony of the situation was not lost on him. Normally, his intentions would be the ones called into question. However, at the moment, he seemed to be the only one with a modicum of restraint. Only inexperience held Amanda back, and she made up for that with eagerness.

"What's so funny?" she asked.

"Amanda," he said in a voice muffled by the light kisses he placed around one nipple. He stroked the other one with the pad of his thumb. "Would you like to return to Baltimore?"

When she didn't immediately respond, he pulled his attention away from her breasts so he could see her expression.

"Baltimore? Do you mean to live?" she asked, her green eyes wide.

What did he see in their cloudy depths? Doubt? Fear? He could have kicked himself for the way he had started the conversation. He should have given the matter his full attention instead of assuming he could possibly think and speak clearly while in the process of making love to her.

"Yes, I could help you get set up in town somewhere."

"Set up?" Suspicion shone in her narrowed eyes.

"Yes, or at least settled. There's no need to return to the farm if you prefer not to."

"But once I am *settled*, what am I to do then?"

He grappled with the question, trying to latch on to the right answer, the one that would keep her in his life.

Independence should be among her options, if that was what she desired. He didn't want her to feel as though marrying him were the only option available to her. She had enough money to live comfortably, independent of any man.

But did she want to be? Most women yearned for a home and family. The idea of her marrying somebody else made his stomach clench, but this was her choice. She would not be forced into marrying him just because she felt she had no other options.

"Whatever you want to do," he suggested. "You could be comfortable for the rest of your life."

She grasped the sleeve of her shift and tugged it back into place. Color rose from her neckline and returned the flush to her cheeks. Her eyes were shining again, and her spine was as stiff as a ship's spar.

"You would set me up as your mistress?" she asked, her voice strained.

"No!" Will lowered his voice when he realized he had come close to shouting. "I simply meant you'd have enough money of your own. Of course, I could make sure you never wanted for anything."

This discussion had not gone at all the way he had intended, but then no discussion with Amanda ever did. She could be more unpredictable than any tempest.

She cocked an eyebrow. "You would give me money for the rest of my life, not expecting anything in return?"

"That's right." His sense of relief in her understanding mingled with disappointment because it wasn't the outcome he was looking for. "I will support you for the rest of your life unless you find a husband. In fact, I could even help you find a husband, if that is what you want."

Like hell he would. He would spend the entire time convincing her to marry him.

She grabbed his feather pillow. "You stupid, stupid man!" Amanda shouted.

"What are you...?" He stood up, hands raised to fend off the attack.

Feathery blows rained down upon his head from the only weapon she could find. Luckily, she hadn't notice the poker standing next to the small warming stove, or he would be in real trouble.

He tried to regain control of the situation and grabbed for the pillow when it came at him again. He held it tightly in one fist, but Amanda refused to relinquish the other end. She glared at him, but tears glistened in her eyes and her lower lip trembled.

Dammit, he hadn't meant to make her cry. Quite the opposite, in fact.

Perhaps he didn't understand women as much as he thought, but then, he had never met a woman like her. He had better remove himself before he made more of a mess out of it than he already had.

He dropped his end of the pillow and strode toward the door.

Will considered locking the door behind him, but it would be pointless. There would be no stopping her if she managed to locate a more damaging weapon and decided to come after him with it. Perhaps he would ask Buck to stand guard tonight—over him!

****

Amanda threw herself into the hammock and sobbed until the pillow turned into a sodden, lumpy mass with feathers squeezing out through the rents in the seams. She tossed it across the room, where it hit the wall with a dull thud and fell to the floor like an old, dead goose. Amanda choked, the sound half laugh and half sob. His pillow looked as pathetic as she felt.

She flopped on her back, letting one arm hang over the side of the hammock, her hand dangling limply from her wrist. Her sniffles subsiding, she stared at the rafters.

The wine had cleared from her head, and her skull felt like it had been stuffed with cotton. To make matters worse, she had never been so humiliated in her life, and her shame heated her skin until she felt like she was on fire.

She hadn't meant to seduce the captain, but somehow she had found herself in his quarters...in her shift...his hand on her breast. Did he think she had arranged it all? He probably thought she had meant to seduce him as a way to get him to consent to her remaining aboard the *Amanda*. Instead he had offered to make her his…his…*mistress* was the kindest word she could come up with.

Or maybe she had read too much into his offer. He had, after all, offered to find her a husband! As though she couldn't find one on her own!

Mistress or hopelessly pathetic—she couldn't decide which idea she found more insulting. She drew in her limbs and curled into a ball on her side, cradling the pain that settled in the pit of her stomach.

As a girl, Amanda had imagined marrying eventually. While she knew not everyone had the opportunity to marry for love, she had been determined to marry an honorable man. One she could respect, and one who would respect her in return. She had always imagined that love, of a sort, would follow.

Now that she had found an honorable man, one she truly loved, she had nurtured a girlish hope that he might eventually love her in return. He hadn't said so in so many words, but he had called her "my love" at supper when he whispered in her ear. She remembered the way the small endearment had warmed her to her toes, a warmth more delicious that Buck's best rum.

"But that was all it was. Just an endearment thrown about lightly, nothing more," she told the pillow lying on the other side of the room.

Perhaps his physical need for her did not match her own either. She knew his attraction to her was real, simmering beneath his controlled facade. She wasn't so naïve that she did not notice the hard length of him pressed against her belly. She had seen the heat in his eyes and felt it radiate from him. Her traitorous breasts still tingled with the memory of his kisses, and her humiliation deepened.

Despite his arousal, if he felt a fraction of what she did, he would never have stopped, certainly not to ask her if she wanted his help in finding a husband.

"Aaaargh!" She flopped to her other side, wishing she hadn't wrecked his pillow. It would have helped her sleep.

She had drunk far too much wine, and the aftereffects were reminding her of why she had sworn off rum. Every inch of her head ached, even her teeth and her eyebrows. The wine and the passions it fueled had muddied her thinking, and she knew nothing would be resolved until the clearer light of morning shone through the windows.

She tossed and turned through the night, tormented by the replay of the evening's events. Unbidden, every word, every action paraded through her memory. In the end, she fell into a fitful sleep. Her one solace was that she lay in comfort on the softest mattress on the ship, while somewhere in the dark roamed a grumpy and probably very tired man, looking for a place to sleep now that she had ousted him from his own quarters. She smiled through her tears when she imagined him trying to squeeze his large frame into her narrow hammock in the doctor's quarters. It would not be an easy night for him either!

Chapter Twenty-Three

"Good morning, sailor!" Will said, in a voice even louder than usual.

Amanda groaned and rolled over in the hammock, pulling a quilt over her head.

Will nudged her hip with his foot. "I'd cut you down, but that's my bed you're in, so I have as much to lose as you do."

She rolled onto her back and opened one eye little more than a slit. Her face had a decidedly green cast to it.

"I'm guessing wine doesn't agree with you any more than rum."

"What is that awful smell?" she groaned, ignoring his jibe.

"That," he said, drawing back the cloth cover from the tray he carried in a dramatic sweep, "is your breakfast, my dear."

"Breakfast?" she asked, her voice raspy.

"I had Cookie make it for you since you were unable to prepare mine this morning. Your just rewards, if I do say so myself."

If anything, Amanda looked greener than she had a moment ago. He let her suffer for just a moment more before taking pity on her. "Of course he didn't make it. I did."

"You made it?" She wrinkled her nose.

"Yes."

He felt rather proud of himself too. The eggs looked passable, the toast a light caramel color, and there were no grounds floating on the surface of the coffee. For a man who hadn't cooked his own meals in years, he had done quite well.

Amanda flopped onto her back and laid a limp hand over her eyes, blocking out the morning light that streamed through the high, curtainless windows. She swallowed, then said in a thick voice. "Well, whoever made it, I'm not eating."

"Yes, you are." Will set the tray down on his desk. "And after you have eaten, we are going into town."

Like a corpse reanimated, she sat up. "For what?"

"You need a new dress."

It wasn't exactly an order, but he hoped she would take it as such. She needed to eat, not talk.

"I have the one you gave to me yesterday."

"Yes, and it didn't fit you very well," he said, unable to avoid casting a glance at the shadow of her breasts under the soft fabric of her shift.

He remembered the gentle curves straining against fine green silk. He could still feel the memory of her puckered nipple brushing the palm of his hand, see the desire shimmering in her green eyes. What a difference a few glasses of wine made. He eyed her puffy lids, wondering if she could see anything through the small slits above her freckled cheeks. Disheveled, stubborn, and cross—certainly not at her best—she still affected him. Fortunately, his long waistcoat hid much of his body's reaction.

"I thought it fit fine," she said with a small pout, crossing her arms in front of her.

"It barely covered you."

A blush crept up her cheeks, and she averted her gaze.

Why didn't she want to go into town? Most women loved shopping, didn't they? Then again, Amanda had already proven herself to be unlike any other woman of his acquaintance.

Will watched her stumble out of his bed, wondering what it would take to make her happy. A few days ago, when he knew her as Adam, he thought he understood her. Now, he realized he didn't know her at all. He would gladly spend the rest of his life learning what pleased her, but at this moment, she represented a mystery deeper than any sea he had sailed.

He pulled out his chair and motioned for her to take a seat.

Amanda drew the quilt about her shoulders, and, giving him a dubious look, padded across the room on bare feet.

She lowered herself to the chair, then her slender arm shot out from beneath the protective quilt and snatched the coffee cup. She took a tentative sip, grimaced, then drained half the cup before setting it down again. Next, she picked up the fork and stared at the eggs. Poking the yolk, she frowned at the bright yellow goo that oozed across her plate.

Perhaps he should have cooked them longer.

But whether she liked the way he prepared her eggs or not, she needed to eat something in order to have the energy to go shopping and to kick off the dreadful headache she was sure to have after last night. He was about to suggest she just eat the toast when she surprised him by taking a small bite of the eggs.

Will hunkered down to wait. Leaning against the wall, he crossed one leg over the other at the ankle and folded his arms across his chest. Amanda cast a frown that said she resented his being in the room, or possibly just resented him altogether. She probably thought he lingered to monitor her progress with breakfast. Partially true, his thoughts were also occupied with a review of his carefully laid plans for the day.

Even if she didn't like shopping, he did want to buy her a new dress. Actually, he wanted to buy her whole wardrobe. If he never saw her again in sailor's duds, that would suit him fine. But more than that, he wanted to set things right between them.

Last night, turning in his temporary hammock like a ship caught in a whirlpool, he had resolved to begin anew with his "options" proposal. Maybe an afternoon spent shopping would afford him an opportunity to speak more plainly. A leisurely afternoon ashore, browsing through—*women's things*—whatever that included, might relax Amanda, make her more receptive to his proposal.

Lying awake in the long, quiet hours just before dawn, listening to the gentle lapping of waves against the ship's hull and trying to unravel exactly where he had gone wrong, it occurred to him that he had not included marriage, not to him at least, among her options.

When he said she could live comfortably for the rest of her life, he had been astonished at her assumptions. He thought she understood she need not rely on anyone, ever again—unless she wanted to, of course. That she would think him capable of offering to make her his mistress had pained him—no, insulted him, to the core.

However, replaying his proposal for the hundredth time, he realized that any woman might make the same mistake. That would be especially true of a woman in the process of being ravished. Well, not exactly ravished, he amended, since she had certainly been doing her part. But if she only knew how much effort he had put into maintaining his composure, she would never have accused him of wanting her for physical pleasures alone.

He gave up on sleep just as dawn filtered through the windows, bringing with it the calls of hungry gulls and eager merchants, and made plans to take her dress shopping. While he left her in the hands of a saleswoman with strict orders to dress her from head to toe, letting her choose whatever she wanted—so long as it didn't include trousers or duck cloth, he would find a jeweler to craft a necklace. It would be a peace offering, and hopefully, a betrothal gift.

He watched Amanda polish off the two eggs and half the toast. She was made of strong stuff. He just hoped she kept it down all the while they were in town.

"That's my girl." He removed the plate in front of her. He reached to pick up her cup, but she snatched it away.

"You can have more of that once you're dressed," he said, prying it from her reluctant fingers.

Amanda stood and looked about. "Where are my clothes?"

Her dress lay over the chair behind her, her undergarments piled on the floor beside it.

"In the gut of a whale by now if we're lucky," he replied, knowing to which clothes she referred. "Wear the dress again."

The dress would be a little formal for Baltimore, but if anyone noticed her, they might easily assume Amanda to be a wealthy foreigner. Her short blonde curls were of a style that a libertine French woman might favor. Certainly the green satin gown, with its lace trimmed bodice that covered her breasts only enough to avoid indecency looked worthy of a French woman.

Will scowled at the gown that lay draped so decadently across the back of his chair. With any luck, the first shop they visited would have a shawl she fancied.

****

"I don't need anything except my old clothes," Amanda protested.

They left the cool confines of Miss Francine's dress shop, an establishment that catered to the more prudish among the well-to-do matrons of Baltimore, and stepped onto the narrow wooden walkway. In many ways a provincial town, Baltimore couldn't boast of many fashionable dress shops, and even fewer with readymade clothing that wasn't second hand or tawdry. It would take some extra coin to ensure Amanda's wardrobe would be delivered by the time they weighed anchor the day after tomorrow. If only she would agree to be reasonable and allow herself to be fitted.

The saleswoman at Miss Francine's had seemed relieved when they left, even though they departed empty handed. Perhaps she hadn't relished the thought of trying to take the measurements of a woman whose crossed arms appeared glued to her chest.

"I threw your old clothes overboard, remember?"

Will said.

Amanda took the arm he offered. Instead of strolling sedately down the street, looking in shop windows, he pinned her hand to his sleeve and strode so she had to walk double time to keep up. He cringed when she cursed her tangled skirts in words she could only have learned aboard his ship.

"Well, then, buy me some new ones if you must, but buy me something that doesn't compel me to fear for my life." She yanked on his arm, obliging him to stop so she could tug her skirt free from her ankles.

"On the other hand, I suppose there is a benefit to all these layers," she said, in a saccharine voice. "If we should have to abandon ship, I will be mercifully saved from a slow death by pounds of petticoats dragging me to the bottom of the Atlantic."

Will ignored her sarcastic remarks and looked over his shoulder for the tenth time in as many minutes. More than just his eagerness to clothe her in something more modest than the gown she currently wore had him dragging her alongside him at such a brisk pace. Some blocks back, he had noticed a man trailing them at a discreet distance.

Will tested his theory by extending the gap between them, rounding a few corners and then slowing to a more moderate pace. After traversing a few steps, he turned to see the man standing less than a block away, perusing loaves of bread through the window of a bakery. He glanced up, caught Will's eye, then let his gaze drop.

Amanda grew more vociferous, extolling the merits of a pair of duck cloth trousers, oblivious to Will's inattentiveness or the old man following them.

Who could he be?

The man appeared elderly, bordering on old, yet he had no difficulty keeping up with them. Despite Amanda's trouble with her skirts, they set a pace that would have left any man unused to physical exertion gasping for breath.

Aside from the uncomfortable feeling of being followed, Will didn't sense any malice from the man. Nothing of the criminal sort anyway. A man intent on doing them harm would lie in wait in one of the many dark alleys between buildings. Even that wouldn't be sufficient since Will could easily overpower the old man. He glanced over his shoulder at the man's bent back and shuffling feet. Hell, Amanda could overpower him.

Then why were they being followed?

Lawyer perhaps? The news had come that morning that the admiralty court had certified his latest prize. Now it was simply a matter of public auction. Could one of the ship's owners be fighting the court's decision?

Amanda stumbled when Will stopped abruptly in front of a small coffee shop, "How about some refreshments?"

"Oh, thank heavens!" she said between dramatic gasps for air.

Will ignored her exaggerated attempts to needle him and directed her ahead of him into the shop.

He settled her at a small table and ordered coffee for her, a small beer for himself, and a plate of sandwiches, all the while keeping an eye out for the stranger.

He didn't see the old man pass by the front of the

shop, but Will sensed his presence. It was like knowing a ship sailed just beyond the horizon, but not being near enough to know whether it was friend or foe.

In all likelihood, their pursuer—if you could call him that—lurked in one of the dark alleys across the street, watching the coffee shop and waiting for them to exit the public place. Will would need to abandon Amanda in the relative safety of the shop while he confronted the man in the street.

He opened his mouth to give Amanda an excuse for leaving her by herself, when the bell over the door tinkled softly. The stranger stepped inside, his intent gaze on Amanda but ignoring Will.

The chatter in the coffee shop dimmed, and the background faded, until Will saw naught but the old man staring at Amanda. Beneath his coat, the muscles in Will's shoulders clenched from his instinct to protect her.

Amanda looked up from her coffee and turned her head to see what had captured Will's attention.

"Father!" she gasped.

In a flurry of satin skirts, she flew from her chair and into the old man's arms, oblivious to the gawking of the establishment's other patrons. Amanda embraced the older man with a familiarity that spoke volumes about her relationship with the stranger, and her affection for him.

Father.

But how could that be? Amanda and Neil had both told him, with utmost surety, that their father had died in the war more than two years ago. He hadn't pressed for details, not wanting to open painful memories for either of them. Now, he wished he had. Perhaps they only assumed their father had died.

With a poorly funded Continental Army and harsh conditions, deserters were legion. But unless someone actually saw a man run during battle, it could be difficult to separate the deserters from the dead. Amanda might even have received word from his regiment. Will had heard of several cases where the military declared a man dead only for him to resurface some years later, often when he ran out of money. Had Amanda's father somehow heard about her service aboard his ship and the small fortune she had amassed?

Amanda grasped her father's gnarled hands and gazed into his weathered face, a face that featured eyes as watery his daughter's.

Will cleared his throat.

"Oh, I'm sorry, Father," said Amanda. "May I introduce you to Captain Stoakes. Captain, this is my father, Joseph Blakely." She whispered his name as if saying it louder would jinx her good fortune, making her father disappear in a puff of smoke.

Mr. Blakely tore his gaze from his daughter. "Continental Navy, sir?"

"No, sir. Privateer."

"Well, that is splendid." Blakely grasped Will's hand and pumped it with more enthusiasm than could be expected from the elderly. "I understand we owe a great debt to those who ply the seas and harass the damned English supply ships." He turned to Amanda. "My apologies for my vulgar language, my dear. I'm afraid I have been with the army so long that my manners have become a bit rough."

Amanda accepted her father's apology with a demure smile, and Will coughed to cover his amusement. If her father could have heard her swearing at her skirts just a moment ago, he would have blushed!

Will invited Mr. Blakely to join them for coffee. He wasn't ready to trust the man yet, and it wouldn't hurt to question him while they took their refreshment. Besides, Amanda still held her father's hand in an anchoring grip, and it didn't look like she would be casting off anytime soon.

Over the next several minutes, Mr. Blakely wove a plausible tale of how he had been injured in battle. In the fit of a fever that lasted for days, he had been separated from his regiment. The fever had left him somewhat addled in the brain and unsure of which memories were real and which were a result of his illness.

He spent the next couple of years in an army convalescent home, of little use to anyone. He couldn't go back to the army. They had no need for a soldier who didn't quite have his wits about him. He couldn't go home because he couldn't recall where home was. It had been a stressful two years, seemingly forgotten by both the army and the family he wasn't even sure he had.

Eventually, small flashes of memory became hazy recollections. Through murky images of events past, he recalled having a daughter and a son waiting for him. It took him several more weeks to recall the location of his farm, but once he did, neither Hell's hounds nor the British could prevent him from returning.

Of course, when he got there, he found the farmhouse abandoned, the fields left fallow, the livestock gone. Not sure what to do, he took lodgings in Baltimore, the closest town of any size, and set about trying to uncover news of his children.

"Is Neil..." His voice trailed off.

Amanda squeezed the hand she still held, "Neil is well. He serves on Captain Stoakes' ship."

"Oh, that is wonderful news," Mr. Blakely said, turning to Will.

Will nodded, noting that Amanda did not mention she also served on his ship. He chose not to share that bit of knowledge either. Until he could verify the man's story, the less he knew, the better.

Blakely's tale rang true, and he certainly seemed to believe it. Moreover, Will trusted his instincts, and he didn't sense anything sinister about Amanda's father.

The tension in Will's shoulders eased. He would leave Amanda in her father's company, while her took care of other matters.

"I wonder if the two of you might excuse me." Will rose from his chair. "I have some things I need to attend to, and I'm sure you have much to talk about after being separated for so long. Shall I meet you back here in say, two hours?" He glanced at the gold watch he produced from the pocket of his waistcoat.

Amanda nodded before turning back to her father. He smiled the indulgent smile of a parent to a beloved child. She returned much the same smile. Will rolled his eyes and tucked his watch back in his pocket. He would not be missed.

Stepping onto the cobbled street, he considered where he might start his search for information on Mr. Joseph Blakely. If his claims were true, Amanda's father would have been making inquiries. In a town like Baltimore, gossip traveled fast and nearly everyone would have heard the story by now.

He would check with one of his business contacts first. They might know of an army office with a record of Blakely and his stay in the convalescent home. Once he assured himself that Blakely had no hidden purpose, he had personal business to attend to. He had a necklace to purchase, and he planned to stop by the dressmaker's himself and order an entire wardrobe for Amanda, whether she wanted it or not.

Will considered the possibility that Blakely's sudden appearance changed matters. With her father alive, Amanda might prefer to live ashore, and her father would surely want a say in her choice of a husband. Although he claimed to owe a debt of gratitude to privateers, that did not mean he considered his daughter suitable payment. Still, he didn't think it wise to give her over to the older man until he had verified his story. Despite his amiable manner and obvious affection for his daughter, something about Joseph Blakely didn't sit right.

He waited for a carriage to rumble past, then crossed the cobbled street in the direction of the bank.

It didn't take long for Blakely's story to be confirmed. At the bank, Will even discovered acquaintances of Blakely's from before the war who testified to his character, and the banker confirmed he was not without funds.

According to Mr. Timms, one of the first things Blakely did when he arrived in Baltimore was stop by the bank to review his accounts. He didn't have a fortune, but frugality over the years had allowed him to set aside enough to keep his children fed and clothed until they were both adults.

The banker tugged thoughtfully at his moustache,

then confirmed that Blakely had seemed genuinely surprised to find the funds he left for his children untouched. Describing Amanda and Neil's father as "somewhat absent-minded," Timms speculated that Mr. Blakely had forgotten to tell his children about the money.

Will could believe it. His impression of Blakely had been that of a "dreamer." No wonder his children were so able to take care of themselves. They had probably been doing so for years.

Timms also shared that, upon discovering the accounts untouched, Blakely had become distraught, convinced his children would not have left the farm without first withdrawing funds unless something dreadful had happened to them.

Mr. Timms was delighted when Will told him Amanda and Neil had been found. The banker asked where they had been staying, but Will skirted the question, saying they had been with friends outside of Baltimore. The story bore some semblance of truth since both Neil and Amanda had many friends aboard ship, and one might consider the Atlantic Ocean to be *outside Baltimore*. More to the point, Will's tale would protect Amanda's reputation should she decide to take up residence with her father in Baltimore.

Thanking the banker, he left and headed down the street to the dress shop where he had purchased Amanda's green satin gown. From the same saleswoman, he ordered a half-dozen gowns in a variety of hues he thought would complement Amanda's fair complexion. He asked her to be sure she chose only the finest materials, and paid extra to ensure the dresses would be delivered to his ship by noon the next day.

He tossed a few more coins on the counter and, emphasizing that the gowns were for his *sister*, reminded her that he wished for dresses that were of a more modest design than the last one she had chosen. The saleswoman scooped up the coins and deposited them into the pocket of her tailor's apron. With a grin so deep it left gouges in the powder on her cheeks, she declared she would take great care in choosing only designs he was sure to approve. Will concluded he had probably just wasted the extra money.

His time almost at an end, he stopped at the jewelers where he chose an emerald necklace with one stone surrounded by small diamonds suspended from a gold chain. It wasn't elaborate, nor particularly expensive as emerald necklaces went, but it would suit Amanda perfectly. The green stone sparkled and changed hue when he angled it just right, reminding him of the way Amanda's eyes smoldered and darkened when she lay in his hammock.

Mr. Johannson, the jeweler, assured Will that a "man of his stature" should choose stones that allowed his wife to show off her station in life.

The old man's watery eyes shone like the gems in his case, leading Will to suspect the jeweler presumed the woman in question to be merely a mistress. Undoubtedly, he found the use of the term "wife" much more effective when selling the more expensive pieces. He didn't bother to correct the man's assumptions.

Jowls aquiver, the jeweler brought out several heavy pieces mounted on a black velvet frame. Taking Will's lack of interest to mean he hadn't found something "exquisite enough" for a "man of Captain Stoakes' excellent tastes" he presented piece after piece, each more ornate and expensive than the last.

In the end, Will stood firm on his first choice, ending the man's obsequious sales pitch by forcing money into his chubby hands.

Holding his purchase up to the light streaming through the shop window, the green emerald sparkled, this time reminding him of the way Amanda's green eyes danced when she was excited. He vowed, if she wanted, he would buy her a more expensive piece, but somehow he couldn't imagine his slender, delicate Amanda weighed down with a necklace that jangled when she walked.

Tucking his purchase into his pocket, he waved a cheery good-bye to the discouraged jeweler and left the shop. Whistling a sailor's ditty, he set off down the street toward the coffee shop.

Chapter Twenty-Four

"What's eating you?"

Will glanced up from his books to find Buck standing in his doorway, a familiar grin pasted across his angular jaw.

"Nothing." Will returned his attention to the leather-bound ledger open in front of him and stared at the sea of figures. Most had a considerable number of zeros.

Will's shoulders slumped when the door closed with a soft click a moment later.

"I knew it wasn't nothing," Buck said.

Startled, Will looked up. "I guess I should have dismissed you formally, but I thought you smart enough to take a hint."

"Oh, I got the hint all right," Buck examined a trimmed and buffed nail, "but barring a formal order, I pretty much do as I please."

He took a seat in the chair across from Will and crossed one leg over the other. Placing his hand on his knee, he grinned and swung a booted foot while he waited for his friend to surrender.

In the face of Buck's infectious grin and tenacious nature, Will had no choice. "Yes, I see that you do."

"So, how about we stop the pretense, and you tell me what's troubling you."

"What makes you think something is troubling

me?" Will ran his finger down a column of numbers.

"I stood in your doorway for ten minutes watching you stare at that ledger. During that entire time, you didn't turn a page nor make a mark. However, you must have sighed a dozen times." Buck gave him a meaningful look. "Now I know the ledger nearly as well as you do, and there's nothing to sigh about in there. Therefore, I must conclude it has something to do with the man on deck with Amanda."

There was no point in evading the issue or his best friend. Will closed the ledger and shoved it away. "Her father."

"Ah..." Buck nodded. "That would explain why she's hanging on the man as though he might run away if she loosens her grip. I understand he has been absent for a time."

"Yes, but now he's back." Will placed his chin in one palm and drummed the fingers of his other hand against the leather bound book.

"How is that a problem?" Buck pinched a piece of lint from his knee and flicked it away.

"It's not a problem." Will ran his fingers along the gold embossed letters on the ledger's bindings. "She'll be leaving with him."

Buck looked up. "She'll be leaving?"

For once, Will couldn't tell if Buck's shock was real or feigned, but it didn't matter. "Of course, she'll be leaving. He's her father."

"Hmmm," Buck looked thoughtful, "I don't know that one necessarily follows the other. Neil told me Amanda is almost two and twenty. She is old enough to live without a father."

Will rose and strode to the line of windows set high

in the wall. While the captain's quarters in a larger ship might have more windows than walls, in a small schooner built for speed, large windows were a luxury.

Still, the line of narrow glass let in a little light and allowed Will to look out over the wide expanse of the sea. On most days, it kept him from getting the sensation of being trapped inside a floating wooden coffin. Today, however, all he could see were the crowded, dirty docks of the Port of Baltimore. He couldn't have felt more trapped had he been locked in irons in the ship's hold.

"I can't keep her aboard ship." Will watched a gull tear pieces of flesh from a fish at the edge of the quay. Its scales glinted in the sunlight as the bird tugged.

"Why not?" Buck asked.

Will turned away from the carnage. "Because she's a distraction for the men."

"Your men?" Buck gave a sharp laugh. "Will, when's the last time you've had a voyage where nobody drank themselves into oblivion?"

Will shrugged. "They have been unusually sober recently, haven't they?"

"Well-behaved, too, I'd say. There have been no charges of disorderly conduct, no dismissals for neglecting one's duties, and if I'm not mistaken, their language has been unusually polite, at least for men of their mark."

Will laughed. Despite the words his crew had inadvertently taught Amanda, he had to admit their language had been tame for a pack of crusty old tars. He had even overheard the occasional please and thank you, something not often heard at sea.

"Have you seen them at the guns lately?" Buck

asked.

Of course he had. His crew made steady progress, decreasing the time it took to load and fire successive rounds at an imaginary enemy.

"Don't tell me she's responsible for that too," Will said.

"She bakes lemon cake for the team with the best time, but that's not really why they work so hard. In battle, they're even faster than they are in practice because she reminds them of what they fight for."

"Some of them fight for nothing more than the money."

Buck scoffed. "You can tell yourself that. Hell, they may even tell you that, but don't believe for a moment that a woman like Amanda couldn't melt the heart of even the most miserly among them."

"Perhaps every ship should have a woman aboard," Will grumbled, and leaned against the wall, crossing his arms over his chest.

Buck looked up at him, his eyes serious for once. "I'm not saying that, of course. Perhaps I'm not even suggesting she become a permanent member of the crew." He rose from his seat. "All I am suggesting is that there is no hurry to be rid of her."

"A privateer is a dangerous place to be." Will's tone dared his friend to dispute it.

"I can't argue that, but land may not be much safer. The war isn't going well, Will, and the British see us as traitors, not a legitimate enemy. You've heard the prison stories. Some of our former comrades seem to have lost their sense of honor. To them, a patriot is no better than a traitor."

"Yes, but she's a woman. So long as she stays out

of their way, no harm should come to her," Will said, even though he knew it wasn't always the case. "Besides, the British still value wealth. She has money. She would be treated differently even if we were to lose this war."

Or the British might discover the source of her wealth and confiscate everything she owned. In the event they decided to prosecute the privateers as pirates, being a woman would not save her from the noose. Will shuddered.

Buck shrugged. "Be that as it may. There are other dangers. Smallpox is claiming even more lives than the war and shows no prejudice toward gender nor the size of one's accounts."

"Did you come in here to make me feel better, my friend? Because, if you did, you're doing a very poor job of it."

Buck rose to his feet "Well, then, perhaps I have overstayed my welcome." He strode toward the door, but turned back, one hand resting on the latch. "Just promise me you will think about it. Everyone is entitled to break the rules every once in a while," he paused, "even you."

****

"Bull, where is Neil?" Will asked, taking a step on deck.

"I believe he's below in the officer's mess studying the log books you lent him," Bull said.

"Have him join me, if you please."

"Aye, sir." Bull disappeared through the hatch.

Across the narrow deck, Amanda and her father strolled arm in arm. They were so busy chattering that he feared for their safety as they neared a pile of rope someone had left coiled in their path.

"Oy! Careful there, Miss!" Martin called out, just in time to allow Amanda and her father to skirt the obstruction before they lost themselves in conversation once again.

Will gave a soft snort. Surely they had covered the two years of missing time by now.

What would Neil's reaction be when he learned his father had returned? Being an adopted son didn't mean the bond would be any weaker. Still, somehow he couldn't picture the headstrong, intelligent boy forming a close tie to this amiable but somewhat vacuous old man.

"You wanted to see me, sir?" Neil asked, climbing through the hatch and stepping on deck.

His gaze flitted to his sister, scanned Blakely, then settled on Will. Recognition dawned in Neil's eyes, but dimmed so suddenly that Will wondered if he had misread the boy's expression. Waiting to hear his captain's orders, Neil kept his gaze fixed on Will, his lips set in a thin line.

"Neil?" Blakely called.

Neil dragged his gaze from Will to his father.

"It is you, boy!" Blakely grasped Neil about the shoulders and pulled him into an embrace that was not returned. Releasing him, he tousled the boy's hair. "I would never have recognized you. You've grown so much."

"It has been several years." Neil's voice held no recrimination, just a simple statement of fact.

Will had thought to invite Neil to dine with them that evening, but instinct told him the boy wouldn't welcome the invitation. To say he was not overcome with the same joy as his sister would be an understatement.

He dismissed Neil, sensing his relief, and ushered Amanda and her father below.

****

With Amanda's father commanding her attention, the task of preparing supper fell to Cookie. He had improved significantly under her tutelage and the meal, although rather bland, was at least edible. Not that Amanda or her father noticed. They chatted nonstop and showed no signs of slowing down.

"You will excuse me?" Will stood.

Amanda gave him a dismissive nod before turning her attention back to her father.

On deck, Neil stood alone at the railing, his gaze fixed on the shafts of moonlight shimmering on the waves. Will doubted he saw any of it.

Will joined him at the rail and nodded a greeting. A man didn't pry into another man's relationship with his father. He would wait for Neil to decide whether he wished to talk. It didn't take long.

"I barely knew him, you know," Neil said, still staring out at the night sea. "He took me in after my parents died. I was grateful and all, but I never really thought of him as my father. He wasn't around very often. Then he went away to war, and I nearly forgot him. I didn't even recognize him at first."

Will listened in silence, watching the intricate dance of waves and moonlight.

"Amanda has been my only family for a long time. She may have been a bit too motherly, but I relished it when I was younger. She could be so annoying at times, but I secretly enjoyed her attention. I knew she loved me and was trying to show it in her own, completely inept way." Neil laughed, the strangled sound a strange mixture of pain and fondness.

Will smiled. He knew exactly what Neil meant. Amanda couldn't be happy unless she had something to do for somebody, whether they wanted her to or not. He had never known the doting affections of a woman, his own mother not being the devoted type. Had he been asked, he would have said he preferred not to have a woman flitting about, seeing to his comforts. Now, he wondered how he would get by without her.

"She was the only family I had until..." Neil choked on his words.

"Until a father you barely knew showed up," Will finished for him.

"No." Neil turned, but stared at the tips of his boots. "Until you showed up, sir. I know we're not related or anything, but you are the man I most admire in this world, and I would give anything to be like you."

With his heart lodged in his throat, Will didn't think he could have responded if he tried so he set a hand on Neil's shoulder and squeezed.

"Sir, will I have to leave the ship with my father?" Neil asked, looking up at him.

"Of course not." Will forced himself to sound unconcerned. "You signed on to my crew and you have an obligation to me and the rest of your shipmates. Bull and Buck would be especially disappointed if you left now after they've worked so hard to teach you what they know."

Relief flooded Neil's face, and Will hoped the boy's father wouldn't make a liar out of him by demanding the boy return home. Will could not keep a minor aboard ship against the wishes of his parents.

"What about Amanda?" Neil asked.

"I'm afraid I don't know the answer to that," Will said, gazing into the night.

He listened to the muffled sounds of the men on night watch and considered the question that had been nagging him from the moment Amanda had called the old man "father."

Buck had offered some very convincing arguments for allowing Amanda to remain aboard. Will had grasped at them like a drowning man might reach for an imaginary piece of flotsam riding the waves. However, as soon as he came on deck and saw them together, he knew none of those arguments were as real as the relationship between a father and his daughter.

Amanda glowed with adoration for her father, and from all appearances, he returned her affections. If she couldn't be more than a foot away from him now, how could Will possibly expect her to be happy with a life at sea? She might not have a chance to see the old man for months at a time.

More than anything, he wished to see her happy. At one time, that would have meant letting her stay aboard his ship. Now, he would have to let her go. He fingered the jewelry box still in his pocket. No longer a peace offering or an early betrothal gift, the necklace would be a farewell token.

Chapter Twenty-Five

"Oh, there you are, Captain." Mr. Blakely emerged from below with his daughter close on his heels. "It's getting late, and I'll be taking my leave of you now, sir. Thank you for a lovely evening."

"You are very welcome." Will nodded, then signaled for a boat to take Blakely back to shore.

A trio of sailors pulled back the stiff tarpaulin covering one of the nearby skiffs. Amanda excused herself, saying she would find Neil so he could bid farewell to his father.

Blakely rocked back on his heels and watched his daughter go, grinning like a man who had secured his place in the world. "I cannot wait to tell my friends what my children have been doing in my absence."

A cool breeze rustled the hairs on the back of Will's neck. "What do you mean?"

"Serving aboard your ship, of course. Why, Neil and Amanda had done more for the cause than I have despite my years of service in the army." His voice held only pride. "They've been rewarded handsomely, too."

The older man's eyes twinkled, and this time, the hair on the back of Will's neck stood at full attention. Had he let his guard down too soon? Would Amanda's father squander her fortune? Squander it the way his mother had done with his own father's?

Blakely's eyes had a faraway look about them. Did

he dream of the day he could relate the exploits of his children to friends, neighbors or anybody else who might lend an ear to an old man?

If Amanda's fortune were at risk, at least it wasn't due to malice or greed. More likely, Blakely would brag about his children's accomplishments and attract the attention of every conman in Baltimore. Amanda might not fall for a con, but if she gave her father access to her accounts, she could lose everything.

He would need to devise a plan to keep her and her money safe from her father's ineptitude. Will glanced toward the far side of the ship where Amanda stood nose to nose with her brother, their silhouettes outlined by the lantern behind them. They appeared to be arguing, though their hushed tones didn't carry across the open deck.

"I'm afraid it would be better for Amanda if you spoke of this to no one. She has her reputation to think of," Will said, offering a line of reasoning that any father ought to appreciate.

"What?" Blakely looked confused for a moment then understanding washed across his face. "Oh, yes, of course, of course," he replied, with a harrumph.

Amanda rejoined them to stand by Will's side.

"I'm sorry, but Neil has duties he must attend to."

"Oh, well, can't be helped, I suppose." Blakely shrugged, then gave Amanda a quick peck on the cheek. "I will see you soon, my dear."

Amanda reached for her father's hand and held it before letting his fingers trail from hers.

Will grimaced when she dabbed at her eyes with a handkerchief aged to a yellowish brown and splotched with dark stains. He would have to check his receipts, for he was certain the saleswoman had charged him for a lady's handkerchief to match her dress. The small square of linen, embroidered with a mermaid combing her hair on the rocks and edged in lace had cost him more than her stockings and silk garters combined.

Buck steadied Blakely, helping the older man over the side and with his first few shaky steps down the rope ladder. Only when he had settled himself on a wooden plank at the back of the skiff did he look up. Amanda waved at her father with her handkerchief before a sniffle had her clutching it to her nose. She stood at the railing, alternately waving and sniffling until the small boat disappeared, swallowed by darkness and the cool mist rolling in from the sea.

"Well, I think I'll turn in," Amanda said, her voice loud in the sudden quiet.

Will didn't have time to reply before she hitched up her skirts and double-timed it down the hatchway. He followed her down the narrow stairs, intending to catch her before she reached her quarters and demand to know why she hadn't gone with her father.

Skirts billowing behind her, she blew past the doctor's cabin and headed for Will's door. She swung it open and ducked inside. Will followed her in and closed the door with a soft click.

She stood motionless in the middle of his quarters, facing away from him. Even in the darkness, he could see her shoulders heaving. She reminded him of a cornered rabbit.

"Mind telling me what you're still doing here?" Will said, keeping his voice calm.

****

Amanda pasted a smile on her lips and whirled

around to face him. "I am a member of your crew, aren't I?"

The question sounded more direct than she had intended. Backing a wolf into a corner might not be such a wise thing to do, but desperation had driven her to the point of recklessness.

"I thought you would be leaving with your father now that you know he is alive. I thought he would insist on it. I would, if I were him."

"He thinks you're an honorable man." Amanda lifted her chin.

"And you? What do you think?" Will's question held a note of uncertainty.

"I think you are as well," she took a deep breath to steady her resolve, "but I'd really rather you weren't."

Amanda waited for his reaction, glad his quarters were lit only by weak shafts of moonlight through the high windows. She hated to think he might witness the desperation she knew to be written on her face. She could hear the despised emotion in her own voice.

She threw back her shoulders and stuck out her chin. She would need courage to carry out her plan. This might well be her last night aboard ship. With her father alive, she had relatives in Baltimore with whom she could be entrusted. Captain Stoakes...Will...need no longer feel guilty for depositing her ashore and sailing off. His last reason for keeping her aboard ship had disappeared with her father's appearance.

She loved her father and was overjoyed to have found him alive and well, but she cursed his dreadful timing. Still, if this were to be her last night aboard ship, she would not leave empty handed.

Her breath came in short, hot gasps as though she

had run a great distance instead of just down a short flight of steps and a few yards beyond. To calm herself, she took a deep breath and blew it out through pursed lips to the count of five. She would not let him see the extent of her need. Not yet anyway.

The silence in the small cabin made the usual soft night noises seem deafening by comparison. Anchored close to shore, waves lapped against the hull in a even cadence almost like a heartbeat. From the town came the faint cry of the night watchman declaring that all was well. The distant rumble of a snoring sailor filtered in through the cracks in the planks. Inside the cabin, two shadowed figures faced off, neither moved, neither spoke.

She had just told the captain she did not want him to be honorable. Had he not understood her meaning? She didn't think she could muster the courage to be more direct. Destiny held her in a vice and no matter how she might struggle, she couldn't free herself. With each second that ticked away, the vice tightened around her heart, and fate brought her closer to the end of her relationship with Will.

Amanda's cheeks burned from her pasted-on smile, and she steeled herself to take what little life offered. She needed more time, but time had run out. Even convincing her father to leave her aboard ship for one more night had been a chore. Men could be so damnably stubborn about propriety at times. Perhaps not for themselves, but where their daughters were concerned, they knew no limits.

That she had spent the last several months aboard ship hadn't swayed him at first. Then she suggested, with great tact, that he might have doubts about the captain's honor. That had done the trick. It had been clear to Amanda from the first that Captain Stoakes ranked right up there with General Washington in her father's eyes.

Nevertheless, one night would not be enough time to prove anything. Even if she could somehow, one night would certainly not be enough to gain what her heart most truly desired—his love. But if tonight was all she had, she would seize the opportunity and not look back.

She would have this one night of passion if nothing more. She must have it to carry her through the rest of her years. No matter how long she lived, she would never love another. She had a vision of herself, old and gray, staring out at the sea from her bedroom window, waiting for a lover who never returned.

Oh, for heaven's sakes, Amanda chided herself, and blinked back accursed tears. She would not let a distant, melancholy future ruin her one night.

The crescent moon slipped from behind a cloud, and Will's form took shape. His eyes glinted like gold nuggets in the soft light.

Amanda gasped when Will crossed the distance between them in two quick strides, lifted her off the ground, and held her against his chest. His mouth claimed hers in a crushing kiss that sealed her fate. She would forever be his, whether he wanted her or not.

Amanda sighed into his warm lips. She wouldn't have to fight to put this part of her plan into action. For tonight at least, he belonged to her as well. She wanted to laugh. Tonight she would give herself to the man she loved for the first time and the last. Her joy formed a barrier against the despair lurking at the darkened edges of her mind, waiting to overwhelm her. Well, despair would have to wait for the morning tide. Tonight, there would be no room for it in her heart.

Will set her back on her feet then cupped her face in his hands. He kissed her, a gentle touching of lips that held both reverence and promise, until desire replaced desolation.

Needing to give as well as take, she turned her face toward his and wrapped her arms about his neck, pulling him to her. His lips on hers were more innocent than erotic, more caring than carnal. She wanted more, needed more. What she couldn't tell him with words, she would explain with her actions. If she only had one night with this man, she needed Will to let go of his carefully maintained control. She would not waste this opportunity.

When Will's tongue touched at her lips, Amanda opened without hesitation and reached out to him with her own. She could taste the wine from dinner, wine she had not shared. His tongue toyed with hers for a moment before retreating as though he dared not force his position. Amanda allowed the retreat for only a moment before offering herself again by flicking his upper lip with her tongue. Will needed no more invitation and flesh met flesh in an intimate prelude to pleasures yet to come.

Splaying her hands against the back of his neck, she ran long fingers through his thick wavy locks. When a fingertip caught on the tail he wore, she tugged at the end of the leather strip and released it. His hair flowed to his shoulders and she threaded her hands through it, savoring the silky feel, cool and smooth, against her palms.

Will closed his eyes and rested his forehead against hers, letting Amanda take her time exploring him. Then his lips were on hers and he pulled her against him in an embrace that left her breathless. She entwined her fingers through his hair and held on when the room spun beneath her feet.

Amanda swayed when he finally released her, and he gave a soft laugh when he had to steady her shoulders to keep her upright.

Her heartbeat quickened when he reached behind her to fumble for the buttons on the back of her dress. She could feel his hands tremble. She gazed into his eyes, answering his unvoiced question, by swaying toward him until her breasts pressed against his lapels. He bent his head to kiss her again. His attention diverted, frustration welled inside her when his efforts with her buttons slowed.

Anticipation of pleasures she could only imagine propelled her to action. Her hands went to his lapels, and she yanked his coat off his shoulders. She tugged, attempting to peel the stiff wool over his elbows while he worked the buttons on the back of her dress. Each time she yanked, his hands were pulled from their task.

"We have to do one thing at a time, sweetheart," he said after a moment of tugging at odds with each other.

She stepped back while he stripped away his coat and tossed it over a chair.

"That's better." She set about the buttons on his waistcoat.

"I would have to agree." He laughed and then worked the last of the buttons along the back of her dress before easing it off her shoulders.

With a little more give and take, she managed to

disrobe him until he wore nothing more than his linen drawers, and she, her shift.

Shadows played across his chest in the moonlight, emphasizing deep, chiseled muscles. Even the occasional scar, pale against the darker surrounding skin, didn't mar his near perfection. She ran the tip of her finger along one thin ridge, wondering what story lay behind it. She sighed, flattening her hand against his chest. If only she had time to learn his secrets.

She brought her other hand to his chest and laid it against the hard, warm flesh, amazing herself with her own boldness. Amanda ran searching hands down the curves of his pectoral muscles letting his hardening male nipples scrape against her palms. She continued her path, feeling the sensitive skin pucker even further when she ran the length of her index finger along them until only the tips of her flesh made contact with his. Then she laid her hands flat and started again.

She sensed him watching, assessing her every move while she memorized his contours. Yet, he remained so still she couldn't even feel the rise and fall of his chest beneath her hands.

What did he think about her actions? Did he consider her boldness a character flaw? Many men would. Would he stop her if she went further?

Needing to taste as well as to touch, she bent forward and flicked one of his nipples with her tongue, smiling against his puckered skin when he released a shuddering breath. She had no idea what made her do such a thing, but given his response, she might do it again if she had the chance. For now, however, her eagerness to explore the rest of him drove her on. She needed to burn the texture of his skin, the shape of his body, the taste of his lips into a memory that would last the rest of her life.

Amanda trailed her hands lower, fascinated by the tautness of the muscles of his abdomen and the contrast of his hard body to hers. She traced the trail of dark curls that ran down his core, then flattened her hands again and ran them out to his sides until his hip bones were nestled in the palms of her hands and the tips of her fingers lay against the hollow of his buttocks.

It took only a gentle tug to bring Will's hips to hers, the bulge of his arousal against the flat softness of her belly. The fabric of their undergarments the only barrier between them, she molded herself to him, increasing the pressure and reveling in his answer to her.

He made a guttural sound in the back of his throat, and she eased the pressure, lifting her eyes to search his face. Had she hurt him in her inexperience?

His pupils were dilated, and sparks danced within as golden eyes caught the rays of dappled moonlight. His gaze held no pain, only a hunger that sent a shudder coursing to her toes. He flashed a grin, teeth glimmering in the moonlight and reminding her that although he appeared docile, she had awakened the wolf. Had she any desire to escape, her opportunity had passed some time ago.

Her eyes locked on his, she bunched her shift in her fists, pulled it over her head and tossed it to the floor. She willed herself to stand before him, letting his gaze drift over her naked form. Only humans felt shame at their nakedness. Tonight, she would be a creature of nature, giving into her basic instincts and letting her human side deal with the consequences on the morrow.

Tonight she would be the wolf's mate, and like the wolf, he would be the only one she ever had.

His gaze roamed over her neck and breasts. Although he didn't touch her, a palpable heat radiated between them and her nipples puckered in response. His gaze dropped to her stomach, the juncture of her thighs, her mound covered in dark blonde curls, and down the length of her legs. Inch by slow inch, his gaze caressed her, a trail of heat rippling in its wake.

Amanda needed more. She needed his hands on her and hers on him. She stepped forward until the crisp curls on his chest teased the very tips of her breasts. A jolt of sensation that ran from her nipples to the pit of her belly almost brought her to her knees.

She ran her hands down his taut back, delighting as his muscles quivered beneath her palms. She could feel his strength, the same way one could sense the power of the ocean in the vibrations of a taut rope. When she reached the cotton drawers tied loosely about his hips, a wave of irritation hit her, and she an urge to tear the offending garments from him.

"I can take them off," Will said with a chuckle that suggested he knew what she had been contemplating.

His words called her back from the instinctual abyss she had fallen into, but need still threatened to drag her back down. She reached for the drawstring on the front of his drawers and tugged, then tugged again. When they didn't give way, she looked down.

"Oh, blast it!" she muttered.

She had managed to turn the bow into a knot and now his drawers were more securely fastened than ever. Why did he have to be one of those men who preferred to wear something under his breeches?

Amanda tried to loosen the knot with her fingernails, but it refused to budge. Finally, she bent her head and nipped at the knot with her teeth. Beneath her cheek, Will's stomach shook with barely contained laughter.

"Oh, shhtop it," she said, his drawstring ensnared between her front teeth.

He held his laughter in check, but while she bent over him, working the stubborn knot loose with her canines, he let his hands roam over her back. She twitched when he inched his hands up over her sides and twisted her torso away when he lingered on a ticklish spot.

She straightened and glared at him. "Do you want out of these or not? I fear I've managed to tie a knot more secure than any sailor in the history of seamanship."

Will laughed. "You tied a decent knot? That would be a first. Still, I won't interfere with your efforts."

She looked into his eyes. They were still dark with need, but laugh lines radiated from the corners. Somehow, laughter in the most intimate of moments only heightened her passion.

"All right, then." She lowered her mouth to his drawstring again, worked the knot until it loosened between her teeth, and then drew the strings open.

"Ahh, sweet freedom." He laughed, stripping off his undergarments. "Would you like to continue your exploration?" Will stood with his arms at his sides. His eyes glowed in the darkness.

Amanda let her gaze travel down the dark line of hair on his belly past his angular hipbones to the dark thatch of hair surrounding his manhood. He looked bigger than she had imagined, but then her best friend, Jenny, had assured her that men swelled to many times their normal size when aroused. She had no idea how Jenny had known this so she assumed her fanciful friend had embellished a tale her brothers had told her. Now she wasn't so sure.

Will's thick shaft stood like the bowsprit of a ship pointing proudly into the wind. Fascinated, she took a step forward.

"Can I touch you?" she asked, her voice a raspy whisper.

"Yes," Will said.

She hesitated then crossed the distance between them until his shaft met her outstretched hand. Will groaned when she curled her hand around him.

Amanda gasped. "Did I hurt you?"

"No." He didn't sound certain, so she eased her grip.

"No," he said again, wrapping his hand around hers, tightening her grip. He didn't let go until she squeezed him harder.

Will scooped Amanda into his arms and carried her to his hammock. He laid her down and then lowered himself on top of her, propping his weight onto his elbows. They looked at each other, not saying anything, both lost in the wonder of the moment.

Amanda bit her lip.

"Having second thoughts?" Will asked, rolling off her as much as the curved hammock would allow.

The question startled her at first, but then she paused to consider. Tonight would change her forever. No, that wasn't quite right. Her time aboard the *Amanda* and with Will had already changed her. She could never go back to the girl she had been even if she wanted to. Even if she lost her nerve and left the cabin, maidenhood intact, she would never be the same. She would forever be the wolf's mate.

"Not at all," she assured him. "It's just that I'm not certain what comes next."

Will threw his head back and laughed. "That hasn't stopped you yet." He kissed her again, taking his time, nibbling her lip.

"Seriously, Will," she pushed at his chest. "I have no idea what to do, and I want this to be perfect."

He pulled back and looked at her, stroking her cheek with his thumb. "I can't promise perfection, but I'll do my best."

The moonlight illuminated the doubt in his eyes. Had she managed to insult him? It hadn't been her intention.

"No, I meant I want to be perfect for *you*," she explained.

"You already are." He placed a light kiss on top of her forehead.

Will nibbled a line of kisses from her ear to her collarbone, and she arched her neck to give him better access. She smoothed her hands along his back, marveling in the curve of hard muscle covered by soft skin and the occasional raised ridge that signified yet another scar.

Will teased one nipple, rubbing the little pink nub with his palm. Amanda gasped again when another jolt of energy coursed from her breast all the way down to the juncture of her thighs, pushing her knees apart with its force.

This was her night, her one night, and she would

leave nothing unexplored, nothing unoffered. She ran her hands down his sides to his buttocks and pulled him to her as she ground her hips against him. Will gave a primal sound signaling the one need even greater than the need for food, the need for one's mate.

She circled her hands to the front of his hips and worked her hand between them. He lifted his hips to give her greater access. She continued the exploration, reaching for his manhood and grasped him. Amanda stroked the head with her thumb, marveling at the silky feel of the skin, the pulsing heat beneath her palm.

"Hey, now. You start doing that and this will be over before it begins."

"Oh, I'm sorry," Amanda said, embarrassed to have done something so obviously wrong. "I told you I didn't know what to do."

"That's not what I meant. I am already on the brink from having you under me, and that may be more than I can take."

"Oh. Then would this be too much?" Amanda giggled and ran a foot up the length of his leg.

When her toe trailed past the back of his knee, her hips splayed beneath his. Palms flat against his buttocks, she pulled him snuggly against her.

The tip of him pressed against her tender flesh. Warm moisture allowed him to slide inside her with ease, yet he held back. Will grunted and raised himself on his knees, straddling one of her legs. Amanda glanced up in confusion, wondering what she had done to make him pull away.

He bent forward to kiss her, and the confusion was forgotten when his tongue tangled with hers. He pushed forward, his hard thigh covered by soft springy curls fueling the fires within. Without shame or regard for her own modesty, she shifted so that her soft folds opened to expose the sensitive nub between them.

Will gave an amused chuckle and reached between them to stroke her more effectively with his thumb. Was he laughing at her again? Amanda no longer cared.

Will rolled off her and onto his side, even as his hand remained in contact with her. He continued to drive her to distraction with his thumb before parting the folds between her legs and gently inserting the tip of one finger. Amanda arched her back when he stroked her inner core.

Lost in a sea of sensation, her own soft moans reached her ears as if from a distance. She rode a wave of pleasure to its crest. In a brief moment of sanity, she cracked one eye open to gauge his reaction to her uninhibited response. Will had his head propped on one hand, his torso supported by one elbow while he made love to her with his other hand. His eyes glowed like golden embers, but his wolfish grin told her he enjoyed this.

The muscles in her abdomen, and those even deeper within, clenched. The intensity of the spasms made her gasp for air. "Will," she called his name, her voice hoarse, "I don't think I can do this anymore."

"You want me to stop?" Will's hand stilled.

"Yes," she said, propping herself up on her elbows. "I mean no. I mean..."

"I know what you mean." He lowered her onto her back and rolled on top of her. He kissed her neck, then settled his knees between her thighs, forcing them open. He lifted his face and looked into her eyes. "Are you frightened?"

Amanda shook her head as she bit her lip. Perhaps she was, but not because of what they were about to share and certainly not of him. However, knowing that she might not be able to make this night last the rest of her life terrified her. She would always remember him and this moment, but she now understood that, once she fully gave herself to him, she would be more lost than ever without him. She would be that lonely old woman at the bedroom window, but at least that woman would have her memories to sustain her.

Will searched her face, and she sensed he needed her assent. The controlled captain had won out, for the moment, over the wolf within. He would send her on her way with no questions asked should she request it. Not trusting her own voice, she smiled her consent before his honorable instincts could assert complete control of him and she lost him forever.

"Wrap your legs around me, my love," he said, and she obeyed.

Never taking his eyes off hers, Will reached down and parted her gently with his fingers before entering her slowly and cautiously. Amanda willed herself to breath lest she pass out and end the evening prematurely. Then Will thrust forward with his hips and easily broke the thin barrier between them.

In an instinctive reaction to the invasion, every muscle in her body tightened. Above, Will's body tensed as well.

"Still doing all right?" he asked a moment later, his breath rustling the curls against her ear.

His voice was tight as though it took great effort to hold himself back. She nodded and he thrust his hips forward then retreated in a slow motion that, at first, matched the rocking of the ship, then in a faster, almost desperate rhythm. To compensate for the curve of the hammock and his lack of leverage, he rolled onto his side and pulled Amanda along with him, and used the strength of his arms as much as his legs to time her movements to his. Amanda gasped when he thrust deeper, filling her completely.

Amanda could sense Will watching her, measuring her response. She knew he would stop if she gave him the slightest sign. It bothered her that at this moment he could maintain that much control over his own desire.

Then her own rational mind deserted her. She reveled in the feel of the muscles of his back and hips working in rhythm under her hands. She slid her palms over them, pulling him to her. With each thrust, Amanda became more aware of her physical being and her surroundings faded until she and Will were all that remained.

Will shut his eyes, and a fierce look of concentration washed over his chiseled features. When he quickened his pace, she stopped her exploration and reached up to grab his shoulders. Will's body thrust against hers, her body responding in kind, the two of them setting the hammock in motion. Her inner core trembled, and reason left her completely.

Will tightened his grip around her and deepened his thrusts, digging his fingers into her hips, straining against her. Then he stilled. His forearms wrapped around her back, his hands gripping her shoulders as though he too were trying to hold himself steady against the waves. He leaned forward, rested his forehead on her shoulder, and released a shuddering breath.

They lay, mingled together, for a few more minutes before Will withdrew. Then he put his arm around her waist and drew her to him, her backside nestled against his hips. Amanda sighed her contentment when he drew his quilt over them.

The hammock, once again swung in time to the gentle rocking of the ship, and Amanda melted into it, into him. Gradually, her awareness of the night noises that surrounded them returned, the creaking of the timbers, her snoring shipmates, the sound of the city just yards away. The warmth of his chest against her back seeped into her, and sleep beckoned her into its depths.

"Will," she said in a hoarse whisper, feeling a desperate need to take full advantage of her final moments of consciousness.

"Hmmm." His sleepy murmur made her wonder if she hadn't lost her last opportunity.

Before she gave into her own need to sleep, she let the words spill from her lips. "I love you," she whispered.

Tears stung the back of her eyelids. She might have put these final blissful moments to better use by bidding him farewell.

Chapter Twenty-Six

Will awoke the following morning in a state of bemused lethargy. His brain mired in a fog, he considered doing nothing more than lying in his hammock all day. As captain, he would normally be up and about before sunrise, but the harsh glare through the high windows told him sunrise had been hours ago.

Will yawned and stretched muscles unaccustomed to use. He considered rising, but only for a moment. Even a captain ought to have the right to sleep in every once in awhile. Hunger gnawed at his belly, but he didn't want breakfast just yet. He glanced at the empty space next to him and gave a wicked little grin. In time, he would teach Amanda that one didn't always need to be so attentive to duty.

The memory of his adventurous she-wolf only intensified his hunger. She had been a fast learner last night, unafraid and uninhibited, just what one might expect from a woman with enough daring to sign on to a privateer. What she lacked in experience, she more than made up for in enthusiasm.

Still, he had vowed to take his time with her, to ease her introduction to lovemaking and give her the leeway to retreat if she wanted to.

A vision of her, pale lashes sweeping against flushed cheeks, lips swollen from passionate kisses, hands reaching out to touch him in the most intimate of ways, made him groan in near pain.

She had enjoyed their lovemaking as much as he. Then, as they fell asleep, wrapped in each other's arms, she had declared her love for him. He would have laughed with joy were it not likely to bring Buck running to see what addled his captain.

Sighing, he considered that he must at least dress. Eventually, he would be needed on deck. He eyed his blue woolen coat, slung carelessly over the back of a chair, a bulge in one pocket marring its crisp lines. In the heat of the moment, he had completely forgotten the peace offering, betrothal gift, farewell gift. That mattered little, he decided. He would have plenty of time to present it to her today—as a betrothal gift. After last night, there could be no doubt she needed him as much as he needed her.

Will stood to dress, taking his time so he might not be fully finished when Amanda returned to his quarters with his breakfast. He would satisfy one hunger at a time.

Alas, the anticipated knock at his door didn't come until he had finished tying his cravat in the small mirror above the basin.

"Come in." The mirror reflected an eager light in his eyes.

Damn, he looked like a man besotted, or at least one well satisfied. He would have to dim his enthusiasm a bit before he went on deck to preserve Amanda's reputation not to mention his own. A ship's captain should not be so affected by a night of passion, or a woman.

Cookie entered, carrying a tray in his chubby hands. "Mornin', sir. Shall I set this on the desk, sir?"

Will nodded. The cook's uncharacteristically formal manner set him on edge.

"Very good, sir." Cookie laid the tray at the edge of the desk, and then proceeded to arrange Will's breakfast things in a way that reminded him of Amanda's attention to detail. Evidently, she had given him precise instructions this morning.

"Where is she?"

"Pardon, sir?" Cookie asked, looking up from the pitcher of cream he had just set next to the captain's coffee.

"Amanda. Where is she?"

"Not here." Cookie rearranged the cup and saucer, adjusting and readjusting the angle of the cup's handle.

"I can see that," Will said through gritted teeth. "But *where* is she?"

"I don't rightly know, sir." Cookie scratched behind his ear and studied the arrangement.

Will drew back the linen cloth that covered his breakfast. The light yellow of hard cooked yolks surrounded by charred whites interlaced with flecks of brown scrapings stared back at him. Cookie's eggs.

"She didn't make breakfast?"

"No, sir, I made it." Cookie's shoulders slumped.

Will wanted to strangle the full truth out of the portly little Irishman, but he grappled with his temper and decided to take it one step at a time. After all, if Amanda had deserted him, he still needed a cook.

"Did you see her this morning?" he asked

"Yes." Cookie nodded, chins wobbling.

Will had hoped for a more effusive response, but at least the man hadn't started out with a lie. In fact, he seemed eager to cooperate. Will suspected he would have said more had someone not given him specific instructions about what not to say. The way Cookie refused to meet his eyes left him no doubt as to the identity of that certain someone.

No matter. Cookie's response so far suggested he simply needed to ask the right questions. Later, he would explain to his cook that orders from the cook's assistant did not outrank direct questions from the captain.

"Where?" The one syllable held both question and command.

"On deck," Cookie said with a slight hesitation, as though he were measuring his answer against a list of things he wasn't supposed to reveal. Cookie tugged at his collar.

"What was she doing when you saw her?" His voice was slow, measured.

A look of panic flashed in Cookie's eyes, and his gaze darted about the room, searching for a means of escape. Will knew he had chosen the right tack.

"Leaving," Cookie said, his gaze dropping to the floor in defeat.

"Leaving?" Will roared, making Cookie jump. "With whom? And did she say where the hell she was going?"

"She didn't tell you?" Doctor Miller asked from just outside Will's door.

The doctor gave a silent signal to Cookie and the cook nodded. He hunched his shoulders and shuffled from the captain's quarters.

"Didn't tell me what?" Will ground out once he and the doctor were alone.

"She left early this morning to go ashore to live

with her father," Doctor Miller said. "I assumed you knew, given that you've been trying to get her off the ship for months now. With her father alive, she has no reason to remain. And there is your rule."

"I don't need you reminding me of my rules, Doctor," Will said, his words laced with warning. He raked his hand through his hair. "She's been a member of my crew for months now as well as my personal cook. You didn't think it odd that I didn't see her off?"

The doctor shrugged. "Well, actually, I didn't see her leave either. I heard from the men when they returned with the transport boat. But don't worry. Martin said they left her safely in the care of Mr. Blakely."

Will stomach clenched. The last time she had been left in her father's care, he had gone off to war, leaving his children to fend for themselves. What's more, he still didn't quite trust the elder Blakely's good sense not to bring his daughter trouble. The man talked too much, and in his experience, those who did were often indiscreet.

It annoyed him that his men would have rowed her ashore without express orders from their captain. His recent conversation with Buck came back to him. Evidently, his men were as eager to please her as they were to serve him. Then he remembered that her new wardrobe had not yet arrived. If she wore that damn green dress again, and he knew that she had since he had dumped everything else overboard, they wouldn't have given him a second thought. When he got her back, he would have a talk with her, and a few of his men, about who commanded this ship.

"Shall I ask Buck to send someone to bring her

back?"

"No, that won't be necessary. Thank you, Doctor. That will be all."

After the doctor left, Will rubbed his hand against the back of his neck and blew a pent-up breath between pursed lips. She had thrown him overboard!

He paced the small confines of his quarters. How could he have misread Amanda? After months in close quarters, and their shared intimacy, he thought he knew her as well as he knew anyone. He had been so certain of her affections, that he had almost convinced himself a formal marriage proposal would be unnecessary. What woman, especially an innocent, would jump into bed with a man she didn't intend to marry?

Yet, she had left him, forever, without so much as a farewell.

Will shook his head, disgusted. He acted like a damn bridegroom, jilted at the altar. Well he wouldn't sit around moping and waiting for his lover to return. He stopped pacing and strode out the door, scaling the stairs to the upper deck in two steps.

The first reaction from his crew did nothing to soothe his irritation. Several men stopped what they were doing to eye him for a moment before they busied themselves, even more diligently than before, with whatever task lay at hand. Even the more slovenly among his crew were unusually hard-working this morning.

"Buck, take us away from this damn coast," Will grumbled. "I need some fresh sea air."

"Any destination in particular, sir?" Buck asked.

Will glared at him. Buck knew he had free rein to improvise when his orders were nonspecific. His request for clarification seemed an obvious attempt to needle his captain. The counsel Buck had given yesterday spoke volumes about his soft spot for Amanda. He probably thought Will had sent her ashore, and now sought to make him suffer for it. He would regain command of his ship, starting with his second in command.

"Don't toy with me, Buck," Will said.

"Wouldn't dream of it, sir," Buck said with nary a trace of his usual good humor. "I just wondered if you had a destination in mind."

"Away from here!" Will exploded.

He gave a snort of disgust and strode to the bulwark. He had to get away from Buck before he did something he regretted and destroyed his relationship with his closest friend.

Did Buck think he had sent Amanda to live with her father? Did he think him capable of leaving her behind? He would let him think that for now. It was preferable to explaining that he had been the one abandoned.

Will clasped his hands at his back and stared at the sea, adopting a stoic expression he hoped did not betray his inner turmoil. Only those brave enough to venture close would be able to sense the tension lying just below the surface, but his men gave him a wide berth.

Damn her and damn them! And damn his small ship!

Sailors loved nothing more than a juicy piece of gossip, setting upon it like a pack of gulls.

From the way they avoided him, his crew might well know he and Amanda had spent the night together. If one man had seen her race into his cabin last night, they would all know by morning. They would also know, even before he did, that she had left him.

Will's stomach clenched, and he was glad he had not eaten Cookie's eggs.

Ever since she came on board, he seemed to be the last to know everything. Perhaps it was better for his crew, and for him, if she were gone. Her very presence undermined his authority, disrupted his ability to command, and weakened crew morale. Despite Buck's assertions to the contrary, he had been right all along, women did not belong on ships.

"My glass!" Will bellowed, startling a sailor who had been careless enough to wander close.

The man retrieved the spyglass, handed it to his captain and then scurried away.

Will snapped open the long tube and held it to his eye. The wind whipping his hair about his face, he scanned the horizon. Buck ordered full sail, and the *Amanda* picked up speed, skipping across the waves, leaving Baltimore behind.

He would give anything for an English ship to appear on the horizon just now, but the crisp line where sea met sky remained unmarred by cloud or sail. He continued to scan, hoping to appear less brooding. He could not let his crew see how much her departure had affected him.

He lowered the spyglass and caught a few of the sailors scanning the horizon as well, their hands shielding their eyes against the glare of the morning sun. His mood elevated ever so slightly. There was nothing like the all-consuming prospect of chasing a British prize to take the focus off him.

Alas, with the aid of the glass, he could see there

were no enemy ships upon which to vent his anger and frustration. He snapped the instrument shut. If only he could have willed a ship to appear. Or better yet, a whole squadron. In fact, prudence be damned, he felt like taking on a ship of war instead of a straggling merchantman. He wanted a fight, and if he couldn't have it with her, the whole of the Royal Navy might do.

Staring out at the empty horizon, Will pondered how best to spend the next month vexing the English and forgetting Amanda. The English forces and the loyal Tories in America were hungry for supplies, and that translated into more opportunities for him. His chance would come.

The mere thought of the hunt sent a primal thrill coursing through him. If he were lucky, he would spend the next month or so, prowling the seas, and not think of Amanda for more than a moment. Will clasped his hands behind his back. With no English in sight, he allowed himself to envision Amanda's future.

She would languish on shore, drinking tea with her father and his acquaintances. She might make a few female friends, provided she could knock off some of the rough edges she had developed aboard ship. He chuckled, wondering if she could manage to keep a civil tongue while playing a game of whist. He doubted she even knew she had a penchant for swearing under her breath when frustrated.

After life at sea, she would be drowning in boredom after a month, probably less. Once he had bloodied a few British noses, he would track her down at her father's home, whence forth she would plead with him to take her back even as a lowly member of his crew. He would, of course, but only after she did a significant amount of apologizing and agreed to marry him.

A joyful possibility crossed his mind. Perhaps she would even be with child! He had taken no precautions. He hadn't thought he needed to. After a month passed, she would surely know, and if she did carry his child, she would have no choice but to accept him.

Of course, if she were pregnant, he would not give her the chance to plead. Nor would he give her the chance to decline his proposal. He would announce their betrothal to the world, and her father, and force her to the altar even if he had to carry her there himself.

"Sail ho, Captain!" Nate cried from the platform above, snapping Will out of pleasant dreams of Amanda's ultimate surrender.

"Where away?" Will called.

"Off the port bow," Nate bellowed.

Will snapped open the glass again and scanned the horizon. A faint silhouette shimmered in the sunlight, no more than a flash of light and shadow before it disappeared again. The boy had excellent vision! Will peered through his glass, hoping it hadn't been light bouncing off a distant wave or the remnants of a low wisp of cloud. His heart leapt when the shadow appeared again. Eyes straining against the glass, he watched it grow larger and resolve into the shape of a distant sail.

He was about to give the order, when Nate called down again, "There's three of 'em, sir!"

Will brought the glass to his eye again. The armada he wished for took form and sent his mood soaring. Three square-rigged ships dotted the horizon. Already at full sail, the *Amanda* gained fast. They were English merchantmen, and from the size of them, all likely to be heavily armed and ready for a fight. Well, they would have it!

Normally, three armed ships would be more than a lone schooner would take on, but the *Amanda* had sailed close enough for Will to see these ships were low in the water, indicating they bore heavy cargo. This and their size made them significantly less agile than the *Amanda*.

A fresh breeze tugged at Will's hair, and he lifted his face to the wind. The blustery weather could be unpredictable, but the *Amanda* had been built to handle herself in capricious seas. The trick would be to disable, perhaps even sink, one of the ships to even the odds. It would mean the loss of a prize, but it would lessen the risk for his crew, and he wasn't about to put the salving of his ego above their safety.

His crew would have to hit the first merchantman "between wind and water"—the underside of the hull, normally below water, that showed when the ship rolled over in the waves. The nine-pound shot from his cannons could do considerable damage if aimed well, and they would have to, because the men of the *Amanda* would not get another chance at it.

Will snapped his glass shut again, his laughter bringing smiles to his crew. This had to be a good omen. Just after making plans to spend the next month vexing the British, the Good Lord had sent him three promising candidates to sink his teeth into. Now, if it wasn't asking too much, perhaps God would see fit to ensure that Amanda would be miserable on land. Not too much, but enough to make her realize where she belonged.

Chapter Twenty-Seven

The trip from the wharf to the home that Amanda's father had established in Baltimore promised to be a dreary one. The small transport skiff bumped against the dock, and the first drop of cold rain hit Amanda's cheek. With an anxious look in his eye, her father reached down with both hands to help her onto solid ground. When she informed him that she had no luggage, he shot her a questioning glance, but said nothing.

Instead, he wrapped her hand in the crook of his elbow, capturing her as though he sensed her reluctance, and led her to a hired coach.

The vehicle appeared as though it had been owned by someone of wealth and status at one time, but had fallen into disrepair. The gilded outlines of a stylized grayhound and a touch of red paint were all that remained of a family crest that once emblazoned the peeling ochre lacquer. Even the two sway-backed horses, with their bent heads, dull eyes, and protruding ribs, looked like relics from a faded past.

How appropriate that such a dreary conveyance would carry her to a new life.

Thunder rumbling in the distance, Amanda's father handed her up into the shadowy interior. She glanced about, letting her eyes adjust to the darkness. Closer inspection did not improve her first impressions. Red velvet curtains, no more than rags really, hung at the dirt-encrusted windows. The gold cushions on the seat were matted and stained. Twin depressions, dark fibers delineating their edges, showed where countless derrieres had perched over the years. Still, she had never ridden in anything fancier than a horse drawn cart, so even in a state of disrepair, the coach would have fascinated her on any other day. Today, however, the dilapidated interior matched her despair.

The carriage swayed alarmingly when Amanda's father clambered up the stairs to sit across from her, and she had to grab the leather strap to keep from tumbling out the door. Clearly, the springs were in no better shape than the interior. She hoped the ride would not be a long one.

What started as a light sprinkling of cold rain turned into a steady drizzle. The driver coaxed the two tired horses into motion. Thunder boomed overhead, and Amanda pressed her face against the glass, peering through the streaks of grit to see dark clouds rolling in. At any moment, the skies might open up and turn the rutted road into a mud path that would make progress impossible. Amanda brightened momentarily at the thought.

The rain beat down in a continuous drizzle that made the roads slow going and uncomfortable, but not impassable even though the rundown carriage seemed destined to find each furrow.

She leaned her head against the side of the carriage and watched the rain beat a steady rhythm against the window. The drops caught, pooled, and fell like dirty tears down the glass.

Sensing her father's anxious gaze on her from the

opposite side of the coach, Amanda sat up. She couldn't let him think her anything but the happiest daughter in the world to be reunited with her father. And she was happy, or at least mostly so. She just hadn't expected to find herself ripped in half when she left the *Amanda* and her captain behind.

Her body still tingled where he had lain against her, still pulsed where his rough hands had caressed her. She had washed in the basin that morning, but the scent of their lovemaking still lingered on her skin.

The coach ground to a halt, and Amanda raised her chin. She cast a questioning glance at her father, then peered out the rain-streaked window. She could see nothing from her vantage point inside the vehicle except a few townspeople, hats and bonnets pulled low over their brows, skittering along the wooden walkway, seeking refuge from what had become a downpour.

Mr. Blakely opened the door to the carriage and leaned out. Gripping the side to steady himself, he spoke to the driver. The wind whipped their words away, and Amanda could not hear the exchange.

He pulled himself back inside, rain running in rivulets from the corners of his hat.

"What is it, Father?"

"Appears to be a carriage ahead of us stuck in the mud," Mr. Blakely said. "Not to worry though. I'll get out and help the driver. We'll be on our way in no time."

"Be careful," Amanda cautioned, laying a hand on her father's sleeve.

Something about the situation set her on edge, but she couldn't explain it, certainly not to her father. With no justification for the uneasiness, she would only give him cause for concern about her soundness of mind. He had enough of his own troubles, having only recently recovered from an illness himself.

"Not to worry dear." He patted her hand before stepping out of the carriage. Rain blew in through the open door, spattering her green silk with dark splotches. "I'll be back before you know it."

He shut the door behind him, leaving Amanda by herself, with nothing to do but wait. She shut her eyes, leaned back against the tattered gold cushions, and listened to the rain beat against the coach, trying not to think about the dreariness of the future that awaited her.

A short time later, the door opened again.

"That was qui—"

The words died in her throat. A burlap sack was thrown over her head and darkness surrounded her. The sack and the pressure of a man's arm around her neck robbed her of breath. She struggled to hold onto consciousness.

****

Will breakfasted the next morning on charred eggs, blackened toast and coffee that could best be described as "grainy." However, neither Cookie's insipid fare nor the pitching of the ship during the summer storm that had rolled out to sea from the nearby coast could dampen his mood.

After a merry chase the previous day, one in which the *Amanda* toyed with her quarry, Will took all three ships in a feat of pure genius, if he did say so himself. The sailing skill of the *Amanda's* crew had managed to confuse the merchant ships until they sailed more closely together than wise. Neil had been the one to spot their error in seamanship, and suggested that, instead of sinking the first ship, they might aim for her main mast.

Will's gunners had steadily improved over the course of the last few months, and he wasn't disappointed. With the first volley, the mast splintered like kindling, crashing into the rigging of her sister ship and effectively disabling the two ships with one shot. The captain of the third ship wisely chose to strike her colors.

Once the first two ships were repaired, he would order three prize crews to take the ships, their prisoners, and their cargo to the court in Boston, assuming the port wasn't currently blockaded by the British. If it were, they would simply sail farther south to one of the lesser courts and be back to a full complement within the month.

Will's good fortune, ironically, caused an unforeseen wrinkle in his plan to take his mind off Amanda. He had intended to spend that month hunting British merchant ships, but the *Amanda* only carried enough men for three prize crews—skeletal ones at that. With all three gone in one shot, the remaining crew could do little more than sail the ship. They certainly couldn't pursue another prize until their mates returned.

Perhaps he would lay low for a week or two, then sail to Baltimore and find Amanda sooner than planned. She belonged with him; surely, it wouldn't take her a month to see that.

Yesterday's skirmish had appeased Will's inner demons, and much of his anger had passed. If she were with child, he couldn't stand the thought of her, for one single moment, wondering whether she would be left to raise his child on her own.

He took a large swig of his coffee, forgetting that Amanda hadn't made it, and grimaced at the layer of grit coating his tongue. He had just picked up a napkin to swab his mouth when Buck entered his quarters.

"Captain, sorry to interrupt your, er...breakfast," Buck eyed the pitch black toast and half-eaten eggs, "but there's a packet ship hailing us."

"Packet ship?" ask Will.

Packet ships delivered the post between ports and the naval ships at sea. However, the privateers that prowled the coast usually had to send a boat into port if they wanted their mail. Unless of course, the more formal branches of the American military forces needed their assistance.

Will threw down his napkin and rose to his feet. If a ship hailed them, it meant she carried an urgent message, perhaps even a special request from General Washington himself. The general, although he knew little about ships or sailing, promoted privateering. He understood just how much the informal naval force offered in the way of support by depriving the British troops of their supplies. Most of the privateer captains, acknowledging the importance of friends in high places, did their best to accommodate the general's occasional special request. This might be a most unfortunate time to be shorthanded.

Will yanked on his coat and followed Buck on deck. When his second handed him the glass, Will held it to his eye, struggling to make sense of the small transport skiff rowing toward them through the driving rain. The boat pitched and rolled on each wave, appearing and disappearing.

Will's heart skipped a beat when he made out the man at the rear of the small transport boat, clutching onto the edge as though he were going to be sick at any moment. The packet ship didn't bear an urgent message in the way of a post. The urgent message would be delivered by the sender himself. A land man such as Blakely would never brave travel in a transport boat in the midst of a storm, unless he wished to discuss a matter of great importance.

Will's heart thumped against his breastbone during the eternity it took for the oarsmen to bring the small boat alongside the *Amanda* and to hand Blakely, legs shaking, up the rope ladder.

****

"She's gone? What do you mean she's gone?" Will bellowed against the wind that howled through the rigging. "When?"

"Yesterday," Blakely choked out.

Wet and shivering from the driving rain of the late summer squall, Blakely's face had lost all color. Will knew he ought to take the man below, get him some dry clothes and something to warm his insides, but Blakely's discomfort served a purpose too. He would have the details out of the old man sooner if he kept him on deck in the driving rain.

"We were in the coach on our way home, sir," Blakely shouted, rain spattering from his lips like spittle. "We stopped for what we thought to be a carriage stuck in the street ahead of us. I got out, leaving Amanda in the coach," he paused to hold his clenched fist over his mouth and swallowed before continuing, "while my driver and I went to see if we could help get the carriage out of the mud."

Blakely pitched forward when the *Amanda* rolled, and Will reached out to steady him. "Where's Amanda?" he asked once Blakely's face returned from green to its normal ashen gray.

"I don't know." His voice held a note of helplessness that made Will want to shake him.

Blakely's eyes were turning vacant, and Will grasped him by the shoulders, forcing him to focus. "What do you mean you don't know? She wasn't in the coach when you returned?"

"No, she wasn't."

"Did you see her leave? Or see anyone who looked suspicious hanging around the coach?"

"Well, the thing is, Captain, my driver and I both received lumps to the head. They knocked us out cold." He sounded at once embarrassed to admit his incompetence yet glad to have an excuse.

The ship rolled again, and Blakely stifled another urge to vomit. Will wondered whether the pitching of the ship had Blakely turning green or if the knock on the head was partly to blame. He would have Doctor Miller examine the man once he had his answers.

"Did you happen to see who hit you?" he yelled against the wind.

"I caught a glimpse. I would bet my life on it they were sailors." He forced the words between chattering teeth.

"Why's that?"

"I'm not really sure, but they seemed a little disreputable."

Will considered the response. The man probably assumed any seedy looking character was a sailor. Normally he would have been irritated at the assumption, but he had far greater concerns at the moment.

"They were English," Blakely added as though to soften the insult.

"You know that for a fact?" If true, that would at least narrow the possibilities.

"Yes, fairly certain, anyway. I heard them talking before we were knocked out. Their accents were definitely English, though not of the well-bred London sort."

The wind swallowed Blakely's words, and the churning seas made it difficult for the man to control the contents of his stomach. Further discussion would have to wait until they were below deck.

Will led Blakely below and settled him in a chair, several blankets about his shoulders. Then he went to the cupboard and poured two glasses of whiskey. He handed one to Blakely who accepted it with obvious gratitude.

Will swallowed half the contents of his glass in one gulp and considered what he knew. Sailors. Common sailors, if Blakely could be counted on to judge their accents correctly. Most likely, he would be dealing with ruffians and not men of consequence.

But what could they want with Amanda? He took another swallow of whiskey, grimacing when it scorched his throat. He hadn't wasted his best on Amanda's father.

His success had made him many enemies among the English naval men and wealthy British merchants over the years. One of them could have made off with Amanda as a matter of revenge, in which case, she could be taken to England or to the European continent.

It would be harder to track her down in enemy territory or on the continent. Not impossible, of course. Just much more difficult.

Common sailors, on the other hand, would be easier to track. Although their ship might eventually be bound for England or some other shore, they couldn't requisition a ship or direct the sailing of one themselves. If their ship was not scheduled to sail immediately, it meant Amanda would remain in American waters longer. It offered only a slight advantage, but it did improve his odds.

Moreover, common sailors, especially those up to no good, loved to brag about their nefarious deeds. With dozens of men all bunked together in the hold of a ship, knowledge of her presence would spread like a fire. That too increased the odds of finding her, although it didn't do much for her safety.

Blakely snuffled and slurped his whiskey, bringing Will's thoughts back to the present.

"Did you happen to catch any of what they said?" Will noted that the color had returned to the old man's cheeks. Perhaps he might remember more now that he did not fear for his life.

"Not anything that made sense to me. Something about catching their own prize and, wouldn't their captain be pleased." He gave an embarrassed grin. "Now that I think about it, I suppose that's how I knew they were sailors."

"I suppose so." Will swallowed the last of his whiskey before setting the glass on his desk.

Blakely raised his glass with a shaking hand and drained the last of his whiskey. He held onto his glass though, turning a hopeful glance toward the bottle on the desk. Will poured more of the amber liquid, hoping to set him at ease. He needed to ask more pointed questions, and he didn't need Blakely getting defensive.

"Did you happen to mention to anyone that you were meeting Amanda at the dock?" he asked, keeping his tone light, inquisitive but not accusatory.

"No one," Blakely replied without pause.

"No one?"

"Well, I suppose I might have mentioned it to a couple of my oldest and dearest friends." He paused at a memory. "Met them when I served in the army."

Will didn't comment that would make his acquaintance with these men less than two years old, and perhaps a distant two years at that. He noted these two "dear friends" as possible suspects, but would come back to them only if there weren't more likely leads to pursue.

"Do you recall where you were when you mentioned this to your friends?" Will asked.

"I believe I might have been playing cards at the time." Blakely's voice held a definite guilty note.

"At the home of one of your friends, or in a public establishment?"

"Just a tavern somewhere," Blakely said, looking even more guilty now. "I don't recall exactly which one."

Had the man drunk too much to remember? If so, Will would add that to the list of things that disqualified him to take possession of his daughter. Asking Blakely to recall who might have been standing next to his table would be a waste of time if the man couldn't even recall which tavern he had been in. He decided to try a new line of questions.

"Did you happen to mention your daughter's recent good fortune due to the *Amanda's* successes?" If the man had been playing cards, he might have asked for a loan, promising future payment once he had access to his daughter's funds.

"No, of course not." Blakely's denial sounded strong, but he didn't look up.

"You told no one about your daughter's funds?" Certain he was lying, Will wanted to choke the truth out of the man. However, if he harmed her father, he didn't think it would sit well with Amanda should he ever get her back.

"No, I didn't, I swear it." Blakely looked up, "But…"

"But what?" Will growled.

"I might have said something…that is, I might have implied." Blakely seemed unable to continue.

Will grasped the man's shoulder, bunching his coat in his fist and forcing Blakely to look at him. "You might have implied what?"

"It's just that everyone is aware of your reputation. I might have implied that you might soon be part of the family."

Will dropped the man's shoulder, and Blakely slumped back in his chair looking as beaten as his wrinkled coat. Had Amanda been taken because of him?

"What else do you remember about the incident?" Will asked.

Blakely pursed his lips and stared at the captain's desk blotter, "Hmm… Oh yes! Something about being serene. What do you suppose they could have meant by that?" He appeared eager to have left the topic of his indiscretion behind them.

"Serene?" Will said, musing over the sound of the word. He didn't suppose it to be a common word for a sailor. A sudden thought hit him like a blow to the gut. "Could the word have been 'Serenity,' perhaps?"

"Yes, I believe it was, now that you mention it. Does it mean anything to you?"

"I'm not sure," Will lied. He reached out a hand to pull a startled Blakely to his feet. "I want you to go home in case she finds a way to escape. She may try to find her way there. I need to check out a few things on my own."

"But, Captain..." Blakely protested when Will drew the blankets from his shoulders.

"I will get your daughter back," Will said, ending the man's sputtering.

He had not lied. He would get Amanda back, but he wouldn't be returning her.

The summer storm, furious while it lasted, spent itself out, and the world sparkled in the sun by the time Will and Blakely stepped on deck. The transport boat, however, had decided not to wait out the storm tied to the *Amanda* and had already returned to the packet ship. Will called for one of his own boats to return Blakely to the ship.

Blakely's eyes told him he would have prefer to remain on the *Amanda*, but Will left him no opportunity to ask. Each time the man opened his mouth to say something, Will shut it with a hard look.

After seeing Amanda's father off, Will returned to his own quarters to think through his next move. He was sorry he had so purposefully intimidated the old man. In truth, he didn't envy his position. Blakely surely loved his only daughter and the idea of sitting at home, virtually impotent, must have been hard to swallow.

Yet, it must be so. Love alone would not bring her back nor keep her safe. Nor was he willing to let the man have her afterwards. He had been reunited with his daughter for no more than an hour before managing to to lose her. At least he had enough wits about him to note a few useful things about her captors. He pondered the word that they had used—serenity. Was it possible? Had Amanda been kidnapped by men from the *HMS Serenity*?

If so, it made no sense. Will had served on the *Serenity* as a boy. Captain Goodman still commanded the ship last he had heard.

It had been years since he had seen his former captain. He had been even younger than Neil when he first joined the Royal Navy and only slightly older when he left. Captain Goodman had gone a long way in replacing the hole left in his heart by the death of his father.

While they were on opposite sides now, he didn't think Captain Goodman bore him any ill will. But even if he did, revenge wasn't his style. Captain Goodman held honor and devotion to duty above all else. He might put Will in chains, if he were able to capture him, but he would never target someone close to him.

"Buck," Will called, loud enough for his second to hear even if he were above deck.

"Yes, sir?" Buck appeared so quickly Will surmised he had been waiting outside the door.

"We sail back to Baltimore."

"Yes, sir!" Buck replied, his hazel eyes twinkling.

Chapter Twenty-Eight

Amanda opened her eyes and coughed, spitting bits of moldy sawdust. Her cheek rested against rough wood and darkness surrounded her.

Raucous male laughter drifted from somewhere above, a distant sound, as if left over from a dream. The room swayed and her stomach lurched, confirming that her surroundings were real enough. She closed her eyes again, swallowing the sharp sting of bile.

How had she gotten here? Her last memories were of riding in her father's coach, the broken springs threatening to throw her to the floor each time the spindled wheels found a rut. The constant drizzle of rain turned into a sudden downpour. Another coach got stuck in the mud and blocked the street. Her father got out to help…

A thousand needles poked at her throat. There had been a man, or more precisely, there had been a man's arm, beefy and covered with crisp hair, curled about her neck. She hadn't seen the owner of the arm. Something rough had been thrown over her head. Burlap, judging from the way her face itched. None too clean, she added, crinkling her nose at the moldy odor clinging to her skin.

Trying until her head throbbed, she couldn't remember more. Her abductors, whomever they were, must have carried her unconscious body to this place.

Amanda opened her eyes, trying to focus on something beyond the plank beneath her cheek. Wherever here was.

After the dizziness passed, she tried to right herself by pushing against the rough-hewn planks with arms that didn't seem to be her own. Looking down, she realized they were bound with a thin rope, almost a twine, wrapped several times around her wrists and pulled so tightly her hands had gone numb. Amanda flexed her fingers to return at least some of the circulation. Then she twisted her wrists trying to loosen her bindings. The rope dug in, tearing at her wrists until they burned.

Amanda licked her dry lips, tasting the musty burlap sack on her tongue. Tiny fibers dug into her face, like pins in a pincushion, making her want to claw at her skin. She bore the pain of movement long enough to bring her bound hands up to brush a lock of hair from her eyes and at least some of the debris from her cheeks.

Finally, the fog cleared from her brain and her eyes adjusted to the darkness. A sliver of yellow light shone through a crack in the planks, illuminating the dust and molds that hung in the air. By its faint light, she could see sacks of grain and other foodstuffs lining the walls. Footsteps sounded overhead, then a shadow passed by the light temporarily shrouding her prison in darkness.

The dull thud of many heavy boots suggested a gathering of some sort. A short burst of laughter, a cheer, then the steady rumble of voices again. Were they playing a game—cards perhaps? She doubted they were eating since she couldn't smell any food. Her stomach growled at the thought.

Were they aware of her presence? If salvation sat less than ten feet away, one loud plea for help might bring them running. On the other hand, the odds were that these men were her prison guards. If she yelled, she might find herself gagged with that hateful sack, knocked over the head, or worse.

The room swayed, tilting on its side as though pushed by an unseen force, then settled back into position. A moment later the pattern repeated. Sway, tilt, settle. Sway, tilt, settle. A familiar rhythm, one to which she had grown accustomed. Her captors had taken her aboard a ship. Beyond the sacks of grain sat row after row of barrels. Some of the larger ones looked like they might hold wine or rum. The smaller ones stacked into mini pyramids looked similar to those used to hold gunpowder on the *Amanda*. Beyond that, she couldn't see clearly, the size of the hold being so large that it might have held the whole of the *Amanda* with room to spare.

She tried to get a sense of how much time had passed, but there were no windows in the hold through which to gauge the time of day. It might have been hours since her abduction, or perhaps even days given the way her head throbbed. The faint light lacked the brilliance of sunlight and probably came from an oil lamp. It could very well be evening, or the deck above might simply be windowless.

Perhaps not too much time had passed. The rate of the rhythmic rocking suggested they were still at anchor in shallow waters. Perhaps they had not set sail yet. She strained her ears for sounds that spoke of a nearby town or city, but heard nothing over the laughter of the men. Her stomach knotted when she considered the possibility they had reached their destination already.

She licked dry lips again and surveyed her makeshift prison. Grain spilled from a few of the sacks around her, and her stomach growled again. She tried to work up enough saliva to swallow and ease the pain in her throat. Hunger was the least of her problems; the dried grain would be useless to her. Without water, she would die of thirst long before hunger claimed her.

Surely, her captors wouldn't leave her down here to waste away. What use could she be to them dead?

A rat nibbled at a nearby sack, tearing a hole and unleashing a stream that formed a golden cone-shaped mound on the wooden planks. She fought back the image of what the rats would do to her if she were to die here among the cargo.

No. She shook her head, instantly regretting the action when white-hot pain stabbed behind her eyes. If her captors wanted her dead, she would be dead by now. But what on earth could they want with her?

She doubted this had anything to do with her father. He was a farmer and a common soldier and simply not important enough for anybody to gather notice.

Could her kidnapping be somehow linked to Will? She had learned from some of the *Amanda's* crew that he had amassed a fortune from privateering. She never knew how much of what her shipmates told her was true and how much they exaggerated. They did have a penchant for expanding a tale with every telling, and she had earned an unfortunate reputation for being gullible. Even so, the story probably held a kernel of truth. According to Buck, she had accumulated a sizable amount of funds herself. Perhaps her assailants would ask for a ransom.

Panic welled anew when she thought of her gentle father coming face to face with the ruffians who had snatched her. He would gladly pay whatever they asked, but he didn't have that kind of money, and she hadn't had time to give him access to her accounts. She prayed he would have the soundness of mind to go to Captain Stoakes for help.

Would Will pay a ransom?

Probably, assuming the *Amanda* hadn't weighed anchor and left Baltimore already. Nevertheless, the idea that Captain Stoakes might be searching for her even now, allowed some of her fear to subside. She leaned against the crate at her back, considering her situation from a more rational frame of mind.

Although comforted by the notion, she also hated the thought of Captain Stoakes being the one to rescue her. She would owe him, and if she had to life her life without him, she preferred not to have any ties binding her to him. Perhaps she could free herself before her captors had a chance to make any demands, then her father and the captain wouldn't be forced to deal with this mess.

Scuffling feet and shouts sounded from the deck above. She tried to make out what they were saying, but the words were muted by the heavy footfalls of numerous running boots.

Had something caught the attention of the ship's captain, something important enough for him to call all hands on deck? Despite her recent resolve to free herself, she nurtured a hope that the something came with piercing gold eyes and dark curly hair.

As quickly as it began, the commotion died away,

and Amanda's hopes died with it. Perhaps it had been unreasonable to expect a rescue attempt so soon.

A second rat gnawed at a bag, tearing through it with sharp teeth. Too bad she couldn't enlist their help with her bindings.

Another rat scurried over to nibble at the grain spilling out of the sack.

What about something else sharp? She spied a nail supporting a coil of rope much like the strands that bound her hands. Amanda struggled to her feet, legs stiff from lying on the wooden planks. She could do little to balance herself with her hands tied and she fell, wincing when she banged her knee on the uneven edge of a plank.

Once upright, she staggered toward the coil of rope. It hung at eye level and, on closer inspection, the square head of the nail appeared rather blunt. She glanced around her confines searching for a more promising option. Finding none, she raised her hands to the nail, grateful they were tied in front of her, making it easier to pick apart her bindings.

She set to work, breaking one or two strands at a time. Her shoulders ached from holding her arms up to reach the nail, but steady progress urged her on. She made a mental note that should she ever need to tie somebody up and stash them in the hold, she would definitely tie their hands behind their back.

****

Will hailed the *HMS Serenity* with a flag of parlay and was soon on the deck of the ship he had practically grown up on.

"Will!" Captain Goodman greeted him. "Or, should I call you Captain Stoakes now?"

"Will is fine, sir," he said with a smile and a bow to his old captain. "Thank you for agreeing to speak with me under the circumstances."

Captain Goodman would have none of Will's formality. He grabbed him about the shoulders and pulled him into a bear hug. The warmth of his reception startled Will, but he returned the embrace with equal affection. He held his former captain in a higher regard than he did any man, including his own father. When independence had been declared, his only regret had been that it might cost him the dearest friendship he ever had.

Captain Goodman released him, a jovial smile on his face and fatherly warmth shining in his eyes. Will knew war could not sever this bond.

"What brings you on board my ship under a flag of parlay? Surely the war hasn't ended, has it?"

"That would be my greatest desire, sir, but I'm afraid that is not what brought me here."

Seeing his old captain again for the first time in years, he knew in his gut the man hadn't changed. Older now, gray about the beard, with a paunch beginning to show where he had once been as lean as Will himself, there could be no mistaking the man behind the warm hazel eyes.

Captain Goodman had nothing to do with Amanda's kidnapping. It occurred to him that he didn't even have solid proof she had been taken to Goodman's ship other than the supposition that a common sailor would not use the word "serenity" unless he referred to the ship.

He needed to broach the subject without impugning the man's honor. "I seem to have lost something, sir,"

Will began, still trying to grasp the right words.

"Lost something?" Captain Goodman looked confused.

"Yes, sir."

"Can you be more specific?"

Will winced. "My wife."

He couldn't tell the man he thought of as a father that he had lost a crewmember—who just happened to be female. It would be akin to admitting he had lost his mistress. Besides, if he ever got Amanda alone again, proposing to her would be his first order of business.

"Your wife?" Captain Goodman's laugh held real humor. "You were the last man I ever expected to be able to find a wife, and now that you have, you lost her?"

A shout from one of the men had both captains turning to see the source of the disturbance.

Green silk glinting in the sun, Amanda emerged from below deck. She blinked several times in succession, looking a bit confused and rubbing her wrists. Then she glanced about, returning the unflinching stares of several dozen sailors who seemed more surprised to see her than she was to see them.

Finally, her gaze settled on Will, looking startled for only a moment before she regained her composure and came to join him. "Hello, Will. Did you come to rescue me?" Aside from her raspy voice and unusual question, she sounded as though they had just met at a local teashop.

He looked down at her, assessing her condition. Her green satin gown smelled a bit musty, and she had little bits of grain stuck to her sleeves and skirt. Her short curly hair looked charmingly disheveled, and a streak of what appeared to be dirt marred one cheek. All in all, she didn't look as though she had been mistreated, nor did she even look frightened. In fact, she did not look like a woman in need of rescue.

"I thought I told you to tie her up!" came a rough English-accented voice from among Goodman's crew.

"I did!" protested another. "With a proper sailor's knot, I did!"

Will looked into the crowd of men around them and spotted two ruffians arguing with each other. So did Captain Goodman.

The men seemed to sense that all eyes were on them, and they stopped their quarreling. Slowly, they turned to find two of the most ferocious sets of eyes, one gold and the other hazel, peering at them.

"Take them below and put them in the brig," Captain Goodman said to an armed Marine sergeant standing nearby.

He turned back to Will. "They are yours to do with as you please."

Will smiled. "Captain Goodman, have the methods of discipline changed much in the Royal Navy since I served aboard your ship?"

Captain Goodman snorted. "They have not."

Out of the corner of his eye, Will saw Amanda, chin raised, assessing Captain Goodman.

"I'm sure whatever you do with them would be far worse than anything I could ever dream of," Will said, focusing his attention on Amanda and wondering what she had planned.

Goodman turned his attention to his unusual guest, and she gave him a dazzling smile. "So this charming lady is your wife, I take it," he said as though they were at a ball and not aboard his ship, with small kernels of barley, oats and some unidentifiable debris clinging to Amanda's gown and hair.

"Wife?" Her smiled dissolved, and her gaze slid to Will before returning to their host.

Will frowned down at her. "Yes."

"I'm not his wife, sir," Amanda shook her head, blonde curls bobbing. Several pieces of straw drifted to the deck.

"You're not?"

"She will be," Will answered for her.

Goodman looked at him for a moment before turning back to Amanda. "Do you want to be?"

"Well I suppose I might," she replied as though considering it for the first time.

"Then why aren't you?"

"Because he hasn't asked me. A moment ago, it sounded almost like he commanded me, but then I'm no longer a member of his crew."

"You were a member of his crew?" Captain Goodman asked incredulously.

"Yes, but I'm not now, so he can no longer command me, can he?" Amanda's chin tilted up a little higher.

Amanda had made him look like a fool at best, and a cad at worst. If only Goodman could hear the full truth of it. He would have asked her last night if she hadn't been so intent on seducing him. How was he to know that she would disappear before morning?

However, the blame didn't rest with her. He should have made his intentions clear before things got out of hand. Still, he didn't care to discuss his shortcomings with his former captain, especially not with an audience of English seamen who, at any other moment, would be happy to slit his throat. They had drawn nearer to the trio standing amidships, circling around them until they closed in on all sides. Like it or not, he had become the morning's entertainment.

"Why aren't you a member of his crew now?" Captain Goodman seemed determined to get to the bottom of this unusual situation.

"Because I am a woman." Amanda's tone implied her response said it all.

A few of the English sailors nodded.

"And you weren't before?" Captain Goodman asked, his lips twisted into a knot.

"No." She paused. "Well, yes, I was. But Will, I mean Captain Stoakes, didn't know that."

"I see." Goodman laughed as it all became clear to him. "So you broke the captain's rule and became a member of his crew?"

"And a damn good one!" Amanda added.

Captain Goodman chuckled softly at Amanda's coarse language while Will cringed. The sailors around them, however, all seemed to appreciate it, and her, immensely. They slapped each other on the back, laughing and admiring their guest.

"So, now that you aren't a member of the crew, you are free to marry him, aren't you?"

"I suppose I am." She didn't sound too certain.

"And all he has to do is ask?"

She hesitated and a look of panic flashed in her eyes before her gaze dropped to deck. "Yes," she said in a voice so low Will had to strain to hear.

"Well, Will?" Goodman regarded Will, a smile on his face but his expectations clear.

If Goodman thought to trap him into doing the right thing, he would have the last laugh. Will stuck his hand into his coat pocket and retrieved the necklace he intended to give her the night before. He held it in his fist so no one could see it, then he turned to Amanda and took her hand in his.

"Amanda Blakely, would you do me the honor of marrying me?"

"Yes," Amanda said in a whisper. Her panic dissolved in a pool of misty, unshed tears that made her eyes sparkle like the gems he clutched in his hand.

Will turned her hand over in his and slipped the necklace into her palm. Finding her wide-eyed look of astonishment gratifying, he closed her fingers over his gift. He turned her hand back over and raised it to his lips to kiss her knuckles.

As the crowd around them erupted into cheers, he said, for her ears only, "I love you. I had intended to ask you last night, if you had given me the chance."

"So, now, when do you intend to get married?" asked Captain Goodman after the clamor had subsided.

Will grinned, recalling that his former captain seldom left an opportunity for escape. "I suppose as soon as we can find a church or a ship's captain willing to perform the ceremony."

Goodman surveyed the expanse of blue sea that surrounded them. "I think out here a ship's captain might be a more likely find."

"I suppose you're right," Will said. "Perhaps you would do us the honor?"

"The honor would be mine, Will."

Chapter Twenty-Nine

For the second time in a week, Amanda had the luxury of a lavender-scented, freshwater bath. Captain Goodman even managed to find a gown suitable to serve as a wedding dress. On a chair next to her bath, mauve satin petticoats shimmered beneath a gown of cream trimmed in the finest French lace.

Amanda reached out from the tub to caress the soft fabric. When she had asked the captain how he could have come by something so fine, he just smiled and said it was sometimes better not to be too curious. The gown's origins were of no matter. It belonged to her now.

Captain Goodman had given her more than he could ever know. She could see his influence in the man Will had become, guiding him through the struggles of a turbulent adolescence, much as Will did for Neil now.

Her heart swelled with love for her betrothed. Even if she had to live much of her life with him at sea, knowing that he loved her in return would sustain her through the many long days ahead. The nights would be harder, she decided, recalling the passion they had shared not long ago.

He might not come home for months at a time, but when he did, he would be hers, and she would make sure she used that time wisely. If she had her way, he would have no desire to go to a tavern or accept any social engagements. She would keep him occupied with more pleasant diversions.

She ran the bar of lavender soap across her breasts, remembering the caress of his palms, his fingers and his mouth. When the soap dropped into the water Amanda let it go and slid soapy hands across slick skin. Her breasts felt fuller than before and she cupped them, testing their weight and running her own thumbs across her nipples, delighting in the rippling sensations that ran to the pit of her belly.

“Thinking of me?” Will asked from just inside the door. He leaned against the wall, his arms crossed over his chest and his legs crossed at the ankle.

Amanda squeaked and ducked down in the tub, splashing water over the side. “I didn’t hear you come in.”

How long had he been there, watching her?

“I didn’t intend you to.” He gave her a knowing grin.

Unwinding his long limbs, he strode to the tub.

“It’s not considered proper for the groom to see the bride on their wedding day before the ceremony.” Especially naked, she added to herself.

Considering the intimacies they had already shared, she shouldn’t be embarrassed. Yet, something about being in the bath with him standing over her went beyond intimate.

“Relax.” Will knelt beside the tub. He cupped Amanda’s chin in his hand and titled her face so he could place a light kiss on her lips. “I had no choice considering you needed rescuing this morning.” He shrugged. “Or so I thought. Apparently, you were well on your way to getting out of that one on your own."

"Yes, but you came when I needed you," Amanda reassured him.

Will laughed. "Don't worry. My self-esteem isn't so weak that a wife who can handle her own is going to unman me." He looked at her seriously. "Any second thoughts?"

"Well," she began. An uncharacteristic expression of doubt danced across Will's features, and she couldn't resist teasing him a bit. "I have considered that perhaps I didn't use the opportunity to its best advantage."

"Opportunity?"

"Yes. I thought you were being forced to propose, but it appears you already had it planned. Perhaps I should have hesitated before saying 'yes' and done a little...negotiating."

"What would you have asked for?" His gazed flickered to her naked breasts, and Amanda rather thought she knew what line of thinking he had gone down.

She bit her lower lip. She had to try one more time. "I want to remain part of your crew."

"Part of my crew?" Will asked, his bemused expression confirming that it had not been the request he anticipated.

Amanda smiled to herself. She had thrown him off. If negotiating naked gave her the advantage, she would have to remember to try it again when the stakes were high.

"Will, you can't marry me and then expect me to go ashore and live out my days without you."

"But, life on a privateer can be dangerous."

"You think I don't know that! I just spent the last

several months on your ship dodging cannonballs and sewing up severed limbs." She punctuated her point with wet hands, splashing water on the sleeve of his coat.

"No one can dodge a cannonball," Will said, "and, as I recall, only one man lost a limb."

"So clearly it's not as dangerous as all that."

"You twist my words, Amanda," Will said, his voice serious. "But, I will make you a deal. You can remain on board my ship, and I suppose as a member of my crew, for now. After all, I have no wish to die of food poisoning, and the doctor says you are the best with a needle he's ever seen."

"Thank you!" Amanda threw her wet arms around Will's neck, heedless of the water dripping from her naked breasts and soaking his waistcoat.

"You can remain a crew member until..."

"Until?" Amanda pulled away searching his face.

"Until you are with child and then you will go ashore, willingly I might add, and live in a house on dry land with a doctor to attend you if it should become necessary."

"Until I am with child. Is that it?"

"Yes," said Will, eyeing her mischievous grin with suspicion.

"You realize, don't you, that you just gave me an incentive to stay out of your bed?"

"You realize don't you," Will said, teasing her with her own words, but with a smile that softened his response, "that it is you who has tried to seduce me twice and once succeeded. I've come to the conclusion that I have so much appeal for you that it would be impossible for you to stay out of my bed."

Amanda ducked further down into the tub, splashing water over the sides and soaking his breeches before he could jump out of the way. The short tub required her to bend her knees and prop her feet up on the opposite side. She wiggled her wrinkled water-soaked toes and studied them.

He was right and she knew it. He had never once taken the initiative, and it mortified her that he had realized it—and mentioned it.

"I certainly hope I won't be the only one to make the effort in this marriage." Amanda crossed her arms over her chest, blocking her taut, pink nipples from his view.

"I can assure you that you will not." Will cupped her face in his large hands. His lips lingered on hers, before he nudged them open with the tip of his tongue.

Amanda wrapped her arms around his neck again, effectively soaking what little dry clothing remained. "Surely there has to be some sort of taboo against doing this with the bride before the ceremony," she whispered against his lips.

"No, there is not," Will said, pulling her to her feet. "At least not on a ship. In fact out here, it is tradition."

Amanda laughed. "You're making that up."

"Perhaps, it is not tradition yet," he said, grabbing a towel, "but traditions need to start somewhere."

Amanda could think of no reply to that strange logic. In fact, she had a difficult time thinking at all. Will dried her legs, slowly, thoroughly, one at a time. Amanda closed her eyes and supported herself with her hand on his shoulder, giving herself over to pleasure. Will ran the rough towel across delicate skin in slow, mesmerizing strokes. She swayed toward him until his dark curls tickled the tips of her breasts.

Amanda bent her head to the top of his, buried her nose in his hair, and breathed in his scent. She would never tire of the way he smelled, a heady mixture of man and sea.

He worked the towel up between her thighs, lingering at the hollow where thigh met hip. She sighed her contentment and widened her stance, hoping to encourage him to continue his exploration.

The heat rose in her cheeks, but not from embarrassment this time. Somewhere in the back of her mind, she supposed she should be ashamed of her wanton behavior with a man she had not yet married. Will dropped the towel and used his fingers to part her soft folds and stroke the sensitive nub beneath. A moan escaped her lips. How could she be ashamed of her actions when he robbed her of all reason with his slightest touch?

Amanda opened her eyes when Will grasped her hips in both hands. He glanced up at her with a look that implored her to trust him. Amanda wondered what he was about to do, but she gave him a smile that told him she trusted him, with her heart, and with her body.

His tongue darted out to tease the very spot where his fingers had stroked her just moments ago, and her knees buckled. Only his firm hold on her hips and her fingers entwined in his hair steadied her against wave after wave of pleasure.

"I didn't know you could do this before or after the wedding," she said, sounding a little out of breath.

Will chuckled. "There is much I look forward to showing you, but perhaps we better take it a little slow today, or we will have to prop you up at your own wedding."

He scooped her up in his arms and carried her over to the hammock. She lay back and watched him undress, enjoying the slow unveiling of the well-built man beneath the formal attire. Will gave her a wicked smile then slowed his pace. He unbuttoned his silk shirt, taking his time with each button then slid it off his shoulders, revealing his broad chest sprinkled with dark curls.

He reached for the buttons on his breeches then gave Amanda a suggestive look, "Are you sure you don't want to help?"

She smiled wickedly in return. "I don't think that would be wise unless you brought a change of clothes. If I had been the one to remove your shirt, you wouldn't have any buttons left."

Will laughed then tugged his breeches down his hips and thighs. When finished, he proudly stood naked before her.

"It's about bloody time." Amanda reached out to take his hand and pull him toward her.

Will sat on the edge of the hammock. "You aren't too tender after yesterday?"

Amanda shook her head, and he lowered himself to her. He reached between them to continue the pleasure he had started earlier, but Amanda would have none of it. She wrapped her legs around his hips and drew him to her.

"You're rather eager," he said, sounding pleased.

"We have a wedding to get to, you know." She kissed his neck. "We have to hurry or they might start without us."

When Will guided himself into her, there were

none of the sharp pains of yesterday. She rose to meet his slow, languid strokes, reveling in the fullness of him.

Desperation building, her breathing grew more rapid, and she grasped his hips trying to pull him closer and take him deeper into her own body. She quickened her own pace, urging him to do the same with her hips and her hands, grasping at a goal that remained just out of reach. Then Will pulsed within her and he took over, thrusting deeper and faster. She let him set the pace, and familiar waves of pleasure washed over her once again. Then he shuddered, collapsing on top of her.

She lay beneath him, listening to his breathing slow and running her fingertips across the sweat slick skin of his back. After a moment, he tried to roll to the side, but Amanda grasped him to her.

"No, not yet. Please." Although he no longer filled her the way he had, her sensitive inner walls still pulsed around him, and she wanted to savor it awhile longer.

He settled against her. She kissed his neck, recalling their recent agreement and the conditions that came with it. *Until you are with child.*

Even now, she could be pregnant, in which case she would only have a few weeks before he would see the tell tale signs, and then she would be off the ship. The thought of leaving him made her want to weep.

"Will," she said, her voice shaking. She nudged his shoulder.

"Hmmm?" He sounded as though he had drifted into a doze.

"I don't think I can do it," she said.

"Now's a fine time to tell me after we've already consummated the marriage," he said, his voice teasing.

Amanda laughed at his attempt at humor. "You can't consummate a marriage before it exists."

"Aaargh," he groaned, kissing the corner of her lips, "You mean we have to do this again?"

She pushed his shoulder to get his attention, "I don't mean the marriage, I mean this."

He withdrew and rolled onto his side. "You didn't enjoy it?"

"Of course I did!" she said. "That's the problem."

"The problem?" He looked thoroughly befuddled.

"Yes, I could be pregnant even now," she said, tears shining in her eyes.

"I hope so," Will said, trailing a finger down the center of her abdomen and then spreading his hand across her taut, flat belly. "I can't wait to see you all swollen with my child."

"But how will you? How will you see me swollen with child if you make me leave the ship?"

"Who said you're going alone?"

"I'm not?"

"Of course not," Will answered. "Getting you pregnant would be only a temporary solution to keep you off the ship. Knowing you, you'd find a way back on, probably hauling our poor baby with you. As I see it, the best way to keep you off my ship is to keep you pregnant, and for that, I need to be there."

"You do?" A tear rolled down Amanda's cheek and Will caught it with his finger.

"Of course I do." Will lifted her, rolled onto his back and settled her against his chest. Amanda crossed her hands over his chest and leaned her chin against them. "I've been at sea for a number of years, and I've probably been one of the most fortunate captains in the business. But for me, it was never about the money." He stared at the ceiling above them.

"For country?" Amanda asked.

"I like to think that was part of it," he replied. "But in truth, I think I have been searching for something missing from my life."

"What were you searching for?"

"Family." He looked down at her. "I never really knew my own father even though I followed him from battle to battle. As captain of his regiment, he mostly interacted with the other officers. Too young to fight, and kind of timid to boot, I was just a lowly drummer. I'm not sure how many of the men even knew I was his son."

Amanda smiled at the image of a young, curly-haired boy with big golden eyes banging away on a drum and trying his best to keep up with full-grown men on the march.

"And your mother?" Amanda asked. She desperately wanted to hear the details of his life, and she hoped the question wouldn't shut down their conversation.

"My mother was a lost cause from the start. She hadn't been born into wealth the way my father had, but she coveted it." Will snorted. "Looking back, I think jealousy was about the only emotion she ever felt. When I was born, she resented my intrusion into her busy life, full of all the social engagements she had never been invited to until she married my father. Then she resented the war for taking him away from her. When he died, I think she lost some of the respectability his presence gave her, and she resented him for abandoning her."

"What did she do?" Amanda asked.

"Spent all his money mostly. I think it was her way of getting her revenge on him."

"And on you," Amanda added.

Will's eyes held real sadness, and Amanda supposed that he mourned for the mother he never really had. She raised her head from her hands, hoping to turn the discussion toward happier times. "So did you find what you were searching for at sea?"

"Yes, as a matter of fact I did," Will said, happiness returning to his face.

He tucked one hand behind his head while he caressed her back with the other. A surge of pure pleasure washed over her and her inner core twitched in anticipation. Surprised her body would respond so quickly after making love, she laid her head against his chest, determined to let him finish his story.

"I already think of Neil as a brother." His voice rumbled in her ear. "In truth, I had even begun to think of him as a son, even though we are separated by less than ten years."

Doing the math, Amanda smiled to herself. That would make him only twenty-five, and she had the suspicion Will might be a couple years older. One day soon, he would discover Neil's true age, but not just yet.

"You know he'll make an excellent captain someday, and I don't intend to ask him to leave the ship with us. Does that bother you?"

"Not at all," she replied, raising her head so he could see she spoke from the heart. "Privateering is dangerous business, but he can hold his own. This is the life he loves. I wouldn't dream of asking him to leave it."

"Somehow, I knew you'd understand." The pride in his voice warmed her in ways words never could.

"Anyway. I've made enough money to pay off the *Amanda* many times over. I can easily hand her over to Buck. He is more than qualified to be a captain in his own right. Frankly, I think the only reason he's stayed on with me is because he expects to be named her captain someday. And, I have enough put aside to outfit a couple additional ships. If I can find decent commanders who have the strength to manage a good crew, I can make enough money to last us well after the war is over and we are allies with the English again." He paused, mulling over the distant future. "After that, maybe we'll go into trade."

"Do you think we will be? Allies with the English, I mean." She had noted the way he said *we*, and wanted to ask if he intended to include her in that, but she also wanted to hear what he thought would happen after the war.

She waited for his answer, unable to resist stretching up to nibble at the stubble along his jaw line, delighting in the prickly feel against her sensitive lips.

"I'm sure of it," Will said, reaching down to cup the back of her thighs in his hands. He drew her legs up so she sat astride him as he continued, "I don't know if you and I will live to see the day, but we are too alike, the English and the Americans. There's a bond between our people that will survive this fight. As equals, I believe we will become invincible partners in the decades and perhaps even centuries to come.

"I hope so," Amanda sighed. She moved against him and he stiffened in response.

She liked Captain Goodman, and it would be a shame to have to continue to fight men such as him. A sudden thought struck her and she stopped her movements.

"Do you think our marriage by an English captain will be recognized?"

"Probably," Will replied, gripping her hips in both hands and guiding her onto him. "But just in case, we'll get married again in a regular church ceremony when we return to Baltimore."

"Hmmm," Amanda murmured. She wasn't thinking so much about the wedding, or anything else at the moment. It had just occurred to her how much easier it would be to make love in a hammock when she was on top and in control. She wondered what other ways they could discover before they were considered late for their own wedding.

****

Amanda decided their ceremony at sea had to be one of the oddest on record. The two ships moored side by side, and they were married on the *Serenity* surrounded by a mixture of English and American sailors. All the men were on their best behavior, but the looks they shot one another across the open deck suggested the truce would be short-lived once the ceremony and associated festivities were over.

When the ceremony ended, the two crews opened up barrels of rum and thought up ways to challenge each other throughout the night. Luckily, Captain Goodman had an ample supply of marines to keep order. By morning, the brigs were full and it took a bit of work to sort out the prisoners on both ships, keeping the ones that belonged and sending the others back to their own ship.

Amanda and Will heard about most of this through Buck. They had slept through it all, too exhausted from their own post-wedding celebrations to join in the fun.

A word about the author...

Mary Jean Adams has been writing romance since she was in middle school—a fact her English teachers didn't always appreciate. She also loves history and telling the stories behind the stories of the founding of America.

Today, she lives in North Dakota with her husband and two children.

Readers may contact her through:

www.maryjeanadams.com.

Thank you for purchasing
this publication of The Wild Rose Press, Inc.
For other wonderful stories of romance,
please visit our on-line bookstore at
www.thewildrosepress.com.

For questions or more information
contact us at
info@thewildrosepress.com.

The Wild Rose Press, Inc.
www.thewildrosepress.com

To visit with authors of
The Wild Rose Press, Inc.
join our yahoo loop at
http://groups.yahoo.com/group/thewildrosepress/

www.ingramcontent.com/pod-product-compliance
Lightning Source LLC
Chambersburg PA
CBHW071647260626
47170CB00001B/271

9781612178783